Home Ground

Brian Cook

TSL Publications

First published in Great Britain in 2020
By TSL Publications, Rickmansworth

Copyright © 2020 Brian Cook

ISBN / 978-1-913294-47-2

Photo (front cover) by Illiya Vjestica on Unsplash
Photo (back cover) by Greg Willson on Unsplash

DEDICATION

To Felicity

They must often change who would be constant in happiness or wisdom.
~ Confucius

Prologue

The last rays of a faltering sun dipped below the bluff on the far side of the dale. The gnarled hand of a working man reached out for the switch of a shadeless table lamp. The lifeless eyes squinted once again at the small print.

Sleepy from an uncommonly large feed, the old sheepdog sighed and shifted position at his master's feet. The hand reached down to reassure him with a rub behind the ear. The paper was returned to the pile and the hand cupped to receive the pills.

A chipped mug of whisky, a series of swallows and the light was clicked off.

1

London, Friday 6th April 2001

Tom Keardon, fashionably dressed down in expensive black, clicked his mouse and waited for his company's share price to appear on the screen. Friday afternoons sometimes produced unexpected shifts in the market as the city throttled back for the weekend.

Not so today. Tiger.com was holding steady. The company Tom had founded barely three years ago appeared to be weathering the squalls of the new economy. Supplying Internet based information about Far Eastern investment was never going to make Tiger a global player. But neither was it likely to go the way of the hope and a prayer dotcoms who had gambled on fooling all of the people all of the time. Most of them had crashed and burned when the bubble burst a year ago.

At 33, Tom was, if anything, a little long in the tooth to be the Managing Director of a dotcom company. In a business where youth and enthusiasm were celebrated, experience was often viewed with nonchalance. But it was a measure of his ability that as well as commanding the respect of the suits in the City of London who provided financial backing, he could also hold his own with the brightest young Turks among his staff.

Tom looked through the glass wall of his office to the large open plan space beyond. Minimalist design. Desks artfully arranged in clusters, ensuring that specialists were grouped together. Economist with economist. Marketer with his or her own kind. Web page designers close by the systems engineers. When Tiger.com expanded into the newly refurbished building in Fenchurch Street at the beginning of the year the layout had been planned with the assistance of a Feng Shui expert. It had been the idea of the public relations consultants they retained, eager to fashion a story which would be picked up by financial diarists. Tom had played along willingly, happy to be described as a firm believer in all things Eastern. Which to an extent he was. Leaving university with a yen to be a journalist, he had intended to see the world before knuckling down to a career. Six months travelling through the Indian sub-continent and South East Asia had left him with a dickey tummy and a severe shortage of funds. Hong Kong offered the means to repair both conditions. A temporary job with an English language newspaper might have been just that if it had not been for So Lin, the delicate beauty who worked there as an interpreter. Within months Tom had caught the bug for a regular wage, a steady job and girlfriend, Chinese culture and the high-octane lifestyle of the roving reporter he rapidly became.

For a while all was well. Tom had originally been accepted, if a little formally, by his girlfriend's extended Chinese family. But once married, tensions began to surface. So Lin had given up her job and now moved mostly in Tom's ex-pat circles. It led to murmurings that she was forsaking her background and turning into a 'banana' – yellow on the outside, white in the middle. The accusation stung, and Lin became increasingly distant from Tom. This, plus Tom's frequent and lengthy absences on assignment for the paper cast dark shadows over their mixed and mixed-up marriage.

Tom couldn't help musing, when sitting in another nameless hotel bar over one too many whiskies, that it was mirrored by the situation Hong Kong found itself in. Acquired by Britain in 1898 under a 99-year lease, the time was rapidly approaching when the colony would revert to the Chinese. Maybe he'd only leased Lin's affections, not acquired them for good.

Out of a firm resolution to put his life back on an even keel grew the germ that was to become Tiger.com. With Britain pulling out of Hong Kong in 1997 and the Chinese growing more ambivalent about their denunciation of capitalism, commercial intelligence about South East Asia would be at a premium. It was discussing these ideas with Lin which brought them together again, professionally if not personally. They both agreed that the marriage had been a mistake but that the business idea was a winner. They managed to fit in an amicable divorce while setting up the Hong Kong offices of Tiger.com which Lin would continue to manage after the handover. Tom then flew back to the UK with a list of venture capitalists provided by his ex-pat friends.

'And now look at it,' murmured Tom, surveying the quiet frenzy of activity at a score of terminals and telephones within his immediate field of vision.

'Look at what?' It was Angie, his Business Development Director who spoke as she sank into a long, low sofa beside Tom's desk. The action caused her Jasper Conran frock to ride up to the limits of decency over her slim legs. She stretched her arms along the top of the sofa and regarded Tom with a knowing expression in her coolly beautiful eyes.

'Sorry, I was miles away.' Tom jolted back from his reverie.

That Tom and Angie were something of an item was an open secret in the company. Open, because Tom took the view that office romances, or in this case flings, were less likely to lead to unprofessional behaviour if they were not hidden. At least that's what he hoped. Privately he regretted having succumbed to her subtle advances. They made a handsome couple, of that there was no doubt, but bed and boardroom he was increasingly discovering did not mix.

'Yes, what is it?' There was coldness in his voice. Angie sat up straight and morphed into efficient businesswoman mode, a mode which Tom couldn't stop himself thinking rang somewhat more true.

'Tom, it's just that I know you won't want to talk shop over dinner tonight, so I wanted to find out what you thought about my strategy document.' Tom tensed at the loaded question and searched for a suitably neutral phrase.

'It's very thought-provoking. But why are you bringing this up again when we've already had it out. You know it's for discussion at next week's board meeting and not before.'

'Yes, but I thought you might tell me whether I can count on your support.'

'Support?' Tom's eyebrows arched. 'It's not an election, Angie. We'll be making critical judgments about the future direction of this company. I've already made it clear that any decisions will be made in the best interests of the shareholders, the staff and our clients.'

'Don't patronize me with platitudes,' Angie flashed, 'particularly ones which you could do well to remember. You may have started this company but it's not your baby anymore. Agreeing to a takeover would serve everyone's interests. I just can't see why you're holding out against it.'

The temptation to engage in the argument was strong but Tom was aware that it would have been an own goal. After a long pause, he spoke evenly.

'Angie, at the risk of repeating myself, the discussion will take place at the board meeting and I will thank you not to try to build this up into a confrontation by bending my ear or those of any other directors before next Tuesday. And here's another platitude. We work as a team. Teams have no room for prima donnas who try to circumvent normal company procedures. Now can we leave it there, please?'

Tom waited for the explosion, wondering if he had been altogether too harsh in trying to bring the exchange to an abrupt end. But to his surprise, if not relief, Angie merely smiled sweetly, brightly chirped 'OK, see you later', and sashayed out of the office.

Tom's relief was short-lived, soon to be replaced by a nagging sense of unease. There was no doubt that his fling with Angie – no let's downgrade that to a dalliance, Tom decided – had been ill-advised. Sharply intelligent, relentlessly efficient, overtly ambitious, she had been quite a catch for the company when Tom had poached her from the marketing department of a major Japanese bank in the City. Tom had not been the only red-blooded male on the staff to speculate about what lurked beneath the ice queen exterior, but he had been the only one allowed a glimpse. First over business lunches, then over purportedly business dinners. Finally, on a shared sales trip to Tokyo, there was the sake, the interconnecting hotel rooms and … stop fooling yourself, Tom rebuked himself. You've got nothing to blame but yourself for giving in to raw sexual attraction and hanging the consequences.

Now, three months on, the relationship – Tom baulked at the word – was on an edge, both personally and professionally. On the personal front, increasingly frequent rows were less frequently made up before the next. Professionally – well, Tom reached into his in-tray to look again at the document which had brought matters to a head.

It had begun as casual pillow talk. Tiger.com's emerging rivals in providing information about the Far East were the international news agencies and management consultancies. They had been slow to take to the information highway but were now throwing all of their not inconsiderable weight behind it. What Tiger lacked in resources it could make up in customized services for its clients, but the choice was clear: survive and hopefully prosper by remaining small, quick-witted and nimble, or cash in by selling-out to the big boys. Angie had pushed for Tom to allow her to use her banking contacts to make discreet enquiries about possible interest in a take-over. Tom had, as far as he recalled, agreed that it might be an idea, but that he would have to speak to the Chairman about it. It had then slipped his mind.

Two weeks later, when said Chairman, Sir Giles Clark, asked for any other business at the conclusion of the fortnightly board meeting, Angie flourished copies of a report. She announced that she believed the board should be considering the possibility of acceding to a takeover in view of the information contained in the document.

Sir Giles had turned to Tom and lowered his half-moon spectacles. 'I was not aware that this report was being prepared. Were you?'

Tom shot a glance at Angie. She remained impassive. Tom rapidly weighed up the implications of saying yes or no and realized that an honest answer was the only option.

'Angie and I had discussed it informally, but I was not aware that a report was being prepared.'

'I see.' The words spoke volumes. Sir Giles picked up his copy of the report and slipping it into his briefcase declared, 'Then we all better read it. In the strictest confidence please, ladies and gentlemen. Let me have your views at the next board meeting. We'll discuss it then, not before. Tom, join me for lunch.'

The meal turned out to be far less of an ordeal than Tom had feared. Sir Giles had served in the diplomat corps throughout Asia, culminating in an ambassadorship in China before putting his wealth of Far Eastern experience to great and lucrative use in the City with a clutch of directorships. Sir Giles knew the value of a soft touch.

'I do hope that rather attractive young thing hasn't got you on a bit of a sticky wicket!' was his mild opener.

Tom was relieved to be able to confide his misgivings about becoming involved with Angie. As Sir Giles listened, nodding frequently and offering the odd word of encouragement, Tom went on to question whether he wasn't beginning to lose his judgment about the running of the company and his objectivity about its future.

When Tom had run out of words Sir Giles leant back in his chair and spoke softly but briskly. 'Well my boy, you're not the first to mix business with pleasure. As far as I can see it seems to be all the rage these days. Always was come to think of it. You've made a rod for your own back, and only you can work out the best way to extricate yourself from the relationship – if that's what you want. As for questioning your judgment, well, thank the Lord that you are. It's the moment that you stop being alert to the dangers of poor decision-making that the trouble starts. Which brings us to the little matter of this report. Damned if I know what the girl's playing at. She knows perfectly well what the correct channels are. Perhaps you've talked to her about your passion for the business and she's assumed that you would block any move to let your bird fly the coop. Let's put it all down to a misunderstanding, shall we? A misunderstanding which I'm sure you'll discuss with her. In the meantime, we'll consider what she has to say and keep an open mind. Now, which pudding takes your fancy?'

'It's playtime!'

Tom looked up to see Ben Simpson, his Director of Technology, slouching against the door jamb of his office. Pushing 30 in reality, Ben still looked like an overgrown teenager, baseball hat askance, baggy trousers at half-mast. Ben had the knack of taking dressing down to new depths. Long-haired and constantly smiling, he was that rarest of creatures, a brilliant computer technician with an engaging personality.

'Not still fretting over that report, are we?' said Ben, seeing the document clutched in Tom's hands. 'Tom, join me for lunch!' he mimicked in Sir Giles' cut glass drawl. 'Did you get a grilling from the headmaster?'

Tom quickly closed the report and returned it to his in tray, taking care to insert it halfway down the pile of papers. 'Piss off, Ben. There's no need to make an awkward situation worse.'

'No. Sorry, mate. I just couldn't resist it. You looked so glum.'

Ben had the ability to breeze through life without ever giving offence, however irreverent he could be and usually was. Tom couldn't help but smile at the valued colleague who had grown to be a good friend. Whenever Tom had a difficult decision to make, he found Ben to be an excellent sounding board. He could think both laterally and logically and knew when to apply which technique.

'Did I hear playtime mentioned?'

'You did, oh great leader. Six o'clock on a Friday night approaches, and your grateful and devoted staff look forward to your presence at the wine bar to stand the first round, not to mention the second, and the third, and ...'

'OK, point taken. I sometimes wish I'd never started the tradition. It was fine with only three or four on the payroll but now...'

'Stop moaning, oh thee of deep pockets and short arms. The wallet moths have waited long enough for liberation.' And with the spin of a heel he was gone.

Tom quickly tidied his desk, powered down his notebook and resolved to put the week's trials behind him with the help of a drink or two. Or maybe three.

Music from Jamiroquai played on the speakers of the packed basement wine bar, but it might as well have been the Dagenham Girl Pipers for all the attention the gathered drinkers were paying. Conversation was the order of the day. Animated, anecdotal, argumentative, conspiratorial, it came in all flavours, talkers and listeners high on the adrenalin of release from a week's work and a weekend's promise.

Tucked away in a corner, early arrivals from Tiger.com had staked out a large area and were vigorously repelling would-be boarders. Tom fought his way from the bar clutching chilled bottles of house white by the neck, two in each hand. Ben followed with as many glasses as could safely be inserted between his fingers. Tom plonked down in his usual seat at the far end of the table which had the advantage of making it difficult to make a return visit to the bar. Ben, ever the life and soul, began to fill the glasses, chattering away in the manner of an obsequious wine waiter in a cod French accent.

And so the Friday night ritual began. The number of Tiger staff swelled to around twenty. Angie was among the last to arrive. She ordered her own cocktail at the bar and fell into deep conversation with Ben. As usual the seat to Tom's right remained free for a while. No one wanted to be seen to be too eager to talk to the MD. To Tom's left was Charles Wright, Tiger's Director of Finance and Administration, formal, old beyond his years, whose idea of dressing down was to remove his suit jacket.

They spent a few minutes discussing the prospects for survival of a retail dotcom whose share price had collapsed following disastrous half-yearly figures. Then a recent recruit, a studious Cambridge economics graduate, took advantage of a lull in the conversation to settle beside Tom and ask him about the possibility of a secondment to Tiger's Hong Kong branch.

He was followed by one of the team of political analysts. She wanted to know if he had any contacts in North Korea, newly opening its borders to the South. Tom was able to point her in the direction of an Australian foreign correspondent he'd known in his newspaper days who specialised in gleaning what little information could be gathered from the strict Communist regime. But as usual, the quality of the discussion decreased in proportion to the consumption of alcohol. It suited Tom well because he himself was not holding back. By 7.30, as some of the drinkers had begun to drift away, a pimple-faced web designer who looked all of fifteen, and judging by the slurring of his words had been a very early arrival in the wine bar, started to badger Tom about buying him a new piece of software. Tom confessed that he hadn't the foggiest idea what the software was or did and suggested that he speak to Ben on Monday about it.

Gesturing at Ben as he did so, he was perplexed to see that Angie was still talking animatedly to him. Excusing himself from the pimpled one, who carried on extolling the virtues of his coveted software oblivious to the lack of an audience, Tom squeezed past chairs to level with Ben and Angie.

'There you are. Can I get you two a drink? Usual?' And without waiting for a reply, 'Give me a hand, Ben.'

The crowd was thinning out and he was able to order without delay. Seconds later Ben appeared at his side. Ever astute to a situation however carefree his manner, Ben asked 'What's up then?'

Tom glanced over his shoulder. Angie was eyeing the pair of them.

'Just interested to know what you and Angie were having a heart to heart about.'

'Two words,' replied Ben. 'Over and take, but not necessarily in that order. She's really got a bee in her bonnet. Hasn't stopped banging on about it for a good half hour.'

The drinks were placed in front of them and Tom fished in his pocket to pay. Ben moved to pick up the glasses, but Tom halted him with a touch of the hand. Inwardly, he was churning. What the hell was Angie doing, flouting his instruction not to canvass support and choosing to do so in front of half the company? God knows what snippets of information those close to her might have overheard. And now what? Confrontation? In public? Less than sober? Or wait until later, over their planned dinner. Some dinner that would be. Tom stared fixedly at the optics behind the bar and ground his teeth. Ben fidgeted beside him, for once sensing that a chirpy remark would not ease the obvious tension.

Reflected in the bar mirror, Tom saw Angie's approach. 'Where's my drink, boys?'

Tom snapped, whirling round. 'What the hell do you think you're playing at?'

'Playing at? This is not a game, you know, this is the real world. The chance to make real money.'

'I thought it had been made absolutely clear that the report should remain confidential and that all discussion should be deferred until the board meeting.' Even in his anger, Tom couldn't help noticing that he was sounding rather pompous. Angie must have sensed an opening, a faltering of purpose. She seized on the basest of weapons. Ridicule.

'Frightened that people might have different opinions to those of our great founder? Tiger? More like a pussy cat!'

Around them the conversation level had dipped. Wine-fuelled banter was straggling to a halt as the gathered drinkers sensed a situation. Ben waded in before Tom could react.

'Look, guys, there's a time and a place and it's not now and it's not here. OK?' Angie and Tom locked unblinking eyes long enough for the noise level to stutter to life again.

When Tom spoke, it was soft, seething and staccato. 'I will not have my company treated like a commodity to be traded to the highest bidder.'

'My company?' Angie pounced. 'My company? It's not your company anymore, Tom Keardon.'

And with that she was gone.

'What the hell was that all about?' Ben asked after what he felt was a suitable pause.

'Why's she doing this?' Tom appealed. 'Forget the personal stuff. That's not been good. But it doesn't explain why all of a sudden she seems intent on provoking me into some kind of disciplinary action. What am I going to do?'

Ben considered a serious response to the question and quickly decided against it. 'What you're going to do, my friend, is knock back that drink, allow me to buy you several more, and then join us at the club we're going to. This time on a Friday night is no time to be fathoming the whys of women and the wherefores of business. By Monday you'll know what to do.'

It might have been the pounding music, or the pulsating lights, or the many bottles of iced lager, but that giggling blonde with the great body and the estuary accent was looking more desirable by the minute. Shouldn't. But face it, Keardon, when have you ever done the sensible thing where women were concerned. Why start now?

2

The first rays of a gathering sun had long since risen above the office complex on the far bank of the Thames. In Tom's converted loft apartment shards of milky light streamed between the blinds, illuminating motes of dust hovering above the stripped pine floor. From outside came the dull wash of traffic. In the bedroom the snoring was abruptly curtailed by the urgent trill of a telephone.

A hand groped from beneath the covers and began a fingertip search of the bedside table. Finding the phone, the hand lifted the handset from its cradle and balanced it on its side. With a Herculean effort, Tom raised himself to a sitting position, lolled against the headboard and clasped his head in his hands. From the corner of his eye Tom spied a splash of bottle blonde hair splayed across the adjoining pillow. He winced and moved the hands down to cover his eyes in a fruitless attempt to evade the returning memory. From the phone he became aware of the distant scratch of a voice. He grasped the handset and tried to say hello. A croak emerged. Clearing his throat, he tried again and was successful.

Tom sat up straight. His brow furrowed. 'He's what?'

The voice continued.

'What did he do that for?'

Tom's head nodded as he listened, occasionally punctuating the flow of the voice with a curt 'Yes.'

'Of course I will. I should be there.' He paused to glance at the bedside clock showing past noon. He gathered his thoughts and calculated. 'I'll be with you late afternoon, early evening Mum … OK.'

Tom replaced the handset and stared into the middle distance. He breathed long and hard, and then with a passion which came from deep within, he exploded. 'Stupid bugger!'

Leaping from the bed in a whirlwind of activity, he pulled on his discarded boxer shorts, opened the Venetian blinds to flood the room with light and bounced back on to the bed to shake his nocturnal sparring partner. He waited until she showed some semblance of consciousness. 'Sorry, love, I've got to go and so have you. Soon as possible, please.'

Four hours and two hundred and fifty miles later, Tom Keardon swung his black Audi TT off the A1 and on to the narrow road signposted to Richmond in North Yorkshire.

Mentally, the journey had proceeded in stages. In his fragile state, safely negotiating the heavy Saturday morning traffic through the tortured twists and turns of the City and then North London had required his full attention. But as he swung on to the M1 motorway his mental fog began to lift and the memory of his previous night's debacle returned to haunt him. Each flashback caused further pain. Angie apparently on a mission to undermine his authority. Ben embarrassed for him. Angie insulting him and walking out. Making a fool of himself in front of his staff at the night club. Treating the pneumatic blonde like a prostitute.

But as the miles slipped away, he made a conscious effort to concentrate on the reason for his journey. His thoughts turned to his destination and his childhood. Middle Farm in Upper Swaledale had been the home, and the living, of generations of Keardons. Perched midway between the lush river meadows of the remote dale and the rock-strewn heights of the vertiginous hills, it was a location which could be idyllic on sunny summer days. But for much of the year, the elements conspired to create conditions so unforgiving that only the most hardy of farmers and their animals could survive. Being snowed under in Winter, inundated in Spring and blown away in Autumn was the circle of life in the Dales.

Tom's grandfather had been called up to fight in the Second World War leaving the running of the sheep farm to his grandmother and their ten-year-old son Bill, Tom's father. As was the way in the Dales, education took second place to the necessity of farming and Bill became the man of the house at his tender age, replacing his father who was never to return. Only when Tom's grandmother succumbed to a fatal illness brought on by a lifetime of hardship did Bill, by then in his early forties, feel the need to find a wife to help him run the farm and to provide a son and heir.

Jean was an unlikely catch for him. She had seen life at university and in London before the acrimonious breakdown of a long-term relationship had led her to seek a new existence in rural isolation. She took a teaching post in an infant's school in the Dales and met Bill at a village dance. Against all the odds, the unsophisticated sheep farmer and the well-educated but unambitious schoolmistress cemented a solid if unromantic marriage.

Tom was that son and heir. An only child, it was a given that he would one day inherit the farm and therefore had to be schooled in the ways of hill sheep farming. Accordingly, as soon as he could toddle, he was helping to tend to the sheep, learning how to mend fences, taking the controls of the tractor. But unlike the many generations of Keardon sons before him, education didn't take second place. The compulsory school leaving age was now 16, and through the wishes and trans-ferred ambitions of his mother, Tom was able to take full ad-vantage of his schooling.

As Tom drove into the cobbled streets of the little Georgian town of Richmond, memories of his teenage years flooded back. The secondary school where inspiring teachers had opened his eyes to a world beyond the daily drudge of sheep farming. Fellow pupils with ambitions to escape to big city universities and experience life to the full. The feeling of being an outsider because, whenever school friends discussed plans for underage pub visits, parent-free parties and casual get-to-gethers to listen to the latest albums, Tom knew that he would be getting on the school bus at the end of each day to return to his lonely and remote farmhouse home. Just in time to help with the evening chores.

Leaving Richmond, following the all too familiar route of that school bus, he powered past the metal sign encased in concrete at the entrance to the Yorkshire Dales National Park. The logo of a stylised Swaledale sheep had always seemed to taunt him on the thousand occasions he had been driven past it as a schoolboy. Goodbye civilisation, hello sheep. Tom remembered one occasion only too well. It was the end of the summer term in his sixteenth year. With good results predicted in the 10 'O' levels he had taken his teachers were encouraging him to return to the sixth form – university material they'd all agreed. Maybe even Oxbridge.

His father had other ideas. Approaching 60 he had for many years been looking forward to the time that his son could share the burden of running the farm full time. Staying at school, he made abundantly clear, was simply not an option. Torn between what Bill described as his ancestral duty and a life beyond which his mother tacitly supported, Tom had been in turmoil. It had been the taunting horned sheep logo that had firmed up his intentions. Goodbye sheep, hello civilisation.

As his car emerged from the trees which thickly lined the road, Tom couldn't help but be stirred by the majestic panorama of lower Swaledale rolled out before him. The meadows in the narrow valley skirting the River Swale were closely flanked by steeply rising slopes, initially wooded but soon giving way to hillside pastures and topped by vertical limestone outcrops – scars as the locals called them.

Cresting a sharp bend an extraordinary sight almost caused him to veer off the road. He slowed down and looked into his rear-view mirror to confirm that he hadn't dreamed it. The carcass of a cow was dangling by its trussed feet from the steel bars of a fully extended forklift truck. It swung pendulously from side to side as the truck trundled across a roadside farmyard. In his solipsistic state it took him some time to register what had been going on. Of course. Foot and Mouth. He'd been following its progress of course, but it was understandably not a major topic of conversation in the circles he moved in in the City. Seeing its effects red in tooth and claw, or rather cloven hoof, had jolted him. In barely six weeks since the first case had been confirmed, the highly infectious disease had spread like a plague to farms across the country. He'd phoned his mother when he'd first read about the outbreak. She'd dismissed the threat saying that it was hundreds of miles away in the South of England. But by early March the television news was reporting the first confirmed cases in the North. When he heard that a hundred cattle and nearly twice as many sheep had been slaughtered near Hawes over the fells in the next dale, but only ten miles away from Middle Farm, he phoned again.

This time his mother had poured out her heart. The first year of her marriage had been overshadowed by the previous out-break of foot and mouth in the UK. As well as having to come to terms with life and work as a farmer's wife and becoming pregnant with Tom, she'd had to live with the gloom which had settled over the Dales as the farming community waited to see if it would escape the slaughter of their animals. That time Swaledale wasn't affected, but this time, she said, his father was convinced that there would be no escape. Tom drove on, now aware of the hastily erected 'no entry without permission' signs at every farm entrance he passed.

Tom drew to a halt at the very spot the school bus had dropped him so many times. Several hundred feet above the chocolate box village, now largely second homes and holiday cottages, Middle Farm was clearly visible. He got out of the car and sat down on bench facing the village green. His head fell into his hands.

So my father's dead. The father who disowned me. Who I haven't spoken a civil word to in maybe fifteen years. The father I failed. The father who failed me. Tom raised his head and took in the scene around him. An early evening breeze was gently bending the daffodils which stretched across the green. A banner on the Black Bull, the village inn, proclaimed a forth-coming folk festival. The near silence was broken by the twitter-ing alarm call of a blackbird. Distantly, just audible, as Tom's urban ears became attuned to the sounds of the countryside, came the bleats of ewes and their new-born lambs.

He looked up to his childhood home. A wisp of smoke trailed from a chimney above the grey stone façade clad intermittently with ivy. The irregular patchwork of dry-stone wall enclosures was dotted with ancient barns casting long shadows in the weak Spring sunshine. Above the crags beyond the farm, dark-ening clouds threatened rain.

A gust of wind caused an involuntary shiver and Tom returned to the comfort of his car. He turned the ignition and the radio sprang to life. *'I know that I'm a prisoner, to all my father held so dear. I know that I'm a hostage, to all his hopes and fears.'* Tom lunged for the off button to silence Mike and the Mechanics. Do I wish I'd made it up to him in the living years, he mused. Maybe, maybe not. It's too late now.

With a fleeting concern about the danger to his car's suspension which he dismissed as wholly inappropriate in the circumstances, he headed for the rough track that would take him to his newly widowed mother.

Tom pulled to a halt at the barred gates to Middle Farm. A sheet of murky plastic had failed to prevent the rain from severely blurring a hand-crafted 'Keep Out' sign nailed to a post. Outside the car his nose wrinkled at the strong smell of antiseptic. A layer of straw had been strewn at the entrance, covered with sacking secured by wooden stakes and dowsed with disinfectant. He opened the gates, drove as slowly as possible across the sacking and bumped across the cattle grid. Returning to close the gates he noticed an old-fashioned enamel baby bath full of milky water. He tentatively immersed the soles of his brogues, fleetingly wondering if the bath had been his own as an infant.

Jean opened the farmhouse door as Tom was retrieving his overnight bag from the boot. He raised his hand to her. She lifted her hand uncertainly in response, forming a brave smile. Tom picked his way across the muddy farmyard feeling strangely detached. What do you say to your recently bereaved mother who you've not had the good grace to visit in years?

'Hi Mum.'

'Tom.' It sounded like a question. He stood before her while she looked him up and down. Then she clasped him in her arms and murmured 'Thank you for coming.'

Tom held her close, conscious of how frail her once robust frame had become. 'I'm sorry, Mum,' he blurted, not knowing whether it was an apology or an expression of sympathy. They parted. Jean smoothed down her dress and surreptitiously brushed a welling tear from her eye.

'Come right in, Tom. Mrs Hardcastle's here. She's been so kind to me. You remember her don't you – from Gawthrop Farm, just down dale. Perhaps not – it's been so long. No, you must do – you were always off to play with her daughter, Sally, when you were little. You grew up in each other's pockets.'

Tom took in the nostalgic smell of the kitchen stove and at once felt like the awkward teenager he'd once been. The old sheepdog opened an inquisitive eye and, detecting no threat, settled back to sleep. 'Hello, Mrs Hardcastle. Nice to see you.'

'Now then, Tom' said the matronly figure seated at the kitchen table in broad Yorkshire. 'Right bad thing to have happened this. I just don't know how your poor mother's coping so well.'

Jean was busying herself with a kettle. 'Tea, Tom?'

'Coffee ...' Tom stopped himself. 'Tea would be lovely, Mum.'

'And another one for you, Rosie?'

Mrs Hardcastle demurred. 'No Jean, I should be getting back now that Tom's here. Is that OK?'

'Yes, of course. I'll be fine now. Thanks so much for being such a support. I really appreciate it.'

'That's what neighbours are for. I'll pop up again soon to see if there's anything we can do.'

'Thanks Rosie. I really mean it.'

Tom escorted Rosie Hardcastle to the front door. She paused outside and looked him hard in the eye. 'This is none of my business, but I just want to say that your father was a good man. I know you two fell out and you've chosen to do other things – very successfully from what I've heard. But farming round here's not about being successful. It's about keeping going. And your father kept it going for a lifetime until he couldn't anymore. I don't hold with anyone taking their own life but perhaps I can understand why he did it. He knew that without you the farm was going to die, and he didn't want to be around when it happened.' Tom found himself looking at a patch of straw, his head bowed. 'Maybe I've said too much, but I believe in speaking my mind. Like it or not you're going to have to take some responsibility for the farm now, even if it's only to sell it. Although goodness knows who'd buy a farm round here these days what with the foot and mouth. But there's the animals to look after for the while and your mother can't do it on her own.'

Tom met her gaze. 'I don't know what to say. I've not had a chance to think anything through yet. It's all come as a bit of a shock.'

Rosie's look softened. 'Sorry, love. I shouldn't be lecturing you when your father's not even buried. Look, I'll send my Sally around tomorrow morning to help with the chores. Now you just go and look after your Mum. She's proud of you, you know, even if your father wasn't.'

Tom watched her stride away into the gathering dusk and closed the door.

In the kitchen his mother brought the teapot to the table and carefully poured the brown liquid into two flowered mugs. 'Sugar, Tom? I can't remember if you take it.'

'Just milk, please.'

Jean smiled weakly at her son. Cupping both hands around her mug, she looked blankly into the distance. The only sound was the faint fizzing of an unseasoned log on the open fire, the contented snuffles of the sheepdog and once again the distant and plaintive calls of ewes and their lambs.

Tom took a deep breath. 'So … what happened?'

His mother continued to stare into space. Tom took in her fine, intelligent features, now framed in strands of grey hair which had escaped from the clasp in her hair. He had never thought of her as old before. She took a long sip of her tea, placed the cup on the table and leant back in her chair.

'He killed himself.' The stark words hung in the air.

'I know that, Mum. I want to know why.'

'So do I.'

Tom toyed with his mug, uncertain how to continue the conversation and aware of the undercurrent of hostility in his mother's terse reply. He realised that she was waiting for him to make the next move.

'Look, Mum. I know I haven't been the son that Dad wanted. And I haven't been a good son to you. I love you Mum, and I know what you went through to stand up for me and help me leave the farm. I've never told you how much I admire you and everything you did for me. But when it comes to Dad, I've just got this blind spot. So stubborn, remote, even selfish. No, that's unfair – he was selfless when it came to keeping the farm going and looking after you. But can't you see that from my point of view he was selfish to try to stop me doing what I wanted to do. Yes, I respect him for his dedication and his achievement in this little world of the farm, but …'

Tom trailed off unable and unwilling to articulate the coldness of his feelings for his newly dead father.

'He was a stubborn one, no doubt.' Jean still hadn't caught his eye. 'But in his 'little world' as you call it, he was a king. A king who cared for his subjects, even if they were mostly sheep. He knew right from wrong and always did the right thing. He was a straightforward, good-hearted man. That's why I fell in love with him. Life was simple for him – never easy, but always simple. You simply had to do what was necessary to scratch a living in a place like this. And I loved him for it. I loved being queen of this little kingdom. But then along came the prince.' Jean turned to look at her son at last. She gave him a weak smile and clutched his hand. 'I'm sorry – I'm making it sound like a bad rehash of Hamlet, aren't I?'

Tom broke in gently. 'Mum, there's so much we need to say to each other. But can you please tell me the facts first. I need to know, before I can begin to understand.'

Jean began to speak in a detached, matter of fact tone. 'I always go to choir practice on Friday evenings. I'd told your father that I'd be late back because we had a lot to rehearse for the Easter services. When I got back he wasn't around, so I just assumed he'd gone to bed early. I watched a programme on telly and then, when I went up, I found him. He was still in his working clothes, lying back on the bed, muddy boots and all. There was an empty whisky bottle on the floor. I was just about to wake him up to give him a piece of my mind when I noticed the pill bottles. Several of them. All empty.'

Tom noticed a tear beginning a journey down his mother's cheek. She continued to speak evenly, as if giving evidence in a court.

'So I shook him. I shouted in his ear. I tried slapping his cheeks. Nothing. I couldn't find a pulse, so I tried the kiss of life. He was cold to the touch. Nothing. I phoned 999 and they said an ambulance would come as quickly as it could, but it would take a good hour to get out here. They told me to how to check for signs of life. I said I'd already done that, but they said I should check again while they hung on. Nothing. So there I was, waiting. And then I remembered Dr. Wilson who moved into the village when he retired. I know him from church. I phoned him, and he said he'd come up right away. He went straight up to Bill when he got here. When he came down, I'd made a cup of tea for him. It had got a bit cold, but he said he didn't mind. And then he said 'I'm sorry Mrs Keardon, but I'm afraid I have to tell you that your husband's passed away."

Suddenly aware of the tears, Jean slowly brushed them away one cheek at a time with the open palms of her hands. 'Dr. Wilson was very kind. He said the police would have to be informed because of the circumstances so he phoned them. They said they had nobody to come out that night but that they'd be here in the morning. They'd call off the ambulance and we should leave Bill's body and the room untouched until they came. I asked Dr. Wilson what would happen and he said that they'd be taking Bill's body away for tests. To see if it was suicide, I asked. He said yes. He asked if he could use the phone to call his wife to tell her to get their spare bedroom ready for me to stay the night. I tried to say that I'd be alright on my own, but he was having none of it. So I went upstairs to pack a bag and say goodbye to Bill.'

Tom shifted in his seat, searching for words. 'Had Dad given any indication that he might be thinking of taking his life?'

'No. But he was very depressed. He was convinced we were going to get foot and mouth this time with it being so close. And we'd got a letter from the bank calling in the overdraft. At first he'd got angry saying they could whistle for it, saying everything would be fine. But then it seemed to sink in that it wouldn't.'

'It was money then! Why didn't you tell me – I've got more money than I need now. I would have helped.'

'I tried to persuade him to let me speak to you, but he was too proud. Too stubborn. After all the battles you two had, what do you think it would have meant to him to come running to you cap in hand? And anyway, it wasn't the money.'

'What do you mean?'

'He was an old man, Tom. Well over 70 and still working in the fields every day. His health had been failing and he was starting to lose all co-ordination. He looked to be wasting away. His speech was slurring as well. It took me months to persuade him to see a doctor and then he only went because a cut on his leg turned septic. The doctor insisted on some tests. The results came through a few days ago. Motor Neurone Disease.'

'There's no cure, is there,' said Tom quietly.

'No. They gave him a 50% chance of surviving beyond a year or so. And the likelihood that he'd need full time care in a matter of months.'

'But ...' Tom faltered, 'that could have been arranged, surely. I would have ...'

Jean interrupted. 'And who'd be running the farm? Me? On my own?'

'Didn't you discuss what could be done – at least telling me?'

'No. He refused point blank to talk about it. You know what he was like. Said he'd have a think and then just clammed up. Carried on as if nothing was wrong.'

Jean rose from the table and crossed to the kitchen dresser. A row of willow-pattern plates clinked as she opened a drawer. 'He left a note. The police were here today asking me questions and doing forensics before an ambulance took Bill's body away. They said they had to take the note as evidence for the coroner's court but they let me write out a copy.'

Tom took the sheet of paper and read his mother's feathery handwriting.

Sorry lass, but it's for the best. There's no future for farm or for me. I can't be a burden to you. That's not right. You've been the grandest wife any man could wish for. Tell Tom to look after you.

Tom re-read the suicide note, deconstructing it as he went. So his father had typically given himself a simple choice between right and wrong. Wrong to be a burden, so therefore right to choose the simplest way to avoid it.

The grandest wife – some epitaph to 35 years of marriage. But any expression of love would have been wholly out of character. No chance of 'tell Tom I love him.' Even less 'tell Tom all is forgiven.' Just a terse command: *Tell Tom to look after you.*

What emotion lay behind those six words? Were they painful to write, an admission of his father's final defeat, a recognition of his inability to continue to do his duty to the farm and his wife? Or was there a hint of victory, in that Tom would now be forced to take on the duty?

Tom became aware that his mother was staring at him, expecting a response. He chose his words carefully.

'He did it for you then.'

Jean shrugged. 'That's one way of looking at it. And probably the way he looked at it. A noble act, maybe.'

'And is that the way you look at it?'

Jean took her time to reply. 'I don't know. I just feel numb right now.'

The old sheepdog's ears pricked as he sensed the anguish in her voice. He hauled himself from the blanketed comfort of his basket and lumbered across to lick his mistress's hand. Jean absentmindedly ruffled the white fur beneath his chin.

'Did you love him, Mum?'

'What a strange thing to say, Tom. Of course I did. He could be exasperating. There were times when I could have wrung his neck. But he was a good, honest, hardworking man with such a sense of … a sense of belief in what he did. And I loved him for it. It was never a grand passion to set the world alight, but yes, I loved him.'

The sheepdog turned to look at Tom, as if awaiting his response, but it was Jean who spoke. 'And did you love him?'

Tom was lost for an answer. Absurdly all he could think of was Prince Charles' infamous remark when asked if he loved Diana. Whatever love is.

Jean saved him from having to reply. 'Look, I've had more than enough for one day. Life must go on and I've got the motherless lambs to bottle feed before I go to bed then church in the morning. It's Palm Sunday.'

'Can I help?'

'What, in those fine city clothes? No, it's my job.' She'd reverted to the brisk, efficient wife and mother he remembered so well.

'But isn't there anything I can do?'

'No, Tom. For the time being it's enough that you're here. Tomorrow morning I'll do the first bottle feed, and then while I'm at church you can check the fields for any new lambs born overnight and bring them in to the pens with their mothers. I'm sure you can still remember what needs doing. And you need to be on the lookout for any signs of fever in the sheep. It's the first stage of foot and mouth. When I'm back we'll sit down calmly and sensibly and talk practicalities.'

'You don't want me to come to church with you?'

'Just get to bed, Tom.' Tom rose and clasped his mother. 'We've said enough for now. Just go to bed. I'll be fine.'

Tom unzipped his overnight bag in his childhood bedroom exposing his laptop and mobile phone. With a jolt he realised he'd not given one thought to his London life for most of the day. Instinctively he checked the phone for missed calls. No signal. He turned it off to preserve the battery. He lay back on the creaking single bed, sinking into the hollow of the mattress. A video of his day fast forwarded in his mind, but before he could focus on it, the late night, the long drive and the rollercoaster of emotions took their toll and he collapsed into sleep, fully clothed.

3

Tom awoke to the sound of rain beating on the window. He looked round uncertainly, taking in with dismay that he had slept in his clothes. His Patek Phillipe wristwatch, bought too cheaply in Shanghai to be genuine, told him that it was nearly 10 a.m. He peered outside and saw that the ancient Land Rover he had parked beside last night was no longer there. He was alone.

Stripping off his crumpled clothes and grabbing his toilet bag he headed for the bathroom to shower. There was no shower, only the roll top enamel bath of his youth. He decided that a quick wash and shave would have to suffice for the moment, especially if he was going to be out in the elements searching for new-born lambs.

Back in his bedroom, he pulled out fresh clothes from his bag. Chinos and a Lacoste polo shirt would hardly do. With some trepidation he walked to his parents' bedroom and opened his father's wardrobe. A musty smell wafted out. He selected a thick, checked Viyella shirt and a pair of beige corduroy twill trousers. Both had seen better days. He put them on with a conscious effort to ignore any symbolism in the act. The trouser turns ups hung a good six inches above his ankles

Downstairs he opened the fridge door to look for something to eat and his father's words came back to him. *'Nay lad. Animals come first. Give them their feed and then thee'll have earned thy breakfast.'*

He opened the door to the porch outside the kitchen door. Hanging above mud-encrusted wellingtons several dark blue overalls hung in a line. Struggling to pull on a pair, he found they pinched uncomfortably around his crotch. The sheepdog had joined him, ready for duty. Guiltily, Tom realised that he didn't know his name, so long had it been since he'd visited the farm. He ventured the name of the dog he'd grown up with. 'Bob?' The animal cocked his head his head to one side, non-committedly, but wagged his tail. Bob would have to do for the moment. He forced his feet into boots a size too small. *'So, finally stepping into thy father's shoes. Eh lad?'* Tom recoiled at the words of his own imagination.

Opening the porch door, Tom was hit by a blast of driving rain. He looked forlornly around, wondering where and how to begin to look for new-born sheep. As he bent forward to tuck the overall trousers into his boots, he heard the approaching sound of an engine above the howl of the wind. Hearing it too, Bob, or whatever his name was, launched himself from the porch in a frenzy of barking, clipping Tom's legs and propelling him face forward into the mud. A quad bike slewed to a halt as Tom struggled to his feet. A slim hooded figure dismounted and approached grinning broadly.

'Tom Keardon, I presume.'

'Sorry?'

'Sally. Sally Hardcastle.' She stifled a laugh. 'I'm sorry, but you look so funny.'

Tom looked down self-consciously at his splattered overalls and wiped his muddy face. 'I was just …'

'Look, can I come in out of this filthy weather?'

'I'm sorry, of course.'

They retreated to the porch with the dog and closed the door. There was barely enough space for the three of them. Sally pulled down the hood of her anorak to reveal a tousled mane of damp blonde hair.

'I'm so sorry about your father, Tom. I know you weren't close to him, but it must be terrible for you. And for your Mum, of course.'

'Yes. Thanks. It's all been … well, I haven't taken it all in yet.'

'Hold still while I get my boots off.'

She grasped his shoulder to steady herself while she tugged at her wellingtons. 'Thanks. Mind if I put the kettle on?' Without waiting for an answer, she moved into the kitchen, removing her anorak as she went. Tom watched her, intrigued at her self-possession. He too rid himself of his boots and wriggled out of his muddied overall.

As Tom entered the kitchen Sally took in his appearance. She giggled. 'Well, what a city slicker!' Tom looked down ruefully at the gap between his socks and the turn ups of his father's trousers. 'And to think that I used to have a teenage crush on you. You do know who I am, don't you?'

'Of course I do.'

'Good. Because I didn't want you to think that I was some mad girl who turned up out of the blue. My Mum asked me to come over to see if you needed any help. I got here just as Jean was leaving for church and she asked me to look for the new-borns as you hadn't surfaced. I've checked and there aren't any today. And no signs of foot and mouth you'll be glad to know. So you can relax – and get out of those silly clothes.'

'Yes, perhaps I should. I feel I'm at something of a disadvantage.'

When Tom returned, face washed, in his fresh clothes, a cup of tea was waiting. He sat down at the kitchen table opposite Sally who smiled broadly at him.

'So … it must be all of fifteen years since I last saw you. You were just off to university. I was just going into the sixth form.'

'Yes, it must be that long.'

'Jean told me you became a journalist in Hong Kong of all places.'

'Yes, that's right.'

'And now you're some sort of big shot in the city.'

'Well, I started up a company providing online business intelligence on the Far East. It's early days, but we're expanding fast.'

'And is this the first time you've been home in fifteen years?'

'No. I came back once to see Mum when I first got back from Hong Kong.'

'Not to see your Dad as well?'

'I never saw him. He took himself off to the fields just before I arrived. Told Mum I was no son of his, and he stayed out until

I'd gone. It got late and he still hadn't come back so I went down to the village inn to stay the night.'

'That bad, eh? I can understand that he was pissed off that you weren't going to take over the farm, but to completely blank you – that's a bit over the top.'

'That's the sort of man he was.'

Tom broke the silence that ensued. 'What about you, Sally? What's your story?'

'I went to Uni in Newcastle to do Business Studies. Did my third-year work attachment at a marketing company in the city and they offered me a job when I graduated. I got myself a flat and a wardrobe full of business suits and became little Miss Efficient. I seemed to be quite good at it, but my heart wasn't in it. I didn't really take to city living and missed the countryside. I started coming home every other weekend to chill out on the farm.'

'Is this one of those weekends?'

'No. I live here now.'

'What made you come home?'

'Breaking up with the boyfriend I'd been living with was the catalyst. I thought hard about what I wanted to do and came up with a way to kill two birds with one stone – help Mum and Dad to make a decent living and set up a business which could actually work out here in the sticks.'

'Was your farm struggling then?'

'No more than every other sheep farm in the Dales. I don't suppose what's been happening here has crossed your radar?'

Tom shook his head.

'Well you must know that it's never been particularly profitable trying to farm marginal land like this, but in the past few years there's been almost a perfect storm of setbacks. What's the old adage about there only being three ways to make a business more profitable? Sell more, charge more, cut your costs. Fat chance of selling more when the EU quotas are limiting the number of sheep we can keep, and we've still got restrictions in force on sheep sales from Chernobyl fifteen years on. Charge more? Lamb prices have collapsed in the last couple of years. Great news for the consumer and supermarket profits, but who takes the hit? Us sheep farmers at the end of the chain. And as for costs, you name it. Fuel, fodder, machinery; everything we can't do without has increased in price. All we need now is for the foot and mouth to hit us and we can all give up and go home. Except the farms are our homes.'

Tom was taken aback by the passion in her voice. 'That was quite a speech.'

She looked at him defiantly, eyes flashing.

'I'm sorry. Ask me about the economic conditions of farming in South West China and I could probably bore you rigid, but I had no idea things were so bad here.'

'Obviously not.'

Tom picked up on the undercurrents of the remark but decided not to go there. 'What was the idea you had? Killing two birds with one stone?'

As she continued to stare at him with accusation in her eyes, he thought she was about to ignore the question and launch into a lecture on his dereliction of duty to his father's farm. But she relaxed and answered.

'I dug out my notes from Uni to help me do an analysis of my parents' business. I pretended it was a course assignment. It didn't take long to rule out any way of making the traditional business model of sheep farming work, so it had to be changed. Diversification was the obvious way to go. But that meant finding finance. I started researching grants and found that we might be eligible for a whole raft of EU and UK government subsidies for improving the farm environment and rearing animals other than sheep, for organic farming, conservation, and encouraging wildlife. But most significantly, I discovered that grants were available for non-farming developments in depressed rural areas like this – campsites and caravan parks, sports activities, arts and crafts, tourism. At first I only thought about out how our farm could use grants to diversify, but then the penny dropped. I realised that because almost every farm round here was struggling just like us, there was a big business opportunity.'

'What, offering consultancy on grants to other farms?'

'No. The last thing I wanted to do was wade through bureaucracy. Anyway, there are plenty of people who can do it far better than I could, although it's good for my business if I know the ropes and can point people in the right direction to get financial help. No. I thought beyond that. If and when all this diversification came to fruition, then it would need to be marketed. And that's where I thought I could use my skills to build a business.'

'What did you do?'

'I started up Dales PR and Marketing Ltd. I approached all the existing tourist businesses in the Dales – holiday cottages and the like. Managed to get a few retainers, and then I started up a website, dales dotcom, and got businesses to sign up to it. It's a single point of contact for anyone searching the web for everything we've got to offer here in the Dales. It's growing nicely and I'm getting plenty of PR for the site. And the spin-off is that I'm picking up loads of marketing briefs - design and print work and the like. Just like your business, how did you put it, it's early days, but we're expanding fast. Although a lot of things have been put on hold since foot and mouth came.'

'What about your parents' business? Have you managed to diversify?'

'Yes. With a combination of grants and loans we were able to convert some old buildings on the farm into five holiday cottages plus an office for me. I live in one of the cottages when it's not let and pop back to Mum and Dad's when it is.'

'I take my hat off to you. You're not just a pretty face!'

Sally's eyes narrowed. 'I'll choose to take that as a compliment rather than the condescending sexist remark it probably was.'

The sheepdog leapt from his basket and rested his front paws on the windowsill, barking madly and frantically wagging his tail. 'That must be Mum back,' said Tom standing up to look through the window. The Land Rover pulled to a halt and the dog rushed to the door to greet his mistress.

In the porch Jean shook the raindrops from her coat and hung it up. She opened the kitchen door and held the palm of her hand out to the dog to prevent it from leaping up. 'Down, Bob – can't you see I'm in my Sunday best?'

Hearing the name Tom did a double take. 'Hi Mum, are you OK?'

'Bearing up. It was a great comfort to see everyone at church. They were all so kind, and the vicar said a special prayer for Bill. Still here Sally? Any lambs?'

'No Mrs Keardon, I couldn't find any. Tom and I have been chatting, catching up. But I should get back now - Mum's doing a Sunday roast. Unless there's anything else needs doing of course?'

'You get away, Sally. You've already been such a help.'

'Yes', said Tom, 'I don't think I even thanked you for what you did.'

'No need.'

'Well can I at least give you a lift home?'

'No thanks. It'll be quicker to walk across the fields, and the rain's not too bad now.'

Tom waited to see her off while she pulled on her boots and anorak. 'Thanks then,' he said. 'And it was good talking to you.'

Sally's head tilted to one side, a faint smile on her face. 'Yeah. See you, slicker.' She spun on her heel and was gone.

Jean was busying herself at the kitchen worktop.

'Quite a girl that Sally.'

'Aye, she's a fine lass. And so good to her parents.' She immediately realised how Tom might take it. 'Sorry, Tom – that wasn't meant to be any sort of jibe.'

'I'd deserve if it was. I couldn't even get up in time to look for the lambs.'

'You're probably just not used to country hours, being away so long.'

'Look Mum, why don't I take you down to the Black Bull for some lunch. Sally talking about Sunday roast has made me hungry and you might enjoy a little break from work.'

'I'm sure I would, but who's going to bottle feed the lambs if we go gallivanting off to the village? It's every four hours they need feeding you know, and it's already overdue. No, let's see if you can manage it while I get changed and make some sandwiches.'

By the time Tom had once again struggled in to the undersized work clothes and reached the sheep pens, the rain had relented and the sun was making sporadic appearances between heavy, scudding clouds. He made up the bottles, carefully reading instructions on the unfamiliar packets of milk replacer. They were nothing like the ones he remembered from his teenage years. Securing the first lamb gently between his knees, he placed the teat in its mouth and marvelled at the intensity with which the frail creature began to suck.

For the first time since he'd received the fateful phone call, he was able to think rationally and take stock of his situation. He was obviously needed here at the farm, at least until help could be arranged. Presumably he could hire someone – but did such things as freelance sheep farmers exist? Then there'd be the formalities following from his father's suicide to be completed. Registering the death, arranging the funeral. Hang on, they didn't even have the body. He had no idea what the procedure was after a suicide.

The lamb had sucked the bottle dry, so he gently released it. It tottered away as he moved on to the next.

There'd presumably be a post-mortem before the body could be released and then a coroner's inquest. And what about the will? Who was the executor and who would inherit? Not him for sure – probably his mother would get the farm, along with all the debts. Ah yes, the bank. He'd have to arrange a meeting.

Tom filled a bottle for the next lamb and turned his attention to London. He couldn't miss Tuesday's board meeting, not with Angie's report up for discussion. He'd have to get back by Monday evening. He could leave the car and take a train. The only saving grace was that with the long Easter weekend coming up, at least he'd be able to return to Yorkshire and stay for a few days without missing too much at work.

Over sandwiches, Jean pulled out a sheet of paper and firmly wrote 'To Do' on the top of it. 'Right, Tom. The first thing I need to know is how long you'll be staying to help me out with everything that needs doing.'

Tom formed an apologetic expression. 'I've been thinking. I can stay for most of tomorrow but then I'll have to get a train back to London in the evening. I've got a monthly board meeting on Tuesday morning and there's no way I can miss it. We've got critical decisions to take about the future of the company. I'll definitely be back for the Easter weekend. Perhaps before if I can sort things out.'

'I see,' Jean said, coldly.

'Look, sorry Mum, but I'm running quite a big operation. I can't just down tools at the drop of a hat and leave everybody in the lurch.'

'So you're indispensable are you, even for your father's death?'

'No, of course I'm not. But ...' Tom stopped himself saying that it couldn't have come at a worst time. 'It's just that we've reached a crossroads in the company. I feel that it's my baby, and I want ... no I need to be there for the meeting. It's crucial. We've even got So Lin flying in from Hong Kong specially for it.'

'Ah, the ex-wife that we never got to meet.'

'Yes. I'm sorry Mum. I would have loved for you to meet her but I didn't think that there was a chance that Dad would have welcomed her.'

'So what went wrong with the marriage?'

'What went wrong?' Tom leant back from the table, clasping his hands behind his head. 'What went wrong was that it was never right. I suppose that going off travelling in the East straight after I left university was partly a way of avoiding having to come home and make my peace with Dad. I knew that there was no way I wanted to take on the farm, so I didn't see any point in coming home and kicking off all the old arguments again. Then, when I fell on my feet in Hong Kong and got a job, part of the attraction of staying put there was that I was pretty much as far away from the farm and Dad as possible.' Tom leant forward. 'But I missed you, Mum.'

'Not as much as I missed you, Tom.'

'No.' Tom could think of nothing more to say.

'I missed you, but when you told me you'd got married, at least it was some sort of comfort. I told myself he's flown the coop and settled down. Not such a bad thing. I always wanted you to make your way in the world, to do things I never had the determination or the courage to do. I took an easy option – some easy option, being a sheep farmer's wife – but you know what I mean. I retreated from the big wide world. No real regrets, but always that nagging feeling that things might have been different.'

'I know how difficult it must it have been for you to fight in my corner against Dad. I appreciate it.'

'Yes, it wasn't easy. But I asked about So Lin. Why did you break up?'

'Don't get me wrong, I fell in love with her and married her because I thought we could build a life together. But, with hindsight, we were too different. I was a gweilo, she was a Hong.'

'And what are they when they're at home?'

'Gweilo's a Cantonese slang word. Usually translated as foreign devil. She came from a family of Hongs. Hongs are powerful business dynasties who pull all the commercial strings out there. We found common ground in the social whirl of all the other displaced yuppies who worked and lived hard, but it was all very superficial. Then when I started to report for the paper all over the Far East and I was on the road more than I was with her, we just drifted apart. She naturally went back to her Chinese friends and family.'

'But you're still friends. And business colleagues.'

'Yes, good friends. I'm supposed to be having dinner with her on Tuesday evening after the board meeting.'

Jean picked up her pen and underlined 'To do' on the sheet of paper. 'So I've got you for most of tomorrow before you disappear. What do you think you might be able to do?'

They agreed that Tom would phone the police on Monday morning to find out what the procedure was for registering the death, when the body might be released so that a funeral could be arranged, and when the inquest might be held. Jean gave him the name of a firm of funeral directors she knew. She thought that Bill had made a will with a firm of solicitors in Richmond. Tom would call them to arrange a meeting. The letter from the bank was retrieved and studied by Tom.

'They're asking for the best part of £80,000. I assume that you – I mean you and Dad haven't got any savings.'

'Fat chance. There might be a bit of life insurance. No pension that I know of. I'll have to dig through his papers. He never let me know what was happening with the finances. He had this old-fashioned idea that women shouldn't or couldn't worry their pretty little heads about money. I got my weekly allowance for housekeeping and that was about it.'

'If there is any life insurance, it might be invalidated if the coroner finds that it was suicide.'

Jean made no comment. Tom realised that she felt pain hearing the word. He continued after a respectful pause. 'Presumably the farm is held in collateral against the overdraft, so we've got three options. One, we put the farm up for sale and pay off the bank with the proceeds – if and when it sells. Two, we hand over the farm to the bank and make it their problem. Three, I pay off the overdraft. I can just about afford to. But that begs the question of what we'd do with the farm after that. Whatever we do, you can't run the farm on your own without help and you need somewhere to live. What do you want to do?'

Jean took a long time to answer. 'What I want to do is live out the rest of my years in peace and quiet. I've earned it. I'd rather it was here – this is my home – but I'd understand if it had to be elsewhere. But somewhere close.'

'I need to find out more. I'll speak to the bank first and depending on what they say, either look into hiring someone to manage the farm or selling it off. Don't worry, Mum. I'll make sure that you're looked after. I want to do it for you.'

'Not for Dad? It's what he asked you to do.'

Tom thought hard about his feelings for his father. 'Let's just say that I'm not ready to make my peace with Dad yet.'

4

It was still dark when the alarm clock Tom had borrowed roused him from a good night's sleep brought on by physical exertion. He'd spent Sunday afternoon helping his mother with the daily farm chores – mucking out the lambing sheds, topping up hay racks and providing fresh drinking water. Together they'd taken the quad bike to the outlying fields to check the sheep for signs of foot and mouth. She'd examined a few who were unusually lethargic and showed him how to look for the tell-tale signs of the disease – blisters in the mouth and on the feet. Thankfully there were none. Then a quiet evening in front of the television during which Tom made a conscious effort to relax and not tax his brain with the range of problems and decisions he faced, followed by an early night.

At first light he joined Jean on a search for new-born lambs. The clear skies promised a fine day. They found several and brought them and their mothers to pens where each family group had its own space in which to bond. To make room for them the lambs already a few days old were transferred with their ewes to larger mothering pens to encourage lamb/ewe recognition in a crowd, a vital skill for lambs' survival.

After another round of bottle-feeding Tom was able to bathe, dress in his London clothes and grab a slice of toast for breakfast. He searched the kitchen cupboards for coffee to no avail, so resigned himself to tea. By 9 a.m. he was by the house phone with pen and paper to begin the round of calls. The first was to his PA at the office. He explained that his father had died – omitting to elaborate on the circumstances – and that he would be back in the office tomorrow in time for the board meeting.

His PA ran through the day's appointments that he would miss. He told her to ask Charles, the finance director, to chair the regular Monday morning operations meeting and he postponed three annual assessments he'd been due to conduct with members of staff. A presentation that he and Angie were due to give at the offices of a prospective client in the city in the late afternoon was more of a problem. He toyed with the idea of asking to be put through to her but shied away from having to conduct a professional conversation as if nothing had happened. Instead he asked to be transferred to Ben.

'Morning, boss. How goes it?'

'Not so good.'

Ben listened intently as Tom gave a brief summary of the weekend's events. 'Oh, I'm so sorry, mate. What a bugger! Are you're going to stay up there to help your Mum?'

'Only for today. I'm not going to miss the board meeting tomorrow. Then I'll have to look at coming back up here as soon as I can. In the meantime, can you do something for me? I don't want to speak to Angie on the phone right now. I'd rather have it out with her face to face when the time's right. Could you tell her that I won't be able to make the presentation we're due to give this afternoon? See if she's happy to do it on her own unless it can be rearranged without upsetting the client.'

'Sure thing. Is there anything else I can do?'

'I suppose you better tell everyone at the Operations meeting why I'm not there.'

'OK. How are you feeling?'

'I'm really not sure. A whole mix of emotions. I think I told you once about all the baggage I've got from leaving the family farm. This has brought it all back. And at the same time I've got to resolve the situation with Angie somehow. That's hanging over my head. Then there's her report to be discussed tomorrow.'

'Well, I'll give you all the support I can – as a friend, as well as a colleague.'

'I know you will. Thanks. I think I'm going to need it.'

Tom replaced the receiver and wondered whether he should have bitten the bullet and spoken to Angie. But what would he have said? Should he be suspending her for her behaviour? Then what about his behaviour? Right now, he guessed, the water-cooler gossip at Tiger.com would be hotting up. Do you know what Angie said to the MD at the wine bar last Friday? Have you heard how drunk he got at the night club? You should have seen the slapper he copped off with. Tom winced at the thoughts. But the word of his father's death would also soon be spreading. How would that play out? Maybe it would win a sympathy vote. He rebuked himself for hoping that it would.

Release from the distressing rumination came in tackling the 'To Do' list. He started with the police and after being transferred several times and hanging on for many minutes he finally got to speak to the officer in charge of investigating his father's death. The officer offered his sympathies and asked after his mother before explaining that the coroner had been informed and that a post-mortem would be carried out in the next day or two to establish the cause of death. But we're assuming that it was suicide, he said – we're not looking for anyone else in connection with your father's death. Tom asked when they could expect the inquest to take place. Probably not for several months was the reply – there was apparently a backlog. Only then could the death be registered, but the body would probably be released after the post-mortem, so a funeral could be arranged. Tom thanked him for his help and gave him his mobile phone number in case he needed to be contacted in London.

Feeling perturbed that it was obviously going to be a long, drawn-out affair before his father could be buried and some sort of line drawn under his death, he moved on to the next call.

The receptionist at the firm of solicitors told him that the partner his mother thought might be the executor of the will had retired some years ago. However, she'd arrange for a copy of the will to be retrieved from their storeroom and someone would phone him back, probably within an hour or two.

He was quickly put through to the manager of his father's bank in Richmond. Tom asked if there was any chance of a meeting that day as he was returning to London that evening and couldn't be sure when he'd be able to return to Yorkshire. After a pause to consult his diary, the manager said he could fit him in at four o'clock for thirty minutes.

Tom wondered about the train times back to London that evening. He could always drive back, but five hours on the road was the last thing he needed if he was going to be in any shape for tomorrow's board meeting. And it made sense to leave the car up North if he would be returning in a few days. He phoned rail enquiries and was relieved to discover that trains from Darlington, on the main east coast line between Edinburgh and London, ran every half hour or so during the early evening. The last train, just after nine would get him to Kings Cross shortly after midnight.

His thoughts turned to arranging help for his mother in looking after the farm. Instinctively he moved to get his laptop to search for information online before he remembered that he'd not brought a modem with him so there was no chance of getting dial-up Internet access. He thought about phoning his PA again to get her to do some research online then thought better of it. It would probably end up as more grist to the mill of water-cooler gossip.

He toyed with the idea of driving down to the village to see if the inn had Internet access. Pretty unlikely, he decided. Who could he speak to who might have the right contacts to find a farm worker in need of a job? He found a telephone directory, looked up a name and called the number.

Rosie Hardcastle answered.

'It's Tom, Mrs Hardcastle. Tom Keardon.'

'Hello, love. Is everything OK? Is your Mum OK?'

'She seems to be fine. She's being very strong.'

'That's good. Do you need any help?'

'Well actually it was Sally I was after. I hope she might be able to help me with some information.'

'She's in her office. I could go and get her unless you'd like to call her direct.'

Tom took down the number and redialled.

'Dales PR and Marketing.' The voice had a sing-song intonation.

'Sally? It's Tom.'

'Tom?' There was a brief pause. 'Oh, Tom. Hiya slicker. To what do I owe the pleasure?'

'It's just that I'm after some information and I thought you might be able to help. I've got to go back to London this evening and I wanted to try and get things moving about finding at least some temporary help for Mum in looking after the farm. I want to employ someone, and I don't really know where to start. I thought you might have some contacts.'

'I could probably ring round some of my clients to see if they've got any ideas. You might be in luck. The lambing season's coming to an end so there could be some casual labour looking for work soon. I'll see what I can do.'

'Thanks Sally. I really appreciate it.'

'But what about the long term? You've got to take responsibility for your Mum. You can't expect her to keep the place going, even with casual labour. Have you thought about looking for a farm manager?'

'Well it did cross my mind, but if the place is losing money without any staff costs, wouldn't that be throwing good money after bad? The bank's already threatening to call in the overdraft.'

'Oh dear! That bad, eh? I don't suppose it's any comfort, but I know of plenty of other Dales farms in the same situation. It's part of what I do in my job, helping them find a way out.'

'It sounds as if you're touting for business.'

'Never miss a sales opportunity! No, seriously, I'd be happy to see what I can do to help out. First consultation entirely free, no obligation. Then once I've hooked you, I can start fleecing you for some of those ill-gotten gains you must have made in the City.'

There was a pause during which Tom said nothing. Sally sounded apologetic. 'Sorry. Am I being insensitive? Giving you all this banter when you've only just lost your father and goodness knows how much you've got on your mind. I apologise.'

'No, Sally. Amidst all the doom and gloom, chatting to you is about the only thing that's cheered me up.'

'Are you sure? You're not just being polite? It's just that seeing you again after all these years, I somehow revert to the gawky sixteen-year-old I was when I last saw you, teeth barely out of braces. You were the glamorous rebel with a cause, about to break free. But try as I might to get your attention, to get you to notice that I'd grown up, you continued to treat me as your childhood chum.'

Further silence from Tom.

'Are you still there? Or have you hung up on my mad rantings?'

'I'm still here, Sally.'

'Well, as I said, I'm sorry. I'll cut out the psychobabble, tone down the banter and promise I won't become your stalker.'

'I know what you mean about reverting. Coming back here, and my father's death, has just thrown up all the emotions and frustrations I felt when I last lived here.'

Tom heard a jaunty ringtone in the background. 'Hang on, I've got a call coming through on my mobile.' Distantly, he heard her answer and tell the caller to wait. She came back to him.

'Tom, I need to take this. I'll phone around about finding help for the farm and get back to you. Give me your mobile number in case it's after you've left.'

Replacing the receiver, Tom tried to take in their conversation. She was a force of nature, no doubt. Fun to talk to as well. But he couldn't help feeling wary of her. He could handle the mickey taking – he probably deserved it – but there had been flashes of disapproval as well.

The harsh ring of the phone interrupted his thoughts. It was the retired solicitor calling to confirm that he was indeed the executor of his father's will. Tom explained that he was returning to London that evening and asked him if there was any chance of a meeting that afternoon. To his surprise, he readily agreed and three o'clock was agreed at his old firm's offices.

Tom looked at his watch and took in that he wouldn't have to leave for several hours. He toyed with the idea of going to help his mother out in the fields, but she had been insistent that she could cope on her own. Anyhow he couldn't face struggling into the ridiculous work clothes, getting filthy and needing another bath before he left. Instead he decided to fire up his laptop and re-read Angie's report which they would be discussing at the board meeting. He acknowledged to himself that he'd never read it dispassionately and resolved to do his duty as a managing director responsible both to his shareholders and staff to take an objective view of the arguments and proposals. He turned over his mother's 'To Do' list and began to make notes on the back of it as he read. An hour later, he had the arguments for and against clear in his mind.

Jean returned, sheepdog in tow, to make herself an inevitable cup of tea. Tom had just finished filling her in on the outcome of his morning's calls when the phone rang again. Tom walked to the hallway to answer it. It was Sally.

'Hi, Tom. I may have a lead for you about help on the farm.'

'That's great. You're a quick worker.'

'I just struck lucky. Have you got a pen?'

Tom thought about the time he would have to kill before leaving for his first meeting in Richmond. He was getting stir crazy cooped up in the farm and Sally's company would lift his spirits. 'I tell you what. Rather than taking the details down now, can I buy you lunch down at the Bull? To say thank you for all you help and, to be frank, I think I could do with cheering up. I don't have to leave for meetings in Richmond until about two and I'm just kicking my heels here.'

'Well, I … OK, you're on.'

Tom took his leave of his mother, promising to be back for the Easter weekend if not before. Jean insisted that she would be fine. 'It's only looking after the sheep for the while,' she assured him. 'Everything else will have to wait for the moment.'

He gingerly negotiated his way across the farmyard between the muddy puddles from yesterday's rain and flung his overnight bag into the small boot of the Audi. Driving carefully down the rough track he was struck by the beauty of the panorama before him. He stopped at a vantage point close to where the Hardcastles lived. He turned off the engine and got out of the car. Below him, the clustered grey stone buildings of the village were wreathed in watery sunshine. Beyond, the silvery Swale meandered through the river meadows. Above, at the peak of the steep grassy slopes on the far side of the dale, three stubby trees were framed in isolation against a clear blue sky, monuments to survival against the odds. To his right, at the same level, the Gawthrop Farm buildings newly converted into holiday cottages were clearly visible. He wondered which one Sally stayed in. Tom turned and looked up at his farm. It seemed to be so much part of the landscape, as if it were meant to be there. For the first time that he could remember, he felt an affinity with the surroundings.

At 12.30 he pulled into the car park of the village inn. Outside an A-frame board proclaimed 'Open all day – walkers welcome. Good food and accommodation.' A further sign boasted 'Under New Management.' Entering, he was struck by the transformation. It was no longer the shabby pub he remembered from his youth but a welcoming, even stylish environment. The flagstone floor and the original Georgian features had been retained but the light oak furniture, artfully distressed, and the modern wall hangings spoke of an expensive makeover aimed at attracting city weekenders and well-heeled walkers.

The bar was empty. He was obviously the first customer of the day. He surveyed the line of hand pumps before pressing his palm on a bell on the counter. A young barmaid emerged from the kitchen. He confirmed that they were serving lunch and, conscious of the driving ahead of him, ordered the real ale with the lowest alcoholic content, a pint of Black Sheep. Rather appropriate, he mused. Choosing a seat by the window, Tom spent five minutes reminiscing about the many less than sober evenings he'd spent in the inn when he infrequently returned home during his university student years. The pub visits were usually triggered by an acrimonious argument with his father, followed by Tom storming out.

He saw a Freelander pull into the car park. Sally emerged and walked briskly towards the pub entrance. He was surprised to see that she was smartly dressed for business in a pencil skirt, a neat white fitted blouse and high heels. No longer the country girl. He rose from behind the table ready to greet her.

'Hi, Tom.' The blond hair was still tousled but carefully coiffured and she had applied light make up to her fresh face.

'My word. You look good.'

'I'm going on to a meeting with a client this afternoon. Gotta make an effort, you know.'

Tom felt a little crestfallen for thinking it might have been for him. 'What can I get you?'

'Just an orange juice, please.'

He bought one at the bar and came back with two menus, returning to order after they'd made their choices. 'You've got a lead then,' he said as he sat down beside her.

'Yes. There's a farmer near Hawes who runs an agency for casual labour and seasonal workers in the Dales. I've heard he's a difficult man to deal with, but he comes highly recommended. He might be able to come up with some temporary help. There's his name and number.' She handed him a slip of paper. 'Do you want me to keep looking for some permanent help – a farm manager perhaps? That's if you want to keep the farm going.'

'It's not so much whether I want to. It's more whether I can or not.'

Sally looked at him quizzically. 'What do you mean?'

'I already told you that the bank's threatening to pull the rug. I've got a meeting with them this afternoon to see what can be sorted out. And I'm seeing a solicitor about my father's will. I haven't seen it, but I can guarantee that I won't be a beneficiary and probably don't deserve to be. I'm sure the farm will pass to

my Mum, along with all the debts so, technically, it's not up to
me to decide what happens to the farm. And we've still got to
get through the inquest before we can start to move on.'

'But if your Mum wants to keep it going, you're going to try to
help her, aren't you? The farm's been in your family for generations, just like mine. Don't you feel some sense of duty?'

Tom was saved from answering immediately by the arrival of
the barmaid with plates of sandwiches which they'd both ordered. They began to eat.

'Duty is a word I've been hearing of lot of lately.'

'What, from your Mum?'

'She's mentioned it. But I've also been remembering my father
using it every time we argued about the farm. It's being ban-
died about a lot at work too.'

'In what context?'

'One of the directors is arguing for us to start looking for a
major company to take us over. Instinctively I don't feel ready
to lose control of the company I started but it's being pointed
out to me that it's not my company anymore. I have a duty to
the shareholders now. It's all a bit fraught at work at the moment. And then on top of that, I've got to come to terms with
my father's death.'

'I can see why you need cheering up.'

'Look – I'm sorry. I shouldn't be burdening you with all my
problems, especially when you've been so helpful.' Tom
glanced down at the contact details she'd given him.

'So are you going to phone this guy?'

'I'll certainly phone him. But I think I'll hang fire on the idea
of a farm manager for the moment – at least until I know what's
happening with the will and the bank.'

There was a brief silence between them, broken by the latch of
the door being opened and a group of elderly walkers entering.
They chattered animatedly as they removed muddy boots and
propped up expensive metal walking poles more appropriate
for an assault on the Eiger than a stroll in the Dales.

'Thank God we've still got some tourists who haven't been
frightened away.' Tom frowned. She saw his puzzlement and

explained her remark. 'It's not just the farmers who are being affected by foot and mouth. All the tourism businesses around here are getting cancellations left, right and centre. The townies all seem to think that we've shut up shop.'

'But surely you can't have people trampling the disease all over the Dales.'

'Of course there are some restrictions. But that shouldn't stop people staying in the hotels, walking on the footpaths and spending their money. That's what my meeting's about this afternoon. It's with the Dales Tourism Association to look at ways we can get some positive PR and use the media to spread the word that we're open for business. Since foot and mouth arrived all my work's been focused on damage limitation rather than development.'

Tom tried to lighten the mood. 'Still, it's good that you can pick up business in bad times as well as good. You can't be doing too badly if you're driving a Freelander.' He gestured out to the car park.

'It's on a finance deal I can just about manage. It's good for the image, and you need 4 by 4 to get around here in the winter.'

'Tell me about your clients.'

Sally warmed to the invitation. Within a couple of minutes she was regaling him with a tale of trying to explain to a farmer what a website was. Tom found himself laughing along with her and swapping stories of his own about the problems of convincing companies rooted in the old economy that the Internet was the way forward, despite the bursting of the dotcom bubble.

Moving on, they talked about old school friends. With Sally being two years below him at the Richmond school – a gulf at that age – they were able to find few that they both recalled, but they found common ground in the teachers who had variously inspired and appalled them. It was Tom who broke the cheerful mood by looking at his watch. Sally looked at hers at well.

'Well, I guess we both need to get going.'

They both held each other's gaze, long enough for them both to become conscious of the prolonged eye contact. Sally broke it first.

'OK, slicker. Thanks for lunch.'

'No. Thanks for your company – and your help.'

They walked together to the car park and stood facing each other between their cars.

Sally held out her hand. Tom clasped it.

'Good luck with the meetings in Richmond.'

'And good luck with your meeting.'

Tom became aware that he was still holding her hand, and dropped it, embarrassed. 'Right. Thanks again.'

Sally smiled sweetly. 'When are you back?'

'Probably for Easter weekend.'

'OK, might see you then.'

5

Tom easily found a parking space in the sloping cobbled market square of Richmond. With twenty minutes to kill before his first meeting he found a country clothes store and bought himself wellingtons and a pair of overalls. He walked back to the car and stored them in the boot ready for his return. He suddenly thought of his mobile phone and turned it on to see if he had a signal. It sprung into life and showed him five missed calls and two messages.

Conscious of the time, he decided to ignore them for the moment and made his way the short distance to the solicitors' office. He made himself known to the silver-haired receptionist and was shown immediately into a meeting room where he was greeted by a sprightly gentleman in his seventies dressed in golfing clothes.

'Thanks for agreeing to see me.'

'My pleasure, lad. There's only so much time you can spend on the golf course without upsetting the wife and I'm glad to have an excuse to exercise the old brain cells once in a while.'

Tom took to him immediately.

'My condolences about your father. We go back more years than I care to remember. I wouldn't say that I knew him well, but we had a good business relationship. He always struck me as a fine man.'

'Yes, he was. We never saw eye to eye, but I respect his …' Tom searched for the word. 'his single-mindedness.'

The retired solicitor looked at Tom curiously but continued without questioning the choice of phrase. He opened a file on the table in front of him. 'Well, he appointed me to be the executor of his will. In short, everything passes to his wife – your mother.'

'I'd assumed that would be the case. But what if she'd pre-deceased him? Surely there would be some arrangement for that.'

'Of course. I was duty bound to advise him to consider that possibility. I asked him about children and he told me that he'd disowned you, his only child, because you'd wanted nothing to do with the farm and had gone off to make a life elsewhere. I asked him about relatives who might inherit, but he said he had few and none that he wished to make beneficiaries. I warned him that without a beneficiary in the event that your mother was to die before him, the estate would probably pass to you.'

'So what did he decide to do?'

'Well, it's irrelevant now that he's died before your mother. She inherits everything.'

'But, what if he hadn't? Are you able to tell me what the provision was?'

'If you insist. He asked for the farm to be sold and the pro-ceeds to be donated to a charity.' The retired solicitor searched for its name on the will in front of him. 'The Royal Agricultural Benevolent Institution. It supports members of the farming community suffering hardship.'

'He really didn't want me to get the farm, did he?'

'So it would appear.'

'I think I should tell you that my mother will be inheriting considerable debts. The bank's calling in around £80,000 worth of loans.'

'I see. Well technically she won't inherit the debt, the estate will. Unless she's a co-signatory of course.'

'I very much doubt that she is. That wasn't my father's way.'

'It will need to be checked, but if she's not, then it's my task as executor to realise any assets to pay off the debt. I assume the only asset is the farm.'

'As far as I know.'

'Then that means selling it – unless the bank can be persuaded to come to a new arrangement.'

They spent a few minutes discussing options and the process of executing the will before Tom thanked him and took his leave.

Back outside he checked his watch, seeing that he had a good half hour before his appointment at the bank. He remembered a quiet spot where he could sit in the pleasant sunshine. Crossing the busy market square, he turned up an alley leading to the Norman castle, a grey stone fortress built on a rocky spur and said to be the oldest stone-built castle in England. He gazed up at the well-preserved keep towering above him and then walked quickly to the path which followed the perimeter of the castle grounds.

On the South side he peered down a sheer drop to the River Swale, turbulent after the recent rain. White water tumbled noisily over the Foss, a waterfall strewn with rocks. Finding a bench overlooking the thickly wooded river bank rising vertically opposite, Tom pulled out his mobile and retrieved the first text message. It turned out to be from the captain of a 5-a-side football team he occasionally turned out for, asking about his availability. He texted the number to say that he wouldn't be able to play.

The second was from Angie, sent that morning.

'Hi Tom. Just heard about your father. I'm so sorry. I owe you an apology over Friday night. I tried to call you over the weekend but your phone was turned off. Can we talk when you're back? Hope you're OK.'

He put away his mobile and set off to complete the circuit of the castle. Yes, they would have to talk. Both the personal and the professional problems needed to be resolved. Tom had no doubt about the outcome he was looking for – to finish the relationship, and to give her an informal warning about her professional behaviour. He made a mental note to have a word with his Human Resources manager about the correct procedure to follow. The question was how, where and when to tackle the two issues. Together or separately? In the office or out of work? By the time he'd arrived at the bank he'd still reached no conclusion.

The bank manager's appearance came as a surprise. Ruddy-faced and tweedily dressed, he looked like a farmer in his market day best. His oak-panelled office spoke of older and simpler times.

Tom declined the tea that was offered and accepted sympathies for his father's death. The manager pulled a file from his wooden in-tray and sadly shook his head.

'I've been at the bank for about thirty-five years now, and I've never known it so bad for Dales farmers. Time was when we would have ridden out the bad times together. We were both in it for the long term. Provided we got the interest on the loans and the mortgages, we weren't too worried about having them paid back. If a farm got into real financial difficulties, I could usually have a word with head office and find a way to tide them over. They valued the local knowledge I had. I'm afraid it's all very different now.'

'In what way?'

'Well the letter your father received is a perfect example. I wasn't consulted. I was just sent a copy. And what a time to be sending out letters like this, in the middle of a foot and mouth outbreak! Although I wouldn't put it past some bright spark at Head Office to figure out that with the government paying out compensation for slaughtered herds, now could be the time to get in on the act. The bank's not run by people anymore. Computers have taken over. Customers aren't real people with real lives anymore. They're just entries on a spreadsheet. In your father's case the computers must have flagged up that his loans fell outside the acceptable risk parameters or whatever they call it, and off went the letter automatically.'

Tom was taken aback by the vehemence in the manager's voice.

'Is that your way of telling me that you're powerless to do anything about the situation?'

'It's more a way of saying that I disagree with the policies my employers have adopted. Not just my bank, but all of them. Profit at all costs and hang the consequences for the people who lose their homes and livelihoods as a result. Or in your father's case, perhaps his life. I can't tell you how much it's been preying on my mind since I heard he may have taken his own life.'

Tom marvelled at the speed with which the news must have travelled by word of mouth. He'd not mentioned the cause of his father's death when arranging the meeting.

'However, I must do my duty and inform you that the bank requires repayment of all your father's outstanding loans – I'm sorry, your father's estate's loans – forthwith. I'm only empowered to discuss terms and timing.'

'And if it's not repaid, presumably the bank will take possession of the farm.'

'Ultimately, yes. But as you can imagine, that's the last thing we would want to do. Your farm is not the only one in a similar situation and if we're not careful we could end up owning half of North Yorkshire's farms – most of them running at a loss. '

'So you'd prefer it if we sold the farm to repay the debts.'

'I think you'd find it preferable as well. If you could find a buyer, the estate would probably end up with considerably more money than if we were to sell. We'd be happy to price it very low for a quick sale. We wouldn't care what it sold for providing we got our money back.'

'There is another possibility. I could pay the debt.'

The manager raised his eyebrows. 'Would you want to do that?'

'I'm not sure. I haven't thought it through yet. But my mother wants to stay on at the farm.'

Tom gave him the name of the solicitor who was acting as executor. Unsurprisingly, given the size of the town and the nature of their businesses the manager knew him well. He promised to give him a call to talk through the situation.

'There's nothing the bank can do until a grant of probate has been given. And I'm sure our solicitor friend doesn't need to be it too much of rush to apply for it.' He tapped his nose conspiratorially. 'In the meantime,' the manager said, 'I'll try to get through to the department that's dealing with the loan, tell them about your father's death and hold them off for the time being. Even I have to go through a bloody call centre now to speak to them. I'm looking forward to retiring in eighteen months, I can tell you. There's precious little I can do on my own authority these days. They've turned us all into glorified salesmen.' He pointed at a rack of glossy brochures across the office. 'I'm not supposed to let you leave without extolling the virtues of our latest financial products and twisting your arm into buying something you don't really want or need.'

Tom smiled. 'If anyone asks, I'll tell them you made a great sales pitch.'

'Don't you dare! It would ruin my reputation as one of the last surviving dinosaurs of the banking world.'

Tom set off on the journey to Darlington. A few miles along the road he spotted a column of dense black smoke rising into the clear blue sky. Approaching its source, he was appalled to see a funeral pyre of cattle in a roadside field. He pulled to a halt and watched as charred limbs detached from blazing carcasses. Sparks showered and flames flared. A sickly smell permeated his nostrils. To the side, stood a phalanx of white boiler-suited attendants. Hooded, their features obscured by goggles and masks, they looked like survivors from a nuclear holocaust. Beyond them a giant digger was putting the finishing touches to a trench the size of an Olympic swimming pool. Tom shuddered at the recollection of similar scenes from grainy films of concentration camp atrocities. He quickly put the car into gear and sped away.

As the London train gathered pace, Tom settled in his seat and spread out a newspaper on the table which he was pleased to have bagged for himself. The train was half empty. Casting his former journalist's eye over the front page he was unsurprised to find nothing which he hadn't already learnt from watching last night's TV news bulletin. In the absence of a late breaking story, Monday's papers tended to be full of rehashes of articles the Sundays had broken after spending most of the previous week preparing them. They also usually carried a higher than normal number of PR-inspired stories to fill the spaces otherwise occupied by political, legal and commercial news during the working week. Turning the page, his eye was caught by a headline: *Outbreak may not have peaked*. It was accompanied by a photo of burning cattle not dissimilar to the scene he had witnessed not an hour before.

The substance of the story was an admission from the Agriculture Minister speaking on a Sunday morning TV news programme that it was too early to tell if the inexorable spread of foot and mouth was slowing.

Tom read on. The rest of the long article smacked of something that had been written on Friday as a banker for the Monday edition before the day of rest for hacks working on the dailies. It summarised the state of play in the fight against the disease. More than eleven hundred farms now had confirmed cases. The National Farmers Union was calling for vaccination instead of the government's policy of 'death and disinfectant.' Good sound bite, Tom thought. The government was trying to deflect criticism by blaming European Community regulations for not being able to introduce vaccination. In parliament the opposition was getting the bit between its teeth about delays in the introduction of countermeasures and transport bans. Veterinary experts were claiming that the slaughtering policy was literally overkill given that the majority of culled livestock were clean of the disease.

The final paragraphs particularly engaged Tom's attention. They outlined the impact on rural tourism and quoted the results of a survey suggesting that two-thirds of people who had booked Easter trips to the countryside had now cancelled. He thought of Sally and wondered how her meeting had gone. She obviously had a fight on her hands. He looked through the train window at the speeding countryside and caught his ghostly reflection, realising that he was smiling at the recollection of her.

With a conscious effort to focus on the fight on his own hands he turned to the business pages. There was no relief from the general mood of gloom. *Recession Bites* proclaimed a headline. The story posited that the fall-out from the bursting of the dotcom bubble was now affecting even those traditional businesses which had resisted the siren call of the so-called new economy. It cited a raft of profit warnings and job loss announcements from companies on both sides of the Atlantic. Tom noted that many were from telecommunications companies and investment banks which had most to lose from the slowdown in the growth of new technology. The article concluded by suggesting that things had reached a pretty state of affairs if Amazon's share price had jumped by a third only because first quarter losses were smaller than expected.

Tom took exception to the proposition. Surely he thought, that was a reason to be optimistic. Didn't the rise in the share price mean that the markets believed in a future for those dotcom companies which had survived? Yes, fortunes had been made and more commonly lost in the fevered dotcom gold rush, but unlike seams of gold the new economy would not be running out. It had already changed the way the world did business and could only grow. The Wright Brothers crashed a hundred and fifty feet into their maiden flight. Did that stop us from developing Concorde? It was an argument he had used several times when presenting to technological disbelievers.

The train drew into York station and he took in the magnificent Victorian metal arches supporting the glass roof above what was once the largest station in the world. He also took in the throng of passengers on the platform and realised that he was likely to lose his sole occupation of the seats around his table. Sure enough his relative privacy was invaded by a young couple both sporting black T shirts emblazoned with the logos of heavy metal bands. He folded his newspaper on his side of the table and they proceeded to fill the rest of the space of with a variety of crisps, snacks and fizzy drinks. Without exchanging a word, they both donned headphones and settled down to play on a Gameboy in his case and to read a celebrity magazine in hers. The tinny buzz from two competing music tracks made Tom regret his decision not to travel first class and he resolved to upgrade for the return journey.

With little room to reopen his broadsheet paper he turned to the copy of the Economist he'd bought at Darlington station and lighted on a piece about the burgeoning Chinese economy headlined *Enter the Dragon*. Taking as its cue China's approach to join the World Trade Organisation, it chronicled the path to the country's current economic boom. It predicted that China would emerge even stronger from the worldwide recession but in the longer term it could lose competitiveness when higher living standards forced up wages and property prices. Tom found little to disagree with in the analysis nor much that he didn't already know. Indeed, he had recently written an article for a business magazine arguing pretty much the same. But it sparked the germ of an idea in his mind. Apart from a visit to the buffet bar for sandwiches and coffee, he spent the rest of the journey thinking it through. By the time the train had reached the suburbs of North London he'd decided on a plan of action.

Rather than join the long queue for taxis at the side of the King's Cross station he ran the gauntlet of the homeless, the drug addicts and the prostitutes who nightly congregated on the forecourt and was able to hail a cab after walking a couple of hundred yards in the direction of the City of London. Fifteen minutes later he was opening the door of his loft apartment.

As always, the night-time view across the River Thames through the panoramic windows was spectacular, but when he turned on the lights the place seemed very empty. Not simply because it had been sparely furnished in minimalist style, but because it didn't feel lived in. Tom carried his bag through to the bedroom to unpack. The unmade bed triggered guilty memories of his drunken Friday night romp. Retrieving his laptop, he walked across the polished wooden floorboards of the long, narrow living room to the desk beside the connection for the expensive new broadband system he'd just had installed. Logging on, he watched as a succession of emails cascaded down the screen. He set about weeding out the spam and then opened the remaining messages. Only one needed his immediate attention, a compilation of departmental reports for the board meeting which his PA had sent as an attachment to all directors.

He went to the kitchen refrigerator and saw that in the absence of a weekend shop it was largely empty. Thankfully there were several bottles of lager, one of which he opened and took back to the living room. He scanned the rack of CDs and chose a favourite Clapton album which he fired up on the Bang and Olufsen system.

He settled down with bottle and laptop in a leather and steel Le Corbusier armchair and opened the attachment to read through the reports. When he'd finished, he crossed to the plate glass window which spanned the length of the living room. Reflections of the streetlights on the opposite bank rippled on the surface of the water. A fully laden barge, impossibly low in the water, doggedly ploughed a delta-shaped furrow against the incoming tide. The murmur of traffic noise was punctuated by a wailing siren and he watched as an ambulance careered into view, blue light intermittently illuminating the darkened buildings lining the southern bank.

He leant forward, feeling the coolness of the glass against his forehead, and wondered how his mother was coping with the first night on her own in the farm in what might be more than thirty years. Once again, a feeling of remorse came over him that he'd selfishly pursued his own ends and career with so little thought for the caring, supportive mother he'd left behind.

He read the time from his watch and resolved to get an early night. He quickly cleared up and retired to his bedroom meaning to change the sheets. But a wave of tiredness overcame him and he decided to leave it for his Filipino cleaner who was due in the morning. He'd slept in far worse during his time in the Far East.

Turning off the bedside light and slipping his hand under a pillow he felt something. He clicked on the light and saw a slip of torn-off paper with a name, a mobile number and two kisses. Kelly. So that was her name. He crumpled the paper into a ball and threw it in the general direction of a waste bin.

6

Just before eight a.m. the following morning a taxi dropped Tom outside the offices of Tiger.com. Climbing the stairs, he greeted several of his overnight staff coming in the other direction. They worked on Hong Kong time to ensure that the website was fully up to date with developments in the Far East by the time UK subscribers logged on in the early morning. One, the team leader, a third-generation Chinese immigrant, stopped to report on the night's work. All was comparatively quiet on the Eastern front.

Tom spent the next hour going through his in tray until he saw through the wall of his office his Human Resources manager arriving at her desk. He gave her five minutes to settle in and then walked across to her. 'Morning, Sue.' She was a homely-looking girl, slightly overweight, who seldom mixed socially with the staff. The nature of her job made too much fraternising difficult, but Tom had never had any cause to complain about her professionalism.

'Hi Tom. I was so sorry to hear about your father.'

'Thanks. I've got a lot to sort out up in Yorkshire so I might have to be away quite a bit in the next few weeks.'

'I'm sure we can count it as compassionate leave.'

Tom smiled. 'That's not what I wanted to talk to you about. Could we have a word in private? I need some advice.' She followed him into his office. He closed the door behind her.

'Sue, I've got a problem with Angie. Mostly of my own making. It can't have escaped your attention that we've been seeing each other – it's common knowledge. Well, I've made a decision to break off the relationship, mainly because I don't think it's going anywhere, but also because it's resulted in us both behaving unprofessionally.'

'In what way?'

'You've not heard anything?' Sue shook her head. Tom was slightly concerned that his HR manager appeared not to have her ear to the ground on office gossip.

'It all came to a head last Friday night. I know you never come to the wine bar, but you're aware that it's something of a company tradition for lots of us to let our hair down there at the end of the week. To cut a long story short, Angie began discussing a confidential company issue against my clear instructions. When I tackled her about it, she publicly flouted my authority in earshot of several members of staff.'

Tom could see Sue's brow furrowing as she struggled to think what advice she was about to be asked for.

'Then, after she'd left, I didn't need much persuading to join some of the lads at a club where I proceeded to get drunk and behave like to fool. So in the course of one evening I had my authority challenged and then probably lost a lot of it through my own behaviour.'

Sue looked faintly shocked. 'Do you want me to advise you on how to resolve the situation?'

'No. I'm not asking you to be an agony aunt. I've already decided that I've got to grasp the nettle and finish the relationship. I'm only asking you for a professional opinion. Do you think Angie's defiance of my instructions warrants a warning – informal at this stage?'

'I'd need to know more about the circumstances.'

Tom filled her in on the takeover report which Angie had prepared without his knowledge and put before the board. He told her that the Chairman had asked for it to be treated in the strictest confidence and explained how he had repeated the instruction to Angie. After clarifying several details, Sue agreed that it warranted an informal warning and advised him to make notes about their meeting in case it were to escalate into a formal warning.

Tom thanked her. 'And as for my behaviour?'

She smiled. 'Tom. You've created a good culture in this company. The staff respect you and I don't think that revealing that you're human once in a while will do you any harm. You can always give yourself an informal warning if you like!'

Buoyed by her comment he watched her walk back to her desk and turned to look into Angie's office at the other end of the open plan floor. She was talking to her assistant. He waited until she was alone, took a deep breath and speed dialled her number. 'Angie, could I see you in my office please.'

She looked up and stared at him across the expanse of the office. 'Yes, of course.'

He followed her progress across the floor. Immaculately turned out as always, he couldn't help but feel a familiar rise in the pulse from the way her hips swayed knowingly as she approached. But the cool, almost disdainful expression which spoke of self-awareness of her attractiveness brought Tom quickly back to his resolve.

'Shut the door please.' She sat down in a chair in front of Tom's desk, tugging her tight skirt down as she did so. 'Angie, first of all can I say thank-you for leaving the message about my father, and for having the decency to admit that you owed me an apology.' She looked at him evenly and made no comment. 'I've been thinking long and hard about the personal and professional issues we have, and I'd like to tackle them head on, here and now. The office is the right place to do it because this is the start of a new relationship which is going to be purely professional.' He paused, expecting a response. None came. 'We've had some good times together, but I've never felt we really connected. There's more to a relationship than fine dining and good sex, and it's become increasingly obvious that it was never going to develop into something more worthwhile. We were almost like fashion accessories for each other.'

At last Angie spoke. 'No need to continue with the carefully constructed speech. I hear what you're saying. It was good while it lasted. I'm sure I'll find another fashion accessory soon.'

Tom looked at her intently. 'So personally, no bad feelings?'

'Only that you finished it before I could. I'm not used to that.'

For a moment Tom sensed a hint of vulnerability beneath her habitual steely self-possession but he refused to be swayed from his resolution. 'Can we now have a purely professional conversation about your behaviour? Discussing your report with Ben in earshot of several members of staff contravened the Chairman's instruction and mine to keep your report confidential. I know we'd both had a few drinks, but that's no excuse for you challenging my authority in the way you did. Humiliating me in front of the staff. It hurt personally, but that's not the point.'

'I said I owed you an apology. I'm sorry.'

'Accepted. But can I trust you to behave professionally in the future? You can take this as an informal warning. If there are further breaches of professional behaviour, I'll have to initiate formal procedures.'

Tom saw that she was struggling to suppress an instinctive attack. Angie eventually thought better of it. 'I've said I'm sorry, and you have my word that from now on I'll not challenge your authority or ignore your instructions.'

Tom was relieved but couldn't help feeling that her contrition was altogether too trite. Bridges needed to be rebuilt if they were to work together in the future. 'Look, Ange. I'm sorry I've had to do this, but it seemed to be the only way. You may think I'm being pompous, but I run this company and I have a duty to keep it on an even keel. We've both been rocking the boat too much and it's my fault as much as yours. In case you feel that I'm not admitting any blame, you should know that I've already spoken to the Chairman about my concerns.'

'What, about what happened on Friday?'

'No, some time ago about us. He said he was sure I would use my judgement to resolve the problem. I hope that now I have.'

'You have.' It was spoken flatly.

Tom rose from behind his desk. Angie stood with him. 'OK. Let's leave it there.'

They stood facing each other, holding eye contact. 'Just one more question. Why are you so set on the company being taken over?'

'I thought the Chairman's instructions were that it was only to be discussed at the board meeting.'

Touché. Trust her to have the last word. She lowered her head in an ironic bowing movement and glided out of the office.

Before he could reflect on how the encounter had gone, his PA knocked on the open door. She'd obviously been waiting for Angie to leave. 'Message from So Lin, Tom. I didn't want to disturb you. Her flight's been delayed, so she might be a bit late getting here for the board meeting.'

'OK, thanks.' She turned away, but Tom called her back.

'Emma. I know that you're very discreet and understand that much of what you become aware of has to be kept confidential, but in this case can I ask you to break the rule?' She looked quizzically at him. 'I'm sure you've picked up on the gossip about me and Angie, and about what happened last Friday night.'

'Well, yes,' she volunteered tentatively.

'Let's just suppose that you were to say that you'd heard that Angie and I had split up. I wouldn't be unhappy about you spreading the word.'

She considered the proposition for a moment then said, 'I hear what you're saying.'

'Thanks, Em. I appreciate it.'

'No problem.'

When Tom entered the boardroom, Charles, his Director of Finance and Administration was pouring a coffee for Sir Giles and bending his ear about an arcane detail of accountancy procedure. Tom greeted them both. Sir Giles looked as if he would have been relieved to have been rescued from the conversation, but Charles ploughed on, so Tom stood aside and helped himself to a coffee. He joined Ben who had, as usual, made an unsuccessful attempt to smarten himself up for the board meeting.

At the far end of the room Angie was talking animatedly to Ranjit Patel, the non-executive director appointed by the venture capitalists who had provided seed money to get the business off the ground. Tom thought of him as a necessary evil. He contributed little to the board, simply monitoring the return on investment for the company's backers – of which he was a major one. Ranjit had been a leading light in the heady first days of the dotcom boom, hosting swish business parties in flash City venues where potential investors paid to be introduced to every Tom, Dick or Harry convinced that their Internet start-up ideas were the greatest things since sliced bread. Tom found Ranjit's ostentatious display of wealth distasteful. He looked and lived like a playboy, with a showy Rolex watch, much expensive jewellery, a Ferrari and a penchant for ordering vintage champagne in VIP areas of exclusive night clubs surrounded by simpering would-be footballers' wives and gold diggers. But if Tom disliked him and his style, at the end of the day he'd put the money together, so who was Tom to complain?

Angie was standing close to him, seemly enthralled by an anecdote Ranjit was regaling her with. Sharply suited and darkly handsome, he was flashing smiles. Angie burst into laughter and reached out to clutch his arm at what was apparently the denouement of an amusing tale.

Extricating himself from Charles' diatribe, Sir Giles called the meeting to order. They took their places at the boardroom table.

'Welcome everyone. As you may have heard, our Director of International Operations has been delayed but I think we should press on rather than waiting for her to arrive. The first item on the agenda is the monthly P & L. Charles?'

Ranjit leant forward in anticipation. It was usually the only agenda item in which he took any interest, often departing with the excuse of another meeting shortly after the profit and loss accounts had been presented. Today though, he would certainly be staying to take part in the discussion on the takeover proposal.

Charles checked that everyone had a copy of the P & L spreadsheet then began to talk though it in a flat tone line by line, focusing on the areas which were significantly below or above budget or target. He highlighted the slowdown in new subscriptions and renewals to the online information service they provided. However, this had been offset by an encouraging increase in consultancy projects. Reaching the bottom line, he summarised by saying that the modest monthly profit was in line with a pattern of slow growth but lagging behind expectations.

Ranjit broke in. 'I'd put it more strongly than that. The investors I represent are very concerned about the rate of growth. At this rate we'd be waiting years to get a decent return. Frankly, the mood amongst them is to look to sell out to the highest bidder and cash in our investment as quickly as possible.'

Sir Giles admonished him. 'Ranjit, we're grateful for your comments, but can we follow the agenda please and save discussion on the pros and cons of a takeover until later?'

Ranjit was visibly annoyed. Before he could reply there was a knock on the door and So Lin entered. She looked surprisingly fresh for one who had just endured a sixteen-hour overnight flight. Tall for a Chinese woman, she was elegantly dressed in a black trouser suit matching the colour of her straight shoulder length hair cut with a curving fringe. She took in her fellow board members with a smile. 'Morning everyone. Sorry I'm late.'

They rose to greet her with a succession of handshakes. She saved an affectionate hug for her former husband. 'Great to see you, Lin.' said Tom smelling her familiar perfume. Once she was seated Sir Giles formally welcomed her and explained that she'd only missed the reading of the monthly P & L accounts which they were just about to review.

Tom was the first to speak. 'Sir Giles, forgive me for mentioning the proposed takeover again. I take your point about saving discussion for the appropriate agenda item, but the prospect of considering whether to sell our business has rather focused my mind on the current state of the company. I too have to admit to being concerned about the figures we've just seen. Growth is far too slow, but I believe there are ways in which it could be improved. I'm proud of what we've achieved in building the foundations of a good business in less than three years but perhaps now is the time to move into a new phase of development.'

Ranjit let out a snort of derision, but Sir Giles' raised hand was enough to prevent him from speaking. Tom continued, addressing Ranjit directly. 'I'll be the first to admit that I've been too consumed with fire fighting immediate problems to see the wood for the trees. What I'm proposing is a back to basics look at our business. I have some clear ideas on how it should be conducted and about a new direction we should take to realise our potential.' He turned to Sir Giles. 'I'll be happy to go into detail, but it's highly relevant to the arguments for and against selling the company so I suspect that it might be more appropriate to wait for that discussion.'

'Well, you've certainly intrigued us,' said the chairman. 'I can see that it's going to be an interesting exchange of views. Unless anyone has any objections, I suggest we do our best to move through the agenda as quickly as possible.'

The monthly departmental reports were presented, and action points were swiftly agreed. It was obvious that everyone was champing at the bit to begin the discussion.

'Well, ladies and gentlemen,' announced Sir Giles, scanning the faces around the table. 'I'm sure you've all read the paper which Angie has prepared. It's come before the board in a

rather unorthodox manner in that it was not formally commis-
sioned, but I took the view that since it had been written it
would be the right thing to do allow it to be discussed. Angie,
do you want to begin?'

'Yes, thank you Sir Giles. I won't go into the arguments I've set
out in the paper - you've all read them - but I would like to
remind you of the summary and conclusions. The company has
survived the dotcom crash intact, albeit with our share price
reduced. We achieved initial success by riding on the coat tails
of enthusiasm for the new economy, but I believe the prospects
for further growth are poor. We're all too aware of the current
economic conditions. As of last month, the United States went
into recession and we're on the brink of it here. Recession is
negative growth, and that's what we too can expect in the short
to medium term.'

Angie paused to survey her audience. no one challenged her
so she pressed on. 'The other major limiter on growth concerns
the difficulty in finding new business and retaining existing
clients. I put it down to two specific reasons. Firstly, we were
ahead of the game in setting up the services we offer, but
increasingly major competitors are getting in on the act. Secondly, whereas it was once a selling point for us to be associated with the new economy, it's now a disadvantage. After the
dotcom crash, we're tarred with the brush of risk and failure.
Potential clients are playing safe and we're consistently losing
out in competitive pitches to more traditional long-established
companies even if the services they offer are not a match for
ours.'

She spread her arms in a gesture of openness. 'Now before
anyone questions my motives for writing this paper, let me say
straight away that it's not an elaborate excuse for any future
lack of performance in my role as Business Development Director. I'm stating the facts as I see them, and I believe that it would
be remiss of us as a board not to face them. I had discussed
these issues with our Managing Director, but I found little
sympathy for my views – that's why I took the unusual step of

presenting the paper directly to the board. I believed it was my responsibility to the shareholders to do so.'

Tom looked sharply at Angie for the implied criticism. She continued, drawing now to a close. 'My conclusions are that the company has reached a crossroads and is faced with a simple choice. Either we beat the competition, or we join them. Trying to beat them in a hostile climate would be a long slow process with no guarantee of success. We owe it to our investors to consider joining them by sounding out possible buyers,' she concluded.

'Thank you, Angie,' said Sir Giles. 'Tom, I think it would be appropriate to have your response.'

Tom had already decided to avoid the trap of rising to Angie's criticism. Instead he calmly launched into a set of carefully prepared counter arguments. 'I can't disagree with the facts which Angie has drawn our attention to. They were already known to me and I suspect to everyone round this table. But I do take issue with her analysis of them. Until now most of our work has been concerned with advising companies who look on China and the Far East as a cheap source for manufacturing their goods. And I accept that during a recession in the West that side of our business may decline. But it also provides us with a great and largely untapped opportunity. China will almost certainly escape the recession and continue to grow apace. I would like to think that Lin would agree with that.'

Lin nodded. 'All the indications are that China will ride out the recession in the West and continue to grow.'

'And if so,' Tom picked up, 'that means improving lifestyles, more consumers able to afford goods, and a rising demand to import those which they can't provide internally. And of course, if we're in recession our exports become cheaper for them to buy. I've got some specific ideas which I'll be exploring with Lin while she's here, but in outline I see a bright future for us in advising Western companies wanting to expand into the largest population of consumers in the world.'

Ranjit broke in, scoffing. 'What, you mean you're going to help companies like MacDonalds open a chain of restaurants there. Fat chance. Have you ever tried eating a hamburger with a pair of chopsticks?' Tom recoiled at the crass remark and its racist undertones. And from a British Asian who should know better.

Lin shot a glance at Tom and then turned slowly to Ranjit. 'I think I'm right in saying that MacDonalds opened their first restaurant in China over ten years ago.'

Ranjit looked crestfallen and tried to recover with a different argument. 'OK, but even if you're right Tom, how long would it take to get this new business and where's the money coming from in the meantime?'

'That's one of the questions I'll be putting to Lin. She'll have a better idea how fast consumerism will grow in China and I'm keen to get her views. But grow it will and clever companies will already be eyeing the opportunities. We can offer our consultancy now, and if we win contracts, we can expect them to be long term. Supermarkets are good example. Imagine if we could persuade one of the big chains to commission a feasibility study on entry into the Chinese market.'

Ranjit tried another tack. 'Alright, but what about the big boys muscling in on our act. Angie's not wrong about that, is she?'

'No, but I don't agree that it's a reason to raise a white flag. Yes, Internet business has suffered a setback, but it's here to stay. Soon all companies big and small will have their own website and will conduct much of their business online. Over time we'll be less and less associated with dotcom failures. In the meantime, we need to capitalise on the credibility and awareness we've built through our web information services, remembering that it's not our core business, just a shop window. Our core business is providing commercial consultancy to companies trading with and in the Far East. Unlike the big boys we're specialists. The competition is growing but so is the market for the service we provide. I'm confident we can hold our own.'

With the two opposing views laid on the table, the discussion moved into more detailed arguments for and against. As Tom had expected, Lin gave him strong support. She summed up her objections to a takeover by saying that she and Tom hadn't founded the company to cut and run at the first sign of a hurdle to be overcome. She believed in a long-term future for the company and thought it would be foolish to cash in before its potential had begun to be realised.

Charles volunteered little to the discussion, speaking only when asked questions, usually from Ranjit, about how overtures could be made to potential buyers and what procedures had to be followed. Whenever asked a direct question about the decision on the table he carefully laid out the pros and cons. He seemed to be sitting on a fence, unwilling to throw in his hat with either opposing faction.

Angie remained remarkably silent for one usually so forthright in her opinions. When asked to comment, she always referred to a section of the paper she'd prepared. Tom judged that she had taken a conscious decision not to engage in the to and fro of the discussion but to let her views expressed on paper stand.

To Tom's relief, Ben also gave him a measure of support. He fully backed the view that the new economy was here to stay and hadn't begun to take off as it surely would. But as for the question of selling or sticking at it he claimed, somewhat disingenuously Tom judged, to be not well enough versed in the mysteries of finance to be able to comment on the advantages or disadvantages. Throughout the discussion which raged over an hour, Ranjit kept reiterating his basic position. The shareholders he represented needed a return on their investment and needed it soon. Sir Giles, as befitted a chairman, restricted his contribution to deftly steering the debate, calming the heat and ensuring that both opposing views had an equal hearing.

At one p.m. the boardroom phone rang. Tom answered and his PA told him that the caterers had arrived and wanted to set out the buffet lunch which had been specially ordered in anticipation of a long meeting. Sir Giles indicated to Tom that the trays should be left outside the room and slowly took in the group of directors gathered around the table, looking at them each in turn. 'Normally I would expect any opposing arguments between directors to be resolved through a discussion like the one we've just held. But in this case, I think it's clear that it's not to be. I think my only course of action is to call for a show of hands. I'd remind you that we're not deciding whether to sell the company or not. That decision can only be made by shareholders if and when an offer is on the table. Your vote is for whether or not we should take soundings about a possible takeover of the company. Those in favour?'

Ranjit's hand shot up. Angie's followed with less indecent haste. Charles looked nervously around, before slowly and rather half-heartedly raising his hand.

Sir Giles looked resigned. The outcome was predictable. 'And those against?' Tom, Lin and Ben's arms rose in unison. 'I'd rather feared that might be the outcome. I'd hoped not to have to make a casting vote. Normally, in the case of a split vote it would be incumbent on me to preserve the status quo, but I'm not entirely sure what that is in this case. The company not being for sale? Which company is ever not for sale if the price is right? I'm conscious that I have two conflicting duties – to support Tom as managing director and at the same time to take into account the wishes of the major shareholders which have been clearly stated by Ranjit. Since this is not an irrevocable decision about the future of the company, merely – how shall I put it – a fishing expedition, I'm persuaded to say that we should go ahead and take soundings about a possible takeover. I'd suggest that Charles and I form a working party to progress it. We'd welcome any contributions of course, particularly from Angie and Ranjit who have already indicated that they may have some leads. Now, I believe there's some food outside.'

The buffet lunch was understandably strained. Two groups quickly formed. Sir Giles, with Charles faithfully at his side, notebook in hand, was being given ideas from Angie and Ranjit for people they thought might be worth contacting. Tom, in conversation with Lin and Ben, took a conscious decision to not to dwell on their defeat and asked his ex-wife to fill him in on developments in the Hong Kong office. Ranjit was the first to excuse himself, and Ben, Angie and Charles took this as their cue to return to their desks.

Sir Giles turned to Tom and Lin and invited them to sit at the table. 'Well, that was a full and frank exchange of views, as politicians always phrase it when there's been no resolution to a problem. I hope you understand the reasoning behind my casting vote. Let me make it clear that it went against my instincts, but I felt it was the right thing to do.' Tom and Lin both assured him that they accepted his decision.

Sir Giles took in their forlorn expressions and spoke warmly. 'I want you to know that you both have my full support and respect for the vision you have for the company, and my admiration for what you've achieved. I'm keen to find out more about these new initiatives you've been talking about Tom. They've rather come out of the blue. I'll look forward to hearing about them when you've put some flesh on the bones. I know this company's your baby. It's still a toddler, but I'm sure it will be walking soon and who knows how far it will run. It's not being put up for adoption yet.'

He rose to take his leave. Tom and Lin stood as well. Lin gave him a peck on the cheek. 'Thanks for your confidence in us.' Sir Giles left the room and they were alone. They were silent for a while before Tom spoke.

'Unfortunate analogy to choose. Our baby.'

'Yes. He knows we were married.'

More silence. 'Do you think things would have been different if we'd had a real baby?'

Tom felt a pang of remorse for the failure of their marriage. He was still very fond of her. 'Let's not rake over past times. You must be shattered after your flight. Why don't you get off to your hotel and rest? Are you still up for the dinner we'd arranged for tonight?'

'Yes, of course. There's lots to discuss.'

'OK. I'll pick you up at 7.30.'

Walking back across the open floor to his office, Tom was somehow comforted to see that all appeared well. There'd been no seismic shift. Everyone was beavering away at their workstations. He checked with his PA for phone messages. He dealt with the couple which required his attention then checked his emails. Having satisfied himself that there were none which couldn't wait for a reply he dug out the slip of paper from his wallet which Sally had given him.

Rather than phone either of the numbers immediately Tom dialled his mother. To his surprise she answered quickly – he'd expected her to be out in the fields. She assured him that all was well.

'Have you had a chance to think about me getting some help for you? It's probably too early to decide about a farm manager but let me hire in some temporary labour. You can't do it all yourself and you can't expect the Hardcastles to keep on popping round – they've got their own farm to run.'

At first Jean protested that she was managing fine but was easily persuaded. She was concerned about whether Tom could afford it, but when he insisted that he could, she eventually agreed. Tom promised to make the call straight away.

The number was answered gruffly. 'Yes?'

'Is that George Outhwaite?

'It is. Who wants him?' The Yorkshire accent was broad in the extreme.

'I'm Tom Keardon. Bill Keardon's son from Middle Farm over in Swaledale.'

'Keardon? Now then lad, what can I do for thee?'

'I don't know if you'd heard, but my father died recently and …'

'Ah, Bill Keardon. Yes, I saw the piece in't Gazette. Topped himself, didn't he?'

Tom winced. Subtlety was obviously not George's strong point.

'Nay, sorry lad. Sorry to hear it. So how can I help?'

Tom recovered and continued. 'I understand that you might be able to supply some casual labour to help my mother out on the farm until we get things sorted.'

'Can't you help her?'

'I live in London.'

'Live in London do thee? Poor lad.'

Tom felt his composure ebbing away. It was like talking to his father all over again. He took a deep breath and steeled himself to fight bluntness with bluntness. 'Look Mr Outhwaite. If you can't help me or don't want my business that's fine by me.'

After a lengthy pause there was a sullen reply. 'What are you looking for?'

Tom explained the situation and asked if a labourer experienced in sheep farming could be found at short notice.

'Not easy, lad. Still lambing time, and all of my men are tied up.'

'Isn't there anyone you could think of?'

George ummed and aahed for a while. 'There is old Sid who's found himself unexpectedly available.'

'What do you mean?'

'He's forgotten more about sheep than I've ever learnt. Used to farm near Crackpot until those bank bastards took it away from him.'

Tom remembered the strangely named place a few miles from his farm. 'But what do mean by unexpectedly available?'

'Fell out with farmer I put him with. Bit too keen on the bottle. But he's a good man.'

'And there's no one else?'

'Not than I can think of lad.'

Tom considered his options. He could start all over again to find a contact for temporary labour. But time was against him. He wouldn't be back in Yorkshire until late Thursday evening and had hoped to get help for his mother in place before left on the following Monday. He was also conscious of the long list of other things to be dealt with – the funeral, the inquest, the bank, the will, the future of the farm. He took the easy option. 'OK, but I'd like to meet him first. Can you arrange it?'

'When?'

'Well I'm not up until Thursday evening so it would have to be Friday. No, that's no good.'

'Why not?'

'Well it's Good Friday.'

'So what. We don't hold with holidays up here, lad. no one's thought to tell sheep.'

'OK then, Friday. I could come over to your farm.'

'I'm not having the likes of you trampling over my land, what with foot and mouth just up dale. Noon at the White Hart in Hawes. Sid'll be there. He always is.'

The phone went dead. Tom stared at the receiver. Hang on, don't you want a number to call me in case there's a problem. What will it cost me, and what's your agent's fee? He toyed with the idea of phoning back but couldn't face the prospect of another dysfunctional conversation with a living ghost of his father. He replaced the receiver and wondered what he'd let himself in for – interviewing an alcoholic for the post of his mother's temporary saviour?

Tom looked out at the familiar view through the floor-to-ceiling plate glass window of his office, taking solace that here was a world in which he felt at home. But did he? Was it simply that he'd learnt how to operate in this world, and had forgotten – or never learnt – how to do so back home? He pulled himself up. No time for cracker barrel philosophy, time for practicality. He retrieved the 'To Do' list he'd prepared with his mother and scanned it. There was nothing further he could do until the post-mortem had been conducted. He phoned his contact at the police to see if there was any information. He was told that the post-mortem had been booked in for Thursday. Great, Tom thought, that probably means a trip up the following week for the funeral. He admonished himself for the thought.

He spent a while tackling his in tray, but his mind wasn't focused, flashing as it was between the implications of the board meeting vote and his obligations to his mother. Eventually he gave up and did what he always did when he lost the will or inspiration to plough through his workload. He went on walkabout.

Tom's staff had become used to his habit of regularly wandering around the office and chatting at random to anyone. They'd long learnt that it was not the boss checking up on them, but an opportunity to tell him what they were working on, bend his ear if so desired or just get his advice or opinions. In was a conscious management style on Tom's part, one which he felt he benefitted from as much as he hoped the employees did. The downside was that on occasion he was drawn into discussions of small details of the business which didn't warrant his involvement. But he always refused to micro-manage and extricated himself by assuring the member of staff that he was sure that they would be able to take the right decision. Generally, he came away from a walkabout buoyed by feeling that he'd been in touch with the lifeblood of the business.

He passed Ben's office and raised a hand. Ben beckoned him in. 'You OK, boss?'

'Surviving.'

'Good, because I know you've got a lot on your plate, what with the board meeting and your father. Heard you'd chucked Angie though.'

Tom raised his eyebrows. His PA Emma had obviously accomplished her mission in double quick time. 'Yeah. It's a relief.'

'She and Ranjit seemed to be getting on pretty well.'

'What do you mean?'

'Nothing. Just noticed it. They seemed to be working as a team at the meeting, almost as if it had been planned.'

'Probably just that they'd both reached the same conclusions about selling out.'

'Maybe. I can understand why Ranjit's so keen, but why should Angie be his cheerleader?'

'Could be personal. Some way to get at me. Anyhow, personally Angie and I are now history. I've got to rebuild a professional relationship with her.'

Tom returned to his office. It was four o'clock. He looked unenthusiastically at his in tray and decided to give the day up as a bad job. He packed up his laptop, told Emma that he would be on his mobile and left for home.

7

Tom walked into the expansive marble-floored entrance hall of Lin's hotel wearing his favourite Hugo Boss suit and a Paul Smith shirt. He asked reception to phone up to her room and sat down on a low leather sofa to wait, keeping his eyes on the stainless-steel doors of the lift. A few minutes later they opened, and Lin emerged, scanning the foyer. Tom rose and she flashed a smile when she spotted him. Her high heels clicked across the floor as she approached, dressed in a body-hugging silk cheongsam, high at the collar, ending on the knee and split to the thigh on one side.

'You could have made an effort,' said Tom, largely to defuse the quickening pulse which he felt.

'So could you,' she said, looking him up and down. She kissed him primly and knowingly on the cheek. Tom resisted the temptation to hug her.

'I haven't booked anywhere because I didn't know what you'd like to eat. There's a great place I've found in Chinatown which serves authentic Chinese food. Not a single Chow Mein on the menu.'

'I eat Chinese all the time. When in Rome … take me some-where which serves authentic English.'

'Right. What about Simpsons. Great roast beef. I'll need to see if we can get a table.'

Tom got the number from reception and phoned on his mo-bile. He was in luck. They'd had a cancellation and could fit them in.

At the restaurant, once their orders had been taken, Lin looked Tom compassionately in the eyes. 'I heard about your father. I'm so sorry.'

'Yeah. It's been quite emotional. My mother seems to be coping well in the circumstances.'

'What's going to happen to her now? She can't run the farm on her own.'

'No she can't – much as she'd like to think she could. I've got a lot to sort out, but it'll all be fine.'

Lin waited for him to elaborate but Tom had already decided not to burden her with the details. Instead he asked after her family.

'They're all fine. I'm getting on with them really well. Actually, there's a reason for it.'

Tom was intrigued, but before she could continue, she was interrupted by the waiter bringing the first course. 'Tom. I've got a little announcement to make. I'm engaged to be married.'

Tom felt a pang of distress and hoped that his change of expression from shock to broad smile had been suitably quick. 'That's wonderful news. Who is he?'

Lin animatedly began to tell Tom that he was a businessman from another Hong family who regularly traded with her own. Both families were delighted, she said. It was obvious from her expression that she was too.

'It's the match your family always hoped you'd make.'

'Oh Tom – we agreed our marriage was a mistake.'

'Yes, it was. But it was probably the best mistake I ever made.'

Lin smiled and grasped his hand across the table. 'We had some good times.'

Tom squeezed her hand and let it go. 'I really am pleased for you. I can see how happy you are. I wish you both the very best.' He stopped himself from saying that she had his blessing, realising how proprietorial it would sound.

'And what about you? I heard you'd been seeing Angie.'

'Not anymore. I ended it.'

'Good. I wouldn't have thought she was your type. A bit too hard. You could do better than her.'

'I did.'

Lin rolled her eyes, then grinned at him. 'Tom Keardon, you are incorrigible!'

The main course arrived as they were reminiscing about their first heady days together in Hong Kong as the clock ran down to the transfer of sovereignty. Lin reminded him of several escapades he'd almost forgotten. The meal was nearly finished before Lin brought up the subject of the day's board meeting.

'Tom, I know we meant this to be just a social evening, but there is – what's the phrase - an elephant in the room.' Lin was a connoisseur of arcane English idioms as only a non-native speaker could be. She'd always taken great delight in getting Tom to teach her strange phrases with which she could pepper her conversation.

'Yeah. What's going to happen to our business? I don't know. One way of looking at it is that there's no downside. If it gets sold, we both make a lot of money. If we keep it, we get what we want.'

'That doesn't mean that you're just going to wait and see what happens though. What about all those new initiatives you were talking about today? The ones you wanted to explore further with me?'

'I want to go through them with you in the office tomorrow. I'm certainly not going to sit back and go with the flow. On the contrary, I'm going to fight to keep control of the company and there's only one way to do it – make it more attractive to the investors to stick with us than sell out.'

'Easier said than done.'

'No one ever said it would be easy, but that's no reason not to try. And we can start first thing tomorrow morning, OK?'

By eight thirty the following morning, Tom and Lin were facing each other across a round meeting table in Tom's office, notebooks at the ready. Tom had kept the morning clear to work with her.

'Right. My premise is that consumerism in China will take off in the next few years as their economy grows.' Lin began to make notes. 'If so, will there be opportunities for Western companies to tap into the emerging market? How much of the demand can be met internally, and what sort of goods and services will the Chinese be looking to import? If we can identify opportunities for Western businesses, then we choose the relevant companies to target, the bigger the better. We put together a comprehensive prospectus then go out and market like hell.'

Over the course of the next few hours they hammered out the issues. To help test the premise Tom called in his chief economist to get his views. Lin twice called colleagues in Hong Kong, catching them just before they left for the day and putting them on speaker phone to contribute to the discussion. Eventually, despite reservations expressed by some, it was agreed that the prediction was plausible. As for opportunities for Western companies, Lin argued that they didn't lie in exporting goods. Many were already being manufactured in China anyway. What China needed to meet the growing demands of consumers were the commercial skills of branding, marketing, distribution and customer service – skills which had not been needed in the days of state-controlled commerce. Companies whose success was built on those skills would be the ones to target.

Convinced that they were on to something, they set about drafting a plan of action. Lin would work with the Chief Economist to prepare a paper on the economic arguments. Lin would additionally write about the political and cultural hurdles which Tiger.com could help companies to overcome. Angie would be tasked with writing a section on the commercial opportunities and drawing up a list of companies to target. Lin questioned whether Angie's heart would be in it given her support for selling the company. Tom insisted that as long as he was managing director, she would do what she was told. Everyone would have ten days to write their first drafts and pass them to Tom, giving him three days to draw them together and write an introduction and summary before the next board meeting. With the plan clear in their minds Tom asked his PA to find out if the other directors and the Chief Economist were able to join them for an impromptu meeting at noon. He was in luck. All were available.

They filed into the boardroom, taking the same seats they had occupied the previous day. Only Sir Giles and Ranjit were absent. Tom slowly scanned their faces before speaking. 'Thanks for coming at short notice. I won't keep you long because I know you're all busy, but I was keen to follow up on yesterday's decision as soon as possible. Time is of the essence, particularly with the Easter break coming up. First of all let me say that I fully abide by the decision to look for possible buyers and I will do everything I can to support that. However, there's no guarantee that one will be found, and in the meantime I'm determined to move the company on in the hope that it will be in the shareholders' interests to continue to back the company rather than sell out. I hope that I can count on all of you, irrespective of the way you voted yesterday, to support me fully in the initiatives I'm proposing.'

Everyone nodded immediately apart from Angie who spoke directly to Tom. 'Of course. You'll have my full support.'

Tom thanked her then explained the thinking behind the new initiative and outlined what was required of everyone. 'I appreciate that it's a lot of work for most of you to do in a short time, but it's crucial that we get this thing moving as soon as possible so that it's on the table for the next board meeting in two weeks' time. If you need any further guidance please speak to Lin or me. Thanks for your time.'

They left. Once again Tom and Lin were together at the table. 'So, the fight begins!' she said.

Tom looked pensive. 'Yes. It does.'

8

At six o'clock on the morning of Good Friday Tom's alarm trilled beside his childhood bed. His intervening time had been spent on scheduled meetings and a concerted effort to lower the height of his in tray. He was conscious of the fact that he was liable to be away from the office dealing with the aftermath of his father's death for several days over the next couple of weeks. Lin had taken her leave on Thursday afternoon to fly to Paris to spend the Easter weekend with an old school friend now working at a fashion house in the city. Shortly after, Tom left for his apartment to pack the most appropriate clothes he could find for the long weekend. He'd set off for King's Cross, pleased that he had remembered to get his PA to upgrade him to a first-class seat to avoid the bank holiday crush on the train.

Dressed in the newly bought overalls and wellingtons which he had retrieved from the boot of his car, Tom strode out to the fields to perform the morning duties on the farm. After much persuasion on his late arrival the previous evening he'd got his mother to agree to take a break for once and have a lie in. Predictably she'd been up before him, ready to coach him in all the things which needed doing.

The day was dawning bright. Down in the dale a thin mist hovered above the river meadows. The call of a peewit caused Tom to raise his eyes skywards to catch a glimpse of its skittering flight. He shaded his eyes against the sun to look eastwards along the expanse of Swaledale, suddenly feeling relieved to be free, albeit temporarily, from the machinations of big business. Firing up the quad bike he set off in good spirits to tend to the flock.

Jean was waiting for him with a fried breakfast when he returned. Normally he would have preferred something healthier, but the fresh air and exercise had given him a good appetite and he devoured the meal.

'Who's this chap you're going to see in Hawes?'

'George Outhwaite. Do you know him?

'Can't say that I do. I remember your Dad talking about him. He used to see him at market. You say he's recommended someone to come and help out.'

'Well, he didn't exactly recommend him. Just said he was the only one he could think of who was available. His name's Sid. Apparently, he used to farm up at Crackpot until the bank foreclosed on him.'

'Sid? Not Sid Lambert? It must be. Well I'll be blowed.' Tom was surprised to see that she had a wide smile on her face.

'You obviously know him then.'

'He was always a wild one, that Sid. He was the life and soul at the village hall dances your Dad and I used to go to. Always playing the fool.'

'Do you think he'd be suitable? I've been told he might have a drink problem.'

'Doesn't surprise me after what he's been through. Lost his wife in childbirth. The baby was severely disabled and died after a few months. I heard he went off the rails, not that he'd ever been on the straight and narrow. Then he lost the farm, but I didn't hear what happened after that. I don't know if he'd be suitable. You'll have to see what you think. There certainly wouldn't be many dull moments if he were to come here.'

Tom changed out of his overalls into the oldest clothes he'd brought with him, wary of George Outhwaite's obvious prejudice against London folk. Likewise, he chose to drive the battered Land Rover rather than the Audi to the meeting, a good choice because the journey of less than ten miles involved negotiating a narrow twisting road over the Buttertubs Pass. He drove across the cattle grid at the farm entrance then over the sack-covered pile of straw, making a mental note to check whether it needed topping up with disinfectant on his return. He turned West out of the village and soon branched left up the narrow lane leading to the pass, steep enough to require him to engage first gear. Grassy fields soon gave way to desolate moorland, the road edged with black and white poles to guide the way in winter and gauge the depth of the snow. Every now and then steel hawsers strung between metal uprights were all there was to protect errant drivers from pitching hundreds of feet into a ravine. Cresting the hill and reaching the plateau, Tom drove past the deep limestone potholes which gave the Buttertubs Pass its name. The idea that Swaledale farmers on their way to market in Hawes had lowered their butter down the potholes to cool it on hot days had always seemed far-fetched, but no other explanation for the name existed.

The road began to descend and the rolling vista of Wensley-dale unfolded. Far wider than Swaledale, it was unusual in that it was not named after the river which threaded through it but for the small village at its easternmost end. Reaching the end of the long undulating descent Tom crossed the River Ure and drove into the small town at the head of the dale. He found a parking space outside the old coaching house in the main street of Hawes a few minutes before noon.

The bar of the White Hart was empty but for a small figure standing at the bar nursing a full pint of bitter. Whippet-thin and dressed in a threadbare tweed jacket with leather elbow patches he was just a few inches over five feet tall. Incongruous-ly a pair of pristine red and white trainers poked from the bottom of the turned-up jeans he wore.

Tom approached him uncertainly. 'Sorry – but are you Sid?'

The figure turned. Tom took in the skin stretched gauntly across a weather-beaten face which creased into a grin. 'The very same, lad. And who's asking?'

'Tom. Tom Keardon.' He held out his hand which Sid grasped and shook vigorously.

'Now then. What can I get you?' said Sid, hammering the bell on the counter to call for service.

'No, please. I'll get my own. You're OK, are you?' asked Tom, eyeing Sid's full pint. Sid held his palms up to indicate that he didn't need another drink. Tom ordered a bitter when the barman arrived and suggested that they sat down at a table. Sid followed Tom, carrying his glass with elaborate care.

'So, George tells me you're looking for work.'

'Happens I am, lad. And I'm told you're wanting some help now that your Dad's gone. I was sorry to hear about it – Bill was a good'un. How's Jean coping?'

'She's managing. You know her then?'

Before Sid could answer the door to the bar was flung noisily open and the large figure of George Outhwaite barged in. Tom turned and took in his imposing girth, checked flat cap and florid red complexion born of many years of being battered by Dales wind and rain. He marched directly to their table. Tom rose and offered his hand. 'Mr Outhwaite?'

George shook Tom's hand with an unenthusiastic grip, grunted an acknowledgement and subsided into a chair. He refused the drink which Tom offered saying that he had to be away as soon as possible for another meeting, so could they get on with business. Tom was relieved that he wouldn't be spending too much time with this boorish man.

'Do you want him then?' Tom was perplexed.

'I beg your pardon?'

'I said do you want Sid to work for you?'

'I've just met him, Mr Outhwaite. I need to chat to Sid and ask a few questions before I make a decision,' said Tom, glancing at his prospective employee who was resolutely avoiding any eye contact by staring at his untouched pint.

'Well, you can take him or leave him as far as I'm concerned. He let me down on last job I found him. Begged me for another chance, promised he'd stay off the booze and what does he do? Get's kicked off farm after two weeks for drinking on't job. Look lad, I said I'd introduce you to him. If you take him, I'll be glad to take my fee for it, but that's where it ends. He comes with no recommendation and if he buggers up again and you ask for your fee back, I'll tell you to whistle for it. And I'll thank you not to complain about it to anybody – I don't know if reputation means anything where you come from but round here, we set store by it. I'm known for supplying reliable men – apart from Sid of course.'

Tom couldn't help but look at Sid to see how he was reacting to the character assassination. His face was impassive, eyes still lowered, fixed on his drink.

'Do I make myself understood, lad? If you take Sid on, it's a case of … what's the phrase?'

'Caveat emptor,' Tom volunteered automatically, regretting it instantly.

'You what?' George fixed him with an expression of disdain.

'Sorry – buyer beware.'

'That's it. Buyer beware. Well I'm not going to waste my time sitting around while you ask him your questions. If you want him, call me and we'll discuss an introduction fee. And Sid,' said George, acknowledging his presence for the first time. Sid nodded imperceptibly but refused to raise his eyes. 'You're on your own now. This is the last time I do anything for you. You've let me down one too many times. If this lad gives you a job, then I don't want a cut. And if he doesn't, don't bother getting in touch. Understood?'

Sid gave no reaction. George stood and took his leave with a curt goodbye, leaving the bar door to slam on its hinges. Tom shook his head in bewilderment and raised his glass to drink before realising that Sid was still gazing vacantly at his pint. Tom felt a wave of sympathy for the little man who had just endured such an onslaught.

'For goodness sake, knock it back!'

'I shouldn't, Mr Keardon. Once I get started, you know. I'm trying to give it up. I didn't mean to buy it. Just thought that I couldn't come into a pub and sit here waiting for you without buying a drink. I was going to get an orange juice, but the barman started pouring it without me asking. He knows me.'

'Pity to waste it,' said Tom gently. 'It's Tom, by the way, not Mr Keardon.' For the first time in many minutes Sid made eye contact. He smiled thinly, raised the glass to Tom and took a conservative sip before replacing it carefully on a beer mat on the table.

Tom decided to get straight to the point. 'Sid, I've been told several things about you, some good, some bad. My Mum told me about the hard times you've had, losing your family and your farm. I've also heard that there's nothing you don't know about sheep. She needs help on the farm urgently, but she's got enough to worry about without employing someone who will only create more problems. George has made it abundantly clear that he thinks you're unreliable. I need you to tell me if you think you can hold down a job.'

Sid looked back down at his pint and took his time in replying. 'I don't think I'm an alcoholic. I can stay off booze when everything's going well and I can work hard. But every now and then it all seems to get on top of me and I just lose it.' He looked up and fixed Tom with a clear, honest gaze. 'The truth is that I can't promise you it won't happen again. But God knows I need to sort myself out. I've burnt too many boats and I'm not going to get many more chances at my time of life. I need a job and if you're willing to give me a try, all I can promise is that I'll try as well.'

Tom thought long and hard. Instinctively he liked the man. He was a loveable rogue. But what were the chances of him changing his spots? Realistically there was little chance of finding anyone else before he returned to London. He didn't want his mother to have to manage on her own for another week and frankly he had enough on his plate without the added problem of looking for another farm helper. In the worst case, Sid would last a while before falling off the wagon and that would at least buy him time. Tom came to a decision.

'OK Sid, I'm willing to employ you on trial on two conditions. First, you'll need to meet my mother. You'd be spending a lot of time with her and I need to find out she'd be happy with that. Secondly, I need to rely on you. I'm very busy in London and can't be checking up on you all the time. What you drink away from the farm is none of my business, but the first time I hear that you've turned up late or that you're less than sober when you're working, that'll be it. Summary dismissal without notice. Is that understood?'

Sid's face broke into an expression of thankfulness and relief. 'Thank you Mr Keardon. You don't know how much that means to me.' He raised his glass to Tom.

Tom clinked glasses. 'It's Tom, remember. But I'm not offering you the job yet. I need to know that my mother would be happy with it. When do you think you'd be able to come to the farm to see her?'

'As soon as I've finished this pint if that's OK with you. It's not as if I've got anything else to do.'

Tom was pleased to feel that it could all be sorted out quickly. 'Well, OK. I'll drive you over and then drop you back.'

'No need Tom. I've got me bike. I'll follow you.'

Tom had a vision of the wiry little man toiling up the long hill on a pushbike but realised that it must be a motorbike. He took the opportunity to get to know him better while they slowly sipped their pints, asking about the farm that he'd lost and his thoughts on the foot and mouth epidemic. Sid turned out to be a lively conversationalist with a wicked sense of humour. He asked about Middle Farm and Tom had to apologise that he was unable to tell him much about it, explaining that he'd left to go to university and had hardly been back since. Sid asked about Tom's job and made a valiant attempt to listen with interest before admitting that he didn't really understand what the Internet was. He confided that he'd only ever been to London once and didn't like the noise and the crowds.

Tom sank the last inch of his pint and was tempted to order another round as he was enjoying the conversation, even though it would send out the wrong signal to Sid. But it was Sid who suggested they should go. They carried their empty glasses to the bar then walked out into the sunshine. Tom saw the bike leaning against the wall of the pub, a vintage, mud-splattered Triumph. He told Sid to follow him and then used his mobile to phone his mother to warn her of the impending visit. Sid donned an antique crash helmet which sat like a pudding basin on his head. He then pulled on a pair of goggles. Tom climbed into the Land Rover and was about to turn the ignition when there was a tap on the window. Sid was standing there looking sheepish. Tom wound down the window.

'Er, Tom. Sorry about this, but I don't think I've got enough petrol to get there and back. And I've only got couple of quid. I know I haven't got the job yet but I couldn't get an advance, could I, so that I can fill up before we go? If you don't give me the job, I'll owe it to you.'

Tom wondered if he was being a soft touch by agreeing but agree he did. Once again, the alternative was to risk losing the opportunity to resolve the problem of finding help before he had to leave.

Sid led the way to a filling station where Tom paid for a full tank, thinking that Sid would need it to make the journeys to the farm in the coming week before being paid. And if his mother wasn't happy with employing him, then he could put it down to charity.

Tom took the lead as they headed out of the town in convoy and up the long hill to the Buttertubs. Arriving eventually at the farm gates, Tom drew to a halt and walked across the disinfected sacking to open them. Sid dismounted and knelt down to feel the straw. 'Bone dry this, Tom. I can hardly smell any disinfectant.' He looked round and saw the enamel bath full of disinfected water. 'Give us a hand to pour this over. I'll come back and fill it before I go, whether I'm staying or not.'

Tom decided not to confess that he'd thought about doing the same and then forgotten. Between them they dowsed the sacking with the milky liquid.

Jean had heard their approach and was standing at the farmhouse door when they parked in the yard. Sid removed his helmet and walked briskly up to her.

'Hello, Mrs K. Long time no see. And you don't look a day older.' Tom could have sworn he saw his mother's eyelids flutter.

'Then I must have looked pretty old last time we met.' They shook hands. 'Come on in. Tea?'

Tom followed them in and decided to leave them alone for a while, making the excuse that he needed to check his emails. He did so in his room having brought a modem with him this time to be able to make a dial-up connection.

When he came down the stairs, he could hear his mother's laughter. They were seated at the kitchen table chatting nine-teen to the dozen. For the first time since he'd returned home Jean's mood seemed to be buoyant, her face smiling and worry free. They continued gossiping while he made himself a mug of coffee from the box of filters he'd thought to bring. Many years of drinking delicate Chinese tea had killed his taste for the strong English varieties. He joined them at the table and waited for a gap in the conversation.

'You two obviously go back a long way.' They both nodded. 'But we need to think about the present. Sid - now my mother's had a chance to meet you again would you mind popping outside for a bit so we can discuss the situation?' Sid winked at Jean, then acquiesced and made his exit. Jean still had a smile on her face.

'Mum? It's obvious that you like him, and he seems to have lifted your spirits. But we've got a serious decision to make. George Outhwaite says he's unreliable. Sid lost his last job for being drunk at work. By his own admission he's got a history of binge drinking when things get on top of him. Are you sure you want to take the risk? We're trying to make your life easier, not creating another problem for you.'

Jean took just a moment to reply. 'He's cheered me up for the first time since your Dad died. He'd be good company for me. I know he can do the job and he needs a break.'

'You're not worried about him hitting the bottle?'

'Let's give him a try. I think he knows what he's got to do to keep the job.'

'OK. I'll go and tell him.'

Tom went outside. Sid was nowhere to be seen. He looked up to the fields and seeing no sign of him, walked towards the barn. Sid emerged from the entrance carrying a large container of disinfectant.

'I knew it'd be somewhere. Found it under pile of tarpaulins. That barn needs a serious sort out.' They sat down on a rusted water tank.

'OK Sid, we've decided to give you a month's trial to see how it goes.'

Sid grabbed Tom's hand and shook it vigorously. 'I'll try not to let you down. Thank you.'

They discussed wages and although Tom was surprised at how little Sid asked for, he managed to conceal it. In the circumstances he could only agree because he had no idea of the going rate. Realising that he also hadn't a clue how much George Outhwaite would demand as an introduction fee, he casually asked Sid how much George normally charged. Usually a hundred pounds, he was told. Tom admonished himself for not having done his research – imagine if he ran Tiger.com as sloppily. He resolved to be nothing but business-like in his future dealings over his mother's farm.

To his enquiry about working hours, Sid looked a little confused and replied, 'Whenever sheep need me.' When Tom asked when he might be able to start, Sid picked up the container of disinfectant, grinned, and said he already had.

Tom watched him stride off towards the farm gates and returned to his mother's kitchen to tell her that he'd employed Sid. He then went to the phone in the hall to call George Outhwaite, determined to behave as a successful London businessman, not the tongue-tied teenager he'd been reduced to when he'd first called him. George answered the phone with a familiar grunt.

'Mr Outhwaite. I've taken Sid on for a month's trial, so we need to agree an introduction fee. What do you usually charge?'

'Right lad. Five hundred will be fine.'

'And that's your usual fee, is it. Strange, because I've been told me that it's normally a hundred. Either they're mistaken or you're trying to take advantage of me. I wonder which it could be.'

'Don't you get cute with me, lad. Who was it that told you? It was Sid, I'll bet. Well, that's the last time he works for me.'

'That'll come as no surprise to Sid, given you said the very same thing to his face a couple of hours ago. Is he lying, Mr Outhwaite? Before you answer, I should warn you that it would be very easy for me to contact other farms you've supplied with casual labour. If I were to find out that the going rate is around a hundred, I wonder what that would do to your reputation which you told me you set so much store by round here. I'll put a cheque for a hundred in the post to you. Any objections?'

Tom heard snorting sounds down the phone. 'I'll take that as a no then. Goodbye Mr Outhwaite,' he concluded and put the phone down. Relieved to have finished the call he'd not been looking forward to, he redialled in a lighter mood. Sally answered.

'Hi Sally. It's Tom. Just wanted to say thank you for giving me that contact. I've just employed someone to help on the farm.'

'That's great! You met George Outhwaite then?'

'Unfortunately, yes.'

'Why unfortunately?'

'He's thoroughly unpleasant.'

'Yes, I've heard he's fairly forthright. The local gangmaster! So who's the farmhand then?'

'A guy called Sid Lambert. He's quite a character. Comes with a lot of baggage, but my Mum knows him and he seems to make her laugh. It's the first time I've seen her looking happy since my Dad died. Do you know him?'

'Can't say I do.'

There was an awkward silence. They both spoke at once, then both apologised. It was Sally who finally took the initiative.

'Tom, I don't know what you and your Mum are doing tomorrow night, but there's a concert on in Reeth as part of the folk festival I've been helping to promote. It might not be your thing but to be honest we need all the bums on seats we can get with all the tourists staying away because of the foot and mouth. Oh God, that sounded terrible. Talk about putting your foot in your mouth! Sorry Tom, I don't think of you as a bum on a seat – it would be nice to see you again. And your Mum. Sorry, I'm sounding like an idiot.'

'No you're not. I'd love to come, although I'll look forward to seeing you more than listening to the folk music. I'll have to ask my Mum if she wants to come. It might do her good to get away from the farm for once.'

9

Tom found it easy to find a space on the cobbled parking area fronting the long line of Georgian buildings on the West side of the village green in Reeth. Disturbingly easy he thought for a bank holiday weekend. He walked round the Land Rover to help his mother down from the passenger door taking in the panoramic view of the Eastern end of Swaledale glowing golden in the low evening sun. With more than half an hour to kill before the concert they entered the low beamed bar of the nearest pub and ordered drinks.

Jean emptied a small bottle of tonic water into her gin. 'You know, Tom, not counting church choir this is the first time I've been out of an evening in best part of a year. Your Dad was never a one for gallivanting as he called it and in last few years it was more than I could do to ever get him off farm. I don't mean to insult his memory by saying this, but now that I've come to terms with his going I feel, I don't know, maybe a sense of release. Is that a terrible thing to say?'

'Not at all. It can't have been easy for you when he started going downhill. Let's hope that we can make life better for you now and you can enjoy a bit of freedom.'

Reeth District Memorial Hall was festooned with bunting. Posters proclaimed a performance by 'one of the North's leading purveyors of traditional folk songs.' Tom steeled himself for what promised to be one of the less entrancing evenings of his life. He bought two tickets at the door and entered the half empty hall with his mother. Jean immediately spotted two old friends and led Tom to seats beside them. He was introduced and exchanged pleasantries then, as the three began to chat, he looked round in the hope of spotting Sally. She was nowhere to be seen.

Only a couple more people drifted into the hall before a bearded refugee from the nineteen sixties shambled on stage to welcome first the audience and then 'the Dales legend who is gracing us with his presence this evening.'

Tom resolved to put his ingrained aversion to folk music on hold and enter the spirit of the evening, but try as he might, he couldn't help but remain a detached observer. Each song was preceded by rambling anecdote and a detailed elucidation of the lyrics. It was then delivered with an import and intensity more suited to Moses reading from a tablet of stone. Most songs concerned inconsequential aspects of rural life. They were pleasant enough and the guitar playing was competent, but the singing was mannered in the extreme. Tom's mind wandered into testing the old cliché that true lovers of folk music had to wear beards. The most enthusiastic applause did indeed come from bearded men, but they were few and far between. The audience was predominantly ladies of a certain age who could well have made up the local Women's Institute. He came to the conclusion that his findings would not be statistically significant. He then amused himself by imagining a similar gathering in a post-apocalyptic parallel world where a group of baseball-hatted and trainer-footed enthusiasts struggled to keep the urban music of long-gone cities alive.

When an interval was announced it came with relief. Tom spied Sally at the back of the hall but she was busy counting tickets and money, so he and his mother joined the queue to buy drinks from a trestle table. A sign informed Tom that it was in fact run by the local Women's Institute. Jean seemed to know most of the people in the queue and soon became the centre of attention as condolences for her bereavement were offered. With a jolt Tom realised that he had almost put his father's death out of his mind. He bought a coffee and a tea which he handed to his mother. Since she was deep in conversation with her friends, he excused himself and went to greet Sally.

'Hi Tom. Sorry I wasn't here when you arrived. I was doing a last-minute trawl of the pubs and guest houses in the village to try to drum up business. Not very successfully, as you can see.'

'Foot and mouth is really keeping the tourists away then?'

'That or I'm no good at publicity! No, all the hotels and bed and breakfasts are saying that this weekend's a disaster. Easter usually kicks off the season, but this year it's dead. The festival is going to lose money, I'm afraid. Just give me a sec – I'll be straight back.' She closed a metal money box and took it to the bearded man who had introduced the evening. They spoke briefly with much shaking of heads before she returned.

'So, are you enjoying it?'

'It's not really my bag to be honest. But I'm happy to be doing my bit for the community and my Mum seems to be really enjoying being out for once.' They both looked towards Jean who was surrounded by a group of women of a similar age. She was laughing and looked every inch the merry widow. On impulse, Tom made a decision.

'Sally, I can think of a much better way of spending the next hour than listening to more hey nonny noes. My Mum seems to be happy with her friends, so what about sneaking off to the pub and coming back when the concert finishes? Can you?'

Sally smiled at him. 'Yes, I'd love to. I've done everything I need to do. But you're sure your Mum won't mind?'

Tom went to check. Jean looked knowingly at Tom and then at Sally who gave a cheery wave before assuring Tom that she'd be fine, and that he didn't need to collect her from the hall – she'd see him in the pub.

Tom brought a pint of Black Sheep and a dry white wine to the table and sat down beside Sally. She raised her glass to his.

'The city slicker has had his fill of bucolic music for one evening then? Missing your drum and bass?'

'No way! Can't stand that either.'

They put their glasses down. Tom could have picked up the cue for light-hearted banter about music, but he felt a desperate need to pour out his heart to someone he thought would be a sympathetic listener and for whom he was feeling a certain closeness.

'Sally, I don't want to bore you, but it's been a hell of a week. You've been brilliant, helping out on the farm and giving me the contact. You're a real friend and ...' The sentence petered out, Tom not being able to find the words to express what he actually wanted from her. Sally retrieved the situation by clasping his hands in hers.

'You've lost your Dad. And whatever went on between you and him in the past, you're having to come to terms with what it means to lose a parent as well as taking on all the responsibilities of looking after your mother. It's only been a week and already you've sorted out a farmhand. If you're also dealing with big problems with your company back in London, then you're the one that's been brilliant. Go on, tell me about it. Don't bottle it all up.' She released his hands and sat back. 'The psychiatrist is in session. I'll tell you when I'm bored.'

Tom hesitated to make himself vulnerable and tried to insist that he was being self-centred and maudlin. Sally would have none of it, so the floodgates opened. He told her of the whirlwind of emotions he was experiencing in the wake of his father's death. Receiving assurances that she was still willing to listen to his litany of problems, he went on to outline his fears that he might be losing his grip on running his business. Significantly he omitted any mention of Angie. Sally listened intently throughout. When Tom drew to a close, she offered to refill their now empty glasses. Tom refused and went to the bar himself.

'So, that's enough about me,' he said on his return, trying to lighten the mood. 'What about you – what do you think of me?'

Sally giggled. 'A very boring man – not! I think I've still got my crush on you, Tom Keardon.'

Before Tom could react, the pub's door opened and a herd of concertgoers entered, Jean amongst them. She approached their table and Tom leapt up to offer her a drink. At first she refused, citing a long evening and an early morning to come, but seeing the drinks which Tom had just bought, she accepted and asked for a Tia Maria. 'Just to keep you two company,' she said.

When Tom returned with the drink Jean and Sally were deep in conversation about foot and mouth. Two more farms in Wensleydale had been confirmed with the disease. They both felt that it was only a matter of time before Swaledale was hit. Jean was keen to know what precautions Sally's parents were taking on their farm. Nothing, it appeared, beyond what all farms were doing - restricting access and ensuring that the feet of each person and the wheels of every vehicle were thoroughly disinfected before entering. Beyond that it was hope and pray.

'So how long are you up for this time?' Sally asked Tom.

'I'm going to drive back tomorrow evening to avoid the traffic. I could really do with a day to myself in my flat before I go back to work on Tuesday. The fridge is empty, the laundry basket's over-flowing and the cleaner hasn't been because of Good Friday.'

'Always keen to get away,' said Jean. 'Still I've seen more of you this week than in the last fifteen years, so I can't really complain. And you'll be back soon for funeral. Why don't you leave your car here and get the train again? It'll be easier to get back when you need to.'

'And I'd be happy to drive you to the station tomorrow,' Sally offered.

Tom considered the suggestion. It was true that the journey was much quicker by train. Anyway, his car spent most of its time in his garage in London. 'OK, that's really kind. Are you sure I won't be putting you out?'

'Not at all,' said Sally who'd noticed that the prospect of Tom leaving and the mention of the funeral had caused Jean to fall silent. She tried to lift her spirits. 'Have you had a good evening, Jean?'

Jean snapped out of her reverie. 'Best for a long time. Lots of friends I haven't seen for ages and everybody's been so kind. Can't say I'll be rushing back for more of that folk music though. But thanks for inviting us – it's been good to get out for once.'

Easter Sunday dawned sunny and bright. Not that Tom was there to see it as his mother had already left for church by the time he came downstairs. He took a bowl of cereal and a cup of coffee outside to sit in the sunshine. Sid's battered motorcycle was propped up in the courtyard. With his breakfast finished Tom walked off towards the fields to find its owner.

The sound of whistling led him to where Bob the sheepdog was corralling the flock into a pen beside the sheep dip, responding perfectly to Sid's commands. Tom approached as Sid was positioning an aluminium gate to secure the pen. Bob was still excitedly bouncing back and forth outside the pen but with one long whistle from Sid he dropped instantly to the ground, panting hard. Sid went over to tickle him behind the ears in congratulation.

'That's very impressive, Sid!'

Sid looked up to see Tom. 'Ah, lad. Good morning to you – and a fine one it is too.'

'You two seem to be working well together.'

'Bob's been well trained – luckily in the same commands I use.'

Tom vaguely remembered that his father had once tried and failed to teach him the traditional set of whistles used to control sheepdogs. He'd not even been able to master the skill of whistling through his fingers, let alone learn the commands. His father had grumpily given it up as a bad job, caustically commenting that it would be easier to train a cat.

'So, how's it going, Sid?'

'Right grand to be back on't job. And so far, so good. I've not touched a drop since we had that pint together in Hawes.'

'Glad to hear it. What are you up to – going to dip the sheep?'

'Yes. As far I can see that's all the lambs you'll have this year. I can't find any more ewes carrying. Seeing as weather's good, they'll have chance to dry off before day's out. I'll check 'em for foot and mouth at same time.'

'Can I help?'

'Not dressed like that, you can't.' Sid looked critically at Tom's outfit of jeans, trainers and T-shirt. 'You'll get soaked, you know.'

Once again Tom's mind flashed back to his childhood, hearing his father's hectoring voice. *'Getting wet never hurt no one – and you're a wet'un to start with.'*

'I'll go and get changed.'

By the time Tom had walked back to the farmhouse, put on the boots and overalls he'd bought and returned, Sid had already filled the dip with water and chemical fluid from large plastic containers.

'So how can I help?'

'Well lad, I'll pick out sheep, check 'em for foot and mouth and get' em in dip. You can keep them there with pole. We'll start with youngsters. They're more valuable.'

'So how do I dip them? I've forgotten everything my Dad taught me about it.'

Sid looked at him quizzically. 'Right. Beginners guide to dipping sheep. They need to be in't fluid for at least a minute. Get their heads under at least three times. They've got to be wetted right through – especially folds and skin at back of neck. You'll need these.'

Sid handed Tom a pair of rubber gloves, goggles and a pole with a crescent of metal on the end. 'I could only find one of these. You better have it,' he said, handing Tom a long, rubberised apron. 'It'll keep worst off you. If you get any fluid on your skin, wash it off under tap straight away. Count the ones that go through. We're supposed to change fluid after every fifty sheep.'

While Tom donned his protective equipment, Sid waded into the holding pen and picked out a lamb. Amidst anguished bleats from the gathered flock he deftly manhandled it to the entrance to the dip where he pulled back its lips to look in its mouth then quickly checked the feet.

'Looking for blisters?'

'Yes. They're the sure sign of foot and mouth. That and fever. This one's fine.'

He released the lamb and pushed it in into the dip. Tom gingerly poked the animal with the pole. It thrashed wildly in the milky water, sending sprays in all directions.

'Nay lad get stuck in, thar's not going to hurt little bugger. Get metal round its neck and push it right under for a couple of seconds. Then hold it firm till you do it again. Remember – three duckings, out after a minute.'

Sid watched Tom struggling to contain the lamb's panicked attempts to break free then went to select and examine another sheep.

'Minutes up, lad. Let the bugger go.' Tom released the lamb and it lurched forward, its feet finding purchase on the floor as it tottered out into the sloping draining area where the fluid poured from its wool back into the dip. 'Let's see how thar handles a big 'un.' said Sid, tipping a large ewe into the dip. This time Tom fared much better. Sid was waiting with another lamb at the end of the minute.

'Not bad. We'll make a country boy of you yet, lad. When draining area's full, let them through into drying pen. Only a hundred and fifty odd to go.'

They fell into a rhythm and Tom found himself enjoying the repetitive manual work and the chance to let his mind go blank while concentrating only on the task in hand. Within the hour the fiftieth sheep exited the dip and he was able to call a halt. Sid turned a valve to drain the water and sat down beside Tom who was leaning back against a dry-stone wall.

'Good work, lad. Thanks. It'd take me three times as long on my own.'

'So far so good with the foot and mouth then. Do you think we'll escape? You've heard that there are more cases in Wensleydale?'

'Are there? Who can say if we'll get away with it? We did in't dale back in '67 but it never got so close then.'

'And what will happen if we do get it on the farm?'

'We'll be put into isolation. Nobody on farm will be allowed to leave. no one allowed to come on. Then men from ministry will come. They'll slaughter whole flock and burn lot of 'em.'

The two of them remained silent for a good minute, deep in contemplation. Tom was picturing the funeral pyre he'd driven past a few days ago. From where they sat the field fell steeply, affording an expansive view of upper Swaledale, vibrant in the bright sunshine. The sky was a brittle blue, dotted with pure white clouds. Trees were just beginning to grow their leaves, translucently green, affirming Spring's annual triumph of new life. It seemed unthinkable that death on an industrial scale might be visited on a place of such beauty, at this time of regeneration, Tom thought.

As if he had shared the same idea, Sid, almost under his breath, murmured 'Let it not be.'

Tom stood up, breaking the moment. 'Shall we then?'

Sid grinned at Tom. 'Sure thing, boss!'

It was after the next fifty sheep had been dipped and they were once again measuring out the chemicals to mix with the water that Jean called out to them. They turned to see her approaching in her Sunday best apart from, incongruously, a pair of wellingtons.

'Hi Mum. How was the service?'

'Lovely, thank you. I just wanted to see what time you two will be able to eat.'

'We're on the last batch, Mrs K. Your lad's been a great help. I'd say about an hour, but I've brought sandwiches with me.'

'Sandwiches? On Easter Sunday? No, it's got to be roast lamb and you're going to join us. And I've told you, it's Jean.'

'Well if you insist ... Jean.'

'I do.'

Jean told the two of them that dinner would be another quarter of an hour so Tom took the opportunity to go upstairs to wash, change and pack, conscious of the limited time before Sally was due to drive him to the station.

Roast lamb, he mused as he folded his clothes into the suitcase. It was a paradox he had struggled with as a teenager, the fierce love that farmers like his father professed and demonstrated for their livestock when the purpose of caring for them was to make them suitable candidates for summary execution at the abattoir. He remembered as a truculent fifteen-year-old know-it-all raising the issue of animal rights with his father. The reaction was predictably extreme, and not unreasonably so. Tom now thought with a sense of remorse for the trial he'd been to his father. He seemed to remember that the row ended with his father storming out of the kitchen shouting at his mother. *'Fine son you given me – now he's turning into a sodding vegetarian!'* Jean had apologised for his father's language saying that he was under a lot of pressure. She'd then tried unsuccessfully to persuade her fractious son to show more respect for his father.

Tom closed his suitcase and was about to go downstairs when another recollection caused him to sit down on the bed. Easter Sunday lunch had always been a significant occasion in the Keardon household during his childhood. His mother's simple but strong Christian faith ensured that Easter was given the import she believed it was due. His father, not a churchgoer, seemed to have an altogether more pagan take on the festival. For him, it signalled the final victory of spring over winter. He'd said as much, in a rare discussion they'd had which had not degenerated into a clash of opinions. And in essence the two approaches were the same. Both celebrated regeneration – the triumph of life over death. Resurrection.

Oh, for goodness sake, Tom thought. Let's not get too deep here. But good that it had occurred to him that the lunch would be very emotional for his mother. He determined to show his father respect in death that he had so seldom given in his life.

In the kitchen Jean was removing the leg of lamb from the oven. Sid was drawing a carving knife back and forth through a sharpener. Jean placed the leg on a serving dish and looked up at Tom as he deposited his suitcase on the floor. 'All packed then? Just in time for dinner.'

'I'd like to carve, Mum. I feel that I should.' She looked at him curiously then nodded her approval. Between the three of them, the food was arranged on the table – leg of lamb, roast potatoes and vegetables, Sid chattering away and pronouncing the fare to be the best spread he'd seen in many a year.

Once seated, Tom dismissed the fact that he'd never actually carved before. His father had traditionally made a show of carving the Easter leg of lamb, always making an impromptu speech on looking forward to a prosperous future and asking for a thought to be spared for the 'sacrificial lamb.' As a teenager, Tom had always raised his eyebrows at what he considered to be a somewhat toe-curling ritual. But perhaps now he felt an empathy with the feelings his father had been expressing.

'Sid, I hope you'll forgive me, but I feel I have to say something before I carve. It's just that I know having lamb for lunch on Easter Day meant a lot to my Dad. It's the last thing he would have admitted, but it was very symbolic to him. I think he thought of it as a sort of milestone in the journey through the seasons.' Tom looked at his mother to see that a tear had formed in her eye. Sid's head was bowed, sensing the emotion in Tom's voice. 'I feel that I should say something about my Dad now. I'm not worthy to say it, but it would be wrong not to.' Tom searched for the words. 'I respect him for all he achieved, for all the work he did, for providing for Mum and me, for his dedication.' Tom faltered, his voice laden with emotion. He was aware of the inadequacy of his words. 'Since long before I was born, the Easter lamb was always carved by Bill on this farm. Can I now carve it in his honour? I'm sure to make a pig's ear of it. It'll be my first time.'

Jean's face broke into a smile. She grasped his hand. 'Thanks, Tom – that was lovely.' He clasped her in a hug and they rocked back and forth.

Sid looked suitably serious. 'Well said, lad.'

As Tom had predicted, his first attempts to carve the leg of lamb were clumsy and the mood lightened as Sid and Jean offered advice and encouragement. The meal was eaten to the accompaniment of much reminiscing from Sid and Jean, talking of mutual friends and old times, bad years and good. Tom was happy to remain a largely silent listener, thanking his lucky stars that in the space of a few days since his father's death he seemed to have got the farm back on an even keel and found a friend as well as an employee to help offset his mother's loss. Provided of course that Sid could resist the demon drink.

Tom checked his watch and saw that he was shortly due to meet Sally for the drive to the station. He made to leave and shook Sid by the hand, thanking him for his work. Sid insisted that it was he who should be thanking Tom for his help at the sheep dip. Jean walked outside to the courtyard with Tom and gave him a farewell hug.

'I suppose you'll be back soon for the funeral.'

'Yes, I will. I'll phone the police on Tuesday morning to see if there's any news after the post-mortem. Call me if there's anything you need.'

'Thanks Tom.'

'What for, Mum?'

'For taking charge of everything and helping me start to get over it. Your Dad would have been proud.' She watched him fondly for a while as he walked away and then turned to go back in the farmhouse.

At Sally's suggestion, Tom had agreed to meet her at the farm gate. No point in coming on to the farm with foot and mouth around, she'd said. Tom had just finished dipping the soles of his shoes in the enamel bath of disinfectant when her Freelander approached and performed a three-point turn. 'Taxi for Mr Keardon! Jump in, slicker.'

'Excuse me – country boy, if you don't mind. I've spent most of the day dipping sheep.'

'I thought I could smell something!'

'That's the disinfectant. At least I hope it is.'

She drove swiftly, with assurance. Down in the village the pub looked to be doing good business with the wooden benches outside fully occupied with walkers and day trippers. The lure of warm sunshine had obviously overcome trepidation about foot and mouth. They crossed the stone bridge on the outskirts of the village and headed out on the narrow road which threaded its way between dry stone walled meadows to Reeth, tracking the twisting course of the river.

'Didn't you ever miss this place all those years you were away? Especially on days like this.'

'Not really. Yes, it's beautiful, but then I was always coming across beautiful places on my travels.'

'Like where?'

'All over the Far East. Thailand especially. The islands off the coast in the South – the ones the tourists haven't found yet. The hills north of Chiang Mai. I remember driving in a jeep on a jungle track through the rain and coming to a clearing by a pool. There were elephants splashing in the water and the most vivid rainbow I've ever seen. The end of it seemed to be just feet away. It took my breath away.'

'I suppose we don't have a monopoly on beauty here. Perhaps I ought to see more of the world. Elephants are few and far between round here although we do OK for rainbows. What were you doing there?'

'I was on assignment for the paper I was working for in Hong Kong. Following up a story about the opium warlords in the Golden Triangle near the Burmese border. The hill tribes up there had been happily growing opium for generations until the Americans funded the Thai government to do something about it. They had the best of intentions, but they created a real mess. I found out that opium poppies can be grown for most of the year up there, so the hill tribes had been nomadic. They harvested a crop and then planted another before moving on to the next location to do the same. It had a minimal impact on the natural ecology of the place.

'What did the Thai government do?'

'They offered the tribes incentives to settle down in one place and start cultivating coffee. It's not easy to grow and takes years to establish. It was never going to work, and it destroyed their way of life, not to mention the environment.'

'A bit like forcing us to stop raising sheep here, I suppose, and switch to, I don't know, arable farming on the hills.'

'Yeah – that wouldn't work either. Although I don't think you need worry about it happening. Sheep aren't quite as dangerous as opium.'

'Fair point. So what did you write about?'

'It was a think piece. I started by describing a skirmish between the warlords and Thai government troops which we got close to. Machine gun bullets were flying everywhere so we beat a hasty retreat and took refuge in a hill tribe village. Approaching the village was like crossing a wasteland. The jungle had been hacked away for about a mile in every direction around the village and filled with coffee plants which looked to be in a sorry state. Instead of living in harmony with the environment as nomads, the tribe was destroying it. They had to walk a mile to find wood for their fires and water was scarce because it was mostly used on the crops. When we got to the village, we discovered that they were in mourning. A young girl – must have been all of thirteen – was lying in state in a longhouse in traditional dress. Beautifully embroidered cloth with strings of coloured beads sewn on and a headdress decorated with what looked like tiny baubles from a Christmas tree.'

'What had happened to her?'

'I got my interpreter to ask them. It turned out that she'd died in childbirth. But here's the thing. The baby had survived, just. It was very weak and the Thai troops who'd been there at the time had called in a helicopter to fly it to a hospital in Chiang Mai. I wrote about how the young mother's death seemed to symbolise the passing of traditional ways and wondered what future there was for her baby. I described the ill-considered collateral damage that resulted from the fight against the heroin trade questioning where the moral high ground was. I didn't really come to any conclusion.' Tom turned to Sally and shrugged. 'As I said – a think piece.'

They had arrived at Reeth, the meeting point of Swaledale and Arkengarthdale. They skirted the triangular village green, catching sight of a traditional game of quoits being played with horseshoes in front of a crowd of intrigued day trippers. Descending to the river valley they crossed the Swale at Grinton and turned left on to the Richmond road.

Sally had been silent for a while, apparently doing her own thinking about Tom's think piece.

'Perhaps I should rephrase my original question. Don't you miss all that travelling, all that excitement? Don't you find it a bit tame being a city whiz kid now?'

'Now and then I do. When I'm stuck in a tedious business meeting, maybe. But I've had my fill of being a roving journalist. I spent the best part of ten years on the road, living out of a backpack and then a suitcase. Of course I miss the buzz you get from arriving in some exotic location on the scent of a story. The challenge of piecing together the facts and filing a report. It was the idea of being an outsider which first attracted me to journalism, but it was the thing that eventually turned me off it. I suppose I wanted to settle down and be a part of something, rather than an objective observer.'

'But judging by the story of the girl you've just told me, you were anything but detached.'

'True. And that was part of the problem. I'd seen too much fighting, too many natural disasters. Train crashes, plane crashes – you name it. I suppose it was getting to me.'

'But surely it's possible to get involved as a journalist. There's a name for it isn't there?'

'Gonzo journalism. Becoming part of the story and writing about it in the first person. Hunter S. Thompson pioneered it. New journalism's similar, but it tends to be for magazines, not newspapers, and certainly not for the English daily I was working for in Hong Kong. The editor hated my piece. Told me that if I wanted to wear my heart on my sleeve then I better go and work for a women's magazine. And he wanted to know what the hell I was thinking about running away from the machine gun fire and missing the real story.'

'Is that why you decided to get out of journalism?'

'Not immediately. I dutifully went back to hard-nosed reporting for a while, but my heart wasn't in it anymore. Or arguably, because my heart rather than my head was in it, it became more and more difficult to do. And my marriage was breaking up at the time as well, so I wanted a change.'

Sally snapped her head round to stare at him. 'Your marriage?' She remembered she was driving and turned back to look at the road. 'You didn't tell me you were married.'

'You didn't ask me. And it must be one of the only things I haven't told you. All I ever seem to talk about when I'm with you is me.'

Sally fixed her eyes firmly on the road for a while. They were approaching the outskirts of Richmond and richly wooded slopes on either side of the road were giving way to houses. She swung her head round again to fix him with a gaze then turned back to the road ahead, saying in a small voice, 'What was she like?'

It was Tom's turn to look hard at her. She smiled sweetly with a tilt of the head, making light of it. 'Just wondered.'

'OK. She was lovely. And still is. We divorced and now she's my business partner, running the Hong Kong operation. And if I can anticipate your next series of questions, we split up because of … cultural differences is the best way to describe it – she's Chinese. And yes, I still love her, but as a good friend now and she's about to get married again so there's no prospect of a reunion.'

Tom noticed that Sally was blushing. 'Am I that transparent?' she said painfully, her perky attitude drained.

Tom thought carefully before replying. He'd been happy to play along with the sparky, tongue in cheek relationship they'd re-established. More than happy – he enjoyed her company enormously. But she was revealing a potentially serious intent behind her flirty facade.

'Absolutely! And that's why I like you so much.'

She broke into a smile and playfully punched him on the upper arm. 'I like you too, kiddo!'

Tom was pleased that the pitch of his response had apparently defused a potentially awkward situation. He'd have to tread carefully. Meeting her again had been a breath of fresh air in an otherwise traumatic week. For the moment, he resolved, let's keep it at the level of friendship, even if she was signalling that she would not be at all averse to raising it a level or two. And would he be averse? Don't go there, Keardon, he told himself. Life's complicated enough as it is. But then again, she seems to make it simpler. Enough! She's a friendly shoulder to cry on in a time of stress. For the moment, no more.

They drove on into Darlington chatting inconsequentially – a new CD she'd bought which she put on the car stereo, a recently released film he'd seen, news of a mutual school friend she'd remembered. Pulling into the station forecourt they parked in a short stay bay and both walked to the platform entrance where the train departures were displayed. Tom's train was on time and due in a quarter of an hour.

He put his overnight case down and turned to face her. 'Sally, I want to thank you. For so many things. For driving me to the station, for helping me to find Sid, for …' He stumbled over his words as she tipped her smiling face up to look deeply into his eyes. He grasped both her hands in his. 'For being such a support to me in such a horrid week.'

She chuckled. 'And I thought you were supposed to be the wordsmith, Tom Keardon. You make me sound like a surgical truss.'

Tom broke into a broad smile. 'Sorry, I didn't put that very well. Just thank you, for being a friend.'

They both looked down at their clasped hands, and then, as if on cue, dropped them to their sides.

'Can I take you out to dinner when I'm next up, to repay you for the lift to the station?'

'That'd be nice. When do you think it'll be?'

'Probably in a few days for the funeral. That's if we get the go ahead from the coroner.'

'I can't say that I'll look forward to a funeral, but I will look forward to seeing you again.'

'Me too.'

Sally folded her arms and made a slow bowing movement. 'Right. You better get your train. Bye, then.' Her body language was a challenge for him to determine the nature of their parting. Tom melted.

'Come here!' He pulled her towards him and encircled her with his arms. Hers snaked around his waist and she snuggled her head into his shoulder. They stood immobile for a while before she tilted her head back to smile coquettishly into his eyes. She touched her index finger to her lips before planting it on his. 'See you, slicker.' She broke loose and walked quickly away, waving a hand behind her without turning around as she exited the entrance hall, confident that Tom would still be watching her. As indeed he was.

10

Tom spent most of Easter Monday in an orgy of domesticity. Rising late with the rare luxury of not having to set an alarm clock, he was taken aback to discover that he felt stiff from the unaccustomed manual labour of the previous day. Was it really only yesterday that he'd been dipping the struggling sheep? Einstein's theory proved, he mused. Distance does indeed affect time.

A leisurely soak in the bath as opposed to his usual hurried shower seemed to do the trick and he set off to walk to a local supermarket to replenish his empty fridge. Not having his car here wasn't such a bad thing, he thought. Normally he would have driven the short distance. Perhaps he needed to start thinking about taking more exercise if just a few hours of physical exertion had made him stiff. Not as young as I used to be, he admitted to himself.

He bought a copy of yesterday's Sunday Times from a corner shop on his way back from the supermarket and stopped off at a pub overlooking the Thames to sup a pint of real ale and catch up with what had been happening in the world.

Back in his loft apartment, Tom microwaved a meal for one and ate it while watching part of a football match on the Sky Sports Channel. He put the plate into the nearly full dishwasher and set it to run. He had to resort to reading the manual for his washing machine to make sense of the knobs and dials. Then a concerted round of tidying, hoovering and bed sheet changing rendered his home into a semblance of the state in which he usually found it after his cleaner had been.

By late afternoon he flopped on to a sofa and considered how he might spend the rest of the day. Suddenly his life felt empty. Here he was sitting in his desirable loft apartment appointed with fashionable furniture overlooking the Thames, surrounded by the latest technology. So what? He was alone. There was work he could do, information he could mug up on online, CDs he could listen to, DVDs he could watch. But he didn't need to. He knew he didn't do downtime well. He only functioned successfully while chasing deadlines, tackling issues and firefighting problems, but this was different.

Remembering Sally's question, his thoughts drifted back to the years he had spent travelling the Far East. Did he really miss it? Yes. But not chasing up stories so much as the rare moments of genuine human contact he'd had with people of all types, all persuasions and of all races in the course of his reporting. He recalled an evening in Penang in the north of Malaysia when, weary at the thought of another night spent in the artificial cocoon of a hotel bar in the company of fellow journalists, he'd set off to wander. He found himself in the Indian quarter, walking down dusty rutted streets between the crumbling concrete facades of ramshackle houses, the source of friendly curiosity from the dark-skinned faces which silently tracked his ambling progress. He knew the people to be Tamils, originally from the south of India, many of whom had been sent as indentured labourers to the farthest reaches of the British Empire in colonial times.

His attention had been attracted by a roadside bar constructed from rough-hewn poles and corrugated iron. Tacked on to one of the supports was a rusting enamelled advertising sign – *Guinness is Good for You*. He crossed the street to get a better look and studied the iconic image of a toucan balancing a pint of the jet black, white topped liquid on his oversized beak, intrigued that an old colonial artefact had survived such a passage of time. Looking into the dark interior of the bar he noticed four old men sitting at a table watching him intently. As he began to walk away, one of them came out and spoke rapidly in what he assumed was Tamil. He turned back, smiled, shrugged and spread his palms wide in the internationally understood gesture for not being able to understand. The old man smiled in return, bowed and beckoned for Tom to come in. On a whim, Tom followed him. The bar owner, if that was what he was, proudly gestured to a shelf supporting a row of dusty Guinness bottles. Tom nodded and one was opened and poured with elaborate care into a plastic cup. He held out a palm full of coins and a few were picked out. Turning to go towards an empty table, his arm was held and the bar owner pointed towards the table around which the other drinkers were sitting. They all beckoned for him to join them.

After much raising of cups and sipping of drinks the group lapsed into an awkward silence. Searching for a way to communicate Tom noticed that the wall was covered with images of cricketers cut from newspapers. Extraordinarily, one of them was none other than Geoffrey Boycott, the Yorkshire and England batsman he had idolised as a small boy and whose picture he had pinned to his bedroom wall. Tom pointed at the yellowing, crumpled image and said 'Boycott.' His companions' eyes followed the direction of his finger before enthusiastically chorusing 'Boycott.' Much nodding ensued along with a demonstration of a forward defensive stroke for which the famously obdurate player was renowned. They looked at him expectantly as he scanned the images. Recognising none of the Indian cricketers, he decided to venture a name. 'Gavaskar?' Bingo! 'Gavaskar!' they all exclaimed excitedly, pointing to the wall.

And so it continued. Long convivial silences, punctuated by the uttering of a famous cricketing name, followed by more reverential nodding. When Tom finally left amidst much hand-shaking and backslapping after several rounds of drinks for which he had insisted on paying, he felt enormously warmed by the unlikely encounter. A rare visit to a real world, as reassuring as it was alien. A brief respite from the transient life he'd chosen to lead.

Tom emerged from his reverie, went to the fridge to find a bottle of lager and came back to stand at his picture window, surveying the urban riverside view.

Sally's first question. Didn't he miss the Dales? Right now, yes he did. His time spent there in the previous week seemed like another visit to a real world. Maybe that was the reason for the feeling of emptiness he now felt in London. Let's hope it's temporary, Tom thought, because I've got a business to run. He went to settle down with an academic book on the Chinese economy he'd long been meaning to read.

Tiger.com's weekly operations meeting, postponed by a day because of the Bank Holiday Monday was brief and straightforward. Thanks to the four days off since the previous meeting, there was very little to update. Tom spent most of the day conducting the staff assessments he'd had to postpone from the previous week.

It was not until mid-afternoon that he was able to make the promised call to his police contact to learn the results of his father's post-mortem. You'll be pleased to know that the coroner has released the body for burial, he was told. Asking about the cause of death, the policeman said that it was for the coroner to decide, but off the record it was barbiturate poisoning – a clear case of suicide.

Tom looked down the 'To Do' list that he and his mother had prepared to find the name of the funeral directors in Hawes she had recommended. He typed the name into Google and was surprised to see that the first result the search engine provided was for a business listings page on dales.com – Sally's website. He clicked the link and a crudely designed page appeared. He scrolled down to find the phone number, made a note of it, then began to surf through the site. Sally could definitely do with finding a better web designer he thought, but it was certainly comprehensive. She'd been working hard.

He dialled the number. It was answered in a suitably lugubrious voice. As soon as Tom mentioned his surname the voice replied, 'Ah yes, Mr Keardon!' as if the call had been expected. Tom realised that it probably had been, given the fact that his father's death had been reported in the local press and the Dales were not overly endowed with funeral direction companies. The costs were discussed, and the arrangements made. The body would be collected and the funeral could be held at the village church on Friday, Tom's suggested day, subject to confirmation that the local vicar was available.

The farm phone rang out for a long time before his mother picked it up. She was relieved that the funeral could go ahead and agreed to call the vicar to book it. Saying that Tom must be busy, she also offered to phone around to invite people and to arrange for the Black Bull to lay on sandwiches for the attendees after the funeral.

With the round of calls complete, Tom brought up his diary on the screen of his laptop to see what he would have to rearrange. He'd need to travel up on Thursday evening. Several internal appointments could be postponed but he'd just have to miss a client meeting unless it could be re-arranged. He made a note to phone them personally to explain the circumstances. An entry on the Friday gave him the most concern – 'drafts due.' He'd given everyone the Friday deadline for the completion of the drafts which he was to turn into the marketing document which would spearhead the proposed new direction for the company. The document on which he believed the future of the company – and the avoidance of being taken over – depended.

There was nothing else for it. He would just have to return to London on Saturday and spend the rest of the weekend knocking it into good enough shape to present to the board on Tuesday.

He was about to go to his PA to discuss the re-arrangements when Ben popped his head round the door.

'Is there any chance we could go for a pint after work, Tom. There's something I need to talk through with you.'

Tom was taken aback by Ben's uncharacteristically serious demeanour. 'If it's urgent we can talk now.'

'No, better over a pint, boss.' Intrigued, Tom agreed.

At close of play they walked some distance from the offices to a pub Ben had suggested. Tom could only assume that he didn't want to risk talking in earshot of any staff who often frequented nearby establishments. On the way Ben solicitously asked Tom about how he was dealing with the aftermath of his father's death up in Yorkshire. Only when they sat down with their pints did Tom ask Ben to spill the beans.

'I'm not sure if I'm doing the right thing here. I've been weighing up the arguments for and against showing it to you but on balance I think I should.'

'You're talking in riddles. Show me what?'

'Yeah, sorry. It's an email. You know the new email and Internet monitoring system I've been trialling. It's mainly supposed to help us track information when several staff are working on the same project. We've told the staff about the trial, but we haven't come to a formal agreement about the terms of its use so I'm probably breaking some sort of data protection law by showing it to you.' Ben extracted a folded sheet of paper from the back pocket of his jeans. 'I was testing the system and thought that it would be interesting to search for the word 'takeover.' Given that we're supposed to be keeping it confidential I thought I'd see if anything had leaked out from those in the know.'

'And has it?'

'No. The good news is that the search only threw up emails from company directors. I don't know if this is bad news or not.' Ben handed him the paper. Tom unfolded it and read:

From: 'Ranjit Patel'
Sent: 11 April 2001 09:36
To: angie.taylor@tiger.com
Subject: Yesterday

Good work yesterday, girl! You're earning your reward. Roll on takeover (and the weekend)!
Ranjit

From: angie.taylor@tiger.com
To: 'Ranjit Patel'
Sent: 11 April 2001 10:09
Subject: RE: Yesterday

Hi Ran,
No problem. See you at the airport tomorrow.
Angie x

Tom struggled to take in the implications on the first read and looked at his Technical Director with a furrowed brow.

'Did I do the right thing?' Ben said and without waiting for an answer continued. 'You see the emails were sent on the day after the board meeting so Ranjit's presumably referring to Angie doing a good job in supporting him on the vote, or perhaps for writing her report in the first place. And tomorrow would have been last Thursday when they were meeting at the airport.'

'So they were going away for the weekend together.'

'Looks like it. And she's put a kiss after her name. Sorry. Tom.'

'No need to be. Personally, we're history now. But either she moved on pretty damn quickly after we split up or else she'd been seeing Ranjit before. You don't go away for the weekend with somebody you just got together with. I only broke it off on the morning of the board meeting for Christ's sake.' He could feel his anger rising. What sort of ride had Angie taken him on? The personal slight of being two-timed paled into insignificance against the possibility that she had only seduced him as part of a plan to persuade him to sell the company. Could she have been in league with Ranjit all the time?

'What do you think '*You're earning your reward*' means?' Tom asked of Ben.

'I'm not sure. I've thought long and hard about it. It's the reason I decided to show you the email. If it had just been about going away together then I wouldn't have wanted to hurt your feelings. It could just mean that he'd promised her a weekend away as a reward if she supported him in the vote.'

'A bit unlikely. What do you really think?'

'Well it's only a theory but there's some evidence to back it up – mostly circumstantial unfortunately. What if Ranjit is really desperate for money? I don't just mean to get a decent return on his investment, but really on his uppers. You know what he's like. Spends money like water and where does it come from? Unless he's got a sideline in dealing coke or something it must come from dividends from all the companies he's invested in and from dealing in the shares. Well, I decided to see what I could find out on the net. Google his name and up come hundreds of results, mostly to do with the companies he's been involved with. Google the companies and one after another they've either gone tits up or their share value is next to nothing. As far as I could tell, we're about the only company he's invested in which has any value to speak of.'

'So you think he enlisted Angie's help to try to force a takeover? Why would she agree?'

'That's what I couldn't work out at first. But I guess it all boils down to love or money in the end. Pretty weird sort of love agreeing to – forgive me, mate – agreeing to act as a sort of honey trap to get you to put your company up for sale. No, I'd bet on the motive being money.'

'So the reward the email says she's earning isn't just a romantic weekend but a fee or a cut of a takeover deal. Ranjit's paying her to engineer a takeover.'

'You said it. I didn't.'

They lapsed into thoughtful silence, drinking the beers that had remained largely untouched during the long exchange. Eventually Ben spoke. 'I didn't give you the chance to answer my question earlier. Did I do the right thing?'

'When I was a journalist the rule was that you never withheld any piece of information you came across from your editor. It was up to him to decide what to do with it. You've done the right thing. I've got to decide what to do about it?'

Their pints were almost empty. Ben went to buy his round. Returning with the drinks, he looked hard at Tom who was deep in thought. 'So what you are going to do about it.'

Tom remained silent, taking a long pull on his pint before speaking. 'Nothing.'

'Nothing? I mean aren't you going to confront Angie or Ranjit or both of them? Or get advice from Sir Giles, or, I don't know, find out from Human Resources if Angie is in breach of contract?'

'Nothing,' Tom repeated.

'Why, for goodness sake?'

'You were right to say that the evidence is circumstantial. Everything else is supposition. If I were to tackle them, they could just deny it. Who knows, there could be some innocent explanation we haven't thought of, although I very much doubt it.'

'Yeah, maybe you're right.'

'And they haven't done anything illegal that I can think of. I can't just sack Angie for making a fool of me. As for Ranjit, he's never made any secret of wanting to sell out. I still think we can win the battle to keep the company fairly and squarely. We've seen their cards and that puts us at an advantage. We'll keep ours close to our chest.'

11

The weather gods had conjured up a suitable backdrop for the funeral. Fine drizzle hung in the air and the colour of the sky echoed the dull greyness of the roof slates on the simple village church. A biting wind swirled the coats of mourners who trudged up the flagstone path past a freshly dug open grave.

In the porch they were greeted by the vicar, a kindly white-haired gentleman with an air of resigned calm. With an eye to the elements and the advanced age of most of the mourners, he suggested that they take their places inside rather than following the coffin in.

Tom and his mother had been the first to arrive, driving down in the Land Rover. They'd told the funeral directors to bring the hearse directly to the church rather than coming on to the farm to pick them up. From his position in the front pew Tom turned around regularly to survey the gathering congregation. He recognised a few of ladies his mother had been talking to at last week's concert in Reeth, but otherwise the only familiar faces were those of Sid Lambert, Sally and her parents, and the retired solicitor from Richmond who was acting as executor.

The organist struck up a sombre march and the vicar slowly led the bearers down the aisle to place Tom's father's coffin on two trestles in front of the altar.

'I am the resurrection and the life,' intoned the vicar. 'He who believes in me will live, even though he dies.' Adopting a more conversational tone he welcomed the mourners and began a short eulogy to Bill. Tom had been offered the chance to deliver one but he'd declined, thinking it would hardly be appropriate given his estrangement from his father. The vicar dealt with biographical details swiftly. After all there were few. Born on the farm, worked on the farm, died on the farm. Moving on to speak of Bill's character, his dedication and his determination, Tom suspected a detailed brief from his mother behind the vicar's words. Bill had never been a church goer and the vicar was unlikely ever to have met him.

They moved on to sing a psalm - with a certain inevitability, The Lord is My Shepherd. Tom had agreed to his mother's request that he give one of the bible readings. The passage he'd been given by the vicar, John 10, continued the ovine theme. He read in a strong, unwavering voice.

'I am the good shepherd: the good shepherd giveth his life for the sheep. But he that is an hireling, and not the shepherd, whose own the sheep are not, seeth the wolf coming, and leaveth the sheep, and fleeth: and the wolf catcheth them, and scattereth the sheep. The hireling fleeth, because he is an hireling, and careth not for the sheep. I am the good shepherd, and know my sheep, and am known of mine. As the Father knoweth me, even so know I the Father: and I lay down my life for the sheep. And other sheep I have, which are not of this fold: them also I must bring, and they shall hear my voice; and there shall be one fold, and one shepherd.'

When Tom had first looked up the passage his thoughts were taken with an absurd vision of Sid Lambert as the hireling fleeing the wolf. On a second reading he decided that it would be best simply to speak the words and not tax himself with trying to understand the meaning, or the reason that the vicar had chosen it. The reason became clear soon after the vicar began his sermon.

'Many of you will know that Bill probably died at his own hand. In the past such people were denied a funeral mass. The church held that the taking of all human life was a sin. The denial of Christian burial was used as a deterrent to teach the living just how grave a sin was the act of suicide. Today we take a more enlightened view, believing that the soul is judged by God alone. We can't know the inner thoughts of a person at the moment they take their life. We can however know something of the circumstances surrounding Bill's passing. He had just heard that he was suffering from a terminal illness, one that would soon render him incapable of being a good shepherd.

Rather than caring for his flock, he would soon need caring for. When he saw the wolf coming in the shape of that disease, did he act like the hireling and flee, caring more for himself than the sheep? Or did he think of himself as the good shepherd, laying down his life for his sheep, the better that they might be cared for? Only God can know, but maybe we can hope that in taking his life Bill 'feared no evil' in the words of the psalm we sang earlier. Perhaps he believed his last act to be one of kindness. We pray that God, in his infinite wisdom and love, will judge him with mercy. Let us pray.'

A queue formed at the entrance to the private function room at the Black Bull where a buffet had been laid out for the mourners. Jean and Tom stood side by side receiving the guests, thanking them for coming and accepting condolences. When all had entered Tom surveyed the crowded room and considered whom he should talk to. Sally caught his eye but he felt he should first thank the vicar.

'Lovely service. I really appreciated your thoughtful words about my father. I see now why you chose the passage for me to read.'

'I'm not sure my old theology teacher would be entirely happy with the way I interpreted it, though. It's not one of the easiest of Our Lord's parables to understand. The verses you read are actually considered to be a warning against false prophets rather than anything to do with honourable self-sacrifice which is the spin I put on it.'

Tom was intrigued that a man of the cloth should use the word 'spin' but he resisted the temptation to question it, thinking it would probably provoke an extended discussion. He followed a simpler tack.

'What you said will have been a great comfort to my mother. She told me that she'd like to think that my father killed himself because he didn't want to be a burden to her. I think you've helped her to believe that it was true. Thank you.'

To bring the conversation to a close Tom shook the vicar's hand and excused himself, saying that he was going to the buffet. By luck he joined the diminishing queue behind one of the few people present he knew, the retired solicitor who was handling the will.

'Thanks for coming. It's very kind of you.'

'I would be dishonest of me to pretend that it's an act of kindness. My round of golf got cancelled because of the weather,' he said disarmingly. 'But I'm glad that I was able to come to pay my respects to your father.'

They both heaped their plates with a selection of sandwiches, sausage rolls and vol au vents and positioned themselves near the imposing Georgian fireplace which dominated the room. 'Has my father's bank manager been in touch?'

'Yes. A very convivial lunch as it happens. We go back some way.'

'He was saying that you might not be in too much of a hurry to get probate.'

'Wouldn't want it to interfere with the golf, would we. I think we can keep the vultures at bay for a while.'

'Thanks, I appreciate it.'

The solicitor took on a serious tone. 'You do realise that all we can do is delay the inevitable, don't you? Give some breathing space to look at the options.'

'I do. And I've said that if it comes to it I'm willing and able to repay the estate's debts to keep the farm. But the businessman in me has yet to be convinced that it would be a sensible investment, even if I take my mother's wishes into account.'

The solicitor eyed Tom, seeming to be appraising him. 'It's not my place to tell you what to do, but perhaps you'd allow me to make an observation. From a business point of view, investing in your mother's farm by repaying the loan is a no-no. It's barely surviving, like most of the farms round here, and will probably never give a decent return on investment. But surviving, and nothing more, is what we're in the business of round here. It's what your father did.'

Tom was at a loss how to reply, so he once again excused himself and moved to a corner of the room. Yorkshire people were renowned for their bluntness and the conversations he'd just had had borne that out. In many ways it was a breath of fresh air. His years as a journalist had made him all too used to dealing with subtlety, disingenuousness and hidden agendas.

Taking stock of the situation, he felt detached from his father's funeral wake. He wondered if his emotional numbness made him a bad person. He was saved from self-analysis by Sally's approach. She was severely dressed in a black business suit, but still managed to convey a self-assured sassiness which Tom found intensely attractive. Instead of one of her trademark breezy greetings she took on an expression of concern and asked if he was OK.

'Fine. Just feeling like an outsider. Not just from the people here – I know hardly any of them – but I seem to be an observer at my own father's funeral. I was just wondering if that makes me cold, unemotional, I don't know ...'

'Tom, whatever you're feeling is real. Don't pretend to feel anything else.' She broke into a smile. 'Come and say hello to Mum and Dad.'

Sally steered a route to her parents. Tom thanked Mrs Hardcastle for coming and shook her husband's hand, saying it was good to meet him again.

'In other circumstances it would have been better, lad. My sympathies. Your father was a good man.' Tom thanked him. 'What's going to happen to farm? Sally tells me you're a big shot down in London now.'

Sally broke in. 'Dad!' Tom had a vision of her as a teenager, thrown back in the same way that he had been so often on his return to the Dales.

'It's a fair question, Mr Hardcastle, and the answer is that at the moment, I don't know. You may have heard that the bank's calling in the loans. I'm not yet convinced that paying them off wouldn't be throwing good money after bad. Maybe I should be looking at doing what you and Sally have done and diversify into holiday cottages.'

'I can tell you that without extra money from what our Sal's set up, bank would be banging on our door. But you doing holiday cottages is a terrible idea.'

Tom looked puzzled. 'Why's that, Mr Hardcastle?'

The sheep farmer's ruddy face broke into a huge grin. 'We don't want the competition, lad!'

Tom joined him in smiling. 'I wouldn't worry, Mr Hardcastle. We haven't got any buildings which are suitable for conversion anyhow. At the moment things seem to be on an even keel. My Mum's in no hurry to leave the farm and I've got Sid helping to run the place.' He nodded towards Sid who had donned his special red and white trainers again and was chatting to his mother. He was balancing a plate of sandwiches in one hand and holding what appeared to be a cola in the other. 'So far, so good. At least I've got a breathing space now before I need to decide what to do about the farm. I can also get back to my work in London. I've been neglecting it. '

'Well, good luck with Sid, lad. And if you need any help, you know where we are.' Ken Hardcastle excused himself and went with his wife to talk to other guests. Tom was left with Sally.

'When are you going back then?' Sally's tone of voice, as well as her folded-arm stance, was challenging.

'I'm driving down tomorrow morning. I've got to pull together a very important marketing paper in time for a board meeting on Tuesday. Several directors should have written their sections by today. I'll have to make sure we're all singing from the same hymn sheet then write the introduction and summary. It may sound callous, but I'm pleased that the funeral is over and I can get back to some sort of normality and not have to take up so much time travelling up and down the country.'

Sally's arms remained firmly folded. Her voice was cold. 'As a matter of fact, it does sound callous. We're all sorry that your father's death was such an inconvenience to you. I'm glad you can get back to the real world now and leave us lesser beings to plough our weary furrows.'

Tom was taken aback and looked uncertainly at Sally wondering if it had been a wind up, but her fierce expression told him otherwise. He went on the attack. 'Just a few minutes ago, didn't you say to me something like whatever you're feeling is real and don't pretend to feel anything else? I'm sorry. Maybe I am callous. But it's what I feel.'

Sally continued to gaze at him then, as if exasperated, turned to look determinedly into the middle distance.

'Look, Sal, I'm sorry. I owe you a dinner for taking me to the station. How about tonight?'

There was disdain in her voice as she replied. 'Don't you think you should spend the evening of your father's funeral with your mother? Call me if you ever decide to neglect your work again and can be bothered to come up.' Without a backward glance she marched off to join her parents.

12

The British Airways 747 banked steeply over Long Island affording Tom a first glimpse of the Manhattan skyline. He picked out the familiar landmarks – the Empire State, the Chrysler Building, the twin towers of the World Trade Centre. He'd managed to sleep fitfully in his reclining business class seat over the Atlantic in the forlorn hope of staving off the inevitable jet lag but had been fully awake since the plane had over-flown the snowy wastes of Newfoundland. For more than an hour now he'd been peering out of the window as the east coasts of Canada and then America unfolded beneath him, mulling over the decisions he'd taken to bring him to New York.

Preparing the prospectus on Tiger.com's proposals to capitalise on China's emerging consumer market had gone smoothly. Tom was pleased with the final proof of the glossy brochure which lay in his briefcase in the overhead locker above him. It had been in deciding on the next steps that Tom and Angie had locked horns.

Angie had wanted to test the water by marketing the idea to UK retailers. Tom had insisted on starting at the top and targeting the world's biggest companies in the sector. That meant going to the States. She'd countered by saying that China was more likely to declare war on the US than welcome their retailers into the country. It was true that Sino-US relations were currently at a low ebb after the recent mid-air collision between a US spy plane and a Chinese fighter resulting in the death of its pilot and a forced landing for the American plane on the Chinese island of Hainan. Tom argued that the incident had already been resolved and would not stop the inevitable march of China into ever closer trading relationships with the West.

Once Angie had unwillingly conceded, she suggested that she should approach the target U.S. companies direct. Tom overruled her, insisting that they should engage the services of a specialist retail consultancy in New York. He instructed Angie to issue a news release to the trade press in the States saying that Tiger.com was looking for a consultancy partner for a major project in the Far East. Finally, he'd rejected her request to accompany him to the U.S. to hear the pitches from the companies who had responded and who had been short-listed. Instead he'd opted to ask So Lin to fly halfway around the world in the opposite direction to join him in New York.

It was not regret over making the series of decisions that was taxing Tom's mind. It was the motives for taking them that he was questioning. On the face of it, at every step of the way Angie seemed to be obstructing progress towards realising the plan which Tom believed could save the company from being sold to the highest bidder. Was that because she was in league with Ranjit or because she genuinely believed, as a marketing professional, that Tom's way was not the best way to succeed? Was I, Tom thought, too determined to smell a conspiracy? Too bent on getting my own back for making a fool of myself with Angie to give her a fair hearing?

Tom's contemplation was interrupted by a steward announcing that the plane was beginning its descent and the captain had illuminated the seatbelt signs. He set to filling in the bizarrely worded card which would assure the U.S. immigration and customs officials that he had never been arrested for a crime of moral turpitude, was not currently involved in genocide, and was not in possession of a dangerous vegetable.

The yellow cab dropped Tom at his hotel on Madison Avenue and 41st in mid-town Manhattan around one p.m. local time. After checking in and unpacking his suitcase in his room, Tom considered how to spend the three or four hours until Lin was due to arrive and they could begin to discuss strategy for tomorrow morning's meetings. Calculating that it was early evening as far as his body clock was concerned, Tom decided that he wouldn't really be breaking his self-imposed rule of not drinking in the daytime if he were to wander off in search of a beer and a burger.

Buddy's Bar a block away looked like a suitable haven to while away an hour or so with the Wall Street Journal and Time magazine which Tom had bought at the street corner kiosk. He chose a window booth overlooking the street and gave his order to the aproned girl who introduced herself as Gail and informed him that she was to be his waitress for the day. As he opened his paper he heard a loud slam on the window beside him accompanied by barked shouts of 'Freeze, freeze!' Tom whipped his head round to catch the panicked eyes of a tall black youth in a hoody no more than a foot away who was splayed against the plate glass. Four of New York's finest were arranged in a semi-circle around him, standard issue Glock 40 calibre side arms held at arm's length. Tom was directly in their line of fire. His mobile phone rang. He answered in a reflex action.

'Hi Tom. It's Sally. Where are you? That was a strange ring tone.'

One of the policemen viciously kicked the youth behind the knees causing him to sink to the sidewalk. His hands rose above him, palms pressed to the glass.

'Hi, Sally. I'm in New York with several guns pointed at me.'

'Oh! Can you talk?'

'Just a sec.'

The youth was frisked and his arms pulled down behind his back. Handcuffs were whipped out and expertly attached to his wrists before he was bundled away. Tom breathed a sigh of relief and shook his head in disbelief at the surreal incident. 'Sorry. OK now.'

'What was that you said – something about guns?'

'No. It was nothing. Good to hear from you. Have you forgiven me?'

'No, but there is a way in which I might consider it.'

'And what would that be,' Tom asked warily.

'Right. Are you going to be back in the UK a fortnight Saturday?'

'I think so.'

'Well I'm organising another event. Don't worry, it's not another folk concert. It's a dinner for the Swaledale Sheepbreeders' Association. I've persuaded the local MP to speak. It's quite a coup with the general election coming up a few days later.'

With all that had been going on in his life, Tom had uncharacteristically been taking very little interest in the upcoming election. It had originally been expected on May 3rd to coincide with local elections but had been delayed until June 7th because of rural movement restriction imposed in response to the foot and mouth outbreak.

'That might be why he's agreed. MPs always return to their constituencies on the weekend before an election. He's after votes.' Tom instantly regretted the put down and tried to recover. 'Sorry, that was cynical. It is quite a coup.'

Sally sounded crestfallen. 'No, you're right. I hadn't looked at it that way. Damn you! I thought I'd been so clever.' Tom did his best to assure her that she had. 'Anyway, the point is, I don't suppose you'd want to buy some tickets, or, if you really wanted me to forgive you, a table? We've still got a few available – well, a lot, to be honest. The foot and mouth is still bad here.'

'Well, I don't know.'

'Come on, Tom. Your Mum was complaining the other day that you seem to have disappeared again. She needs you and it's time you came up and faced up to your responsibilities. And ... well ... I'd like to see you again.'

Tom groaned inwardly. This seemed very close to emotional blackmail. 'I'm not sure I know enough people to invite on to a table.'

'There are a few people I could invite for you who it'd be good for you to meet. You say you feel like an outsider up here. What better way to start to get accepted? Although, of course, there's always the danger that they might think that you're a flash Londoner, buying a table'

'Do you think so?'

'Possibly. But there's a way round it. We could say that it's my company's table.'

Tom had the distinct feeling that he was being suckered. 'Sally, I don't believe you! Let me get this straight - you want me to give you the money for you to buy a table?'

'Well, I suppose you could look at it that way, but if you don't ask, you don't get. And you owe me a dinner.'

Tom couldn't help laughing down the phone, shaking his head and smiling at her chutzpah.

'And I'd forgive you,' she murmured in a wheedling sing song voice.

'Damn you! Alright. Email me the details and I'll get back to you.'

'Oh thanks, Tom. You're a good mate!'

'And a gullible one.'

'Surely not! Give 'em hell in New York. Bye!'

Tom still had a puzzled grin on his face when his waitress for the day returned with his burger and beer.

Tom and So Lin took the elevator to the 15th floor of the building on Madison Avenue for their first appointment of the day. They'd met up the previous evening in their hotel and over drinks and dinner had poured over the written responses from the three companies on the shortlist to provide consultancy in approaching the American retail giants. They'd both felt that chemistry would be as important as track record in making a decision. They also debated how much of their plans they should divulge to the potential consultants. So far they had been deliberately vague, not wishing to risk competitors being alerted on the grapevine. They decided that they should continue to play their cards close to their chest, simply saying that they were looking initially for introductions to companies interested in major retail opportunities in the Far East, with the carrot of a contract to represent them locally once a retailer had bought in to their proposals.

The elevator doors opened on to a marble-floored foyer, its walls bedecked with faux Warhol canvases of various products and brands. Lin's high heels clacked echoingly as they approached the semi-circular reception desk. An immaculately coiffured receptionist rose to greet them.

'Mr Keardon?' Tom nodded. 'And Miss So? Welcome! I'll tell the vice-president you're here. Can I get you a coffee, a water?' Tom and Lin demurred. 'Then please take a seat.' They settled into black leather and chrome chairs as the receptionist made a call. Within seconds, as if he had been waiting in the wings, an overweight balding man in a shiny suit and a loud tie burst through the wood-panelled double doors.

'Tom! May I call you Tom?' He grasped Tom's outstretched hand in both of his. 'And Lin – you're so welcome – or should I say welcome So Lin.' He made an absurd bow to her with his hands clasped together. 'Please, come and meet the team.'

Tom and Lin exchanged raised eyebrows as he led them through the doors and down a corridor into a boardroom where he made introductions to four of his colleagues standing in a line. After once again refusing coffee, water and this time pastries, they took their places around a long glass-topped table. The picture window running the full length of the room gave on to an uninspiring view of the skyscraper on the other side of the avenue.

The vice-president called the meeting to order. 'May I formally welcome our international guests who have graced us with their presence today. From London, England, Mr Tom Keardon – wotcha, mite.' The last words were spoken in an accent even

Dick Van Dyke would have been ashamed of. 'And from Hong Kong in the People's Republic of China, Miss So Lin – huan ying!'

She looked at him condescendingly. 'Thank you. But we speak Cantonese in Hong Kong, not Mandarin.' Tom supressed a grin. That's my girl, he thought.

With barely a frown, the vice–president continued. 'Before we discuss the details of your requirements, I'd like to present our retail marketing credentials by showing you this short video.'

He flamboyantly waved a remote control and, in a series of actions which would have done justice to a Bond villain's lair, blackout curtains descended to cover the window, a screen unrolled from the ceiling, and a projector sprung into life accompanied by booming audio.

In the darkness, as the flashy video hyperbolically extolled the quasi-messianic achievements and capabilities of the company, Tom felt a gentle kick on his leg from Lin. He returned the kick. They knew each other well enough to know exactly what was meant. All that was required now was to extricate themselves as quickly as possible.

The second appointment fared little better. The old-fashioned elevator which transported them to the top floor of a converted warehouse in Tribeca clanked and groaned upwards before depositing them at the entrance to a large open plan office. Drawing back the two metal latticed gates, they stepped onto heavy wooden floorboards. The brick walls were largely bare, apart from a selection of native American hanging rugs and, at the far end of the space, an outsized portrait of Einstein with his tongue hanging out, looking more like a candidate for the funny farm than the father of modern physics. Desks were few and far between, most of the room being taken up by meeting areas composed of overstuffed antique sofas arranged around low rough-hewn coffee tables. If the first company they'd visited seemed to be stuck in Madison Avenue's heyday of the sixties, this one had at least moved on a decade.

A tall long-haired throwback to the seventies dressed in jeans and T-shirt rose languidly from one of the sofas and came to greet them. 'Hi, there. Great to see you, come on in. I'm Jeff, the senior creative.' Tom inwardly winced. He hated the way that the advertising and marketing industry had taken the adjective and turned it in to a noun. 'Hey you guys, come and join us – Tom and Lin are here.' He beckoned to two of his colleagues who took their place on the sofas.

This time the meeting took the form of a relaxed chat rather than a full-on business presentation. They were intrigued to hear more about what Tiger.com were proposing, saying that they wanted to be sure that they could deliver what was required. Tom appreciated the modest position they were adopting and warmed to them as individuals, but the more he heard from them, the more he felt that they wouldn't be the ones to provide the introductions he was looking for. As brand development specialists they had excellent contacts with the major retail players and displayed creative flair, but he couldn't see them successfully lobbying for the strategic commercial decisions which would have to be made if a retailer was to buy in to Tiger's proposal. Neither did he consider them to have the style, skills or indeed the inclination to represent them locally in a long-term implementation of the plans. They parted on good terms, with the unspoken understanding that they were not right for each other.

Tom and Lin found an Italian restaurant close by to have lunch and take stock.

'Two down and one to go then.'

'Looks like it,' said Tom. 'I liked the feel of that last company but that's probably just the old hippy in me. I mean, could you see them getting to grips with all the political and bureaucratic detail we'll be wading through if this thing comes off?'

'No way. And as for that first lot. Welcoming me in Mandarin! I felt like smiling sweetly and saying something extremely rude to him in Cantonese.'

'You should have.'

'It's all down to your journalist friend then.'

'What do you mean, friend?'

'I was listening in on a conference call to the meeting when you were choosing the shortlist, remember? Angie was arguing that you only wanted him included because he was a journalist, rather implying that that's what you still are rather than a businessman.'

'He's a retail consultant as well as a journalist. And as a journalist he's been writing a column in the biggest retail trade magazine in the States for about 20 years. Apparently, he can be pretty acerbic and he's looked upon as something of a guru. He knows US retailing better than pretty much anyone.'

'But does that mean he's the right guy to help us achieve what we're trying to do? What does he know about China?'

'Remember what Lord Northcliffe said about journalism?'

'Lord who?'

'He was the first media baron in Britain. Pioneered tabloid journalism. He said that journalism is a profession whose business it is to explain to others what it personally does not understand. So who better than a journalist to communicate our message?'

'Well I hope so, because if we don't like him it's back to square one.'

The cab dropped Tom and Lin outside a brownstone terrace in Brooklyn. They climbed steps to a front door and pressed a bell beside a verdigris bronze sign heralding Bob Schwartz Associates. A dog began to bark wildly.

Bob himself flung open the door restraining a large chocolate Labrador by the collar. 'Come in, come in! I hope you don't mind dogs. He's very friendly.' The animal did indeed display leanings in that direction by substituting loud barks for deep-throated growls while schizophrenically thrashing his tail from side to side. Tom readily made a fuss of him, but Lin cowered uneasily in the background.

'Back in your bed!' The dog meekly obeyed Bob's command and followed his master's pointing finger to a basket at the end of the hall where he settled down to chew a rubber bone.

'Sorry about that. Shoulda shut him in the back – I always forget.' Bob's nasal accent suggested that he'd been brought up not far away. He reminded Tom of an academic – corduroy jacket, opened-necked dark shirt and a mass of wavy pepper and salt hair above his craggy, open face.

The impression of academia was reinforced by the state of the front room office into which they were ushered. Floor to ceiling shelves overflowed with books, magazines and boxes of files. Bob cleared piles of paper from two chairs and placed them for Tom and Lin to sit facing an antique desk, behind which he sunk into a chair. It took him some time to search the cluttered desktop for a file which he opened and studied for a while.

'Ah yes - Tiger.com,' he murmured, nodding his head, as if only just remembering what the meeting was about. He looked up and smiled benignly at his guests. 'So you guys think you can pave the way for a major US retailer to expand into China.'

Tom was flummoxed. 'I beg your pardon?'

'No need to be coy. Reading between the lines it's pretty obvious. You're specialists in economic intelligence about the Far East with pretty good links to the Chinese authorities from what I can see, and about to get even better. Congratulations, by the way.' Bob was addressing Lin.

It was her turn to be flummoxed. 'What do you mean?'

'I've got a few contacts out in Hong Kong, so I asked around. Your engagement was announced in the papers, so the fact that you're marrying into one of the most well-connected business families in the region is in the public domain.'

Despite having been put on the back foot the journalist in Tom was impressed. He decided to try to gain the initiative. 'So you've done your research on us. That's very diligent of you. But what makes you jump to your conclusion about what we're trying to do?'

'This article for a start.' Bob fanned out the papers in the file in front of him and located a photocopy of a magazine article.

Tom craned his neck to read the title and the by-line. It was his own. 'You wrote this last December – it was a look back at the year 2000 in the Far Eastern economies. Nice concluding paragraph!' Bob donned a pair of half-rimmed spectacles and read aloud. *'Aptly, the first year of the new millennium was the Year of the Dragon in China. And it is the Chinese dragon which must soon be asserting its dominance over the tiger economies of the Far East. As the world's largest population are tentatively introduced to capitalism, could consumerism be hot on its heels?'* Bob removed his spectacles and tapped them on the article. 'It's pretty clear the way you're thinking.' Tom went to speak, but Bob jumped in. 'And then there's the wording of your brief.' He retrieved the paper from the file and put the glasses on again. *'Tiger .com is looking for a partner in the US to help them develop a major retail initiative, etc.* Well, either you're thinking of opening a chain of Chinese laundries ...' Bob fixed them with a gaze. 'Or you've decided to stop just commentating on economic development in the Far East and get a slice of the action by persuading one of the big retail corporations to expand into China with you as their advisors. Am I right or am I right?'

Tom and Lin both looked uncomfortable. Tom took the plunge. 'If I confirm that you're right, can we count on your confidentiality?'

'Tom – you've been a journalist. You know perfectly well that there's no such thing as off the record. But if you're asking if I'm going to splash it all over my column, the answer is that I'd be a damn fool to do so if I wanted your business – and I do. I'm a consultant as well as a journalist and I'm well versed in managing potential conflicts of interest between the two roles.'

'And what if you don't get our business?' So Lin countered. 'What's to stop you writing about us?'

'Good point. You better give me your business.' Bob grinned and spread his hands wide.

Tom was warming to this guy's no-nonsense approach and he was enjoying sparring with him, but he wasn't willing to let the issue of confidentiality drop. 'We're very concerned to get a clear run at this initiative. We're a minor player compared to some of the big boys in our field. Our strength is our specialism and the fact that we can steal a march on the opposition by being the first to step up to the plate.'

Lin looked questioningly at Tom and he realised that she probably hadn't come across the Americanism. He could be sure that it would be added to her collection of idiomatic phrases when he explained it.

'Sooner or later the question will be asked about whether it would be safer to pursue the initiative with one of the international management consultancies rather than us. And sooner or later those consultancies will get wind of what we're proposing and try to muscle in. In both cases, we need it to be later rather than sooner.'

'Understood. So you're confirming it.'

'I'm not denying it.'

'OK, so hypothetically, if you were to be targeting a corporation to expand into China, who's top of your list?'

'We'd want to start at the top and work down until we get a bite. Supermarket chains are top of the list so it would have to be Valco – they're the biggest.'

'I've got plenty of contacts there, but we're getting ahead of ourselves. You still haven't answered my original question.'

'And what was that?'

'I asked if you guys think you've got what it takes to pull this thing off. If and when you find a company willing to give it a go, do you really think that you'll be able to get the go ahead from the Chinese government?'

'Who's interviewing who here?' Tom said sharply.

Lin laid her hand on his to curb his aggression and responded calmly. 'Mr Schwarz. It's understandable that you want to be convinced of our abilities before considering working with us. We may be a small company and a young one, but we've got our finger on the pulse of the consumer revolution which we're convinced my country is on the brink of. The fact that almost all the major banks and most of the international management consultancies subscribe to our online service speaks for itself. We're a primary source of information on the ground in China and I'd find it difficult to believe that anyone is better placed than us to carry it off.'

Bob looked at Lin with respect. 'OK, I'm sold. If I can arrange an introduction to Valco, what will you be pitching them?'

Tom fished in his briefcase and brought out the proof of the brochure. Bob flicked through it. 'Great – can I keep this?'

'I'm afraid not – it's the only proof copy and of course it's confidential. If you'd like to read the introduction and summary now it should give you a good idea of our pitch.'

'OK. Bear with me.'

Bob donned his spectacles and began to read. Lin looked at Tom and tilted her head in the direction of the door. Tom understood that she wanted to speak in private.

'While you're reading, Bob, do you mind if we pop outside for a chat?'

'Be my guest. Mind the dog.'

Out in the corridor with the office door closed, the Labrador eyed the couple suspiciously but opted to continue in his mission to demolish the rubber bone.

'I thought we were going to play our cards close to our chest – isn't that what you said? And now you've let the dog out of the bag.'

Tom grinned at Lin. 'Cat out of the bag. It's not like you to get an idiom wrong.'

'Yes of course. I've got dogs on the brain. You know I've never liked them. We used to eat them, remember, until you Brits stopped us in Hong Kong.'

'Ah, the civilising influence of colonialism – one of our more memorable achievements.'

Lin punched his arm. 'What's got into you? Be serious, will you? This guy's running rings round us.'

'Yes, he is, and that's why I want to go with him. He's one sharp cookie.'

'He's what?'

'An Americanism. It means on the ball. You can't pull the wool over his eyes. No flies on him.'

'Stop it – plain English, please.'

'He's very bright and perceptive, and I like his style.'

'So do I, but is he right for the job? We've got to find if he can really deliver. It's time that we asked some questions.'

'Yeah, you're right. Let's give him the third degree.'

'Will you stop using idioms you know I won't understand? You're a bully! For God's sake, Tom, this is the future of our company we're dealing with, and all you can do is play the fool.'

'I'm sorry, Lin. But after the last two meetings I was getting really depressed. Now I'm feeling really upbeat about the whole thing. Sorry.'

'Just get back in there and give him hell, you bastard!'

'Yes, ma'am. Anything you say. God, but you're attractive when you're angry!'

She once again punched him, but there was a resigned smile on her face.

Hell it may not have been, but Tom did question him closely about his contacts in the major supermarket chains and his ability to provide on-going support should a contract be signed. Bob appeared to have a direct line to most of the senior managements, a product, he said, of his many years of being a thorn in the flesh of the industry through his widely read column. Support, he said, could be provided if necessary. While he operated as a one-man band, he had a wide circle of researchers and freelancers who he regularly employed on a project basis. Most interestingly, he confided that now could be a very opportune time to approach Valco. Their chief executive was due to retire within the month and the promotion to the helm of the current vice-president for business development suggested that they might be sympathetic to expansion.

The meeting drew to a close. 'Thanks, Bob. I think we can do business. I'll have to run it past the board at the next meeting, but I hope we'll be working together very soon.'

Tom paid for his frivolity with a comprehensive ear bashing from his ex-wife that evening before they flew off in opposite directions the following morning.

13

The board meeting on the following Tuesday proved to be a sobering affair for Tom. Keen to press ahead with approval for the next stage of his plans in the States, he was soon thrown into a dark mood.

The monthly P & L accounts were scrutinised. They told a sorry story of further decline. Then, with departmental reports noted and discussed, Sir Giles moved on to the substantive items on the agenda.

'So, let's find out what progress has been made on our two major initiatives. We agreed that Charles and I would make initial soundings on a possible takeover while Tom and Lin would spearhead the approach to US retailers about expanding into China. Let's hear reports, starting with you, Charles, please.'

Charles shuffled his papers and cleared his throat. Tom noticed that Ranjit and Angie both leant forward in ill-disguised eagerness to hear what he had to say.

'I'm grateful to Sir Giles for taking the lead on this. He made the initial contacts and came up with a list of possible companies who might help us find a buyer. We discussed them and decided to hold an exploratory meeting with PMJK.'

Tom did a double take at the mention of one of the top international accountancy firms. 'PMJK? I know that they've got a great track record in facilitating takeovers but they're also a potential competitor. They're exactly the sort of company who might muscle in on our initiative.'

Ranjit jumped in aggressively. 'And that's the problem with your initiative, Tom. There's no copyright in ideas and why should any of the US corporations get into bed with the likes of us when they could play safe and go with the big boys.'

Sir Giles interrupted. 'Gentlemen! Can we return to Charles' report, please?'

Charles looked around nervously and continued. 'For the record, Tom's initiative was not mentioned at the meeting and it will be irrelevant to discussions unless and until it looks like coming to fruition.' Tom felt suitably admonished by his Finance Director and realised that his ill-considered outburst had done him no favours.

'At the meeting with PMJK we explored the type of companies who might be interested in acquiring us. We also looked at the sort of valuation which might be put on our company. They're fully aware of the potential for commercial opportunities for Western companies in the Far East – and before you ask, Tom, they volunteered that, we didn't alert them to it.'

Tom assured Charles that he hadn't been about to question it.

'In summary, they feel that we would be an attractive acquisition. However, on valuation, they were far less positive. I don't need to tell you that we've burnt through considerable start-up capital. We've provided very little return and have yet to move into significant profit. PMJK feel that the pre-dotcom crash days of valuing companies on their potential are largely a thing of the past. The upshot of it all is that they reckon they could find a buyer but that the price wouldn't be very attractive to shareholders. It would be a matter of unloading liability rather than making a decent gain.'

Ranjit sat back in his chair and crossed his arms, sarcastically muttering, 'Great!' Angie shot him a glance.

There was a long silence which Sir Giles eventually broke. 'I wonder if I might make an observation. We've agreed to pursue two separate initiatives of looking for potential buyers and trying to land a major contract which might negate the need to sell. I'm concerned that this board is splitting in to two factions drawn on the lines we voted at the last board meeting. It seems to me that it would be better for the company, and for the shareholders whose interests ultimately I must represent, that we should be pursuing the initiatives in tandem, with complete co-operation between the two factions. If we were to secure a long-term contract, then the company's valuation would be dramatically increased. Surely that's in everybody's interests whether we sell or not. Are we in agreement?'

Sir Giles looked around the board members one by one – Tom, Ben, Charles, Angie and Ranjit. He received acknowledgements from all. 'Tom, I'll trust you to pass that on to Lin. If we go ahead with contracting PMJK to search for a buyer, then effectively we've fired the starting gun to a resolution of some kind. What might that be? We find a buyer at our current valuation, or we secure a major contract and either our shareholders agree to a takeover at an increased valuation or decide that they'd be better off continuing to back us. Or, and this needs to be clearly understood ...'

Once again Sir Giles scanned the faces around the table. 'Ranjit has made it clear that the investors he represents are currently unwilling to stick with us. The banks are also unlikely to play ball in the present climate. So, if neither a buyer nor a major contract is secured then we face a round of cost savings, redundancies and ultimately, possible liquidation.'

Sir Giles paused to let his words sink in. There was a prolonged and awkward silence. 'So Tom, what news of your trip to New York?'

Tom's chin had sunk into his chest as he'd listened to Sir Giles' stark analysis of the company's situation. He made a concerted effort to appear to be upbeat, raised his head and beamed at his fellow directors. 'Good news! I think we've found a partner to help us. We held meetings with the three companies we shortlisted, and Lin and I had no doubt about the one to work with - Bob Schwartz Associates. Our initial concerns were that he might not have the necessary resources and that his role as a journalist might prove to be problematical. Lin and I were reassured on both counts. The reason for me wishing to go ahead and contract him is that he has a razor-sharp mind and, from 20 years of writing a column in the leading US retail trade magazine, contacts within the industry which are second to none.'

Angie questioned him. 'What's he like personally? I'll be working closely with him if we go ahead.'

Tom wondered whether her statement indicated that she had taken Sir Giles' call for co-operation between the two factions seriously. Or, knowing her, maybe just wanting to appear that she had.

'Looks a bit like Norman Mailer.' Angie looked blank. 'The American writer. Bluff, no nonsense sort of chap. I think he'll be fine to work with. I doubt if he suffers fools gladly, but then you're no fool.' Tom smiled sweetly at Angie, and it was her turn to try to fathom hidden meanings.

Sir Giles stepped in. 'Does everyone feel that they have enough information to make the decisions to appoint PMJK to look for a buyer and Bob Schwartz to act as our retail industry consultant in the States?' All nodded. 'Does anyone wish to speak against the proposals?'

Ranjit looked around the table as his fellow directors shook their heads. 'Sir Giles. You said that by appointing PMJK we'd be firing a starting gun. I'm interested to know how long the race to a resolution is going to be.'

Sir Giles frowned at Ranjit and with more than a hint of sarcasm said 'I'm afraid I've forgotten to bring my crystal ball with me. What's your point?'

Ranjit shifted uneasily in his seat. All he saw were pairs of eyes boring into him. He shrugged. 'Sorry – no point really. Silly question. I'm in agreement with you all.'

'In which case,' said Sir Giles, 'then let's go ahead and retain both parties.'

Tom returned to his office when the board meeting broke up and went to phone Bob with the good news. But with his hand on the receiver, he stopped and thought of Angie's statement about having to work closely with the American. Not fully involving her in the new initiative would be perverse. She seemed to be expressing her willingness to bury the hatchet after having been knocked back on her wish to contact US retailers direct. If she had been in league with Ranjit in engineering a possible takeover, then presumably she had fulfilled any arrangement she'd had with him. Did it matter anymore if she'd gone behind his back? Probably not. Could he trust her now to do her best to win the new business? Probably, and anyway he needed her input. She was the Business Development Director after all, and as Managing Director he did have the little matter of overseeing the day to day running of the company and managing existing business to consider. He picked up the receiver and made an internal rather than an international call.

'Angie, I'd like to join me to make the call to Bob Schwartz so that you can speak to him and discuss the way forward. Can you come to my office?'

As Tom waited for her to arrive, he reflected that this would be the first time since he'd given her the informal warning that he would be alone with her. He'd taken care to ensure that all communication since then had been conducted in the presence of others.

She knocked on his open door. Tom had been pretending to study a spreadsheet on his screen from the moment he saw her approaching. He looked up and took in her svelte figure in an immaculate business suit, hair, nails and make up just so. Same old Angie. Or was it? There was an unusual expression on her face. Normally supremely self-assured, even haughty, her demeanour was one which Tom could only describe as tentative.

'Can I come in?' That was a first. She had customarily swanned into his office as if she owned it. Tom beckoned her in, turning back to his screen and closing down the spreadsheet he'd been using as a prop. She closed the door behind her and sat down on the sofa, crossing her long legs sheathed in the sheerest nylon. Tom made a conscious effort to shift a surge of nostalgic desire to the back of his mind. Angie had her own props – a black A4 notebook which she opened and in which she wrote something then held her pen poised, looking expectantly at Tom.

Tom sternly held her gaze. She was the first to blink and dropped her eyes. Against his better judgement, Tom melted. 'How are you, Ange?' he said softly.

Going someway to recovering her composure she answered 'Fine' and smiled weakly.

The awkwardness of the situation hung in the air. Tom looked quizzically at her. 'Really?' She looked anywhere but into his eyes. 'Anything you want to tell me?'

The moment of vulnerability passed, and Angie snapped into her business-like self. 'What on earth do you mean?'

Tom recognised that he'd lost the opportunity to connect with her and was actually rather relieved that he wouldn't have to confront the issue of her involvement with Ranjit. 'Nothing. I'll make the call. Assuming that Bob's happy to come on board, you can have a chat with him. I'd like you to fly out for a meeting with him, but only when he feels he's had time to generate some good leads. We need to find out when that might be.' Angie bowed her head in acquiescence.

Tom checked his watch, calculating the time in New York and picked up the phone.

The call was answered by Bob himself. 'Hi there, Tom! Good to hear from you.'

'Morning, Bob. Can I put you on speaker phone? I'm here with my Director of Business Development, Angie Carter.' Bob agreed and Tom hit the relevant button on the receiver. 'Bob, we've just finished a board meeting in which we discussed the potential partners we approached over there. The good news is that we'd like to go with you.'

Bob's crackly voice emerged from the speaker. 'Hey! Good news indeed! It'll be a pleasure to join the team.'

'Great to hear it. Welcome aboard! You'll get a call from Charles Wright, our Finance Director, to sort out the contract details, but I'm keen to get things moving straight away. Can I pass you to Angie?'

Tom watched Angie closely as she greeted Bob and proceeded instantly to charm him. She told him how she'd heard how impressed Tom and Lin had been with him and then chatted about an article of his she'd read on the Internet. Clever girl thought Tom. He'd never doubted her abilities, only questioned her motives. Still the nagging feeling remained that every one of her actions was calculated, never spontaneous. In no time at all, she and Bob had established a rapport and she turned to business.

'So Bob, I'd like to come over to meet you in New York soon to discuss our strategy, but I think it would make sense for you to sound out your contacts and generate some good leads before that – how long do you think that might take?'

'I'd say about a fortnight to be safe.' They both consulted diaries and agreed on dates.

Tom broke in. 'Bob, you'll remember that Lin and I impressed on you the need to tread carefully. Sooner or later what we're trying to do will become public knowledge and then our competitors are sure to try to muscle in. The longer we can keep it quiet the better. I appreciate that it will restrict how you go about creating leads, but it's imperative.'

'No problem, Tom. As a journalist you should know all about milking contacts for information without revealing your agenda. Trust me. They'll just think I'm digging around for a story.'

They finished the call and Tom smiled as warmly as he could manage at Angie. 'Thanks. It's good to be back on the same team and chasing the same goal. You haven't lost your touch.'

Angie looked to be searching for barbs behind the comments, but apparently finding none and rejecting any impulse to rake over the coals, she smiled genially in return. 'No hard feelings?'

Tom considered his reply very carefully. 'Not anymore.' There was a long pause while both waited for the other to speak. Tom broke the hiatus. 'Thanks, Ange – keep me in the picture on anything you get from Bob.'

She nodded and left the office. Tom watched her leave, fighting back the frisson brought on by her delectable rear end, and resolutely concentrated on how he felt about their apparent professional reconciliation. He decided to accept the truce at face value and maximise the input she could bring to what had become their common interest.

Emma, his PA, popped her head round the door. 'I took a call while you were in the meeting, Tom. Sally Hardcastle. She wouldn't tell me what it was about, but she said she was a friend of yours. I said I'd let you know she'd called.'

'OK, thanks Emma.' Instead of returning to her desk, Emma remained by the door. Tom realised that she was hoping for more information about Sally. Since he'd taken her into his confidence during the acrimonious split from Angie and asked her to spread the word of their break-up, she'd become very protective of him, if not proprietorial.

'She's an old friend who lived on the next-door farm to me up in Yorkshire. I'm helping out with a charity dinner she's organising up there at the weekend.'

Emma seemed to approve. 'She left her number – do you want me to call her for you?'

Tom guessed what Sally's reaction would be to being called by his PA, but decided to give Emma the pleasure she'd presumably get from making the call.

Moments later Tom's phone rang. 'I have Miss Hardcastle for you.' 'Thanks Emma.' She put him through.

'Get you! Tom Keardon's personal assistant calling! I do hope I'm not causing the wheels of commerce to grind to a halt by intruding on your valuable time!'

Tom couldn't help breaking into a smile, not only because of the predictable sarcasm, but also because it was good to hear her voice again. He'd sent the cheque for sponsoring a table and told his mother that he would be up for the weekend some time ago but hadn't had time to think any more about it or speak to Sally.

'Lovely to hear from you, Sally. I can probably afford to give you a couple of minutes of my time without the stock market crashing.'

'Are you still OK for the dinner Tom? My table – I mean your table all's arranged with lots of people looking forward to meeting you. You are going to make it, aren't you?'

'Wouldn't miss it for the world.'

'Don't take the piss!'

'I'm not – I'm looking forward to seeing you.'

'Really?' Sally's voice had lost its impishness, replaced by softness. Tom felt the need to reel back. He spoke more impersonally.

'I'm driving up on Saturday and taking Monday off to drive back. I'm sure you'll be up to your ears at the dinner and we won't have much of a chance to talk, so perhaps we can meet up on Sunday to catch up.'

'Funny you should say that, because my parents suggested that you and your Mum and Sid join us for Sunday lunch. Well, to be honest, I suggested it to them.'

'Mum and Sid?'

'Yes, didn't you know? Sid's moved into the spare room on your farm. It saves him the rent on his place and all the travelling back and forth. Don't worry, I don't think anything's going on – she likes his company and he's out of harm's way without the temptation of the demon drink.'

'I didn't know. Serves me right for not speaking to my Mum for so long. Sunday lunch would be very nice.'

'OK, slicker. I'm sure that even now captains of industry are clawing at your office door to hear your pearls of wisdom, so I'll let you go. By the way, don't dress up too much for the dinner. Tweed jackets and slightly soiled cavalry twill trousers will be the order of the day. See you!'

She disconnected before he could reply. He was left looking at his phone and marvelling at her force of nature.

Tom replaced the receiver and, making a supreme effort to concentrate on the business in hand, he once again checked his watch, calculating the time in Hong Kong. Eight hours difference meant that it would be late at night, with the office long closed. He dialled Lin's home number. She answered with a cheery hello. He could hear music and laughter in the background.

'Lin, sorry to call you so late. Is it convenient to talk?'

'Hi Tom. Yes I can talk.'

'It sounds as if you've got company.'

'Yes, Chong's here with a couple of friends.'

'Chong?'

'My fiancé. Remember?'

'Of course, I remember. I'd just forgotten his name.' Another burst of laughter was audible in the background. 'Look, do you want me to call tomorrow?'

'No – I want to catch up on the board meeting. Just hang on – I'll put this phone down and take it in the bedroom.'

Tom waited until Lin spoke again, this time without noises off, and he filled her in on the decisions which had been taken - Sir Giles' call for common purpose between the warring factions, and Angie's apparent enthusiasm to progress the initiative with Bob Schwartz. She asked for clarification on a couple of points but seemed generally pleased with the outcome. Tom made to say goodnight, but she interrupted him.

'Actually Tom, I was going to phone you tomorrow morning anyway. Not only about business, but about the wedding. Chong and I arranged a date a while ago – it's July 14th – but I didn't want to tell you until I'd resolved the issue of whether you could be invited.'

'Issue? What do you mean?'

'Well, it's – it's just that you still mean a lot to me. And I felt that by coming to the wedding you'd somehow be giving your blessing. I know it sounds silly.'

Tom was taken aback. He chose his words carefully. 'And you still mean a lot to me,' he said softly. 'But I've already given my blessing. I'm very happy for you, and I don't want to be a source of contention between you and Chong.'

'You won't be. Both our families thought it was pretty weird that I wanted to invite my ex-husband – and I suppose it is in a way – but anyway, I've convinced them. I persuaded them that you'll be coming as my well-connected business partner rather than an ex-husband. Hongs are always looking for a business opportunity.'

'Are you sure? I'd be honoured to come if you're really sure.'

'I'm sure. And the business opportunity is genuine. I've already spoken to Chong's family about our initiative and they're keen to meet you. Perhaps you could come over a week or so before the wedding and see if we can really get things moving at this end. By then we should have some leads in the States if all goes well.'

'OK, you're on – I'm due to come out to the Hong Kong office around then anyway, so it will all fit together nicely.'

'Great.'

'Oh, and do something for me, please. Pass on my congratulations to Chong. Tell him he's a very lucky man.'

Very lucky, thought Tom, after he'd said his goodbyes. But then, so had he been. No – stop it! No regrets, remember? That was then, this is now. With a shrug, Tom reached for his in tray.

It had diminished by far less than he'd hoped by the time that Ben poked his head round the door at the end of the afternoon.

'Fancy a pint, boss? I feel the need to chew the cud over events, dear boy, events.'

They once again walked some distance to a pub where they would be unlikely to bump into any members of staff. They jostled through the throng of city workers to order pints and eventually found a small table to sit at. Ben came straight to the point.

'As I understand it, we're all one big happy family again, joined together in adversity, fighting for the common good.'

'So it would appear,' Tom acknowledged phlegmatically.

Ben spoke with exasperation in his voice. 'Come on. What happened to the Great War of Independence? One skirmish, then capitulation. We've put up the for-sale sign.'

Tom looked pained and took a hefty swig of his beer. 'You can't fight a war without weapons. You've seen the figures. The company's not making enough profit. I've got to live in the real world. If anything, I should thank Angie for bringing me to my senses.'

Ben leant back and folded his arms, then took on a resigned expression. 'Yeah, I take your point. I don't suppose you've got any choice. But it's still hard to swallow. Particularly about

Angie. You've welcomed the traitor back into the fold, have you?'

To Ben's surprise, Tom smiled widely and chuckled. 'Back into the fold,' he repeated. 'Where you keep the sheep safe. It's what my Dad used to say to me when he was trying to persuade me to stay on the farm rather than go off to university. We need you in the fold to survive he said. Probably thought of me as a traitor. We need Angie back in the fold and I'm willing to welcome her just as my Dad would have welcomed me if I'd ever gone back like some sort of prodigal son.'

Ben leant forward and sympathetically touched Tom's forearm. 'Sorry, mate. It's easy for me to sit back and criticise. I should be more thoughtful. You've been through a lot, haven't you? Losing your Dad on top of all the shenanigans at work. How are things working out at the farm?'

'Not too bad. I've got a farm hand in to help my Mum so it's ticking over OK. But I've still got to sort out the will and the bank situation. Which reminds me – I need to fix up meetings for Monday. I'm going up on Saturday for a long weekend. I got conned into buying a table at a farmers' dinner on Saturday night.'

'Doesn't sound like you, parting with your hard-earned cash. Trying to ingratiate yourself with the locals?'

'Funny you should say that – that's exactly what the lady who persuaded me to do it said I should do.'

Ben raised his eyebrows. 'A lady? Anyone I should know about?'

'Not really,' said Tom, smiling at the memory of Sally.

'Aha – I detect a smile?' Ben crossed his arms again. 'Confess all.'

'Nothing much to tell. She's an old friend who lives on the next-door farm. I've known her since we were kids. She helped with sorting out my Mum's farm. She runs a little PR agency in the Dales and asked me to support the event she's organising.'

'So why the smile?'

Tom hesitated, then decided to confide in his trustworthy friend. 'Because I enjoy her company and the thought of seeing her again makes me smile. She's a breath of fresh air with no side to her.'

'Not smitten are we?' asked Ben with a certain degree of relish.

This time Tom's smile was embarrassed. 'I hadn't really thought about it,' he lied.

14

To be fair, while thoughts of a relationship with Sally had crossed his mind on several occasions, he'd always been quick to dismiss them as an unnecessary complication to his already complicated life. To say that he'd never really thought about whether he was smitten with her was pedantically correct. However, on his journey northwards on Saturday morning he considered for the first time the implications of taking their friendship a step further. By the time he drove into the Dales the myriad reasons not to get involved had been overwhelmed by the acknowledgement that he was indeed – to use Ben's wonderfully old-fashioned word – smitten.

At the beginning of June, the Dales were looking their best. Pastures were blanketed in yellow seas of swaying buttercups. Even the ubiquitous grey stone walls had taken on splashes of colour from the lichen and moss which were making the most of the season. The leaves on the trees were a bright but delicate shade of green, glowing in the warm sun which fitfully appeared between threatening clouds. They contrasted with the lush green of the river meadows and the flat washed-out green of the rock-strewn hills above. The colours constantly changed as cloud shadows journeyed across the landscape. If Eskimos have a hundred words for snow, mused Tom, shouldn't dales folk have more for green?

It was mid-afternoon when he drove into the farmyard. Jean
must have heard his approach because she was standing at the
farmhouse door to welcome him. Tom was delighted to see that
his mother looked to be in good health and the best of spirits.
He greeted her with a heartfelt hug. In the kitchen, Sid was
boiling a kettle, looking for all the world like the man of the
house. 'Now then, lad. Yous'll be wanting a brew after all
driving. We got some coffee in – your mum tells me you don't
like tea.'

'That's right, Sid. Strange, I'm sure you think, but true. How
are you?'

'In the pink, lad. You saved my life by giving me this job.
Kettle's boiled. I'll make the tea for me and Mrs K, but you
better make coffee. Not sure I know recipe!' he grinned.

The three of them took their drinks to the old kitchen table and
Tom was given a progress report on the farm. Things were
going as well as could be expected. The lambs were growing
well and there'd been no further outbreaks of foot and mouth
in the vicinity for a while. Everything now depended on live-
stock movement restrictions being lifted in time to sell the
lambs. If they were, then prices could be good when so many
flocks had been slaughtered.

Sid finished his tea and excused himself to go back to work.
Tom watched his mother smile as he left. 'You look to be happy,
Mum.'

The smile continued. 'I suppose I am. I don't want to speak ill
of your father but for years before he died, it was such a struggle. No fun. I'm not saying that we're struggling any less now,
but – I don't know …' Her sentence petered out, as if she was
not willing to voice what she was implying. Tom did it for her.

'It's fun having Sid here?'

'Yes. It is,' she admitted. 'We're just two lonely souls who
enjoy each other's company. I was worried that people would
think I was some kind of scarlet woman inviting him to live in
with your father so recently gone, but then I thought to hell
with them. It makes all the sense in the world. Running a farm's
not a nine to five job and having Sid here all the time means that

we can get so much more done. It saves him rent and petrol and he's contributing to buying food. I did phone you to ask what you thought about it but your office told me you were in America. I didn't like to bother you. You don't disapprove, do you?'

'Not at all. It's great to have you happy again and to see Sid turn over a new leaf. I assume there's been no falling off the wagon?'

'Not a drop. Apart from going to Hawes for the weekly shop we never leave the farm. So no opportunity. But more importantly, no inclination as far as I can see. He's always singing your praises for giving him a last chance.' There was a short silence, during which Jean's face took on a serious expression. 'So far, so good. And thank-you Tom for sorting things out. But we're not out of the woods yet, are we? What's happening with the bank?'

'Nothing at the moment, but when it does, you don't need to worry about it. I've arranged to see the bank and the solicitor on Monday before I go back. And remember, if it comes to it, I'm willing and able to pay off the loan.'

Jean took his hands between hers. She said nothing, but her warm smile spoke volumes. She released his hands and looked at him impishly. 'So, a busy weekend for you. Dinner with Sally tonight and then we're all invited to lunch with her and her parents tomorrow.' She cocked her head to one side and raised her eyebrows. To his surprise, Tom felt his cheeks flushing.

'Yes. I'm looking forward to seeing her. I enjoy her company.' It was his turn to raise his eyebrows, challenging his mother to respond.

'She's a lovely girl, Tom. A lovely girl.' She nodded her approval and gathered up the cups, moving to the sink. 'Oh, I hope you don't mind,' she said as she began to rinse the cups. 'It seemed unfair to put Sid in the little bedroom when you're so seldom here, so he's moved into your old room. I've moved your things. Is that alright?'

He rose and hugged her from behind. 'No problem, Mum. I'll take my bag up.'

Tom had considered carefully what to wear for the Swaledale Sheepbreeders' Dinner, conscious of Sally's advice not to dress up too much. But on balance, he'd decided that it would be absurd to wear country clothes which he anyway didn't possess. He didn't want to pretend to be what he was not, so he donned a sober suit and a tie, a formal one rather than one of his more fashionable designer items.

Tom said his goodbyes to Jean and Sid who were happily ensconced in the living room watching early Saturday evening TV and went out to his car, noting with dismay that the weather had broken, and the temperature had dropped dramatically. By the time he crested the Buttertubs pass he could barely see through the fine mist which hovered beneath an angry sky. He was reduced to driving at little more than a jogging pace, navigating by the snow posts which lined the narrow road. Descending into Hawes the mist thinned, only to be replaced by a fine drizzle which hung motionless in the air.

Taking the road out into Wensleydale he spotted the signs to the auction mart on the outskirts of the town where the event was being held. He parked on a vast expanse of uneven concrete and shivered his way to the marquee which had been set up in a corner of the car park. Lights illuminating the way were haloed by the suspended drizzle. The entrance to the marquee was a wide opening which allowed the rain to blow inside and the concrete floor, Tom could see, was wet through. Not that it seemed to have bothered the gathered throng who were packed around a makeshift bar, engaged in animated conversation. Tom navigated his way through the tightly knit crowd in search of Sally, emerging into rows of trestle tables covered with white paper tablecloths and decked with vases of wildflowers. He spotted her beside a low stage where a DJ was playing music quietly. She was deep in conversation with a small dapperly dressed man. Tom recognised him as the MP for the area who also held a senior shadow ministerial position. Tom stood at a distance, not wishing to intrude. So much for not dressing up! Sally was wearing a figure-hugging blue satin strapless dress which ended just below the knees and matching high heels. She looked sensational.

Tom was still thinking impure thoughts when she turned and spotted him. 'Tom! Great to see you!' She beckoned him to join them. 'Tom – meet Richard Buckley. Richard, this is Tom Keardon, a good friend of mine from London who works in the City.' They shook hands, and at the same time a woman dressed as a caterer approached Sally, asking for a word. Sally excused herself, leaving the two men alone.

'The City, eh? What do you do there and what brings you up here?' asked the MP with an easy charm for which he was noted.

Tom was careful to be brief, not wishing to take up too much time. He was well aware that the politician would be keen to speak to as many people as possible for as little time as was necessary to appear interested and concerned. 'I run a dotcom company specialising in commercial information about the Far East. I'm Dales born and bred on a sheep farm. I started coming back here when my father died recently, and I had to take on responsibility for the farm. Sally persuaded me to come tonight to meet some people.'

'Ah, Sally! Quite a livewire, isn't she? She has considerable powers of persuasion – hence my presence tonight.' The journalist in Tom sparked. No follow-up on either the company or the farm which could lead to a long conversation, but a pleasant remark about Sally after which he could reasonably move on to speak to someone else – particularly a voting constituent, which Tom was obviously not. To his surprise, the MP asked a penetrating question which left Tom feeling guilty about his cynicism. 'You're a rare creature then, with knowledge of both international commerce and sheep farming. Do either give you insights into the other?'

'I've never really considered it. But now you ask, I suppose I'd say that while both share the same business imperatives of controlling costs and maximising profits, otherwise they're chalk and cheese. Commerce, particularly internationally, is all about adapting and changing and exploiting the latest market opportunities. Sheep farmers have one basic product, hardly any opportunity to change, and precious little ability to control costs or influence sale prices. As a Conservative you may not agree, but I'd like to see subsidy and price regulation tipping the scales in favour of the little men and women up here who struggle to make a living on their farms. Maybe they do something that's far more worthwhile than any of the money-grabbing businesses we run in the City.'

The MP looked at Tom with respect. 'I've got a lot of sympathy with what you say. Politics is all about searching for a balance between vested interests and I would agree that at the moment the scales are tipped against the farmers round here. All I can say is that I'll aim to represent the interests of my constituents to the best of my ability. It was a pleasure to meet you Tom, and now if you'll excuse me.'

Richard Buckley MP set off purposefully to enter the fray around the bar and was immediately in conversation. Tom felt a grudging approval for the man's smooth operation. Tom followed in the direction of the bar, conscious that he needed to pace himself because of the drive home but feeling in need of a beer right now. He fought his way through the crowd and patiently waited some time until a gap appeared and he was able to order a pint. Squeezing back out into space, he once again scanned the marquee for Sally. She was at the buffet still talking to the caterers. He rejected the idea of hovering close to her again as undignified, so occupied himself with sipping his pint and taking in the scene. Sally had been right. There was a preponderance of tweed jackets worn by the farmers but the dress code for the many women and youngsters present was more varied, ranging from jeans and T shirts to party dresses. Many of the young girls looked to be dressed for the disco in short skirts and low tops, oblivious to the shivering temperature. He'd envisaged a business dinner, but this was obviously primarily a community event which looked like developing into a well-oiled knees-up once the dinner and speeches had been finished. He felt a tap on his shoulder and turned to see Sally's smiling face.

'Hiya, slicker.' She leant up and pecked him on the cheek. 'Thanks for coming. I hope it's not too grim for you.'

'Well, it's not exactly the Ritz, is it, but it's worth coming just to see you.'

'Flatterer! I don't believe a word of it. Anyhow, you're here to meet people, not stand around like a wallflower. Come and say hello to someone who's on our table.' She searched round and spotted a group nearby. 'There they are – some of my clients.'

Sally broke into their conversation and had just finished the introductions when the DJ's voice boomed over the PA system, calling for order and introducing the Chairman of the Swaledale Sheepbreeders' Association. He gave a short speech, full of thank-yous and comments about individuals, presumably in-jokes judging by the gales of laughter they produced. To Tom's surprise, the spectre of foot and mouth was not mentioned at all. Perhaps tonight was meant to be a rare occasion to forget the problems which were besetting the Dales. Instead the chairman launched into an unnecessarily complicated explanation of how everyone should go up to the buffet in table number order.

Tom was pleased to find that his party was on table two next to the top table, not so much because he was eager to get to the array of homemade pies and rolls, chili, curry and rice which made up the buffet, but because it meant they would be sitting well away from the entrance which was still allowing cold wind and drizzle to permeate the marquee.

Tom took his place beside Sally at the table along with four of her clients and their partners who, out of deference to the outsider, began by asking all about Tom's company. But he was quick to turn the conversation to their common interests, the tourist trade in the Dales and the effect that foot and mouth was having on it. All had sorry tales of cancelled bookings at their holiday accommodation and activity centres. When the table fell quiet with all the clients looking glum, Sally spoke. She'd obviously been choosing her moment.

'I may have some positive news for you.' She was instantly the centre of attention. 'As you know, I've been working with the Dales Tourism Association to get some positive media to encourage tourists to come here and also lobbying to get some form of assistance from the government and various quangos. Amongst other things, I sent a paper to Richard Buckley's office laying out a range of initiatives we thought might be investigated. When he arrived here I cornered him and had a long chat. I didn't expect that he would have read the paper with everything focused on the general election but he was aware of it and seemed to be fairly well-briefed on it. Anyway ...' She paused for effect. 'He's agreed to throw his support behind it.'

There was a chorus of approval around the table. Sally beamed briefly then held up her hand to quell the congratulations. 'Let's not get carried away. We don't even know if he'll be an MP a week from today.' One of the clients ventured that they could pin a blue rosette on a sheep round here and it would get elected. Sally responded. 'I agree that a 20,000 majority is unlikely to be overturned, but the problem is we don't know who we'll be dealing with in the new government. However, Richard has promised to take our case up with whoever ends up as Minister of Tourism at the earliest opportunity. And ...' she once again paused, shamelessly milking the moment. 'He's invited me down to London to meet one of his researchers to discuss a strategy. So I think we can say that our voice will be heard down in Westminster before long.'

The clients and their wives and husbands began talking amongst themselves with a new-found optimism leaving Tom able to talk to Sally for the first time since they'd sat down.

'Wow! I'd thought that Richard Buckley was the only smooth operator round here. I take my hat off to you!'

She turned to meet his gaze with supreme confidence in her eyes. 'Not just a pretty face, slicker.'

Tom was overcome with a desire to kiss her there and then, but, in view of their public situation, thought better of it. Instead he held her softening gaze, until she demurely dropped her eyes, simultaneously clasping his hand out of sight under the table. Tom squeezed it affectionately and continued to hold it.

'Just a thought,' he said on impulse. 'If you'll be coming down to London soon, could I invite you to stay with me?'

Sally took time to take in the implication then broke into a wide smile. 'You can. And I'd love to stay with you.' She squeezed his hand in return, let it go, and turned to engage the client on her left in conversation.

There. It's done, Tom thought. He'd crossed the threshold of a relationship with Sally. And he felt exhilarated.

The DJ's voice boomed. 'Ladies and Gentlemen,' he intoned, reading the words laboriously from a sheet of paper. 'Will you please welcome your Member of Parliament, the Right Honourable Richard Buckley.'

The raucous buzz of conversation and laughter took some time to subside. The MP looked uncertainly around the marquee, aware that for most of his audience his speech would be an unwelcome intrusion into the serious business of drinking and socialising. Accordingly, he began by reassuring his listeners that he would be brief and that they would soon be able to return to their revels, richly deserved, in view of the miserable chain of events which had beset the Dales this year. I've just three simple messages for you, he said.

Tom smiled, recalling a story told to him by a fellow journalist who'd once interviewed Harold Macmillan, the British Prime Minister who'd tried to persuade a population still emerging from the long shadow of war that they'd never had it so good. Macmillan had been reminiscing about his maiden speech in the Commons way back in 1924, which had ranged far and wide across the various issues of the day. Coming out into the lobby he'd hung around hoping that someone might come up and compliment him. Lloyd George, only recently replaced as Prime Minister, approached him and said that he hadn't actually heard the speech but that MPs in the bar were saying that he'd spoken well. Macmillan had said that he'd swelled with pride. 'Only one problem,' Lloyd George had cautioned. 'When

I asked them what you talked about, no one seemed to be able to tell me. A word of advice, lad, when you get up on your hind legs in the chamber as a backbencher, make just one point. Allow yourself two if you become a minister, and in the exceedingly unlikely event of you becoming prime minister of this land of ours, you can indulge yourself in three.'

The principle was obviously still being taught in modern day media training. Buckley launched into his three key messages. One, the Dales farming community had a proud and noble history of surviving adversity and would surely survive the present troubles. Two the Labour party had thoroughly mismanaged the response to the foot and mouth outbreak. And three, if he was afforded the honour of returning to parliament, he would fight for the interests of the farming and tourist industries the Dales.

The applause that followed his speech was warm if not enthusiastic and the chattering and laughter rapidly returned to its previous level. Sally had leapt up to the side of the stage at the start of the clapping and ushered the MP back to the top table where he shook hands with the Chairman and received his thanks. She then deftly threaded him through to the marquee entrance, courteously deflecting the couple of guests who were hoping to pick him up on what he had said. She was rewarded with an effusive appreciation of her help and a reassurance of his support before he was whisked away in a chauffeur-driven car. Returning to the table, Sally sank down beside Tom and immediately kicked off her shoes.

'Thank God for that. Give me wellies any time. I'm not cut out for high heels.' Sally leant towards him and whispered in his ear. 'I'm off duty now, and they've started to clear the tables away to make room for a dance floor for the disco. If I say my goodbyes, will you take me to a pub where we can thaw out?'

Tom was only too pleased to agree. She put her shoes back on and sprung up to take her leave of those at the top table. Helpers who had been clearing the tables from the far end reached them and Tom had to stand up along with Sally's clients and retreat to the side of the marquee. They had dispersed by the time she returned, so the two of them were able to escape.

At the entrance they paused, looking with dismay at the persistent drizzle which was now being driven by a bitter wind. Sally snuggled into his arm against the cold. It's going to be really nasty over Buttertubs,' said Tom. 'I could hardly see my way when I drove here and it's silly to take two cars. Why don't you leave yours here – we can pick it up later in the weekend. Why don't we drive straight to the pub in our village then I'll drop you off at your cottage. I don't fancy driving over the pass after another drink.'

'OK,' she agreed nonchalantly and reached up to kiss him primly on the lips.

'Then wait here while I get my car,' said Tom walking gingerly into the swirling drizzle.

The journey over the narrow twisting pass was indeed perilous with visibility down to a matter of metres. Nothing was said. Sally leant her head on Tom's shoulder and allowed him to concentrate on the road. The Audi's heater soon raised the temperature and a CD played quietly as they drove. It wasn't until they descended the steep hill into Swaledale that the mizzle lifted and Tom was able to relax.

'So … a drink in the Bull?' he asked.

'I think we deserve one.'

The bar was fairly full with both locals and weekenders. In deference to the unseasonably cold evening a log fire had been lit and was generating welcome warmth. Tom ordered drinks and joined Sally at a table as close to the fire as they had been able to find.

'Successful evening?' Tom asked.

'I think so. The clients seemed to be happy and I certainly came up trumps with our esteemed MP. I just hope he can get things moving. It's one thing to pledge to fight for our interests when he's after votes but it may not be at the top of his priority list in a new parliament. And given that he'll probably still be in opposition, it's questionable how much he'd be able to do even if he tries.'

'At least you'll be able to hold him to his pledge,' said Tom.

'How's that?' Sally questioned.

'Well his pledge is in the public domain. You and I and a hundred others heard him make it. You need to make a matter of public record. A news release will do the trick. It'll have to be after purdah, of course.'

'After what?'

'The period in a run up to an election when there are restrictions laid down by the Representation of the People Act on what the media can report. Mostly to do with balance. They couldn't run the story before the election without finding stories of equal weight from all the other candidates. The RPA is well-meaning, but it often has the effect of stifling democratic discussion particularly in constituencies where the sitting MP has a big majority. I mean, why should Buckley risk a gaffe and give oxygen to his opponents by agreeing, for example, to a debate on the local radio station? If he or any other of the candidates refuses, then it can't happen.'

Sally looked at him curiously. 'You've got some very weird chat up lines,' she ribbed.

Tom was flustered. 'Sorry. I was just trying to help. And I don't mean to sound pompous.'

'You are.'

'What, helping or being pompous?'

'Both actually,' she grinned. 'So what about the news release?'

'Well, 'Local MP returned on pledge to support Dales tourism and farming' is the headline you're after. So a release saying how happy the Swaledale Sheepbreeders and the Dales Tourism Association are that Richard Buckley has promised to fight their cause in parliament should do the trick. That way, any time he slacks, you just need to speak to the media and remind them of his pledge and he'll be shamed into acting. And of course, saying in the release that you're off to Westminster to help develop the strategy won't do your reputation any harm.'

Sally bowed her head to Tom in deference. 'Good thinking. I thought I was supposed to be the PR guru round here but now you're talking like one. Don't journalists despise PR people, at least until they've failed in journalism and moved into PR.'

'Or until they set up a company like mine. Yes, I used to look down my nose at them when I first started out in journalism with grand ideals. Sooner or later you give in to being handed a story on a plate and you tell yourself that it's OK because you can still put your own spin on it. But then you're on the slippery slope to lazy journalism.'

'Is that why you quit journalism?'

'Because I became lazy? No, not quite. But I did find it more and more difficult to avoid the temptation of taking the easy route. The fearless searcher-out of the truth became more and more the hack who attended press briefings and colluded with other journos in comfortable hotel bars well away from the action to agree on the story. And I became disillusioned over the real difference that I, or most journalists could make. Expose corruption and it would spring up elsewhere. Take a politician to the cleaners and, depending on how good a politician they were, they'd either bounce back or be replaced by another one equally interested in promoting their own vested interests. Maybe it was simply that I got tired of seeing so much human misery. Wars, earthquakes, accidents, murders. I suppose I could have stopped being a roving reporter and become a sub-editor flying a desk, but it would have been a cop-out. That's not to say that what I'm doing now isn't a cop-out, but I'd like to think that it has some merit – employing people and helping in some small way to improve the lot of people in the Far East.'

Sally took some time to decide how to respond. 'I seem to remember that you accused me of making quite a speech a while ago. Well, that was certainly quite a speech.'

'Sorry. I'm sure you could argue that all I'm doing now is helping to fill the pockets of Western shareholders rather than improving the standard of living in the East.'

'I'm sure I could, but I won't. Because in my small way I think I'm helping to improve standards of living as well. It's just that I'm doing it rather closer to home than you.'

Tom reacted to the implied reproach. 'We're not back to me shirking my responsibility to take over the farm, are we?' he retorted, with perhaps more aggression than he'd meant.

Sally defused the situation by taking one of his hands in hers and stroking his cheek with the palm of her other. 'Still a bit prickly over that, are we? It's water under the bridge and you should have absolved yourself of any guilt by the way you've taken things on since your Dad died.'

She leant over and kissed him briefly but tenderly on the lips, then sat back and clapped her hands together.

'Right slicker. You've got two choices. We can get another drink, lighten up and talk about inconsequential things at the end of a long hard day, or you can drive me back now. Which is it to be?'

Tom grinned. 'Mine's a pint.'

Before he could stop her Sally had leapt up to go to the bar, and despite his protestations, insisted on buying the round. The next half an hour did indeed pass in inconsequential chatter before they left the pub and drove the short distance to Sally's cottage on her parents' farm. Pulling up, Tom peered out of the window at the row of farm cottages which had been spruced up for the tourist trade. They smiled at each other, both waiting for the other to speak. Sally broke the silence, speaking in a tender tone of voice.

'Thanks Tom, first for coming up here to the dinner, secondly for driving me home, and thirdly – well, for being such a nice guy.'

For the first time it was Tom who initiated physical contact. He pulled her towards him across the car and held her tight while their lips met in a deep and lingering kiss. Eventually, Sally pulled away and smoothed down her dress. 'I'm not going to invite you in, Tom Keardon, nice as it would be. We've got plenty of time. See you at lunch tomorrow.'

Before he could remonstrate, she kissed him again quickly and climbed out of the car. Tom waited until she had opened her front door, blown a kiss, and quickly closed it behind her. He set off for his own farm with a grin etched on his face.

15

Fickle as ever, the weather gods had contrived to paint the sky clear blue in the morning. Devoid of any hint of cloud or wind, it promised to be a perfect early summer's day in the Dales. Tom woke early and was down to take breakfast with his mother before she went off to church. Sid was already working in the fields, so he found himself alone. With several hours to kill before they were due for Sunday lunch, Tom opted to go down to the village to buy a Sunday paper. He went to the hall table to pick up his car keys but on opening the front door and taking in the warmth, the stillness and the brightness, he returned the keys to the table and set off briskly to walk to the village.

On a day like this, he thought to himself as he climbed the track to the farm gate, a man should be able to forget all his problems and simply enjoy being alive. Sadly, I'm not that man he acknowledged ruefully. As if to confirm his gloomy self-assessment, the disinfectant foot baths and carpets at the gate hoved into view. He carefully doused the soles of his shoes and pressed on, taking mental stock of his situation. On the negative side was the threat to his company. But how negative was it in reality? If the initiative in the States came good, then all would be well. If not, the company would be sold and while there would be a lot of pride to be swallowed, he'd either be kept on by the new owners or would receive a tidy sum for his shares plus a pay-off. On the positive side – and he suddenly realised that everything positive in his life was currently here in the

Dales – his mother was happy, the farm was surviving for the moment, and then there was Sally. Tom crested a bend in the track and saw the village below bathed in shimmering sunshine, the grey stone buildings nestling beside the sparkling river. He broke into a wide smile at the thought of seeing her again in a couple of hours. She'd said that she'd had a teenage crush on him. Now here he was, a thirty something, feeling like a teenager looking forward to a first date. He tried to think rationally about whether it was wise to enter into a relationship but had to admit to himself that he didn't care. And anyway, the die was cast.

Tom's route to the village shop took him past the tiny church, looking in the strong sunshine so very different from the dismal day that his father had been laid to rest. The melody of a hymn was faintly audible, and Tom was overcome with a need to visit his father's grave. Immediately he felt guilty that the thought had been spontaneous – a dutiful son would have planned to do so. He walked up the flagstone path looking for a new gravestone amongst the many weathered stones engraved with names of generations of farmers and their families who had lived and died in the Dales. A fresh posy of wildflowers had been laid on the grave, no doubt placed there by his mother that very morning. Tom knelt down and battled a maelstrom of emotions, trying to find a way to express his feelings coherently. Tears welled in his eyes, and eventually he formed the words he wanted to say. *'I'm looking after her, Dad.'*

The sound of conversation broke the moment and Tom rose to see the congregation emerging from the church door. He wiped his eyes self-consciously and formed a fixed smile to nod to the churchgoers as they passed. His mother was one of the last to appear and she paused to chat to the vicar whom he recognised from the funeral. He approached and caught his mother's eye.

'Tom! What are you doing here?'

Jean took her leave of the vicar and slipped her arm in Tom's to walk down the path.

'I walked down to get a paper and thought I should pay my respects to Dad,' he said ingenuously.

'Oh, that's nice, Tom.' They paused by the grave and she reached down to rearrange the flowers.

'I told him that I'm doing my best to look after you.'

She rose and hugged him. This time the tears were in her eyes. 'You are, Tom. You are.'

They walked together to the Land Rover which Jean had driven down in. 'Where's your paper?' she asked.

'I won't bother. I won't have time to read it before we go to the Hardcastles.'

Back at the farm Sid was in the kitchen dressed in what looked suspiciously like Tom's father's tweed jacket and twill trousers at least a size too big. Once again, the incongruous red and white trainers had made an appearance in honour of the occasion. Within the hour they had all piled into the Land Rover to drive the short distance to the neighbouring farm.

Rosie and Ken Hardcastle were sitting outside their farmhouse at a trestle table beneath a giant umbrella providing shade from the sun. They greeted Tom, Jean and Sid and poured them a cooling glass of lemonade. The conversation immediately turned to the welfare of their respective flocks. Tom tuned out, impatiently fretting about Sally's unexplained absence and frequently turning to view the holiday cottages where he assumed she was. He didn't have long to wait.

Sally came out of her cottage. She was dressed in a rose patterned white summer dress, tight above the waist, floaty below. She had placed a wide-brimmed straw hat on her ash blond hair, tousled as ever, and walked with a skipping step towards the farmhouse, waving eagerly to Tom when she saw his gaze. Whether or not the delayed entrance had been contrived, Tom didn't care. Its effect was not in question. He was beguiled.

Tom stood up as she approached but she chose to first greet Jean and Sid with quick pecks on the cheek. Then she turned to stand directly in front of Tom. She looked warmly into his eyes then took both his hands in hers and went on tiptoe to kiss him gently. Tom was aware of an exchange of embarrassed glances and felt the need to make light of the situation.

'What happened to that little girl I used to play with,' he said.

Wrong move! His remark triggered a flood of reminiscences from his and Sally's mother, out-doing each other with tales of their childhood escapades. Ken and Sid feigned interest for a while then began to discuss the prospects for lamb prices when the restriction on sales would be lifted. Tom and Sally listened to their mothers with dutiful laughs in appropriate places. At the first opportunity Sally offered to bring the food out from the kitchen and asked Tom to help her.

The kitchen table was laden with plates of cold meats, bowls of rice and salad wrapped in clingfilm. As soon as they were out of sight of the others, Sally playfully punched Tom.

'What was that for?'

'For leading me astray when I was seven and getting me to steal apples with you.' They'd just heard the story from their mothers.

'I'm very sorry.'

'Well, I'm going to get my own back now.'

'How?'

'By leading you astray,' she said coquettishly. Tom moved to take her in his arms, but she wriggled away. 'Mr Keardon! Methinks this is neither the time nor the place.' She grabbed plates in both hands and exited the kitchen. Tom did likewise, emerging into the bright sunshine slightly flustered by the exchange.

The lunch was relaxed and convivial. The conversation ranged from mutual friends and shared good times to popular TV shows and sporting achievements. Everyone contributed and no one ventured to broach any subject which might cast a shadow on a perfect summer's afternoon. Eventually, the plates were cleared away and Jean and Sid made to make a move, citing a need to replenish the sheep's water troughs. They said their goodbyes, and Ken and Rosie went into the farmhouse leaving Tom and Sally alone.

'Thanks for inviting us,' said Tom. 'I don't think I've felt so relaxed for ages.'

Sally leant back and stretched out her arms to soak in the sun, still strong in mid-afternoon, then clasped her hands behind her head before speaking impulsively.

'Let's go for a walk down to the meadows! They're at their best at the moment. Fancy it?'

'What about your car? Don't you need a lift so you can pick it up?' Tom asked.

'No need. Dad's off to Hawes in the morning so I can go with him. Come on – let's go.'

Tom remembered the meadows only too well as a playground of their youth. Now designated a Site of Special Scientific Interest for the species-rich array of wildflowers which they supported, they always became a tourist attraction in the short period in which they burst into bloom.

Approaching the meadows on the outskirts of the village they found themselves walking against the flow of many visitors, dressed for the day in shorts and T-shirts and now returning to their cars. As they passed them, they picked up several foreign languages, testament to the fact that the Dales were still attracting tourists from far and wide despite the deterrent effect of foot and mouth. As Tom and Sally walked down the narrow flagstone path crossing the first field the traffic thinned and they soon found themselves alone. To either side a riot of colour sparkled in the sun. The yellow of meadow buttercups and the red and purple of clover dominated in such abundance that they all but obscured the emerald green of the grass below.

They squeezed through a narrow opening in a drystone wall to enter a further field and Tom knelt down to make a closer inspection of the flowers. In no more than a square metre he counted maybe ten different plants.

'Do you what all these are?' he asked Sally.

She knelt down beside him and ran her hand gently across the flowers to reveal some of the smaller varieties hiding beneath the dominant buttercups. 'I don't pretend to know which are which but I remember some of the names. I did a school project on the meadows. They've got lovely names. There's lady's mantle and globeflower and wood crane's bill. I think the white ones are called pignut, and these are melancholy thistle.'

'I'm impressed. Why melancholy?'

'A potion used to be made from them to treat depression.'

'On a day like this, all you'd need to treat depression is come down here and look at them.'

'True, but how many days like this do you get around here. It's not difficult to see how people got depressed in the depths of winter.'

Hand in hand they walked on to the end of the field where a stile led to the bank of a rock-strewn stream flowing down to the river which skirted the village. Tom climbed over first and turned to help Sally. She put her arms around his neck and kept them there when she stepped down. Her smile was as bright as the sunshine and she melted into him. Tom kissed her – a long and deep kiss.

She pulled away and sat down on the riverbank. There was a distracted expression on her face. Tom sat down beside her. 'What's wrong?' he said.

'Nothing's wrong.' She picked up a stone and threw it into the water. 'It's just that ...'

Tom thought better of pressing her and waited until she spoke again. She was still looking into the middle distance.

'I've made it perfectly obvious how much I like you Tom. In fact, I've probably been altogether too obvious. We live in different worlds. I need to know if you think of me as more than someone you can just have a quick fling with. I don't want to get hurt.'

Tom searched for the right words with which to reply. Was this the real thing or had he just been seduced by the breath of fresh air that she'd brought to his troubled life? Before he was able to respond, Sally turned to him with all her customary bravado restored.

'That's not to say that I'm not up for a quick fling if that's all you want, slicker.'

Tom spoke softly. 'I can't promise anything, but all I can say is that right now, you're the best thing in my life. You make me happy. I look forward to being with you. With you, I can escape from all the problems I've got.'

'But that's exactly why I'm worried. Being a means of escape may be fine for a while, but sooner or later you – or we – would have to come to terms with reality and deal with problems, not escape from them.'

Tom shuffled along the bank to sit directly beside her and wrapped his arms around her. She snuggled into him. 'No promises, but I'd like to think that together we could tackle problems so much better.'

She nuzzled his ear. After a long silence she whispered, 'That'll do for the moment, slicker.'

They sat locked together, watching the tumbling progress of the brown-tinged water over the riverbed rocks. In the distance, along the length of the small dale which spurred North from Swaledale, the sun was losing its bite. Shadows were lengthening, defining the landscape, and the vibrancy of colour with which the overhead sunshine had seared the Dales gave way to a softer palette.

Little needed to be said on their slow walk back to Sally's farm. They were both lost in their own thoughts. Approaching the row of holiday cottages, Sally perked up.

'Would you like to see my cottage? I've tidied it especially for you.'

'In that case, how could I refuse?'

She flung open the door. 'Ta da!'

The door led straight on to a small living room, tastefully but sparsely furnished.

'I can't really have many of my own things here because I have to go back to the farmhouse when we let it out. Can I get you a drink? I've got some beers.'

She brought out two cold lagers from the kitchen. Sitting on a small sofa they clinked glasses and settled back to chat.

Much as he would have liked to stay, Tom felt that he should spend the evening with his mother, having seen so little of her on this visit, so they soon walked up to the farmhouse where Tom thanked Sally's parents for lunch. Sally said goodbye to him outside. They held hands facing each other. The evening sun was low in the sky. For the first time that day, a bank of high cloud had appeared above the horizon.

'It's been a perfect day,' said Tom, 'in more ways than one.'

'I'm going to miss you. I'll be straight on the phone to the MP's office after the election to fix up my trip to London.'

'If you can't arrange it soon, why not come down for the weekend anyway?'

'That'd be nice.'

They parted with a slow kiss and Tom set off across the fields to his farm. Turning around when he reached a stile, he saw that she was leaning on a fence, watching him go. They waved a fond farewell.

16

Tom arrived back in London on Monday evening, driving down after his morning meetings with the bank manager and the solicitor. Both conspiratorially assured him that things were proceeding as slowly as they could manage but repeated that it was only a matter of time before probate would have to be declared and the bank would start to press its claim. The one piece of news came from the solicitor who had heard from a contact at the coroner's office that Tom's father's inquest had been pencilled in for August.

Back in his apartment Tom couldn't help looking at it through Sally's eyes. He imagined her irreverent tone. *'Get you! Quite the bachelor pad for today's man about town!'* His thoughts remained with her until he fell asleep.

Tuesday morning saw him at his desk in the office shortly after eight. He was soon immersed in the daily challenge of doing his best to keep the company on an even keel. It was late afternoon when his PA put through a call from Angie who'd flown out to New York the day before.

'Hi, Tom. I'm with Bob right now and he's got some good news. He's managed to have a conversation with the new chief executive of Valco and he's interested in our proposal. He's not willing to see us himself – that's understandable given that he's just taken over the reins – but he's suggested a meeting with the vice-president for business development who's got his old job.'

'That's brilliant! Can I speak to Bob?'

'I'll put him on speaker phone.'

Bob's Bronx voice greeted Tom, echoing slightly through the transatlantic connection and the acoustic of his office.

'Great work, Bob. Just how good a lead do you think it is?'

'We're only at first base, but I'd say that a home run is not out of the question. The Chief Exec told me that expansion into China is on Valco's agenda but very much on the back burner. It's only part of a long-term strategy at the moment because they're not yet convinced that the time is right. I ran a few key points from your proposal past him, hinted that some of his competitors were looking to steal a march by getting in ahead of Valco and suggested that he was in danger of missing the boat. That seemed to do the trick. As Angie said, he's happy for us to meet with his Business Development VP. And given that the guy's new in the job, I'd say he'll be keen to make a mark by taking our proposal on board.'

'When do you think that will happen?'

'We've already put in a call to his office. I said that Angie's only over here for a few days, so we've asked for a slot in his diary later this week.'

'That's great! Angie?' She acknowledged him. 'Is there anything you need from this end before the meeting?'

'I don't think so, Tom. They've already seen the executive summary of our proposal. If the meeting goes well, then we can give it to them in full.'

Tom hesitated before answering, weighing up the pros and cons of playing all their cards so early in the game. He had a nagging concern that maybe Angie's hidden agenda had not changed and that her professed willingness to fully support the new initiative was less than genuine. Surely she should have spotted the danger inherent in giving Valco everything on a plate with no guarantee of partnership.

'I'm not so sure that we should move so fast. What's to stop them taking all of our ideas and then developing them without our involvement?'

Bob answered. 'Good point. I think the thrust of the meeting should be persuading them that Tiger.com is uniquely placed to advise them on entering the Chinese market. Detailed discussion of our proposal should come further down the line.'

'I agree. Angie, what about you?'

There was a pause until she answered with a reluctant 'I suppose so.'

'OK, let's stand by to see if we get the meeting. If so, then we should press for some sort of commitment on their part, and only then make a full presentation of the proposals.'

When the call ended, he pondered Angie's manner during the transatlantic phone call. Was she still a traitor as Ben had described her? Surely she can't have expected him to sanction releasing the full proposal without any commitment. It was probably just an uncharacteristic lack of judgement, but he determined to remain aware of the possibility that she was still following Ranjit's agenda.

On Thursday the country went to the polls in the general election which had been postponed because of the foot and mouth outbreak. All the opinion polls were predicting that Labour would retain a large majority. Tom's day was taken up with a long and detailed meeting with PMJK who presented the results of their initial trawl through companies who might be interested in buying Tiger.com. Tom steeled himself to be as co-operative as possible even though his heart wasn't in it. They eventually agreed on a prioritised hit list. Emerging from the meeting, he found a message from New York confirming the Valco meeting for Friday morning.

Tom watched the election night special on TV that night in his apartment, losing interest at around 2 a.m. when the first burst of declarations slowed, and it was obvious that the government would be returned with pretty much the same majority. Indeed, hardly any seats at all were changing hands. It looked very much like business as usual for the next five years. He was fast asleep when his bedside phone rang. Struggling into conscious-ness and checking the time on his clock radio his first thought was that it would be an international call at that hour, but the voice he heard when he answered was Sally's.

'Hiya, slicker! Are you watching?'

'Watching what? It's nearly five in the morning!'

'The declaration, grumpy. It's just coming up – we'll see if Richard's back in.'

Tom's sleep-befuddled brain finally slipped into gear. 'Sally – it's probably the safest Conservative seat in the country. Couldn't you wait until the morning to find out?'

'It is the morning. It's been light for ages. Don't you know we get up early in the countryside? Alright, I did set my alarm a bit early to catch it. Go on, turn on a telly, you're missing it.'

Tom groped for the remote control on his bedside table and turned on a small TV standing on a chest of drawers. By the time the picture appeared the declaration had begun, and he saw a self-important returning officer intoning laboriously in a thick Yorkshire accent. '... Bathhurst, Kevin Alan, Monster Raving Loony, 412.' A feeble cheer went up from the floor of the hall and a candidate wearing a chicken costume performed an elaborate bow. 'Buckley, Richard Henry, Conservative, 25,842.' The crowd erupted in a roar and the familiar figure of the MP raised a hand in acknowledgement and smiled modestly. Tom heard a whoop down the phone from Sally. 'And I duly declare …' He turned down the sound.

'What are you, a rabid Tory or something?'

'Not at all. Just pleased that my mate Richard's got back. It means I can get on the phone first thing Monday and start chasing about my meeting in Westminster.'

'That soon? We don't even know who the Tourism Minister's going to be yet.'

'Doesn't matter. The quicker I can get a hearing for the Dales, the quicker something might get done. And more to the point the quicker I get to come to stay with you.'

'Yes, I'm looking forward to it as well.'

Tom considered getting up when they finished the call but decided that three hours sleep would not be enough if he was to be on good form to hear the report on the meeting with Valco.

The call from the States came through late in the afternoon. Bob's voice was first on the speaker phone.

'Well, buddy, I think you're going to like what we've got to tell you. Angie, do you want to be the bringer of glad tidings?'

'As Bob would say, I think we just reached second base. The VP is willing to see a full presentation. If he likes what he hears he'll table it for discussion at their next board meeting provided we agree to their conditions. They're looking for exclusivity and confidentiality – they want us to guarantee that we won't approach any of their competitors until they decide whether or not to go ahead. And we have to keep the fact that we're talking to them strictly confidential'

Tom considered the request. 'We'd need something in return to agree to that.'

'That's what we said at the meeting. We said that we'd require a guarantee that any information we gave them in advance of committing to work with us would be treated in confidence and would remain our copyright.'

Tom frowned. 'Confidence, yes, but I'm not so sure about copyright. You can't copyright facts or opinions which is what most of our proposal is made up of. What do you think, Bob?'

'I know these boys – they play hard ball, and their lawyers would find a way to sidestep any agreement if they chose to do so. Look, if these guys choose to screw us over, then there's probably nothing we could do about it. But it's a gamble you've got to take, and I can't see why they'd want to queer the pitch right now when they've accepted that Tiger can provide what they're potentially looking for.'

'So how did you leave it at the meeting?'

'We suggested that an exchange of letters might be appropriate at this stage. The VP said he'd be happy to speak to his legal department about it and we said we'd talk to our lawyers. Speaking of which, I think you could do with some representation over here. These guys are cute, and you could do with some big guns on your team. There's a law firm I could recommend, but they don't come cheap.'

Tom played out various options in his mind. 'When's their next board meeting?'

'The week after next,' Angie told him.

Tom remembered Sir Giles' comment about the race being on. The process of finding a buyer for Tiger was well advanced. There was no time to lose if a contract with Valco was to be secured before a takeover offer was in place. It also occurred to him that So Lin's wedding was a little over a month away to be followed by an extended period of leave for her honeymoon. He wouldn't have her essential support to call on unless they moved fast.

'Bob, what are the chances of getting the letters in place and making a full presentation in time for the proposal to be considered at that board meeting?

'It would all have to happen next week. I'm willing to give it a shot.'

Tom wondered if he was pushing too hard and decided to give himself breathing space to take stock. 'OK, you've both done good work. I want to run it all past the Chairman. I'll call you as soon as I've spoken to him. Are you going to be there for a while?' They told him they were about to go for a late lunch, but Bob would have his cell phone with him.

Emma, Tom's PA, tracked down Sir Giles at his home in the country. Tom soon heard his cultured tones. 'Well, my boy, what can I do for you? Not bad news, is it? I've had enough for one day with those damned socialists waltzing back into power!'

Tom was soon able to bring him up to speed with events in the States. 'Go for it,' Sir Giles said. 'Yes, these American corporations can be buggers and they're sure to wriggle on the end of the line before you land them. But faint heart, etc. We should give your initiative a fair crack of the whip.'

Reassured, Tom considered a plan of action. Bob would have to set up a meeting with a law firm in New York for early next week. There'd be no time to make a choice between several firms – Tom would accept Bob's recommendation. He'd need Lin to be available to join him in New York for the presentation. He checked his watch to work out the time in Hong Kong. Well past midnight. He debated whether to wait until late evening when the eight-hour time difference would mean that she was up, but decided that her enthusiasm to keep the company in their own hands would be enough to excuse such a late call.

She answered sleepily after several rings. She was enthused by the opportunity which Bob had set up and readily agreed to stand by to fly to New York. She was concerned that her diary was very full, trying to get as much done as possible before her wedding, but she accepted that the trip should take priority. She would just have to rearrange things at short notice.

Tom dialled Bob's cell phone. It was answered with the sound of a lively restaurant in the background.

'We're going to go for broke on this one, Bob. First, how soon do you think you can set up a meeting with your law firm?'

'I can phone them as soon as we finish talking. They'll jump at the prospect of new business so it could well be on Monday.'

'What about getting a date for the presentation to Valco? Assuming we sort the exchange of letters out, would they see us towards the end of next week?'

'I think there's a good chance. How long would you want with them?'

'An hour minimum, longer if they're willing.'

'OK, I'll call the VP's office.'

Tom felt vindicated in his decision to contract Bob. His no-nonsense can-do approach was exactly what was needed.

'Right, call me back when you've firmed things up so that I can book a flight. I'll take over from Angie - can I talk to her please?'

Angie listened while Tom explained his plan of action. 'I'll fly over and pick up the reins from you on Monday. Well done for getting us this far. You'll be able to come back tonight as planned.'

Angie's reply was flat. 'OK, Tom. If that's what you want.'

Half an hour later Bob called with the news that a meeting was on for Monday afternoon at the law firm's offices and the VP had agreed to give them an hour for a presentation on Friday morning. Tom called Emma into his office and asked her to look into flights to New York on Sunday and to check availability at the same hotel where Angie had been staying.

Ben poked his head round the door. 'Busy? Shall I come back?' Tom beckoned him in and gestured to the sofa. He finalised the plans with Emma and turned to Ben who was celebrating dress down Friday in shorts, flip flops and a Tottenham Hotspur T-shirt.

'Friday, close of play. Mean anything?'

'Sorry? Oh, the wine bar.'

'Indeed, oh great leader. The numbers have depleted since you've stopped coming and buying rounds, but your absence has been noted. It's ages since the Angie incident. Don't you think it's time you put in an appearance to rally the troops? They're beginning to think that you're a figment of their imagination.'

Tom reflected that he had been neglecting his staff in the whirlwind of events of the last few weeks. He felt guilty because he'd always prided himself on being approachable and having his ear to the ground. Maybe he should revisit the Friday evening drinks session. He didn't regret it. At first the staff kept their distance even after Tom had bought a round for them, but as their numbers swelled and the drinks flowed, Tom

found himself once more in serial conversation with his employees, catching up on the latest trends, patiently hearing the
usual moans and offering advice wherever he could. Deciding
to take his leave at the time that the group was dwindling down
to the more hardened drinkers he took Ben aside. 'Thanks, Ben
for persuading me to come. I haven't enjoyed anything work-
related for ages. I've just had my head down trying to keep the
company afloat and forgotten what it is we actually do. I
mustn't lose sight of that.'

'No problem, boss. Glad you were enjoying yourself. Talking
of which, how did it go with that lady you went to see up North?'

Tom smiled. 'None of your bloody business!'

'Ah,' Ben grinned 'Say no more!'

17

The elevator doors swished open to reveal the reception area of
Ellis and Steinberg, Attorneys at Law, 25 floors above the busy
pavements of Broadway. Tom and Bob approached the receptionist who asked them to take a seat. Moments later, two
fresh-faced young men bounded through double oak doors to
shake their visitors a little too enthusiastically by the hand.
They were dressed identically in understatedly expensive grey
suits. Only the colours of their diagonally-striped ties distin-
guished them – Harvard and Yale, Tom was later to learn from
Bob.

Pleasantries over, comfortably seated in an oak-panelled
meeting room on studded leather chairs of the deepest burgun-
dy, Bob took the lead.

'OK, guys, you know the score. We've got until the end of the
week to get a basic agreement between Valco and Tiger which
keeps them sweet but doesn't put us at a disadvantage. We

want to know how you think you might achieve it and how much it will cost. Right Tom?'

'I might have taken rather longer to say it and put it more elegantly, but in essence, yes.'

'Remember these guys charge by the hour, so you gotta use shorthand and cut the bullshit.' Bob smiled sweetly at the two junior attorneys who had been assigned to them. They looked uncertainly at each other. Nothing at law school had prepared them for this. The one in the blue and white tie decided to play Bob at his own game.

'OK, here's the no BS version. One, you give us a proper brief so we know what you want. Two, we knock up a draft of the letter of agreement. Three, assuming you're happy with it, we meet Valco's legal department and we wave our dicks at each other for as long as is necessary for us both to believe we've got the best available deal. And four we send you a large invoice for the work we've done charged at $600 an hour. Plus expenses.'

Tom broke in. 'Gentlemen. Forgive me, but I'm used to conducting business in – how can I put it – in a less testosterone-fuelled atmosphere. I'm happy for us to start working as a team …' Tom paused until he'd seen grins begin to spread across the attorneys' faces, then continued. '… provided you'll reduce your hourly charges to $500 an hour.' It was his turn to smile sweetly. 'If we pull off this deal with Valco then we can renegotiate fees and both make a bunch of money. Shall we give you the brief?'

Later, sitting in a coffee shop opposite a Broadway theatre advertising a Tony award-winning play, Tom and Bob replayed the meeting.

'Sorry if I'm a little too forthright for your liking,' said Bob.

'Not at all,' Tom replied. 'I didn't hire you for your diplomacy. Quite the opposite.'

'It's just that all that Ivy League privilege gets up my nose. I get a kick out of playing the Bronx bruiser, and now and then it seems to get results. And how about you pulling that fast one and getting them to knock a hundred dollars an hour off the tab. Respect, man.'

They clinked coffee cups. Bob leant back and eyed Tom. 'Do you feel like clinking glasses of something stronger this evening? I don't know if you like jazz and blues but there's a club I go to every Monday evening downtown. Most of the pros who work the bars get Monday off, so they all meet up at the club for a jam.'

At 10 p.m. after dinner in his hotel, Tom hailed a yellow cab to take him to the address Bob had given him. The desire to take to his bed after dinner had been strong as his body clock insisted that it was the middle of the night, but Tom had long ago learned that the best way to minimise jet lag was to adjust to local times straight away. The cab dropped him in a narrow street in Greenwich Village. Tom found Bob inside the club nursing a drink at a table close to the low stage. The music had yet to begin. Tom ordered a beer and Bob called for another bourbon.

'Can I ask a question?' Bob asked. Tom nodded. 'Why the indecent haste to get this deal? You're pushing it like a teenager trying to get into the sack on a first date. What happened to the gentle art of seduction?'

Tom considered being economical with the truth but decided he could level with Bob. 'The survival of Tiger.com in its present form depends on it. Our investors are losing faith with us and want to cut their losses by selling the company. The Valco deal is my last throw of the dice to avoid it. I need to pull it off before we get taken over – and that could be soon.'

Bob let out a low whistle. 'Jeez! Big stakes then.' He drummed his fingers on the table, deep in thought. 'No wonder you're hot to trot.'

'Can I ask you a question?' Tom asked in return.

'Fire away.'

'What's your take on Angie?'

'Clever girl, and damned attractive if you like her type. Why do you ask?'

'How committed do you think she is to getting the Valco deal?'

Bob looked at him with interest. 'That rather implies that you might think she's less than committed.'

'Let's just say that I have reason to believe that she would prefer the company to be taken over.'

Bob thought for a while. 'There were times when she argued against the value of a Valco deal. I didn't think much of it. I thought she was just playing devil's advocate. Why would she want a takeover?'

'I think she might have a financial interest in it.'

'What – as a shareholder? If your company's in difficulty, then the takeover share price isn't going to be great.'

'No. It's not that.'

'I'm intrigued. Do you want to tell me about it?'

'Not really. It's only supposition on my part. All I'd ask if that you let me know if you come across anything which might confirm my suspicions.'

'OK. If that's what you want.' Bob returned to his bourbon, puzzled.

They fell into a conversation about music. Tom professed to listen to a wide range of styles. Bob admitted to a few guilty pleasures but argued that jazz and blues were the only genres worth listening to if you wanted authenticity, not commercial hype. Tom countered that he wanted to get pleasure from music, not authenticity and anyway hadn't jazz and blues been commercially hyped. The debate meandered on for a while until they were distracted by an announcement over the sound system. On to the stage wandered several casually dressed musicians – a drummer, pianist, upright bass player and a guitarist. On a count of four they launched into a twelve-bar blues which Tom recognised from the opening riff as 'Night Train.'

The standard of playing was superb. Solo after solo was taken, and then, in the manner of a relay race, musicians began to replace each other. A second drummer performed a slick ma-noeuvre to take over from the first without missing a beat. A pianist slid onto the stool to segue seamlessly from the original keyboard player. Up came a sax player for several solos, then a trumpeter, then a trombonist.

'What do you think Tom?' enquired Bob in the comparative quietness of a double bass solo.

'Brilliant musicians. How long do they go on playing the same number?'

'Can be hours. Usually until all the musos here have sat in.'

'In that case, Bob, I may have to leave before it ends. I'm sinking fast. I'm afraid.'

'No problem. I'll hang on here and call you in the morning.'

Bob's was one of a string of calls which Tom received in his hotel room in the morning. The first was from the law firm saying that they had faxed a first draft of the proposed letter of agreement to his hotel. As he put down the phone, he heard a knock on the door. He opened it to find a bellboy with the fax on a silver plate. He fished a dollar out of his wallet and gave a tip. He'd just finished reading through the letter when Bob rang. He too had received a copy of the fax. 'Looks good to me,' he said, 'but then I'm no lawyer.'

'Neither am I,' replied Tom. 'But it seems to cover all we're looking for. I'll tell them to send it off to Valco.'

He duly called the law firm and gave his approval for the draft letter to be sent. They promised to call him with any news.

Around lunchtime Tom's PA called from London. Emma had a list of messages and questions for him. Most he managed to deal with immediately. The rest he promised to resolve via email.

His mobile rang and he answered with a cursory 'Tom Keardon.'

'Funny ringtone again! Where are you this time, slicker?'

'Oh, hi Sally. I'm in New York?'

'Oh.' She sounded deflated. 'Are you going to be back for the weekend?'

'I'm hoping to get a flight back on Friday evening. I'd be at Heathrow on Saturday morning.' The penny dropped. 'Oh no – don't say you've fixed up your Westminster visit already.'

'I thought you'd be pleased.' Sally's voice was cracking. 'I didn't know you'd be jet-setting off around the world, did I? It doesn't matter. I'm sure it's more important than seeing me.'

Tom kicked himself for not being more sensitive. 'I'm sorry, Sally. Of course I'm pleased that you've fixed the meeting. When is it?'

'Thursday,' she said, flatly. Tom's heart sank.

'So what's the problem? Can't you stay over in town – then we could meet up on Saturday.'

There was a long silence from Sally. 'It doesn't matter,' she eventually repeated.

'It does matter, Sally. I want to see you. But I can hardly drop everything and fly back. I've got a crucial meeting here on Friday.'

'And I want to see you. But I don't want to kick my heels for two nights in London all on my own in some horrible hotel which is all I'll be able to afford.'

'I'll pay for you to stay somewhere nice.'

'I don't want to feel like a kept woman.'

Tom thought fast and an idea formed in his mind. 'Look, why don't you stay at my place? My cleaning lady's got a key and I can arrange to get it to you. And as for being on your own, there's a great friend of mine I work with called Ben. He could take you out, perhaps show you some sights or get some theatre tickets. How does that sound?'

Sally hesitated. 'I suppose I could. Are you sure?'

'Of course I am. I've really been looking forward to you coming to stay. If I can't be there when you come down, I'll do anything I can to keep you in London until I arrive.'

'OK, slicker.' Sally's usual breezy mood had returned. 'You're on.'

He first phoned Ben. 'What are you up to on Thursday and Friday evening?'

'Are you asking me for a date? This is all very sudden, Tom. I thought you'd be in New York.'

'I will be. It's just that my friend from Yorkshire is coming to stay for the weekend'

'I knew it. I could tell from the lovelight in your eyes.'

'Shut up, Ben! Yes, I do like her a lot. The problem is that she's coming down on Thursday for a meeting and I won't be back until Saturday morning. I was wondering if you could keep her entertained until I get there.'

'Isn't that a bit dangerous. My debonair charms are legendary and she could fall for me, you know.'

'Ben – how can I put this? I don't think you're her type. But you are great company and I just don't want her stuck in a strange city all on her own. Could you meet up with her on Thursday evening and let her in to my flat. I'll get the keys to you. Then on Friday evening perhaps you could take her to the theatre. On me of course.'

'Well, in that case, how could I refuse?'

'Thanks, Ben. You're a mate!'

Tom gave Ben Sally's mobile number and phoned his cleaner to ask her to stand by for a courier bike to come to pick up the key. He then phoned Emma to arrange a bike. He considered how much to tell her about Sally given her new-found proprietorial interest in his private life and decided to play down any suggestion that he was in a relationship with Sally.

'Hi, Emma. You remember that old friend of mine from Yorkshire who was organising the charity dinner? Well she's going to be in London on business for a couple of days and I've said she could stay at my place while I'm away. Could you get a bike to pick up my keys from my cleaner and give them to Ben?'

She happily agreed and Tom imagined her frantically reading between the lines. Let her think what she wants, thought Tom.

Within an hour of Sally's first call he was able to phone her back and confirm the arrangements. He then opened his laptop and began the process of turning Tiger's proposal into a Power-point presentation for Friday's meeting.

So Lin flew in on Wednesday and booked into the same hotel as Tom. She joined him in honing the presentation, deciding which sections of it they would each present. Late in the afternoon, the law firm called to say that they had reached agreement with Valco on the form of words for the exchange of letters and had a final copy for him to sign. A courier came to the hotel and waited while Tom checked it. A few points had changed from the original draft and many paragraphs of impenetrable legalise had been added, but he was happy to trust the lawyers and returned it, signed, to the courier. Tom offered to take Lin to dinner but she declined, citing the need to get an early night after her long flight. Tom was also still feeling the effects of jet lag and was quite pleased to order a meal on room service and also take early to his bed.

They went to Bob's house the following day for a full rehearsal, with Bob acting the part of Valco, trying to view the proposals critically through their eyes. A projector and screen had been set up and Tom and Lin launched into the presentation. Tom led off, giving Tiger's credentials and an overview of the commercial opportunities that the rise of consumerism in China presented. Lin followed, outlining the political and cultural hurdles that any Western company would have to overcome. Tom picked up, explaining how Tiger could use its expertise and connections to smooth the path for Valco's expansion in China. Finally he focused on the commercial potential which China presented – a vast population, a growing middle-class, rising standards of living and an inability to meet consumer demands without the support and involvement of Western companies.

When they finished, Bob launched into a series of penetrating questions. Why should Valco do business with a Communist regime hostile to capitalism? What sort of infrastructure was there in China to support distribution of goods? How could profits be taken out of the country and what level of taxation could be expected?

Tom and Lin fielded to the best of their ability until Bob came out of character.

'Not bad, guys. It's pretty convincing. But could be better.' He consulted the notes he'd made and began to make suggestions for improvement. Appropriate changes were made to the Powerpoint and they moved on to consider other aspects of the presentation. It was decided that Lin would wear a Chinese silk dress rather than a business suit to emphasise her ear to the ground in the Far East. Bob would make introductions before the presentations.

'OK guys. One last thing. Have you thought through what will happen if they accept the proposal and their board gives the go-ahead? I can't see them signing on a dotted line straight away. They never commit more than they need to with any supplier – they always build partnerships slowly. What would a next step be?'

Tom and Lin exchanged glances, both realising that in focusing so strongly on the presentation they'd not thought past it. Tom turned the question back on Bob. 'You know the way they operate. What do you think they'll be looking for?'

'I'd say they'd want to find out for themselves if what you're saying stacks up. Some sort of fact-finding mission on the ground. You probably need to invite them out to Hong Kong and take them into China to see for themselves what's going on.'

'OK. We need to think it through.' Tom looked questioningly at Lin and she nodded her agreement.

Bob had recommended a family-run Italian restaurant just a block from the hotel and it was there that Lin and Tom went for an evening meal. They settled into a booth and took stock of the situation.

'So what about this fact-finding mission that Bob's suggesting,' Tom said.

'No problem – I could set it up. The only thing is that if it happens – what's the expression – sod's law it will be just around the time that I'm getting married.'

'Then we'd just have to do without you.'

'Although ...'

'What?'

'Chong's family would be involved in helping us deal with the Chinese authorities if we get the Valco deal. You know what Hongs are like – business first, everything else a poor second. They'd be happy to invite anyone from Valco to the wedding and it would actually put me in good stead with them to bring such a prestigious guest.'

'So you're actually suggesting that we make any visit coincide with the wedding. Are you sure?'

'Tom, if it helps us to keep our company, I'm happy to do it.'

'OK. Let's see what happens. Thanks again for inviting me by the way.'

'I want you there. By the way, will you be bringing anyone?'

'What do you mean?'

'Well it's usual for a wedding invitation to include a partner as well.'

'What makes you think I've got someone I'd want to bring?' Tom racked his brains to think of anything that she could have heard. Nothing came to mind, so maybe it was just female intuition.

'Just wondered. Why, is there anyone?'

Tom hesitated then said no. It was obviously unconvincing.

'Come on. Have you met someone?'

'OK. There is someone, but I've only just met her. No, that's not true. I've known her since I was a kid. Her parents own the farm beside ours.'

'Not the girl next door? Doesn't sound like your style.'

'I suppose it's not. But in a way, that's the attraction. She's like an antidote to all my problems and pressures. But I've not even ... I mean we haven't even got together yet.'

Lin gave him an old-fashioned look. 'I can't imagine what you mean.'

Tom felt himself blushing. 'She's coming to stay for the weekend. But I think it might be a little premature to invite her to the wedding.'

'Well she's very welcome if you want to.'

Tom, Bob and Lin were ushered into a presentation room at Valco's headquarters on the 103rd floor of the South Tower at the World Trade Centre. They'd asked for a quarter of an hour to set up their equipment before the meeting was due to start. Tom connected his laptop via a tabletop input to a projector in the ceiling and fired it up. The plate glass windows gave a panoramic view over the East River to Brooklyn and beyond. He located the controls which would black them out when the presentation began.

At precisely the appointed time the door opened and Bob jumped up to greet the Valco's vice president for Business Development and his two assistants. 'Tom, meet Elliott Paul – Elliot, Tom Keardon, Managing Director of Tiger.com. And this is So Lin, their International Director who's flown in from Hong Kong to be with us today.' They shook hands with the well-groomed vice-president who flashed a wide smile revealing too perfect teeth. He in turn introduced his assistants and then gestured for all to take their seats around the table.

'Welcome to Valco,' he said, and raised both hands in the direction of the screen. 'The floor is yours.'

Tom stood, pressed the button to lower the blackout blinds and launched into the presentation speaking clearly and confidently. Every now and then Elliott broke in to clarify a point. The detail he picked up on suggested that he had briefed himself well on the issues.

Lin took over and for the first time Tom was able to observe their audience. Elliott maintained an expression of polite interest, while the two assistants were taking copious notes. Tom caught Bob's eye who nodded his head in approval.

Finally, it was Tom's turn to summarise.

'Gentlemen. It's appropriate that we're standing here in the World Trade Centre. Later this year, the World Trade Organisation will be holding its Fourth Ministerial Conference in Qatar. It will launch negotiations to make globalisation more inclusive by lowering trade barriers, thus increasing international trade. Also on the agenda is China's application to join the organisation. There could be no clearer sign from the Chinese authorities that they foresee a future in which China plays a full part in world trade. They can only do that by liberalising the rules which restrict the expansion of Western companies into the country. Companies which are quick to grasp the opportunities will reap rich rewards. We urge you to act quickly and allow Tiger.com to partner you in the enterprise.'

Tom pressed the button to raise the blinds and daylight flooded into the room. He presented the Valco team with printed copies of the proposal before returning to his end of the table. Elliott consulted with his two assistants in a low voice. Finally he looked up to Tom.

'I'd like to thank you and So Lin for an impressive presentation. As you know the decision to proceed is not one I can make – that will be for my board to decide. However, I will be recommending your proposal to them. Just one question for you, because I'm sure it will be asked of me at the board meeting – if we were to look to develop a partnership, what would the next steps be?'

Tom silently blessed Bob for having anticipated the question.

Lin replied. 'I'd like to extend an invitation for you to visit my country to see for yourself how China is changing. You could meet our team of experts in Hong Kong who can provide you with the commercial intelligence you'll need, and I can introduce you to our business associates who have strong links with the Chinese authorities. I'd also like to arrange a fact-finding trip to the mainland in Guangdong Province which is our most economically advanced region and could provide a model for the rest of China.'

Elliott thanked Lin. 'That sounds like a very attractive proposition, ma'am. We shall see what the board decides.' He glanced at his watch. 'Now if you will excuse me, I have another meeting.' There was a quick round of handshakes and the Valco team exited the room.

Bob leapt up and high-fived Tom and Lin. 'Hey! How about that? Well done, guys!'

'This calls for a rather good lunch,' said Tom.

18

Tom paid off the taxi and climbed the stairs to the door of his loft apartment. He'd called Sally while waiting at the baggage carousel at Heathrow so he knew she'd be expecting him. He slid the key into the lock and deposited his bags on the floor. There was no sign of her, so he called her name. She emerged from the kitchen pulling off one of his aprons and ran to greet him, jumping up into his arms, wrapping her legs around his and kissing him deeply.

Tom disentangled her. 'Whoa! That's quite a welcome.'

'No more than you deserve. I've been having a great time!'

'Without me?'

She took him by the hand and led him to a sofa where she sat facing him, tucking her legs up under her and looking in a simple belted summer dress which emphasised her slim waist like an excited schoolgirl.

'What have you been doing,' Tom asked.

'Well – the meeting went well in Westminster. They think they might be able to get us in front of the new Tourism Minister. Then I met Ben at your offices and he took me for a drink. He's a funny guy isn't he? We came here and ended up ordering a takeaway. I'm afraid we drank most of your beers but don't worry I've been out and bought some more. Oh – would you like one? What sort of hostess am I? Oh, sorry – you live here, don't you!'

She skipped away to the kitchen leaving Tom marvelling at her cheeriness. She returned with two open bottles of lager and continued at a breathless pace.

'I had a nice lie-in yesterday morning and then went up to the shops. I bought this dress in Oxford Street. Do you like it? Then I went to the National Gallery. I loved the Impressionists – it's so amazing to be just inches from all those beautiful pictures. I just wanted to reach out and touch them. Then I walked up into Covent Garden and watched all the street performers. Oh, I bought you some candles – they're over there on the shelf. I came back here to change and then met Ben at the theatre. We went to see *Les Miserables*. It was brilliant!'

She leant over and kissed him quickly. 'I've had a great time without you. It's going to be even better now that you're here.'

'Well, I've had a good trip. We achieved all we were aiming for. Now I'm looking forward to forgetting all about work for the weekend and concentrating on you.'

'I'm going to be concentrated on, am I?' She tossed her head back and spread her arms wide. 'Concentrate all you want!' she giggled.

Tom leant forward and kissed the swell of her breast just above the low neckline of her dress. 'I fully intend to!'

'Mr Keardon!' She pulled the back of her hand to her forehead and closed her eyes in mock indignation.

Tom broke the moment and leapt up. 'Come on you! I need to grab a shower and unpack my bags.'

'I've made a salad for lunch. I'll put it on the table ready for you.'

The afternoon was spent wandering hand in hand along the stalls of a street market with Sally persuading Tom to buy vases and dried flowers for his apartment – it lacked a feminine touch, she said. In the evening they dined at a crowded local bistro. Tom bumped into some friends at the bar and they agreed to share a table rather than wait to have ones of their own. The conversation and the drink flowed freely. Eventually, Tom and Sally returned to the apartment.

'Drink?' Tom asked as they flopped on to the sofa.

'I think I've had more than enough already. Thanks, Tom, for a lovely day.'

She kissed him and they clasped each other closely. The kiss developed into a longing caress, Sally slipping her hands inside

Tom's shirt and Tom cupping her breast. Eventually they parted.

'Shall we go to bed?' Tom suggested.

'I thought you'd never ask! I've waited a good fifteen years. I used to fantasise about going to bed with you when I was sixteen.'

'Well I hope it's going to be worth the wait. No pressure, then! Do you want to use the bathroom first?'

Sally left to prepare for bed and Tom reflected on the way their relationship had developed to the point at which they were about to make love. Knowing each other so well as children then picking up their friendship so easily. Slipping so naturally yet inevitably into – what was it? Love? Who knows, Tom thought.

Sally was lying on the far side of the bed with her back to him when Tom slipped in beside her, naked. She was wearing one of his shirts. He listened to her breathing, too quick for her to be asleep and gently pulled the shirt up to reveal the curve of her back. He softly ran his fingers down her spine, tracing each vertebra.

'Ow! That tickles' She span round and tickled his armpits. They wrestled playfully until she brought it to an end by straddling his stomach and pinning his arms to the pillows.

'I always use to beat you when we had tickle fights when we were kids,' she laughed.

'Only because I let you. But you were quite a handful to control.'

She released his arms and sat up straight, strands of blonde hair falling across her face. She was suddenly serious. 'Sorry, Tom. I'm being silly. We're not kids anymore.'

'Good thing too. You didn't have these then.' He reached to undo the single button which held the shirt together revealing her breasts still rising and falling from the exertion. 'A considerable improvement, I'd say.'

A salacious smile played on her lips and she shrugged off the shirt. Reaching behind her back she felt for him. 'Now that's what I'd call a real handful.'

Tom awoke to find Sally smiling at him. She looked like the cat who'd got the cream. 'Morning, slicker. I've been lying here watching you sleep for ages.'
   'You poor thing! Can't have been a pretty sight.'
   'It was. You're beautiful. And I've come to a conclusion.'
   'What?' asked Tom, slightly alarmed.
   'That my body likes your body.'
   'Phew! That's a relief.'
   'In fact, I don't suppose I could trouble you to make love to me again, could I?'

It was past noon when they finally rose. They ate brunch prepared by Sally on the tiny balcony of Tom's apartment which made up for what it lacked in space with an extravagant view of a sparkling River Thames and the towers of Canary Wharf standing proud in the distance. To take advantage of the warm summer sunshine they wandered down to a marina and sat with coffees taking in the yachts and the passers-by. Only when they returned to the apartment was the spell broken. Sally was due to catch the early evening train home to Yorkshire. She reluctantly packed her bags while Tom went to retrieve his car from the underground garage.
   'You didn't tell me much about your meeting with the MP's researcher,' said Tom as they set off for King's Cross station.
   'Not much to tell. She was very interested in what I had to say. She wants me to try to contact tourism associations in other areas hit by foot and mouth so that we can present a united front. At the end she said she'd suggest to Richard that he wrote a letter to the new minister for tourism asking either for a meeting with the Dales Tourism Association or preferably a visit to the Dales to see for himself what's going on. She thinks that he may well agree given that he's new in the job and will want to make his mark.'

'He may not be that keen. There aren't many Labour voters in the rural areas with outbreaks.'

'You're such a cynic!'

'Just a realist.'

'Oh, by the way, I got a call from the Chairman of the Dales Tourism Association on Friday. He was really pleased that we'd made the front page of the local paper thanks to that news release you encouraged me to write. If ever you need a job in PR, give me a call.'

'Right now, that doesn't seem like a bad idea.'

They drove on in silence, both lost in thought. By the time they arrived at the station with a quarter of an hour to spare, Tom had made a decision. He parked the Audi and turned to Sally.

'It's been wonderful having you here. I can't wait to see you again.'

'I've loved it too. So when can I see you again?'

'I've been thinking about that. I've got to go to Hong Kong in a fortnight for a week or so. I go out every three months to keep up to speed with our office there and I'm hoping that this time I'll have some prospective clients flying in from the States for a visit.'

Sally's face fell. 'So I won't see you for the best part of a month. Is that what you're saying?'

'No – I don't think I could wait that long. There's something else going on when I'm out there. My ex-wife's getting married and I'm invited. She asked me if I'd like to bring a partner. I'd like it to be you.'

Sally spluttered. 'You want me to come to Hong Kong with you?'

'I'd have to leave you to your own devices most days because of business but we'll have the evenings together. There's so much I'd like to show you. I don't know if you'll be able to get away from work at such short notice but maybe your clients ...'

Sally interrupted. 'Tom! Hang my clients! Will you stop babbling so that I can say yes? I'd love to.' She gave him a smacking kiss on the lips.

19

Tiger.com's regular Monday morning operations meeting came to a close just before midday and Tom asked the three directors, Angie, Ben and Charles to stay behind.

'I just wanted to update you on the New York meeting. Lin and I made our presentation to the Valco VP and he's agreed to put it before their board for discussion. We should hear if they want to proceed by the end of the week.'

'That's great, Tom,' Ben enthused. Angie and Charles nodded in less enthusiastic agreement.

'Let's not get too excited though. The decision they'll be making is only whether to continue a dialogue with us. Any contract or partnership agreement would be a long way down the line. So let's keep it amongst ourselves for the moment, please. I don't want to raise false hopes and Valco are very touchy about any of this going public. Anyhow, thanks for all your work which has got us this far with them."

Tom called Ben back when he made to leave with Charles and Angie.

'I owe you several pints for looking after Sally. Thanks, mate.'

'Just the price of the theatre tickets will do! No, it really was a pleasure. What a great girl! Far too good for the likes of you. I told her about all your filthy habits and suggested that she'd be far better off with me, but it didn't seem to do the trick. You've got a good'un there.'

Late that afternoon Emma buzzed Tom.

'Call from the States for you. Dave Travis from USA Retail Weekly.'

Tom frowned, recognising the title of a rival trade magazine to the one which Bob Schwartz wrote for. 'OK, you better put him through.'

A voice full of false bonhomie came down the line. "Well hi there Tom. Great that I could get to speak to you. How are you today?'

'Fine, thanks,' said Tom non-committedly.

'That's great, Tom. My name's Dave Travis and I write a column called 'Rumour Mill' for USA Retail Weekly. I'm running a little piece on Tiger.com and wondered if you wanted to comment.'

Tom's hackles rose. As a journalist he'd made similar calls himself. He knew the game - write a story and at the last minute phone the subject of the story, catch them off guard to get an ill-considered quote or, just as good, get a no comment which would be tantamount to having the story confirmed. Tom replied, choosing his words carefully. 'Would you care to enlighten me as to what you intend writing about?'

'It's just a little rumour I picked up about your company looking to do business with one of our retail big boys.'

Tom cursed inwardly. How the hell had he found out? Who had he been speaking to?

'Now I wouldn't want to print something that isn't true, so I just wondered if you could confirm it. Just a quick comment, my deadline's very tight.'

Tom knew that ploy as well - the false excuse of a deadline to pressurise a spokesperson to give a quick answer off the cuff. He needed to employ delaying tactics. 'I'd need to see the story in full before commenting. E-mail it to me.'

'Well now, I can't do that before I've written it, can I?' Dave's voice was a model of reasonableness.'

'In which case you better start writing now if your deadline's really that tight. I'll give you half an hour to get it to me and then I'll issue a statement through my New York lawyers within an hour.'

'Now Tom!' Dave's voice was beginning to lose its bonhomie. 'I just need a quick comment ...'

Tom cut across him. 'Half an hour, Mr Travis. Goodbye.'

Tom was tempted to try to fathom out where the leak might have come from, but his head told him that he should act fast to get a response in place. He thought of phoning Tiger's PR agency but decided to handle it himself. He phoned Bob Schwartz's home. Luckily he answered straight away.

'Bob, we've got a problem. I've just had a call from Dave Travis at USA Retail Weekly. Do you know him?'

'Of course I do. We've been writing rival columns for years. What did he want?'

'It looks as if he's got wind of the Valco deal. He wants a comment from me?'

'Jeez, Tom. How the hell did he get hold of it? Was it Angie by any chance? You told me about your suspicions.'

'I don't know although I want to get to the bottom of it in good time. Right now we're in damage limitation mode. If Valco think we've been talking in breach of our agreement to keep everything under wraps it could blow any chance of their board agreeing to work with us.'

'Too right it could. What did you tell him?'

'I said I wouldn't comment until I'd seen the story. He claimed he hadn't written it yet and used the old trick of a tight deadline to get a comment, but I called his bluff and gave him half an hour to email it to me. I said that I would ... hang on.' A soft ping came from his laptop speaker. 'Surprise, surprise. He's just sent it. Fast writer, eh?

'What's it say?'

Tom read the short piece out loud. '*It was only a matter of time before US retailers would begin to eye the commercial opportunities presented by China's burgeoning economy and the rise of consumerism in the most populous country in the world. Could that time have come? British Far Eastern experts Tiger.com have been visiting our shores trying to drum up consultancy business and could be close to a deal with one of our biggest retail players. Tiger's Managing Director, Tom Keardon commented...* That's it!

'At least he hasn't said it's Valco,' said Bob. 'But it's all true.'

'I said I'd issue a statement through our US lawyers within an hour of seeing the story, so we need to decide what that will be – pretty quick.'

'Good move – we journalists don't like lawyers breathing down our necks. But in an hour Tom? That might have been a bit reckless.'

'Maybe, but the longer we take to respond, the more it will look like we've got something to hide. When do they put the magazine to bed?'

'Tomorrow evening – Tuesday. It hits the newsstands on Thursday. At least that's after the Valco board meeting on Wednesday. What are the options?'

'I think we've got to warn Valco about the story. If they see it without being warned, it would be more difficult for us to claim that we had nothing to do with leaking it.'

'You're probably right. This is strange for me – as a journalist I'm used to being on the other end of a situation like this. Not easy to think as a gamekeeper rather than a poacher.'

'I know. Look, I want you to alert the lawyers. I'm forwarding the email to you now.' Tom clicked on forward, typed in Bob's address and pressed send. 'I'll put a call into Elliott Paul and see if we can agree a statement for us to put out. You might like to see if the lawyers think it's a good idea for them to talk to Valco's legal team.'

'OK. Any ideas about what the statement might say?'

'We don't want to confirm or deny it, so I'm thinking along the lines of saying that we're always looking for international business opportunities, but we currently have no US clients. But we need Valco to approve anything we say.'

'The email has just come through. I'll get on to the lawyers and phone you back as soon as I've got any news.'

Tom put the phone down and buzzed Emma asking her to get Elliott Paul on the phone immediately. Once again, his mind turned to the question of where the leak had come from. Who had known about the meetings?

Emma buzzed him back. 'Mr Paul's in a meeting, but I've got his assistant on the line.'

The assistant asked how he could help. Tom recognised his name as that of one of Elliot's team who had attended the presentation. He explained the situation quickly and carefully, impressing the need for a quick response from Valco. He was beginning to think that maybe he had created a hostage to fortune by bullishly imposing the hour's deadline on himself. He forwarded Dave Travis' email to the assistant who promised see if he could break in to his bosses' meeting.

Tom drummed his fingers frantically on his desk, desperately thinking what else he could do. He went through to the adjoining office where Emma worked and explained without going into detail that there was a bit of a crisis on. He told her to clear all calls other than those from Bob Schwartz or Valco. If one came through when he was talking to the other, she should put them on hold and tell him immediately.

He'd just returned to his office when she buzzed again. "Bob Schwartz, for you.'

'Bob?'

'I've got the lawyers on conference call.'

'Hi Mr Keardon.' Tom recognised the voice of the Harvard one of the two.

'Right. Elliott Paul's in a meeting. I've explained the situation to his assistant and he's trying to get a message to Elliott to call me. Has Bob talked about contacting Valco's legal boys?'

'He has, and we think it makes sense, particularly if there's no guarantee that Mr Paul will get back to you within the hour. How important is it to hit that deadline?'

Tom knew only too well how much journalists hated it if a promised call was not made in time. It was a sure way to alienate them and risk getting a rougher ride in any story which was written. 'It's crucial. Maybe I should have given us more time, but there's no going back on it. Look on the positive side – we're much more likely to get a resolution to the issue when the pressure's on rather than get into a prolonged debate.'

'OK, Tom. I'll call our contact at Valco. Bob gave me a rough idea of the statement you're thinking of – shall I put it to them?

Tom looked up to see Emma hovering at the door of his office. 'Wait a sec,' he said.

'I've got Mr Paul on hold.'

Tom held up his hand to Emma and spoke to the lawyer. 'I've got a call from Elliott Paul – are you happy to hold while I take it?'

'Sure thing, Tom.'

Emma returned to her office to swap the calls and Tom heard Elliott's voice, calm and collected.

'Tom – now what's this all about?'

Tom made a conscious effort to speak casually.

'Elliott, thanks for getting back to me. Sorry to pull you out of your meeting but I thought we needed to resolve this problem as soon as possible. Has your assistant explained the situation to you?'

'Yes, and I've read the email.'

'Can I assure you that the last thing we wanted is for the terms of our agreement to be breached and for our discussions to go public. We obviously wouldn't want to prejudice the outcome of your board's decision. We'll be launching an investigation into the unlikely possibility of a leak from this end, but I'd like to assure you of our good faith at this stage and also ask you to consider that the leak may well have come from a source other than within our company. My feeling is that we should concern ourselves now with deciding how to respond to the story.'

'It's certainly putting us in an embarrassing situation.'

'Not necessarily. The story doesn't mention you by name and I would assume that Valco wouldn't wish to make any comment. That would only confirm that you were the retailer the story alludes to.'

'True.'

'And for us to make no comment would be taken as confirmation that we were indeed talking to a major US retailer. So what I'd suggest is that I put out a statement which neither confirms nor denies the story.'

There was a long pause before Elliott replied. 'OK, I accept your logic. What would you suggest your statement should say?'

Tom repeated the form of words he had already formulated. 'I'd like to say that Tiger.com is always looking for international business opportunities but we currently have no US clients. It has the advantage of being true without adding any fuel to the fire.'

Another pause. 'I suppose in the circumstances that would be acceptable to us.'

Tom felt a wave of relief. 'So how would you like to proceed? I'd like to issue the statement through our lawyers, but I need your formal approval for the words. Shall I get them to speak to your legal team?'

'Hell no, Tom. You'll never get anything out within an hour if those guys start to pick over the bones. Send me an email with the statement you've suggested and I'll approve it. I've nailed my colours to the mast on this initiative and it won't do me any favours if it all collapses before we've even started, just because some journalist has floated a rumour.'

'I appreciate your faith in us, Elliott. Thank you.'

'OK, Tom. But from now on, don't give me any hassle.'

Tom put the phone down and called out to Emma to put Bob and the lawyers back on the line. He told them what had been agreed and received hearty congratulations from Bob and a lukewarm response from the lawyer who was presumably mourning the evaporation of several hours' worth of billing. He then fired off an email with the statement to Elliott with copies to Bob and the lawyer. Five minutes later an email of approval came back. Tom called the lawyers to confirm that they had received both emails and they went ahead with issuing the statement to the magazine.

Tom felt drained and leant forward on his desk, clasping his head in his hands. What the hell was that all about? Who had tipped off the journalist? Was it a deliberate attempt at sabotage or just an inadvertent chance remark from someone in the know? He pulled himself together and went to thank Emma for her help, assuring her that the crisis was over. Then he called Ben and asked him to come to his office. Ben arrived and was surprised to be told to close the door behind him.

'Not like you to close your door, boss. What have I done?'

'Nothing. It's just that you're the one person I think I can confide in. Perhaps the only one I can trust.'

'Blimey! What's up?'

Tom ran the events of the past hour past Ben. 'I've managed to put a lid on it. Hopefully, it won't bugger up the chances of Valco deciding to stick with us. But now I want to find out where the leak came from. I need your logical mind on the case.'

Ben raised his eyebrows. 'I'm no Sherlock Holmes but I suppose being a computer nerd is the next best thing. OK, let's not jump to conclusions and start by eliminating the least likely culprits. Who knew about the Valco discussions? Two groups of people – us and Valco. Or three if you consider Bob Schwartz as belonging neither to us or them.'

'Why would Bob leak the story? It's in his interests for the deal to go ahead. He'll make a lot of money out of a long-term contract with us. And why would he tip off a rival?'

'True. No motive there. What about Valco? We've no idea how many of their staff knew about it, and there could be some internal politics going on. Maybe a grudge. Suppose someone was passed over for the job of vice-president of Business Development and wanted to queer the pitch of the guy who got the job.'

'Good theory, but how could we possibly test it.'

'I don't see how we could.'

'We've forgotten the lawyers. They knew. But once again, why would they throw away the chance of business. It doesn't make sense, so that brings us back home.'

'OK. Can we assume that the leak came after the presentation we made last Friday? The story only said we were touting for business in the States.'

'Possibly, but it said that we were close to a deal. It stretches the facts, but it would be even less true to say it after Angie and Bob's initial meeting.'

'Let's assume the leak came after the presentation. Who knew what, and when?'

'Obviously me, Lin and Bob immediately after the presentation. We've ruled out Bob, it wasn't me and surely it can't have been Lin. She's as keen as me to secure the deal and save the company from being sold.'

'So the first that anyone else knew about it was when you told me, Angie and Charles about it after the Ops meeting this morning. And you told us to keep it under our hats.'

They both considered the obvious conclusion. Tom attempted to avoid it. 'Charles did vote for a take-over. But why would he want to sabotage my initiative?'

'He's as straight as a die. And I don't think he'd have the imagination.'

Tom drew a long breath. 'So – Angie.'

Ben hesitated. 'Not necessarily. She might have told Ranjit, and he could have tipped off the journalist without her knowledge.'

Tom considered the suggestion. 'If they really are in league as you've suggested, then that could be the answer.'

Tom looked hard at Ben. He was quick on the uptake. 'You want me to check out her emails, don't you.'

'And her phone calls, if that's possible.'

'It's possible. We monitor the numbers rung from each extension but don't record the conversations. But what about the Data Protection Act? Aren't you asking me to do something illegal?'

'No. Remember that I issued new terms and conditions of employment after the trial of email monitoring. They included phone call monitoring.'

'OK. I'll do it.'

'How long will it take?' Tom looked at his watch. It was past six and most of the staff had left.

'Fifteen minutes or so. You'd like me to do it now?'

'I'd be grateful. And then can I take you out for a meal? To say thanks, not the least for looking after Sally for me?'

Ben went off to his workstation, leaving Tom to appraise his actions of the past few hours. He was torn between congratulating himself for being so decisive and worrying that he had acted rashly. He found solace in thinking of Sally. He dialled her number. Hearing her voice sent a wave of comfort through him.

'Hi Sal. I'm missing you. It was a great weekend.'

'Missing you too. What's the matter? You sound down.'

'Just a tough day at the office.'

'Want to tell me about it?'

'No. You're my release from all the crap I have to deal with.'

'You silver-tongued devil! No one's ever called me a release from crap before. How romantic!'

True to form, talking to Sally was lifting Tom's spirits. 'So how are things up there?'

'Not bad, actually. We've got two of the cottages rented out with last minute bookings. I think people are beginning to think that foot and mouth could be on the wane – there haven't been any cases near here for a while. And I've been contacting other regional tourist associations today about lobbying the Tourism Minister. Getting a good response.'

'Anyhow, I just wanted to hear your voice, and it's done me a wonder of good.'

Tom walked across the now empty floor to Ben's office where he was staring intently at the monitor on his desk. 'Any luck?'

'Not yet. I've been through her sent emails and there's nothing suspicious. Likewise on the phone numbers she called, although that's not to say she couldn't have used her mobile to make calls. Just about to check her in box.'

Tom waited while Ben's fingers flew across the keyboard. After a couple of minutes he shouted 'Bingo!'

'What is it?'

'An email from Ranjit. Sent at 2.15 today. Have a look.'

Tom read.

From: 'Ranjit Patel'
Sent: 11 June 2001 14:15
To: angie.taylor@tiger.com
Subject: Info

Thanks for the info.
Ranjit

'So what does that tell us?' asked Ben.
  'Let's go eat and think it over.'
  'What do you say we go via Angie's office?'
  'Why?'
  'I've got a hunch.'
They entered her office and Ben made straight for a bookshelf where a pile of trade magazines were stored. He sorted through them until he triumphantly flourished a copy of USA Retail Weekly.

At a nearby steak house Ben took mischievous delight in ordering the most expensive fillet on the menu. Tom opted for a sirloin.
  'All we know is that Angie gave Ranjit some information. We don't know what, or even when. Not a lot to go on, is it?'
  Ben agreed. 'Pretty circumstantial, but if it doesn't confirm our suspicions, it certainly doesn't rule them out.'
  'And as for the magazine, wouldn't it be surprising if Angie hadn't got hold of a copy when she was researching the American retail market? There were other US trade mags in the pile.'
  They both considered the evidence carefully. Tom spoke first. 'OK, try this for size. Ranjit's desperate to cash in his investment in Tiger because he's made big losses in the dotcom crash.'
  'Why doesn't he just sell his shares in us?'
  'He knows that he can't unload too many without depressing the share price. He'd get a much better return with a takeover. He knows that Lin and I are dead against selling the company, so he offers Angie some incentive to create a situation whereby we're forced to consider a takeover.'
  'And then you and Lin throw a spanner in the works by coming up with the US initiative. But surely if it comes off, the share price will rise, and his investment will be worth more.'
  'In the long term, yes. But he needs cash now, remember. And if we're right that Angie has been offered money, he won't have it to pay her off until, and only if a takeover is complete. So she

has to look for a way to sabotage the Valco deal. She knows about the confidentiality agreement and when she hears that the Valco board is going to consider our proposal she decides to leak news of our discussions to the trade press. Rather than do it herself and risk it being traced back to her, she gives Ranjit all the ammunition and he, or maybe someone else he's set up, tips off the journalist.'

Ben nodded, testing the theory in his mind, looking for a flaw. 'You'd know this better than me, but wouldn't a journalist have to check out the tip-off to see if it was true?'

'Yes, he would – even for a piece in a column called Rumour Mill. But all he's said is that is that we've been trying to drum up business with retailers. Right back at the beginning of this initiative I asked Angie to issue a press release to the US trade press saying we were looking for a consultancy partner for a major project in the Far East. USA Retail Weekly would certainly have been on the list of recipients.'

'But he also wrote that we're close to a deal.'

'No – he said we could be close to a deal with big retail player. He was calling me to try to get confirmation of it. Provided I didn't specifically deny it, he could still run the story.'

Tom winced. Ben asked what the matter was.

'I've just spotted a flaw. The reason I was able to wriggle out of the situation was that Valco wasn't mentioned by name. Surely Angie would have wanted them to be named. It would have been much more likely to produce the desired effect. Why wasn't the journalist tipped off that it was Valco?'

Ben took some time to come up with possible answer. 'Maybe he was told that it was Valco and decided not to name them. Presumably any trade mag has to keep a retail giant like Valco sweet. Perhaps he didn't want to take the word of whoever tipped him off and didn't want to check it out with Valco.'

Tom fell silent and attacked his steak, deep in thought. Eventually he came to a conclusion. 'I think we're whistling in the wind, Ben. Everything is supposition. We've got no hard evidence against Angie or Ranjit and I can't confront them without it. I'm going to pull Angie off any involvement with the States for the moment, saying that I need her to concentrate on finding new bread and butter business. God knows, we need it right now.'

Tom received a call from Bob Schwartz at lunchtime on Thursday to say that USA Retail Weekly hadn't run the story. Tom thanked his lucky stars and accepted Bob's back-handed compliment when he said that more people like him going around killing stories would put honest journalists out of business.

Shortly afterwards he took a call from Elliott Paul.

'Morning Tom. I see that the story didn't run. I'm very pleased about that. But I think you're going to be even more pleased by what I'm going to tell you. The board is minded to continue to investigate the possibility of expansion into China, and I'd like to accept your invitation to visit Hong Kong.'

Tom punched the air but controlled his voice to reply evenly. 'That's great news Elliott.'

'No promises. It's early days yet, but we've got the go ahead to move this thing on.'

'I understand. But we'll do our best to convince you of the value of our involvement when you join us out East. I'll get So Lin to call you to sort out the arrangements.'

20

The Cathay Pacific jumbo from Heathrow to Hong Kong via Dubai broke through the clouds to reveal a first glimpse of the island, the ranks of towering buildings stacked like tombstones up the steep slope of Victoria Peak. Sally gripped Tom's arm and smiled excitedly at him before pressing her nose to the window to get a better view of the spectacular city towards which the aircraft was hurtling.

Tom felt no need to peer out of a window. He'd experienced the breath-taking approach more times than he cared to remember, including once from a cockpit. In those days Kai Tak airport placed great demands on pilots. Once voted the sixth most dangerous airport in the world, landing at Kai Tak involved flying the plane directly towards the mountainous peak and at the last moment banking sharply to pick a way between skyscrapers and descend within feet of rooftops to land on a short runway jutting out into Victoria Harbour. Tom had always been intrigued as to how the residents of the dilapidated blocks of flats which crowded the path to the final approach managed to live with the wheels of planes constantly passing just inches above the washing lines strung across their roofs.

But on this occasion, they were landing at Hong Kong International Airport which had replaced Kai Tak just three years ago. Constructed on Chep Lap Kok island and a full 30 kilometres from the city centre, it offered a safer but far less exhilarating entry into Hong Kong.

Joining a queue for a taxi, Tom rued the passing of the old airport where vintage Rolls-Royces emblazoned with the logos of the finest hotels on the island would wait to ferry their guests the short distance to the city centre. Not that he'd ever been such a guest – until now. Lin had booked selected wedding guests into the world-class Mandarin Hotel in the heart of the city, Tom and Sally included. Tom had protested, saying that he was also visiting on business and the company should pay for a less expensive hotel, but she insisted that Chong's family were paying for it and would be insulted if he refused.

The taxi drew up at the entrance to the Mandarin and a team of doormen and porters snapped to attention. Tom paid the taxi driver and they walked with porters in attendance to the reception desk at the side of a sumptuous foyer. Tom gave his name and a hovering manager leapt to greet them. He assured them of his utmost service and, after Tom and Sally had shown their passports and checked in, he led them to the lifts. Ascending to the fifteenth floor with the porters in tow, he showed them into a small suite and explained the various lighting, heating and television controls before leaving with a generous tip from Tom.

Sally wandered about, seemingly dumbstruck. She peered through the picture window which afforded a panoramic view across Victoria Harbour with its green and white Star ferries plying their trade. She read the labels on the clutch of expensive cosmetics arrayed on a shelf in the bathroom. She bounced on the king-sized bed in the spacious bedroom. Eventually she returned to the lounge and joined Tom on a long sofa.

'Alright. I give in. I'm impressed. So this is how you live when you're swanning around the world.'

'I stay in good hotels but never anything as good as this. Chong's family must be filthy rich to afford to put us up here.'

'What are we doing today? We've got most of the afternoon and all of the evening before you go to work tomorrow.'

'I feel a little guided tour coming on.'

Tom was in his element, relishing the opportunity to show Sally the city he knew so well. Telling her that she could visit the shopping malls and main streets on her own the next day, he led her into the bustling back streets. A riot of colourful signs in Cantonese and English competed for attention in every direction. Goods for sale spilled out into the narrow thoroughfares with shop owners entreating passers-by to enter their stores. Delivery bikes laden with boxes threaded their way through the crowds and pavement stalls selling every imaginable type of food. Tom pointed out some of the more exotic fare – deep fried pig intestine, snake soup, sea slugs and chicken feet.

Emerging into a main street where gaudily decorated trolley buses trundled past, Tom pointed out a dingy building where he'd rented a room for his first few months in Hong Kong. Nearby were the offices of the newspaper he'd worked for and he suggested a drink in a bar frequented by its journalists. Sure enough, several of his former colleagues were there and they spent a pleasant hour chatting about old times.

In the evening Tom and Sally boarded a Star Ferry for the ten-minute journey across the harbour to Kowloon. As the boat pulled away from the jetty a million lights of the city's dramatic skyline twinkled in the dusk, reflections playing on the rippling water. Sally looked on, spellbound. They found a table at one of Tom's favourite restaurants off the tourist track and they feasted on authentic Cantonese cuisine.

Back at the hotel they lay in bed, the harbour visible through the panoramic window. Sally snuggled up to him. 'Thanks for inviting me. I've had a wonderful day, and it's only the first. I can see why you found it so exciting living here. The Dales can't compare.'

'Maybe if we'd got together fifteen years ago, I would never have left.'

'Fifteen wasted years! We've got a lot of time to make up, slicker' she said sliding her hand down his body.

Tom arrived at Tiger's Hong Kong offices early the following morning and, as was customary on his quarterly visits, he spent the first couple of hours chatting to the staff, meeting new recruits and renewing acquaintance with familiar faces. Mid-morning Lin's senior team gathered in the meeting room where Tom gave a company update, focusing on their performance with existing customers and highlighting the need to need to increase profits from their current lacklustre levels. He finished by stressing how much rested on acquiring the Valco business and urged the team to pull out the stops for the impending arrival of their vice president. Before discussing arrangements for the visit, Tom sat through a presentation prepared by the commercial manager reviewing the Hong Kong office's performance over the last three months and setting out the targets for the following quarter.

They broke for lunch and Tom joined Lin to eat a sandwich in her office.

'Looking forward to the wedding? I really appreciate you working so hard up to the last minute.'

'No problem. Both our families understand that you can't let the little matter of a marriage ceremony get in the way of business. They didn't get so rich by thinking that way.'

'Did Elliott Paul take much persuading to come to the wedding?'

'He was a little taken aback when I first suggested it, but I explained that it's traditional for business associates to be invited to weddings between families like ours and that he would be an honoured guest. The fact that Chong's family would be working with us liaising with the Chinese authorities if we get the contract was an added incentive for him to agree. In fact, Chong and his father have invited Elliot and you to dinner tomorrow evening if you can make it.'

'Of course I can. Presumably it's a business dinner so I can't bring Sally.'

'I don't think so. Men only – even I'm not invited. How's Sally enjoying Hong Kong? I'm looking forward to meeting her.'

'She loves it. And I'm looking forward to meeting Chong. In fact, how about the four of us getting together for a drink or a meal this evening? I know it's short notice, but it would be good to get to know him before we meet for the business dinner.'

'I'd like that. I'll call him.'

They reconvened in the meeting room to thrash out final details for Elliott Paul's visit. Lin handed out an itinerary for everyone to study. He would be flying in early the next day, Thursday, and would be met by a limousine which would take him to the Mandarin where he would also be staying. Tom would get a call warning of his arrival so that he could be in the foyer to greet him. Elliott would be given a couple of hours to freshen up then the limousine would take him and Tom the short distance to Tiger's offices where Tom and Lin would give him a tour. A buffet lunch would be laid on in the meeting room where they would be joined by Chong and his father, Huang Li. Lin would then give a presentation looking at the practical aspects of doing business with the Chinese followed by Chong who would focus on the introductions and support which his family could provide on the mainland. The dinner hosted by Huang Li would take place in the evening. Friday would be taken up by a visit to Shenzhen on the mainland to see at first hand the thriving economy there. Tom would be available to take Elliott for dinner in the evening unless he preferred time to himself. On Saturday he would attend the wedding and fly back to the States on Sunday.

Tom asked to see the presentation which Lin would be giving and suggested a few amendments. They then reviewed a copy of Chong's presentation before Tom brought the meeting to a close and wished everyone good luck for the days ahead. Just before he left for his hotel, Lin was able to confirm that she and Chong would love to meet up for a quick bite and would pick Tom and Sally up at eight.

Sally was lounging in a chair reading a paperback when Tom let himself into their suite. Tom saw that it was Tai-Pan, James Clavell's novel about the British seizure of Hong Kong after the Opium War in the 1840s. She closed the book, jumped up and kissed him. 'Hard day at the office, dear?' she said teasingly.

'Harder than yours by the look of it,' Tom said, nodding at the pile of bulging plastic bags strewn across the sofa. 'I see you've been doing your bit to boost the local economy.'

'Things are so cheap here if you avoid the big international shops. I got something for you.' She sorted through the bags and pulled out a pale blue tailored shirt.

'It's great,' said Tom holding it up against him. 'I'll wear it tonight. Talking of which, we're seeing So Lin and Chong for a quick meal. They're picking us up at eight.'

Sally looked concerned. 'Isn't that going to be a bit awkward – I mean me meeting your ex-wife and you meeting the man she's going to marry.'

'We'd all be meeting up on Saturday at the wedding anyhow. Much better to get to know each other informally beforehand. And you know that Lin and I are good friends now.'

'But what if you don't like him?'

'What if she doesn't like you?' Sally punched his arm. 'She's told me she loves him, and that's good enough for me.'

'And what have you told her?'

Tom recognised that he'd painted himself into a corner. 'I could hardly have told her that I loved you when I haven't told you.' Sally looked crestfallen. 'Yet.' Tom added.

'There's no time like the present,' said Sally in a small voice, her eyes lowered demurely.

Tom caught his breath. Another threshold to cross. He took her hands in his and she looked anxiously up at him. 'I love you, Sally Hardcastle. You're the best thing that's ever happened to me.'

'Really? You're not just saying that because I forced you to?' Tom shook his head. She flung her arms around his neck and whispered in his ear. 'And I love you, Tom Keardon.'

At five minutes to eight they stood waiting at the entrance to the hotel enjoying the evening sunshine. Sally had agonised over what to wear but Tom had assured her that something casual would do. She'd chosen white slacks and a striped top. Tom wore Chinos and his new shirt. Minutes later a dark blue open-topped Bentley Continental pulled up behind two waiting taxis. Chong got out of the driver's seat and went round to open the passenger door for So Lin. As they walked towards them Tom could see that Chong was even taller than Lin, with longish hair, fine features and a self-confident gait. Lin gave Tom a peck on the cheek and turned to introduce her fiancé. Chong shook Tom firmly by the hand and told him he was glad to meet him. In turn Tom introduced Sally.

'I thought we'd pop down to the yacht club. How do you feel about that?' asked Chong.

'Sounds good to me.'

Chong gestured to his car and as they walked towards it he engaged Sally in conversation, asking her how she found Hong Kong. Tom and Lin followed a short distance behind. 'Good looking girl.' Lin murmured conspiratorially.

'Pretty cool guy,' Tom replied.

The short ride in the leathered luxury of the Bentley was notable only for the losing battle which Sally had in the back seat to control her hair as the convertable picked up speed along the waterfront dual carriageway. Tom knew the exclusive Royal Hong Kong Yacht Club as a haven for the rich and privileged in the city. He well remembered going there as a junior reporter to conduct an interview and having been re-fused entry because the shirt he'd been wearing was collarless. There was no such problem this time. The security barrier at the entrance to the club was raised without question on the ap-proach of the Bentley. The car was parked, and they found an outdoor table amongst palm trees at the Bistro on a terrace giving a breath-taking view of the harbour, the water seared red by the setting sun.

With drinks and food ordered and pleasantries exchanged, Tom congratulated Chong. 'I'm very happy for Lin. She's told me how much you mean to her.' Lin and Chong gave each other affectionate glances. 'Tell me, where did you two meet?'

Chong laughed. 'Actually when we were young kids. Our families knew each other well. They did quite a lot of business together.'

Sally chimed in. 'We met as toddlers as well! We grew up together on adjoining farms. But how did you meet this time around?'

'Here at the yacht club,' said Lin. 'A mutual friend invited me to come and crew on his yacht.'

'And you made a complete pig's ear of it,' Chong said. Tom wondered if Lin had been schooling Chong in her favourite subject of English idioms. 'I had to take personal charge of you to avoid you sending us on the rocks or falling overboard. And I rather enjoyed it!' They swapped further warm looks.

'What about you two,' Lin asked.

'We met up again this Spring when my father died and I went home for the first time in years,' said Tom. 'Sally was a tower of strength in helping me to cope. We've only been together a few weeks.'

'I'm really looking forward to the wedding ceremony,' said Sally. 'I was reading about Chinese weddings in one of the guidebooks. Is yours going to be very traditional?'

'A mixture of old and new, I suppose,' said Lin. 'Our parents wanted it to be very traditional, but we've picked and mixed the customs we like and given some of the weirder ones a miss.

For example, a red sedan chair used to be sent to the bride's house and she'd be carried to the groom's family home accompanied by servants and a band with flutes and gongs. We thought that would be a bit over the top so Chong's sending a limo.'

'I read about brides having their hair brushed for good luck. Are you doing that?'

'Yes, my Mum was insistent. Actually, it's a lovely romantic idea. I have to sit in front of a moonlit window and have my hair brushed four times. The first brush is supposed to represent lasting good qualities, the second a harmonious relationship right into old age, the third for children and grandchildren and the last brush for prosperity and a lengthy marriage.'

'That's the mistake we made,' said Tom, smiling. 'No hair brushing!'

Sally admonished him. 'Tom! That's not very nice!'

Lin was unconcerned. 'Don't worry – he never was very romantic.'

'What will you be wearing?' asked Sally.

Before Lin could respond, Chong broke in. 'This sounds like girl talk to me.' He turned to Tom. 'Why don't we leave the ladies for a while? Let me show you my yacht.'

They strolled down to the marina and Chong pointed out a 60-foot ocean-going yacht, bobbing gently on the swell. Tom made polite comments about it but was more interested in talking about Lin.

'You're a very lucky man,' he said. 'She's a beautiful person and she deserves more than I could give her. I'm sure she'll be very happy with you.'

'I hope so.' Chong replied. 'She's told me a lot about you and she still speaks fondly of you. I guess it just wasn't to be. Mixing cultures is always difficult.'

'And that's why I'm happy that she met you. You share the same background.'

'Is that why you're now with Sally? East, West, home's best – isn't that what they say?'

'I hadn't really thought of it like that. We come from the same home, but we live in completely different worlds now. She's back on her farm while I live in London and fly all over the world. Different cultures as well, in a way. If we're going to last, then one of us will have to give up what we do. Right now we're in the first flush of being together but sooner or later reality will bite.'

Chong decided against commenting, somewhat uneasy with the depth of the conversation, and chose instead to suggest that they returned as the food would be ready.

As they approached the table a gale of laughter came from their partners. The girls appeared to be getting on famously. The food had indeed arrived and as they ate the chatter turned to the six-week honeymoon cruise which Chong had planned. They would be taking the yacht and its crew across the South China Sea to island hop in the Philippines.

As they walked back to the car after the meal, Lin asked Sally if she'd like to join her for drinks at her apartment the following evening when Tom and Chong would be at their business dinner.

'It's not a hen night, as such,' she said. 'We won't be getting up to any of the things I've heard happen in the UK – just a few girlfriends and relatives coming round. I'd love you to join us.'

Sally was flattered to be asked but protested that she didn't want to impose. Lin insisted and the arrangements were made.

Dropped off at their hotel, Tom and Sally were happy to fall into bed for an early night to try to sleep off their jet lag. 'I can see what you saw in her,' Sally murmured sleepily. Tom was already asleep.

21

Tom got the call to warn him of Elliott Paul's imminent arrival soon after 9 a.m. and went down to the hotel lobby to wait for him. A short while later a gleaming Mercedes limousine with blacked out windows pulled up at the entrance. The red-coated doorman leapt to open the rear door and the vice-president emerged, shading his eyes against the fierce morning sunshine. Tom came forward to greet him.

'Welcome to Hong Kong, Elliott. I hope you had a good flight.'

'Hello Tom. A long one, but I managed to get some sleep.'

'That's good, because we've got a packed agenda for you and you'll need all the energy you've got.'

He ushered Elliott to the reception desk and introduced him to the waiting manager who guided the new guest through the check-in procedure. Walking to the lifts with luggage porters in tow, Tom took his leave, telling Elliott that he would give him time to settle in and would see him in the lobby at eleven.

Back in the suite, Sally was immersed in a guidebook. 'Have you decided what you're doing today?' Tom asked, sitting down beside her and putting his arm around her shoulders.

She turned back through the pages. 'I'm tempted by the Jade Market but I'll only end up spending more money, so I'm going to take the ferry across to Kowloon and go here.' She pointed to a page featuring the Hong Kong Museum of History. 'I'm really getting into Tai-Pan and it's got me hooked on the history of this place.'

'I'm ashamed to say that in all the years I was here I never went there. Too tied up in current affairs rather than historical ones, I suppose.'

'Well I'll tell you all about it. Big day for you?'

'Yes – gotta impress the VP. But I don't have to see him again for an hour or a half or so. Any ideas on how we could fill in the time? I fell asleep on you last night.'

Sally closed the book and pretended to think deeply. 'OK, I've got an idea. Follow me.'

Tom took the lift down to the lobby to meet Elliott hoping he didn't look too flushed from the hot shower he'd only just stepped out of. The black Mercedes was waiting and it whisked them to Tiger's offices where So Lin welcomed them at reception. They took coffee in her office before she led them on a tour of the building. Various team members had been primed to explain their roles to Elliott. He met the economists who monitored the stock markets and commercial activity in China, tracking the relentless shift of state-owned companies into privatised enterprises. The political team showed him how the state-controlled press and media were continuously analysed for signs of liberalisation which would open up commercial opportunities. The web content experts demonstrated how the gathered intelligence was converted into simple-to-access and understand online pages. Elliott showed a keen interest throughout, asking searching questions and occasionally testing the quality of information by asking for specific figures or trends.

When they entered the meeting room where the buffet lunch had been laid out Lin's heads of department were already in attendance along with Chong and his father. Tom first introduced Elliott to Chong, explaining that he represented the associates they proposed working with in Mainland China. Chong in turn introduced his father. Huang Li bowed deeply and greeted Elliott in deeply accented English. Unlike Chong who wore a sharply tailored Western suit, Li was dressed in a high-collared grey jacket which wouldn't have looked out of place in a line-up of the Central Politburo of the Communist Party of China. So Lin then introduced Elliott to her senior team.

Conversations struck up amongst the various groups and Tom found himself beside Huang Li. 'Thought I'd dress up for the occasion, old boy,' he said amiably. Tom did a double take. The accent had all but disappeared. 'I always find that it's good to play up the stereotypes with the Yanks. Give them what they expect. My son can put on the modern face of China – I can appear to be the link with our old-fashioned friends across the border. Good to meet you by the way. I've heard good things about you.'

Tom grinned. 'And I'm delighted to meet you. Can I thank you for putting us up at the Mandarin? It really is enormously generous.'

'My pleasure. The least I can do for Lin's friends. Now tell me, how can I help you to close this deal with Valco? We're very excited about the prospect. There are fortunes to be made for all.'

'At this stage it's all about instilling confidence, I think. They're not going to enter into a partnership lightly and they'll be looking at other potential partners to see if they can offer them more than we can. We just need to prove to them that we're their best bet.'

'Understood. Well, let's see if I can help.' He made a beeline for Elliott.

Tom soon found himself alongside Lin. 'Your future father-in-law's an old devil, isn't he? Putting on that old Chinese duffer act when he's really sharp.'

'As a cookie.' Lin added. 'Thanks for teaching me the phrase. Yes, I love him to bits.'

'Going well so far?'

'So far. I was really pleased with the team. I think they impressed Elliott.'

The buffet was cleared away and all took their seats for the presentations. Tom rose to his feet. 'Elliott. I hope that this morning's tour of our offices and the chance to chat with some of the senior members of our team has given you an insight into the way we operate. This afternoon we want to map out the route we think will need to be taken to achieve our common goal of establishing Valco supermarkets across China. I'd like to hand over to So Lin.'

Lin proceeded to make her presentation with characteristic fluency. Chong then took the reins, making a convincing case for his family business to be the ones to help Valco deal with the authorities across the border.

They drew to a close mid-afternoon. Elliott expressed his thanks and declared himself to be very impressed with the quality of the presentations. Tom accompanied him back to the hotel and arranged the time for them to meet up to go to dinner.

Sally returned to the hotel suite shortly after Tom, laden with more plastic bags.

'I thought you were trying to avoid spending money,' said Tom.

'The museum was fascinating but then I went looking for a few gifts to take home. I really got into bargaining – I knocked almost everything I bought down to about half the original price.'

Tom knew that a 50% discount was the least to expect when haggling with a Chinese shopkeeper but didn't want to spoil her obvious pleasure.

'What did you get?'

Sally began to retrieve the presents from their bags. 'I got this for my Mum,' she said displaying a small jade figure of a dragon mounted on a rosewood stand, 'and a selection of Chinese teas for Dad. Might be a struggle to persuade him to try them, but the tins are nice. He can always fill them up with the Yorkshire tea he's always drinking. This is for your Mum – it's a tablecloth with beautiful embroidery, and I think this is perfect for Sid.' She held up a Chinese mug with a lid and a tea strainer.

'Nothing for yourself?'

'I couldn't resist this.' It was a traditional Chinese brush painting of fruit and flowers flanked by delicately drawn calligraphy. The colours were vibrant against an off-white background.

'I'm going to hang it in my cottage to always remind me of this trip.'

'It's lovely.'

'How was your day?'

'Don't think it could have gone better. The team put on a great show for Elliott.'

'Well I hope tonight goes well too.'

Tom put Sally into a taxi to take her to Lin's flat and shortly after rendezvoused with Elliott. Huang Li had invited them to a restaurant on Victoria Peak and rather than drive up in the limousine Tom had suggested that they take the funicular railway the 400 metres to the top. They walked the short distance to the lower terminus on Garden Road, Tom chatting about his time living in Hong Kong. He pointed out the imposing façade of Government House, the seat of British Colonial rule for 142 years until the Chief Executive of Hong Kong had taken over residence on the handover of the dependency to the Chinese just four years previously.

The doors of the Peak Tram swung shut, the cables tightened, and the dark red vehicle began its lumbering climb, initially threading its way under flyovers and between tower blocks, brushing the overhanging trees as it trundled upwards. For much of the journey the view towards Victoria Harbour was obscured by the wall of city skyscrapers, but towards the end a spectacular vista across the water to the Kowloon peninsula emerged. Tom was able to point out various landmarks and did his best to answer Elliot's many questions about the geography of the area spread out before them.

The blacked-out chauffeured Mercedes was waiting for them at the upper terminus to take them the last 150 metres up the peak. Tom marvelled at the efficiency of the clockwork-like operation which Chong and Lin had set up. They arrived at the exclusive restaurant and were ushered onto a private terrace. Huang Li and his son were already there, Chong dressed casually in a beige linen suit but Li resplendent in a purple high-necked tunic brocaded in gold. He bowed deeply and, with

Chinese inflection restored, exclaimed 'Welcome to our honoured guests. It gives my son and me great pleasure that you could join us.'

'The pleasure is ours,' said Elliott, bowing uncertainly in return.

'Tonight,' said Li, beaming, 'I have laid on a traditional banquet which I hope will be to your taste. Our great philosopher Confucius, who as you know had a saying for just about everything, held that diet and lovemaking are the primal needs of every human being. The latter I would hesitate to provide but I can promise you the very best of our cuisine. Can I offer you an aperitif to begin with?'

Li clicked his fingers and two hovering waiters approached bearing trays laden with drinks in delicate porcelain bowls. Chong spoke to Elliott. 'It's our tradition that the host chooses the wine and liquors to be drunk at a banquet. I think you'll enjoy these, but of course if you would prefer something else – a whisky or a beer perhaps – we would be happy to provide them.'

'No way,' said Elliott. 'I want to experience this as it should be.' He took a proffered bowl.

They stood chatting and taking in the view at the edge of the terrace in the evening sunshine until Li called them to the table laid with an array of cold dishes. They took their seats and Li raised his glass. 'We always begin a banquet with a toast. Gentlemen, please raise your glasses. To partnership, to success in business, and to prosperity!'

They drank the toast. Tom knew from having attended formal banquets in the past that it would be bad form to start eating immediately. As he waited, Chong took it on himself to guide Elliott through the meal. 'After the toast we traditionally engage in what is called the ceremony of beginning. The degree of politeness a guest shows increases the longer he waits to start eating, but in this case we would not be offended if you were to start. We always begin with an even number of cold dishes, usually eight, or in this case, ten. We have a long way to go, so please don't feel that you have to taste each one.'

Chong named each dish in turn and showed Elliott how to use chopsticks. Elliott found them difficult to get to grips with but refused the offer of a fork, insisting that he wanted to persevere.

Shark's fin soup followed, served by Li as the host, as was the custom. It was accompanied by further toasts, to international co-operation, to good luck and, from Elliott, to the generosity of his hosts. Further courses followed – decorative meats, lobster, Peking duck with scallion brushes, scallops and chicken – interspersed with a variety of sweets. Tom paid elaborate compliments to the food throughout, knowing that custom required it of him.

There was a lull in the supply of dishes and thinking that the meal was at an end, Elliott professed himself to be full.

Chong jumped in. 'I'm sorry to have to tell you this, Elliott, but we still have one final course. Banquets always finish with a dish with which the host pays his respects to the guest of honour. I'm afraid that we'll have to ask you to take at least a mouthful.'

A waiter approached and laid a whole fish on the table, its head pointed to Elliott. Elliott's eyes widened, but gamely took a small portion and did his best to appear pleased to eat it.

With the plates cleared away Li pushed back his chair and smiled benignly at his guests. 'Elliott, I congratulate you on having survived the ordeal I've visited upon you.'

Elliott protested, insisting that he had never enjoyed a meal so much.

'I'm honoured that you found it to your liking. Now gentlemen, may I suggest that we take our chairs to the edge of the terrace and indulge in two of my favourite vices. For all the wonders that Chinese cuisine can offer, nothing compares with the Western tradition of following a meal with brandy and cigars.'

They sat in a semi-circle overlooking the lights of the skyscrapers below which mirrored the myriad stars burning in a clear black sky. Waiters brought out a tray of generously-filled brandy snifters and a box of oversized Havanas. Tom and Chong refused the cigars, but Li and Elliott completed the rituals of cutting and lighting and were soon happily puffing away.

Li peered through drifting smoke at Elliott. 'I wonder if you would indulge an old man by listening to a story. It's the tale of my own life but also that of my country. Perhaps if you hear it, you will understand why I am so keen to work with you and your company to bring further prosperity to China.'

Chong caught Tom's eye and raised his eyebrows as if to say here he goes again, but Tom was fascinated to hear what was to come, as was Elliott.

Li settled into his chair and stared out into the night. 'I was born in 1930 in a village perhaps two hundred miles north of here. My parents were poor farmers, eking out a living from a small herd of cattle. It was three years after the start of a civil war between the Communists and the Nationalists which was to continue on and off for more than 20 years. They both wanted to unite China and break the pattern of grinding poverty in which so many peasants lived, but because they had different ideologies millions were to die at the hands of their own countrymen. When I was seven the two sides side formed a fragile alliance to fight the common enemy of Japan who invaded the North. The Japanese employed what they called the three-all policy - kill all, burn all and destroy all. Millions more died, victims not only of the Japanese but of starvation.'

Li paused to take a sip of his brandy and a draw of his cigar. 'When the Second World War ended and the Japanese were defeated, the civil war resumed. I was in my teens and I joined the Nationalist forces. Not through any firmly held ideology - more because my province was a stronghold of Nationalism. I fought without distinction until the victorious Communists proclaimed the People's Republic of China in 1949. Facing the prospect of persecution, I fled here to Hong Kong and in time prospered, building the successful business which I now lead. But across the border, my family and relatives suffered under the misguided rule of the communists. Mao Tse Tung's Great Leap Forward, far from transforming the economic conditions, resulted in the deaths of perhaps 45 million from starvation.

The Cultural Revolution resulted in the persecution and displacement of any who were considered traitors to the class struggle. It was only after the death of Mao that government control over people's lives began to be loosened and China took the first tentative steps towards the mixed economy that exists today.'

A waiter approached with the bottle of brandy offering to top them up but all declined. Li turned to address Elliott directly. 'So you see, my friend, for most of the twentieth century China was beset by conflict, poverty and famine. Communism there, and in all its shades in other countries around the world, has been shown to have been a well-intentioned but misguided experiment. Its battle with capitalism has been lost and while capitalism has many faults, being the cause of mass starvation is not to my knowledge one of them. I've always had a nagging guilt about abandoning my family in the village to save my own skin all those years ago. Call me an old fool, but that guilt might be somewhat assuaged if in few years' time I could return to my village in my dotage and take a group of my relatives to a nearby Valco supermarket to buy them a weekly shop, knowing that I had had a hand in making it possible.'

It was Tom's turn to raise his eyebrows. Such a banal ending to a moving story would surely expose Li's calculated intentions in telling it. But it seemed to have had the desired effect on Elliott.

'Sir, if it comes about, I'm sure my company would be honoured to feel that it had helped to improve the living conditions of the people of your country.'

Li brought the evening to a close. 'We have a heavy schedule tomorrow, gentlemen. We leave for the border early so maybe we should depart.'

Elliott was effusive in his thanks and shook Li and Chong firmly by the hand.

'I won't be joining you tomorrow,' said Chong. 'I'm sure you'll understand that I need to attend to other things on the day before my wedding.'

'Of course. I appreciate the time that both you and Lin have given me today.' Elliott turned to Tom. 'A thought – Lin tells me that you've brought your girlfriend with you to attend the wedding. Rather than for her to miss the opportunity to spend a day in China, I'd be happy for her to join us tomorrow – that's if there's room for her.' Chong assured him that there would be. Tom was able to say that he was sure that she'd be delighted to join them.

As they walked to the waiting car, Huang Li murmured to Tom out of Elliott's earshot. 'You don't think I overdid it, do you, old boy?'

Tom smiled broadly. 'Didn't Confucius also say that you should study the past if you would define the future?'

'I do believe he did. Although he may not have been thinking about the development of a chain of supermarkets when he said it.'

Sally was in bed reading Tai-Pan when Tom returned. He flopped down on the bed beside her. 'How was it at Lin's?'

'Lovely. A real girly evening. Lin's got some lovely friends and relatives and they really made me feel at home.'

'What did you talk about?'

'Weddings mostly. And men. It must be the same the whole world over when girls get together.'

'What about you?'

'I've eaten the most fabulous banquet. In fact, I don't think I'll be able to eat another thing before we have to do it all again at the wedding. And Huang Li was extraordinary. He made an impassioned speech about the horrors of Communist rule in China then all but implied that it was Valco's humanitarian duty to save the Chinese people from further famine by opening supermarkets. It seemed pretty contrived to me. Not to mention in questionable taste.'

'How did Elliott react?'

'He seemed to buy it.'

'Everything on track then?'

'Seems to be.' Tom turned on the bed to look at Sally. 'Have you decided what you're doing tomorrow?'

'Yep. All sorted.' She pointed to the guidebook on the bedside table, pages marked with slips of paper.

'I don't suppose you'd like to come to China instead, would you?' said Tom nonchalantly.

'What?'

'Elliott suggested that you join us.'

'What – on your day in China?'

'The very same.'

'But won't I need a visa or something?'

'You'll be able to get a day's tourist pass at the border.'

'Nah, don't think I'll bother.'

It was Tom's turn to exclaim 'What?'

'Only joking, slicker. I'd love to,' and she threw her arms round his neck to kiss him.

22

Tom introduced Sally to Elliott when they met up the following morning and they walked to a waiting black Mercedes which this time was of the stretch variety. Huang Li emerged along with a sober-suited and muscular Chinese man who he introduced as a trusted aide. The aide held the rear door open for them and returned to the front passenger seat alongside the chauffeur. Elliott sat beside Li in the rear seats with Tom and Sally facing them.

'Tell me more about where we're going today, Tom,' Elliott requested as the car sped across the Western Harbour Crossing.

'We're going just over the border into Shenzen. Li was talking last night about China taking first steps towards economic liberalisation after Mao died in 1976. Deng Xiaoping took over and started introducing reforms, most significantly the setting up of Special Economic Zones with tax incentives for foreign investment and greater freedom for international trade. Shenzen was the first zone, probably chosen because of its proximity to Hong Kong. It was rapidly transformed from little more than a village into one of the fastest growing cities in the world. Now it's home to a major stock exchange, high-tech companies and a massive container port to export all the goods which are manufactured in the province.'

The limousine sped along the Kowloon waterfront before entering a tunnel through the hills. Sally was keen to make an impression and appear more than a token girlfriend. She asked Elliott if it was his first visit to the Far East.

'Sure thing. I've been to Europe and South America, but this is all new to me.'

'Me too. I'm finding it fascinating. I've been reading up on the history and there were as many American traders here in the 1840s as there were British, all competing for the lucrative trade with China. If things had worked out differently Hong Kong might have become an American territory. I suppose the Brits were a little more ruthless. They had plenty of experience of exploiting colonies, including the States of course.'

'But you Americans got your own back eventually,' said Li. 'The sun set on the British Empire and the USA became the pre-eminent global power. I don't wish to suggest that your days are numbered but the progress you'll see we've made today may give you pause for thought.'

Tom was concerned that the turn of conversation might suggest to Elliott that China would be presenting a challenge to America's position in the world. 'That's not to say that we think China presents a threat. On the contrary, our analysis is that the days of any country being able to act solely in its own commercial interests have passed. We're becoming interdependent. The US is in danger of becoming too reliant on cheap imports from China. Now's the time to redress the balance by selling to China the expertise which it needs and which you can provide.'

As they approached the Chinese border a long line of vehicles and a straggling queue of pedestrians came into view. They pulled up and Li pressed a button to lower the glass partition to the front seats. He spoke to his aide in quick-fire Cantonese before turning to Tom, Sally and Elliott. 'I hope it might to be possible to expedite a speedy crossing. Could you give me your passports, please?' He collected them and passed them to the aide who walked away to the border. A few minutes later, he returned with a uniformed Chinese official who checked their passport photographs and nodded them on. The car overtook the queue and was waved through the border. Li looked pleased with himself and with a certain smugness commented that it was good to have friends in high places.

The skyscrapers of Shenzen came into view and Elliott craned his neck to get a better look. 'Jeez! You're telling me this was a village just twenty-odd years ago? It looks like downtown Chicago!'

Tom had done his homework and was able to reel off a stream of facts. 'It's said that over the last decade they were building one high rise a day and a boulevard every three. There are a dozen skyscrapers over 650 feet, and one is in the top ten of the world's tallest buildings. Over three million population and one of the biggest provincial GDPs in China.'

'It's a matter of great pride that we've been able to grow so fast,' Li added, 'but I don't want you to run away with the idea that the whole of China is like this. Most of our vast land will always remain rural. But urbanisation is gathering pace. All of our cities and towns are growing and that's where your opportunity lies.'

They drew into the car park of a large supermarket. 'Shall we take a look at the local competition?' said Tom.

Elliott hesitated. 'Love to. But I don't want to go in looking like part of a delegation. Equally I don't want to be on my own. Tom, could I borrow your lovely lady? That way we would look like a couple of tourists rather than an inspection team.'

Elliott took off his tie to add to the illusion and he and Sally marched off to the entrance, Sally slipping her arm into his and chatting away happily.

Tom and Li got out of the car and sat on a bench in the sunshine. The aide and the chauffeur stood by the car lighting up cigarettes.

'I hear your company's up for sale, Tom.'

Tom was initially startled but then realised that Lin must have discussed it with Chong, who would certainly have told his father.

'It's true. It's not what I wanted, or Lin, but our investors are running out of patience to get a return. We were forced into considering a takeover. I should have told you rather than leaving it for you to find out.'

'No matter, Tom, but you should have realised that I would get to know. It does put the importance of this deal into sharp focus. I should tell you that Chong has sounded me out about the possibility of buying your company for Lin's sake.'

'And what have you said?'

'My heart tells me that I should consider it if my son wants it for his new wife. My head tells me that I haven't amassed a fortune by listening to my heart.'

Tom felt inadequate. Out of his depth. Such was his commitment to sealing the Valco deal that he had been in denial about the possibility of failure and having to come to terms with throwing in the towel and accepting a takeover. Could Li be some sort of lifeline? He considered his reply very carefully.

'I wouldn't wish or expect you to make a decision on anything but sound business principles. At the moment I'm feeling confident about the prospects of securing the Valco business. If we do, then my company will be back on an even keel and you'll stand to benefit as well. If not, and a takeover becomes inevitable, I, and I'm sure Lin, could think of no one else rather than you I would be happier to have as the new owner.'

Li rose from the bench and paced around in thought. He returned to sit beside Tom. 'I'm an old man, Tom, and maybe the time has come to let my heart speak. If it's what Chong and

Lin desire, then maybe I should think of it as a wedding present to them. I'll ask my team to open negotiations with whoever is representing you. No promises, no guarantees you understand. I hope, of course, that we catch this American fish so that it will not be necessary.'

Elliott and Sally were approaching, laden with bags and conversing merrily. They stood to greet them. 'So much for all this talk of international trade,' said Sally breezily. 'I've helped Elliott to do something far more important and buy presents for his family.'

'Yes – I can look forward to a good reception when I get home,' said Elliott smiling at Sally, seemingly charmed by her. 'I'm terrible at buying gifts – always more interested in pricing, packaging and display. Sally's been my saviour.'

They drove to a restaurant on one of the main boulevards for lunch. In contrast to the traditional fare of the previous evening it offered Western-style bistro food.

Securely seated in a booth, Tom asked for Elliot's take on the supermarket he had visited.

'I was impressed by the range of goods, but the layout and the lack of marketing was appalling. They could double their profits if they employed some of the basic techniques we use. Fresh food near the entrance, shelf position, special offers and the like.'

'And the customer service was pretty poor,' Sally added. 'Maybe the language problem and the fact we're foreigners didn't help, but no one seemed in the slightest bit concerned to help us.'

'But getting the marketing and customer service right is only part of the problem,' said Elliott. 'Sourcing suppliers and organising distribution are the keys to building a successful retail business.'

'I don't see that distribution will be a problem in the coming years,' Tom replied. 'China has amassed huge reserves through its exports and they're ploughing them into a major programme of investment in roads and railways.'

'And as for suppliers,' Li added, 'the days of everything being state-controlled have passed. There's a new wave of entrepreneurs we can put you in touch with who are capitalising on the new opportunities. They're organising farmers and producers and they'd jump at the chance to work with you.'

After lunch Tom suggested that they spent some time walking around the city. Li declined, saying that he would rest in the car, but Tom, Sally and Elliott set off with the muscular aide walking at a discreet distance behind them, on hand to help with any problems they might encounter. Elliott soon transformed from businessman to tourist. After having been suitably impressed by the business district he asked to see a street market. The aide, who it turned out spoke excellent English, guided them to Jiadele Huimin market where Tom was able to provide a running commentary on the goods on display and school Elliott in the art of bargaining. Elliott tested his newfound knowledge by bartering for a pair of antique Mandarin vases which took his fancy. He asked the vendor for his best price and, following Tom's advice offered 10%. The price was immediately halved. In an exchange of offers and reductions the vendor stuck at 35%. Elliott looked at Tom who gestured for him to walk away. 'Are you sure this will work?' he asked.

Before Tom could answer the vendor came running after them and invited them to take tea with him. 'Bad idea,' murmured Tom, 'it'll just give him more time to wear you down. He wants you to think of him as a friend.' They refused the offer of tea whereupon the vendor reduced his price by a further 5%.

After a lengthy stand-off from both parties they finally agreed on 30% of the original price. Elliott fished out a large wad of dollars, but Tom held out his hand to stop him.

'I wouldn't advise paying in foreign currency – he'll give you a terrible exchange rate. None of us have any Yuan but maybe our minder might be able to help. If you give him dollars, I'll see if he can get the right amount of Yuan. While we're waiting, perhaps we can take up the offer of tea.'

Tom called the aide who'd been hovering in the background and explained what was required. Elliott gave him a suitable amount of dollars and he went off in search of a money changer. The vendor brewed up the tea and they sat drinking it while the vases were wrapped. After a few minutes the aide returned with Chinese currency and a number of dollars which he returned to Elliott, apologising that he had not been able to get the best rate in a short time, but confident that it would certainly be better than the vendor would offer.

Walking back to the car Elliott seemed to be in high spirits. 'Doing business here is certainly different from the States. We have plenty of training courses on negotiating skills, but I don't think they would have helped me much there. Thanks for getting me a good deal – I can see how important local knowledge is.'

Back in Hong Kong Tom, Sally and Elliott were dropped at the hotel and they gave their thanks to Li who told them he was looking forward to welcoming them to the wedding the following day. Elliott refused Tom's offer to meet for a meal that evening but agreed to a drink before they parted. They ordered cocktails in the M bar high in the building with sweeping views of Victoria Harbour.

'So,' said Tom, 'from now on we can relax and enjoy the rest of our time here. But may I ask for your reaction to everything we've been able to show you. I'd like to get an idea of whether you'll be interested in continuing to work towards a partnership.'

Elliott looked out of the window, choosing his words. 'I'm impressed by your operation, Tom. And Huang Li seems to be quite a player. Let me level with you. I like what I see, and I could be happy to business with you. But the decision isn't mine. My board is used to dealing with much bigger companies than Tiger.com and I can't promise that they won't be looking elsewhere for support if we decide to move into China. We're also concerned about the viability of your company. We've been checking you out and we're aware that you've retained PMJK to look for possible buyers. It doesn't inspire confidence.'

Tom looked crestfallen. Sally came to his defence. 'But you still decided to make this trip. Why would you do that if you didn't think Tiger might be the partners you're looking for?'

Elliott regarded Sally with respect. 'A good point, little lady. As I said, I'd like to do business with you. I'm willing to give you the benefit of the doubt at this stage.'

Tom spoke with as much confidence as he could muster. 'I appreciate that you have doubts about us. Our company does have problems. We're only three years old and we've yet to make the level of profits which our investors have been looking for. But securing a contract with Valco would make them keep faith with us. I can assure you that we'll do everything in our power to come up with the support service you need.'

'I'm sure you will. Tom. But all I can promise right now is that I'll keep faith with you for the time being. We'll see what develops.'

Elliott finished his drink and took his leave.

'Little lady!' Sally exploded when Elliott had left the bar. 'Patronising bastard! Is that all he thinks of me?'

'I think not. I'm sure it was just a turn of phrase. You two seemed to have got on famously. You've been a great help today. I think he might fancy you.'

'Now you're being patronising.' She tossed her head and stared out at the view.

Tom felt an overwhelming need to be close to her. 'I've gone a whole day without telling you I love you.'

She continued to stare through the window but then a smile played on her lips. Without turning to him she said, 'Do you?'

'Probably'

She swung round to confront him, her eyes blazing. 'Probably!'

Tom was grinning. 'Maybe definitely then.'

She shook her head in exasperation.

'Alright. I give in. I love you, Sal.'

She melted. 'Well I probably love you too, slicker. But don't count your chickens. This little lady's no pushover.'

23

A fusillade of firecrackers fizzed and snapped to herald the arrival of Chong and Lin at Huang Li's palatial estate. The wedding guests were gathered on a long seafront terrace festooned with brightly coloured banners waving gently in the warm sea breeze. The white Rolls Royce in which Chong had been driven to Lin's parents' house to pick up his bride to be had been decorated with pink ribbons and an elaborate arrangement of paper flowers covered its long bonnet. Lin was dressed in a red Qun Gua, a beaded high-collared tunic over a floor length skirt. Both were exquisitely embroidered with a golden phoenix and dragons. On her head she wore a tiara-like headdress of gilded silver decorated with feathers and pearls. Chong was less elaborately clothed in a black silk coat over a dark blue robe also decorated with a dragon, and a black cap with red tassels.

They approached the terrace through an avenue of flowers to the sound of clapping from the guests and the music of a band playing flutes, gongs and drums. Tom and Sally were standing with Elliott towards the back of the crowd, Sally on tiptoe to catch a glimpse of the couple. An iron basin containing glowing charcoal had been placed at the entrance to the terrace and Lin leapt over it. 'Why's she doing that?' Elliott asked of Tom.

'It's supposed to bring prosperity and keep evil spirits away,' said Tom. 'I've been to a few Chinese weddings and almost everything that happens is steeped in symbolism. I'll try to explain it as we go along.' Sally caught Tom's eye and gave him a knowing look, aware that he had spent half an hour with her comprehensive guidebook the previous evening mugging up on Chinese weddings.

The bride and groom walked past the welcoming guests and approached their families who were seated on a row of ornate chairs. Li and his wife were at the centre beside Lin's parents. On either side relatives were seated, the oldest nearest the middle, the youngest out on the flanks.

'This is the actual ceremony coming up,' Tom whispered. 'More of a ritual really, but it's equivalent to our wedding vows. They'll bow three times, once to heaven and earth, then to their parents and that tablet you can see which honours their ancestors, and finally to each other.'

They watched, captivated.

'It'll be the tea ceremony next,' Tom said softly. Chong and Lin took bowls from a nearby table, bowed to Chong's parents, and offered them with both hands.

'It's a sweet tea which contains Lotus seeds and two red dates. The Chinese set great store by homophones, words which sound the same but have different meanings. Lotus sounds like year, seed like child and date like early. The tea should help the newlyweds to have children early in their marriage and have them every year.'

'No wonder China's got the largest population in the world,' said Elliott flippantly.

'I think you'll find it had more to do with Maoism. Population growth was encouraged, and it almost doubled under his leadership. It's all changed now. One of the reforms Deng Xiaoping introduced was the one child per family policy. It's estimated to have reduced growth by around 300 million since it was introduced.'

'Why haven't Lin's parents been served tea?' Sally asked.

'They'll have already been served tea by Lin at their home before she left. It's done there so that she can give them her respect and thank them for raising her. What they're doing now is serving tea to all of Chong's relatives in order of seniority.'

'And what are those red envelopes they're being given in return,' Elliott queried.

'They're Lai See which means lucky. Red is a lucky colour and they're stuffed with money which represents a wish for good fortune.'

The tea ceremony ended, and the families and guests mingled. They were approached by So Lin's brother. 'Tom! How are you?'

'Wei! I'm fine, and you're looking well.' Tom turned to make introductions. 'This is Wei, Lin's brother – meet Sally, a good friend of mine and Elliott who's over from the States. We're hoping to do business with him.'

'Pleased to meet you. What a wedding! It's a bit different from when you married Lin.' Elliott did a double take and looked at Tom with curiosity. It was not lost on Wei. 'Sorry, have I spoken out of turn?'

'Not at all,' Tom reassured him. 'Sally knows I was married to Lin. I hadn't told Elliott. Yes, Lin and I had a simple Western-style civil ceremony - with no Lai See!'

'Well it's great to see you. How long are you here for? It would be good to meet up.'

'Flying back tomorrow I'm afraid. But next time I'm over – I come every three months or so.'

'I'll look forward to it. Nice to meet you,' he said to Sally and Elliott and took his leave.

Elliott watched him go then turned to Tom. 'I take my hat off to you, Tom. I could no more work with my ex-wife than fly to the moon. You two seem to get on pretty well.'

'We still great friends. If anything, we get on better profession-ally than we ever did when we were married. She's a great girl.'

'Certainly is, and a bright one. But don't you feel a bit odd being here?'

'A bit strange, perhaps. But Lin insisted that I'd be welcome so I'm happy to be here. Talking of which, I really ought to pay my respects to Lin's parents. Would you excuse Sally and me for a moment?'

Tom found them still sitting on the chairs where the ceremony had taken place. He hung back waiting for them to finish a conversation until Lin's mother saw him and beckoned him over. Close up she looked older than when Tom had last seen her, but she still had the twinkle in her eye which he remembered so well. 'Tom! How nice to see you!'

'And it's good to see you.' He gave her a peck on the cheek and shook her husband's hand. 'We just wanted to say thank-you for allowing us to come to the wedding. This is Sally by the way, my girlfriend.'

Sally bowed. 'Thank-you. It's a wonderful experience for me.'

Lin's mother looked her up and down and seemed to approve. 'So how long have you and Tom been together?'

'Just a few months. But we've known each other since childhood.'

'Ah. Just like Lin and Chong. Our families have been close for many years.'

'I'm so pleased for Lin,' said Tom. 'Chong is a fine man and I'm sure he'll make her very happy.'

She looked at him sympathetically. 'There was a time when you made her happy, Tom.'

Lin's father who'd always been formal in his relationship with Tom was less sympathetic. 'Well, that's all in the past, now. How's the business going? Lin tells me that it's in the balance.'

'We're confident that we can pull through.'

'Well, anything I can do, please let me know.'

Tom thanked them again and they made to leave. Lin's father turned to speak to the relative on his right, but her mother used her index finger to summon Tom close. 'Don't be put off by my grumpy husband. You'll always be welcome in our house and I wish you happiness.' She looked up at Sally. 'Perhaps with your childhood friend?'

'Perhaps, Mrs So. I hope so.'

Walking back to search for Elliott Sally questioned Tom. 'What did she say to you?'

'She wished us happiness.'

'Oh, how nice. She's lovely, isn't she? He was a bit abrupt though.'

'Always was.'

'You said you felt a bit strange being here. I know you say you've got over Lin, but have you really?'

'Well of course it's a bit strange coming to your first wife's second marriage. But yes – I've got over her, even though there'll always be a place in my heart for her.'

'Leaving enough room for me?'

'Plenty of room for you.'

No sooner had they found Elliott than the guests were called to take their seats at the ranks of red-clothed tables which had been laden with food. Once introductions were made it became clear that Huang Li had seated all his business associates together. Of their immediate neighbours in the seating plan one owned a group of manufacturing companies in nearby Guangdong province. Another was a flashily dressed young man from Shenzen who described himself as an entrepreneur. A third and fourth were a Hong Kong banker and his wife. Elliott was understandably cagey about revealing the true purpose of his visit simply saying that he was over from the States looking for investment opportunities.

'Brace yourself, Elliott,' warned Tom. 'I'm afraid you're about to be subjected to another banquet. Not very good for our waistlines!'

'Will we be eating the same dishes?'

'Pretty similar, but it common with everything else at a Chinese wedding, even the food is full of symbolism. I'm pretty certain we'll be getting chicken and lobster. You saw the embroidery on Lin wedding clothes, a phoenix and a dragon? Well a phoenix is considered to be female and a dragon male. The word for chicken also means phoenix and it'll probably be cooked in red oil for luck. Not many dragons around to eat these days but the Cantonese words for lobster literally mean dragon shrimp. By eating the male and female foods we'll be symbolising the union of Chong and Lin.'

'Do modern Chinese really believe in all this stuff?'

'Most would probably say they don't, but it doesn't stop them from following a lot of the old traditions. Fortune tellers still do good business working out the most auspicious days to do different things. And have you noticed that almost all the expensive cars have eights on their number plates? Eight's a lucky number.'

The food arrived course by course. Elliott took the opportunity to find out as much as he could about the businesses of those sitting close to him, trying to get a feel for their reaction to Western investment. Tom was pleased to be temporally released from the pressure of having to entertain Elliot and was able to join the conversation which Sally was conducting with the banker's wife. They were talking about the Yorkshire Dales and Sally was describing the problems of foot and mouth. The banker's wife countered with tales the Hong Kong flu pandemic of 1968 which had killed an estimated one million people worldwide. It had returned in a different form as bird flu only four years ago, but that time the health authorities had been quick to trace the source to domestic poultry. They ordered their wholesale slaughter and over a million and a half chickens, ducks, geese, quails and pigeons were culled in a move which successfully prevented an epidemic but caused economic disaster for Hong Kong's farms and markets.

It was early evening when Chong and Lin who had been doing the rounds of guest tables reached theirs. All rose to give their congratulations. Elliott once again thanked them for his invitation, saying that he would remember the day for the rest of his life.

'It's been an honour to have you here, not only for our wedding, but for the business trip as well,' said Lin. 'I'll be away now until the end of August on our honeymoon so I won't be in contact before then, but I'm sure Tom will be working hard to develop the relationship between our two companies. Dare I hope that there could be a contract to look forward to on my return?'

'You'll know that I can't promise that, but I will be writing a very positive report on my trip for my board to review. I'd hope to be able to get back to you in three or four weeks. We're getting into the holiday period so it's difficult to get decisions made quickly.'

Lin turned to Tom and smiled. He leant forward and kissed her cheek. 'I'm so happy for you,' he said.

'And I'm so pleased that you've met Sally. I've enjoyed meeting her.' She gave her a hug. 'Come and see us again soon.'

Tom shook Chong's hand, thanking him and his father once again for their hospitality. 'I hope you won't think us rude if we leave soon. We've got planes to catch early tomorrow morning.'

Chong gave his approval and he and his new wife continued on to the next table.

Tom, Sally and Elliott were ferried to their hotel in one of the ever-present Mercedes limousines and said their goodbyes in the lobby. Tom and Sally completed their packing and went for a final walk down to the waterfront. The lights of the city played on the water as they sat on a bench overlooking the ferry piers.

'I could get used to this lifestyle,' Sally said, resting her head on Tom's shoulder. 'Exotic locations, posh hotels, amazing food. And great shopping of course.'

'Really? You'd give up the Dales?'

'No, I don't think I could. This doesn't seem real. It'll be difficult to think that all this will still exist when I'm back home. Not a figment of imagination. Could you give up all your travelling?'

'I'm not sure. It's all I've known for years and years.'

They fell quiet before Sally asked tentatively 'So where does that leave us?'

Tom found a way to dodge the implication of the question. 'In love?' he ventured.

24

Three weeks later Tom drove North, buoyed by the prospect of seeing Sally but sobered by the fact that he would be attending his father's inquest. In his mind it would mark an end to the period of grace after his father's death and a time to face up to the hard decisions he would have to take about the future of the farm.

The inquest in the North Yorkshire county town of Northallerton was a perfunctory affair. Tom sat in the coroner's court beside the solicitor dealing with his father's affairs, the only ones in the public seats. Jean had declined Tom's offer to take her. Dr. Wilson who'd attended on the night of Bill's death and who had signed the death certificate gave a succinct account of his involvement. The police officer who had been Tom's contact gave evidence about the discovery of bottles of pills beside the body and confirmed that they had not looked for anyone in connection with the death. The coroner noted that the pathologist's report had given the cause of death as barbiturate poisoning and asked if there were any relatives present who wished to question the witnesses. Tom stood and said that he had no questions. The coroner gave his verdict. Suicide.

Tom and the solicitor left the court and stood outside in the summer sunshine. 'I don't suppose you fancy a pub lunch, do you? No golf today and the Golden Lion is nearby.'
   They drove to the hotel on the market town's main street and both ordered a ploughman's lunch. 'Well my boy,' said the solicitor, 'I hope that it's given you some sort of closure.' Tom agreed that it had. 'The problem is that I can't delay probate any further and neither will my friend at the bank be able to stop the loan being called in now. I'm afraid that unless the money can

be found to pay the estate's debts, then you – or technically your mother – will lose the farm.'

'It's no more than I expected,' replied Tom.

'What are you going to do?'

'I've told my mother that I can repay the debt. That's what I want to do.'

'I understand that you want to look after your mother, but have you thought it through in the cold light of day. Forgive me, but she won't last for ever and sooner or later you'll be left with an unprofitable farm with no one to run it. Not a sensible investment.'

Tom took his time to answer. 'Maybe it's time to repay a debt to my father as well.'

Tom had called ahead to Sally and she was already at Middle Farm when he arrived. Tom greeted his mother with a hug, shook Sid by the hand and gave Sally a kiss. The inevitable tea was brewed along with a coffee for Tom and they sat around the kitchen table.

'So what was the verdict,' asked Jean.

'Suicide, as expected.' no one spoke for a while. 'The solicitor was there and I had lunch with him. He's got to declare probate now.'

Sid spoke. 'Sorry, but what's a probate?'

'It's the process of validating the will so that the executors – the solicitor in this case – can administer the estate. Ownership of the farm will pass to Mum along with all its debts which the bank will call in. I'd like to pay those debts.'

'Isn't there any alternative?'

'The only other thing we could do is hand ownership of the farm to the bank. They'd then try to sell it to recover their money and they wouldn't be bothered how much they got for it provided it covered the debt and their costs.

'It's in their interests to sell it as a going concern so I wouldn't have thought they'd be kicking us out,' said Jean. 'Couldn't we rent the farm back from the bank until they sell it?'

'Would you really want all that uncertainty?' said Sally. 'Having it hanging over you that sooner or later the farm would be sold.'

'Sooner or later Sid and I will be too old to run the place. That, or we'll be gone.' Jean gave Sid a friendly glance.

'Plenty of life in us yet, old girl' he said with a reassuring smile.

Tom held up his hands. 'It's all irrelevant anyway. I want to pay the debt. I want to do it for you Mum. And for Dad.'

'But all that money,' said Jean.

'I can afford it.'

'And then what? After I've gone and left you the farm what will you do with it?'

Tom took his mother's hand in his. 'Let's not worry that far into the future, shall we. My mind's made up.' She went to speak but Tom stopped her. 'No more discussion. I'll speak to the bank tomorrow.'

Carrying his overnight bag and taking the short cut across the fields Tom set off with Sally to walk to her cottage. Tom had broached with his mother the question of whether he should stay on the farm or with Sally. Jean had said that they had presumably been sharing a bed in London and Hong Kong, so why not in the Dales. Far be it from her to be old-fashioned about these things, she'd said.

In high summer the colours of the Dales had been subdued by the bleaching of the sun. The ground was dry, with cracks appearing in exposed earth and grass tinging brown. They reached the gate which separated their farms and opened it, scattering the sheep grazing close by. One trailed behind, moving with difficulty.

'Shit!' exclaimed Sally.

'What's the matter?'

'That ewe. She's limping isn't she?'

Tom looked carefully at it. 'I think you're right. Why the language? It's not like you.'

'Because limping's a sign of foot and mouth. They get blisters on their feet and it makes them limp. Help me catch her.'

Tom ran to overtake the sheep and herded it back in the direction of the gate. Without the ability to move quickly it was soon captured. Sally straddled it to prevent it struggling and examined it. 'Shit!' she repeated. 'Look at those.'

Tom peered closely and saw a cluster of sores around the animal's mouth. 'That's not good news, is it.'

'Could be something else but I'm not holding out hope. We better get my Dad to have a look.'

They found Sally's parents in their farmhouse kitchen. 'Now then Tom!' said Ken Hardcastle rising from his chair. 'Welcome, lad.'

'Hello Tom,' said Rosie. 'Cup of tea?'

'Er, not now thanks.' Tom looked anxiously at Sally.

'Dad, there's a ewe limping up in top field. She's got blisters. I think you better check.'

Ken seemed to deflate. He looked despairingly at his wife then left without a word.

'Maybe we will have some tea,' said Sally and went to busy herself with the kettle.

Tom sat down across the kitchen table from Rosie who was staring distractedly at the door through which Ken had made his exit. 'I thought foot and mouth was pretty much over.'

Rosie took a deep breath and turned to Tom. 'So did we. We were only saying last night that we might have got away with it, weren't we Sally?'

'Yes, Mum,' Sally agreed, laying out four teacups.

'It could be something else wrong with the sheep,' suggested Tom in an attempt to lift the gloom.

'We'll wait and see.' said Rosie flatly with a finality which implied that she was in no mood to speculate. She resumed staring at the door, her teeth worrying a fingernail. In the absence of speech, Tom became acutely aware of the humdrum sounds of the kitchen. The bubbling of water as the kettle boiled. The clink of china as Sally removed the lid of the teapot and poured the liquid over the tea leaves. The scrape of her chair on the stone floor as she sat down to wait for it to brew.

She gave Tom a nervous smile. He responded with a shrug of sympathy.

'You're happy with tea?' she said incongruously. 'I know you prefer coffee.'

'Tea's fine,' Tom assured her. She rose and went to pour three cups and handed them round.

'I'll leave Dad's in the pot until he's back, Mum,' she said quietly, standing behind her mother and putting a hand on her shoulder. Rosie responded by patting it.

Ken's return was signalled by a bark from his sheepdog. He came in and without breaking stride marched purposefully to the door through to the hall saying, 'Better call veterinary.' Rosie got up to follow him.

'He thinks it's foot and mouth then?' Tom asked Sally.

'Enough to call the vet.'

'Is there anything we can do?'

'Like what?' Sally said sharply.

'Sorry. Silly thing to say.'

They sat in silence, listening to the murmur of Ken's voice through the open door. They heard the sound of the receiver being replaced and Ken and Rosie returned. 'Veterinary thinks he can be here before dark. He says he'll have to inform authorities and he wants no one to enter or leave the farm until he's done his tests. Sal, can you see if that family's in the holiday cottage and tell them. If they're not there, you'll have to get them on their mobile and warn them that if they come back, they might not be able to leave for a while.'

Sally went to a notebook where details of holiday lets were kept and copied the mobile number. She beckoned to Tom who picked up his bag and followed her out into the farmyard.

'We're confined to the farm then. How long is that likely to be?'

'If it's confirmed then it could be anything up to a fortnight. It depends how long it takes to slaughter all the sheep and burn them. Why, are you desperate to get away?'

'No. I've taken three days off, but if it goes much beyond that it might be difficult.'

'Not as difficult as it going to be for us losing all our sheep!'

'Yes. Sorry. That was insensitive.' She gave him a withering look.

They reached the door of Sally's cottage. 'Make yourself at home. I'll see if that family's in.'

Tom took his bag upstairs to the bedroom then returned to the living room, spotting the painting that Sally had bought in Hong Kong in pride of place above the mantelpiece. A few minutes later she returned and slumped down on the sofa beside him. 'He's not a happy chappy,' she said. 'The family weren't in so I called his mobile and told him he wouldn't be able to come back on the farm. He hit the roof.'

'Doesn't he understand the situation?'

'I explained that as far as I know it's a legal requirement for farms to be quarantined if foot and mouth is suspected. I've even seen police guarding entrances to farms where it's been confirmed. I told him that we'd look after their things for the moment. He said he'd be calling the police himself to find out if I was telling the truth.'

Sally offered a drink and went off to find two bottles of lager which they mournfully clinked together. 'Had I better phone my Mum?' Tom said. 'They should know.'

'I think you should. Use my landline.' Tom rose to get the phone and Sally let out an expletive.

'What is it this time?'

'I've just thought. We always let the sheep out on to the fells this time of year when the grass in the fields is getting low. Sid has as well. The flocks have been in contact.'

'So they could all have it.'

'Possibly.'

Tom phoned his mother who listened with concern then transferred him to Sid who said he'd go out to the fields straight away to inspect the sheep.

An hour later, they heard a car driving past the cottage. Looking out of the window Sally confirmed that it was the vet's. They gave it a quarter of an hour and then walked up to the farmhouse to join Rosie in waiting for the verdict. Eventually

Ken and the vet came in. Tom had been expecting a tweed-clad James Herriot figure. Instead the vet was a floppy-haired young man in jeans and a sweatshirt. They looked at him in anticipation.

'I'm sorry to say that it looks like foot and mouth,' he said. 'Can't be sure until I get the test results, but I've seen so many cases recently that I wouldn't bet against it. I'm going to have to impose a three-kilometre protection zone round the farm.'

Tom introduced himself. 'That would put my mother's farm in the zone. It adjoins this farm and apparently there could have been some contact between the flocks.' Ken confirmed that there had been.

'In that case you better tell your mother that no one can go in or out of her farm either. Have there been any signs of infected animals?'

'They're checking now,' said Tom.

The vet looked out of the window to see that dusk was falling. 'It's too dark for me to go there now. I'll call you first thing tomorrow morning to get an update.'

'What happens now?' asked Sally.

'The results should come through in three or four days. If they confirm foot and mouth, then I'm afraid the flock will have to be culled. Most of the slaughter teams have been stood down in this area – we thought we'd pretty much beaten the disease - so it could be a while before it can be arranged. That's if it's necessary, of course. I'm sorry.'

The phone rang shortly after the vet had left. Ken went to answer it and they heard his concerned tones in the distance. 'It was Sid,' he said returning to the kitchen. 'He's found a couple of ewes with blisters. Looks like they've got it as well. Not that it makes much difference. Chances are that they'd cull his flock anyway because it's so close.'

Rosie's shoulders trembled and she let out a sob. Ken moved to comfort her. 'Nay lass. Don't fret. Thee'll only get me going too.'

Tom looked awkwardly at Sally who gestured that they should go. She went to put her arms round both her parents. 'There's nothing we can do but wait. We'll go to the cottage.'

Rosie gave a weak smile through watery eyes and Ken nodded his head. 'OK lass.'

Tom and Sally walked back dejectedly. Sally slammed the farmyard gate in frustration. 'Everything they've worked for their whole lives. About to go up in smoke.'

'It's not confirmed yet,' said Tom limply, aware that he was clutching at straws.

'Don't kid yourself,' countered Sally with surprising vehemence. 'You heard what the vet said. It's going to devastate Mum and Dad.'

'My Mum and Sid as well, don't forget. I'd better call her.'

Back in the cottage Sally was distant, slumping down on the sofa and putting her head in her hands. Tom chose to sit way from her, not wishing to intrude. Eventually she looked up with a weak smile and came to hug him forlornly. 'I was going to make you a special meal tonight but it's too late now and I'm really not up to it. I'll stick a pizza in. I'm going to open the wine though.'

She disappeared to the kitchen and Tom dialled his mother's number. 'Hi Mum. I heard Sid's news. It doesn't look good.'

'No.' The depth of emotion with which she managed to imbue a single syllable made Tom wince.

'I don't know what to say Mum. It just seems so unfair when everything seemed to be sorting itself out.'

'Life's not fair, Tom. I'm sure the Lord has some purpose in visiting it upon us.'

Tom fought back his instinct to argue, knowing that his mother's unquestioning faith would be the one source of comfort to her. 'I'll come and see you tomorrow, Mum. If both farms have got it, it can't do any harm. Is Sid looking after you?'

'It's me that's looking after him. He's inconsolable, saying that it's his fault for not being more careful with all the precautions. He feels he's let me down.'

'If it will be any consolation, tell him how much I appreciate what he's done and that it's silly to think that he's at fault.'

'OK, I'll try.'

Tom could tell that his mother was in no mood to talk further. He told her he loved her and finished the call.

Sally came into the living room bearing two large glasses of white wine. They sat side by side on the sofa.

'How's your Mum?'

'As you'd expect. She sounds numb. Said that God had done it for a reason although I'm buggered if I can see what it could be. He's either a vicious bastard or an incompetent fool - if he exists that is.'

'Not a believer then!' said Sally.

'No. But I respect my mother's belief. It got her through my Dad's death and it will probably get her through this.'

'And how will we get through this?'

'What do you mean?'

'I don't mean us personally, at least I hope it doesn't affect us, but it does rather alter the playing field. If the sheep are culled both our farms are going to start from scratch again. My parents are just about young enough to build everything up again if that's what they want. But it's different for Sid and your Mum, and for you. If you pay off the bank what will you be left with? A bit of compensation and a farm with no sheep. Would you really want to start building up a flock?'

'With Mum so old you mean?'

'I didn't want to say it, but yes.'

'There's Sid to consider.'

'It's very noble of you and I know your Mum loves his company, but he's only a hired hand. You haven't really got any obligation to him.'

'I suppose from a business point of view it would be pretty perverse to start sinking money into the farm knowing that it would probably continue to make a loss. Although you could say the same for your parents.'

Sally made no reply, absent-mindlessly swirling the wine in her glass. Tom framed a question carefully.

'Have you ever discussed with your parents what will happen when they're too old to run the farm? You're an only child as well. Do they expect you to take it over?'

She gave a hollow laugh. 'I think they always expected me to marry a farmer.' She got up and went to the tiny kitchen. Tom followed her, cut by the insinuation. 'What's that supposed to mean?' he said with irritation.

'Nothing.' She opened the oven door and inspected the pizza. 'Needs more time.' She pushed past him avoiding eye contact and returned to the sofa, drawing her knees up between her arms and rocking back and forth. Tom stood in the doorway, uncertain whether to approach her. 'I'm sorry, Tom, but it obviously doesn't mean as much to you as it does to me. You're just worried you might get stuck here and won't be able to get back to your precious company.'

'No, that's not fair.'

'Isn't it? Can you honestly tell me that losing the sheep will affect you as much as it will my parents and your Mum and Sid? And me?

Tom realised that it would be futile to pretend. 'No,' he said quietly. 'I'm sorry.'

'For what?' she said aggressively.

'For being insensitive. For being too concerned about my business. For not being a farmer.'

There was a long silence from Sally. She let out a long breath. 'No, I'm the one who should be sorry. I'm just upset. I shouldn't be taking it out on you. Let's just eat and get an early night.'

25

The dry high summer weather had broken. A warm rain was falling gently as Sally and Tom walked up to the farmhouse after breakfast. Rosie was in the kitchen alone.

'Where's Dad?' asked Sally.

'Up in the fields, isolating sheep with symptoms. For what it's worth.'

'I'll go and see if I can help. Has the vet called yet?

'Not yet. Do you want to phone him, Tom, to tell him what Sid's found?'

He went to make the call and the vet arranged to meet him within the hour, agreeing that in view of the contact there had already been it would make no difference for Tom to go from one farm to the other.

Tom walked with Sally to the fields and they found Ken and Sid talking on opposite sides of the boundary gate. Tom filled them in on the conversation with the vet and then set off with Sid to his farmhouse, leaving Sally to help her father.

'Now then, lad,' said Sid. 'Right bad business this. I thought I'd been so careful with precautions.'

'Don't blame yourself, Sid. I sure you know more about it than me, but can't the disease spread in all sorts of ways which you can't control? Bird droppings, for example.'

'Yes. But I can't help but feel guilty.'

'Don't. I'm very proud of what you've done on this farm. You should be proud as well.'

'Proud of getting all sheep slaughtered? That's probably what's going to happen, and then what?'

Tom remembered what Sally had said the previous evening about him having no obligation to Sid. It was true. Having taken him almost literally out of the last chance saloon and put his trust in him Sid had repaid him in spades, so they were even. But Tom still felt a something like a duty of care for him. 'Don't worry, Sid. You're almost part of the family now. We'll try to get through this together.'

The vet soon arrived. Sid took him off to examine the blistered sheep leaving Tom with Jean. She still gave the impression of being drained of all emotion. 'It's a funny thing to say, Tom, but I'm glad your father's not here to see this happening. I'd like to think that he died thinking things would get better without him.'

'I'm sure he did.' Tom said gently.

'How are Ken and Rosie taking it?' asked Jean.

'Rosie's pretty cut up. Ken's putting on a good show of coping. But I'm sure it's only a show.'

'It's worse for them, I suppose.'

'Why's that?'

'Because they'll want to start again if they lose their sheep. I don't want to. Let's face it Tom, your father was right when he said there was no future for this farm. Maybe this means it will cease to be a working farm sooner rather than later. Foot and mouth is only bringing forward the inevitable.'

Tom was distressed by his mother's uncharacteristic fatalism. 'That's not like you Mum – to give in without a fight.'

'Your Dad did.'

Tom was lost for a reply. Jean rose from her chair and went to a cupboard to pull out a vacuum cleaner. 'Anyway, I need to get on.'

Tom went outside. The rain had abated but the overcast sky threatened more. He mindlessly kicked at a stone sending it scudding across the courtyard. He thrust his hands deep into his pockets, tipped his head back and closed his eyes trying to cleanse his mind of emotion. He opened them with a determination to think logically. Was he simply a victim of circumstance or could he influence events? Not as far as the disease was concerned. If it was confirmed an inevitable series of events would follow – the culling of the sheep and his detention on the farms until the authorities lifted quarantine. As Sally had witheringly pointed out, him not being able to leave was the least of their problems, but he had to be concerned with the race between a Valco deal and a possible takeover coming to a head. What could he realistically do to make things better? Make promises about keeping the farm going? No, he couldn't be a hostage to fortune and hadn't his mother just told him that she didn't want that? The only thing he could do, he decided, was to give as much support to everyone as he could muster, to

Sally in particular. She had helped him out of his crisis. He had a duty to help her. After all, he loved her, didn't he?

Tom watched Sid and the vet as they approached across the fields. They came into the courtyard with expressions which told the story. 'Bad news?' Tom asked. The vet nodded.

'I'll go and tell Jean,' said Sid walking away.

'Can I get you a tea, a coffee? The vet declined Tom's offer.

'No thanks. I better get off. I've left my car outside the farm gates. Do you want to walk up with me?'

They began the climb the track. 'Are you able to estimate how long it will be until the quarantine will be lifted?' asked Tom. 'It's not important in the scheme of things but from a practical point of view I need to know. I run a company in London. I'll have to try to put things in place if I'm going to be away for a while.'

'My best guess is up to two weeks. Assuming it's confirmed of course, but I don't want to give you false hope.'

'And there's no way round it?'

'I'm afraid not. It's a legal requirement.' The vet stopped and gave him a stern look. 'Not to mention a moral responsibility. You wouldn't want to risk carrying it elsewhere, would you? Passing on this hell to another farmer?'

Tom felt small. 'I'm sorry. Of course not.' They continued walking. 'It must be hell for you as well.'

'It's certainly not what I became a vet for – travelling around passing death sentences on whole flocks and herds of live-stock.' He stopped once again and looked back to the farm. 'But what really gets to me is when I have to give a diagnosis. Guys like Ken and Sid, they know the score. They wouldn't call me in unless they were 99% certain that the sheep had foot and mouth. But when I've examined them and I turn to confirm what they already know, I can still see that 1% of hope in their eyes. I have to dash it.'

Tom put his hand on the vet's shoulder in sympathy and they walked on to the farm gate. The vet washed his boots thorough-ly in the disinfectant and went to his car to retrieve an official notice which he attached to the gate. 'It's an 'A' notice,' he said. 'No entry or exit for anyone except me or another vet and the slaughter team eventually. It'll remain in place until all the sheep are culled and burnt. The police will be informed and they'll be enforcing the quarantine.'

'What do we do for food?' Tom asked.

'You'll have to ask someone to get supplies and bring them to the gate.'

'So nothing to do now but wait.'

'That's about it. I'll call as soon as I get the results.'

Back in the farmhouse Tom phoned his office and told Emma about his involuntary incarceration, asking her to inform everyone. She passed on a number of messages and then said that Charles wanted to have a word. Tom asked to be put through to his Director of Finance and Administration.

'Morning, Tom,' he said. 'PMJK have just been in touch. We've got two interested parties for a takeover. One is Sinclair Rhodes, the management consultants. They're already quite big on Far Eastern business and seem to be quite keen. The other party is a private company in Hong Kong, Huang Enterprises. They've asked for more details from PMJK. Do you know them?'

'Yes. So Lin's new husband is the son of the owner. I met him when I was out there and he said he might look into buying us. I didn't think much of it at the time.'

'Well it's only an expression of interest at the moment whereas Sinclair Rhodes want a meeting as soon as possible. When are you back?'

'Not for some time. It looks like we've got foot and mouth on my parents' farm and we've been put into quarantine. I'm not allowed to leave.'

'Oh, I'm sorry to hear that,' said Charles lightly, obviously not registering the seriousness of the situation. 'When will you be able to get away?'

'Perhaps not for a couple of weeks. Look, go ahead and arrange the meeting. I'm sure that you and Sir Giles can handle things at this stage. If they want to speak to me it's going to have to be by phone.'

Tom felt depressed that a buyer was in the frame but initially took some solace from the fact that his enforced absence might delay progress. Any comfort was soon cancelled out by the thought that the same might apply to advancing the Valco deal. In fact, he pondered, was there anything to feel happy about? With the farm about to go out of business and his company on the brink of being sold, he failed to think of anything positive. He went to look for his mother and found her changing sheets upstairs.

'Mum, is there anything I can do here, because if not I'll get back to Sally's. I've got some emails to do and she's got an ISDN line in her office.'

'Whatever's that?'

'It means I can connect to the Internet much quicker than by using an ordinary phone line.'

'I'm sure I don't know what you're talking about but go on – get back to her. What's there to do here but wait for the Angels of Death?'

'Now I don't know what you're talking about.'

'That's what we used to call the slaughtermen the last time foot and mouth was here. Help me with this sheet will you, then get off. I'm OK.'

The rain had returned as a light drizzle as Tom walked back across the fields. In the distance the sun was bursting through broken clouds and a rainbow had formed. The sheep he passed were grazing contentedly and to all appearances all was well with the world. If only it were.

Sally was working at her laptop on a desk in the small outbuilding behind the cottages which she had converted into an office.

'It's good to see that someone's got work to do,' Tom said grumpily.

'What do you mean,' she said, breaking off from typing.

'I've just heard that a company's very interested in taking over my business. Coming on top of the foot and mouth it's pretty depressing.'

'What about the deal in the States. Any news?'

'Not a thing and it's nearly a month now. How's your business going? That'd be all we need if you've got problems as well.'

'It's doing OK.'

'Couldn't give me a job, could you?' He slumped on to a chair, crossed his arms and let out a sigh. The body language made his mood plain.

Sally came to join him. 'Cheer up, slicker. We'll get through this somehow.'

'At the moment I'm buggered if I can see how. If we get taken over there's no guarantee that I'll keep my job. Even if I do, I'd have to report to some corporate structure. I don't think I'd be very good at that. Everything's falling down around our ears.'

'We've got each other. We'll get through it together.'

The days waiting for the test results dragged by. Sally arranged for a friend to bring supplies from a supermarket to the farm boundary and busied herself with work for her business. Tom did what he could to keep in touch with his company via email and phone calls. He also phoned the bank to say that he was willing to pay off the debt. The manager had heard about the outbreak on the farms and refused to progress repayment until the situation had been resolved. 'The least I can do in the circumstances,' he said. Sid and Ken continually examined the flocks, finding more signs of infection and separating the diseased sheep from those without symptoms despite knowing full well that it would make no difference. Jean and Rosie found consolation in endless rounds of domesticity with clothes washed, meagre meals prepared, and vegetable plots tended.

The call from the vet came after four days. The tests had proved positive. The ministry had been informed and would be sending a team within a few days.

Shortly after Emma phoned Tom in Sally's cottage.

'I've just had a call from Elliott Paul at Valco. I told him that you were out of the office but that I'd contact you and you'd call him back. I didn't say anything about the foot and mouth.'

'Did he give any indication of what he wanted to say?'

'No – just to call him as soon as possible.'

'OK, I'll do it now.'

Tom put the phone down and called to Sally in the kitchen. 'Valco want me to call.'

She came to stand beside him. 'The moment of truth?'

'Probably.'

'I'll go and sit outside while you make the call. I'll cross my fingers for you.'

Tom pulled up Elliott's number on his laptop and dialled. After a short delay he was put through. 'Hi Tom, how are you?'

'Fine thanks, good to hear from you.'

'Recovered from all that Chinese food yet? I swear I put on five pounds out in Hong Kong.'

'Just about recovered, thanks.'

'And how's Sally?'

Tom was getting frustrated with the pleasantries. 'She's fine thanks.'

Finally, Elliott came to the point. 'Sorry it's taken so long to get back to you but the board's now made a decision. We'd like to take you on initially for a year.'

Tom felt a wave of relief. 'That's great news! What do we need to do to finalise it?'

'I've already asked my legal boys to start drawing up a contract and I'm sure yours will want to go through it carefully before you sign, but in the meantime I'd like to get things moving straight away. We'd like you to second a couple of your people to base themselves in our offices for the duration of the contract. Could you come over so that we can sit down and agree a plan of action?'

'Er, I can't personally. I'm actually stuck on a farm right now and we've got an outbreak of foot and mouth. It's been put under quarantine and nobody's allowed to leave.'

'Foot and what?'

'I think you might call it hoof and mouth over there. It's a highly infectious disease that cattle and sheep get and when they do they usually have to be killed.'

'Yeah I vaguely remember that we used to have it here. There was last an outbreak back in the nineteen twenties, I think. So how long until you can leave?'

'A week, maybe two.'

'Then can you send someone else over?'

Tom thought quickly. Not Lin – she was sailing in the Philippines and only halfway through her honeymoon. Charles? No. He didn't know enough about the operations side of the business and was anyway not a client facing person. Against his better judgement it would have to be Angie.

'I can my send Business Development Director over,' he said. 'You met her with Bill Schwartz at the initial meeting – Angie Carter.'

'Yes, I remember her. OK, so be it. If you really can't make it she'll have to do. Perhaps you can join us as soon as you're able and hopefully we'll have a contract to sign by then.'

'I'll do that. I'm really sorry that I can't come now but it's completely out of my hands – I'd be breaking the law to leave. I'll get Angie to call you to make the arrangements.'

'OK, Tom. I'll look forward to doing business with you.'

Tom went outside to find Sally sunning herself on the bench outside the cottage. She looked at him expectantly. 'We've got the business,' he said calmly.

Sally leapt up and hugged him. 'That's brilliant! Well done! At last something to lift the gloom.'

'The problem is they want me over there now. I've told them I'll have to send someone else.'

'That's not too much of a problem is it?'

Sally was unaware of Tom's suspicions about Angie and he thought this was no time to burden her with them, so he simply acknowledged that it wasn't.

'Will it be enough to prevent a takeover?' she asked.

'I don't know. Time will tell, time being the operative word. I just need to get the Valco deal signed and sealed as fast as possible.'

Tom toyed with the idea of phoning Ben or Bob, the two people involved who he looked upon as trustworthy allies, but decided that it would be only proper to speak first to his chairman.

'Good afternoon, my boy,' drawled Sir Giles. 'Still stuck on the farm? Charles told me about it when he was fixing the meeting with Sinclair Rhodes. What damnable luck to have the disease.'

'Yes, still confined to the farm, Sir Giles, but I've just spoken to Valco. It's good news – they're offering us a year's contract.'

'Good news indeed! Well done!'

'How do you see it affecting a possible takeover?'

'You're very transparent Tom.'

'You know I don't want to sell.'

'Well I understand from Charles and PMJK that Sinclair Rhodes are close to making an offer but the price per share will be based on our current valuation without the Valco deal. If and when it's announced the share price will certainly rise.'

'What's the position on telling Sinclair Rhodes about the deal?'

'Interesting point. If we tell them they presumably won't want to make an offer before the deal is signed.'

'And if we didn't tell them and they made an offer, we might not be able to recommend it knowing that the share price was liable to rise.'

'I'm not sure how ethical that course of action would be, Tom. Anyway, when they evaluate our assets under due diligence a marketing audit would reveal the approach to Valco. No, we'll have to tell them.'

'That's what I hoped you'd say. So we can probably count on them not making an offer before the deal's signed.'

'Well let's see what happens.'

Tom felt relieved after the conversation ended. At least the pressure to secure the Valco deal in advance of a takeover offer was probably off. His mind turned to the Angie problem and he phoned Bob Schwartz in New York to give him the news. Bob responded with his congratulations.

'No, I should be congratulating you, Bob. You're the one who made it all possible. But there is a problem you can help me with. Valco wanted me to come over straight away to hammer out the deal and get started on planning but I can't come.' Tom explained the quarantine to him. 'Anyhow, Lin's on honeymoon so the only person I can send is Angie and you know my reservations about her loyalty. I'd like you to be my eyes and ears when she's with you, just being on the lookout for anything she might do to scupper the deal.'

'Sure thing,' said Bob. 'But I still don't understand why she could possibly want to do that. All you told me is that she might have a financial interest in it. Can't you tell me anymore?'

Tom decided that there was no harm in explaining at this stage. 'It's all supposition, but I think our major shareholder is strapped for cash and needs to sell his shares. He's got too many to unload them without the price crashing, so he wants to sell the business. I suspect that he's offered Angie money if she can bring about a takeover. She was the one who set the hare running about being up for sale and now we're damned close to it happening. We've got a company on the point of making an offer and she knows that the Valco deal could stop the offer being accepted.'

'Jeez, Tom. You're sure that you're not being a little bit paranoid?'

'I wondered that myself but there's just too much evidence to believe otherwise. The problem is that none of it is conclusive, so I can't confront her.'

'If you say so. OK, I'll keep my eyes open.'

Tom took a deep breath and phoned Angie. 'It looks like the Valco deal's on. A year's contract.'

'Wow! Hey, that's great!' Her reaction suggested that she was either a pretty good actress or he'd been barking up the wrong tree about her. No matter at the moment.

'They wanted me to fly over straight away to close the deal but as you know I'm stuck here and Lin's on honeymoon. I need you to go out. Is that possible?'

'Well, yes, I suppose so. You want me to drop everything and go?'

'Yes please. We need to get this one in the bag as soon as possible.'

'Right, I'll see I can get a flight tomorrow. What'll I be doing out there?'

'Finalising the contract. You'll have to liaise with Charles and our New York lawyers over that. Bob Schwartz is on board with what's needed and you can base yourself with him. At the same time you'll be working with Valco to put a plan for the year together – objectives, targets, timescales etc. I'll organise any resources you need from this end. What I'd like is a daily report to keep me updated. I'll come over as soon as I'm able and with luck the contract will be ready to sign by then.'

Tom had just finished composing an email updating all senior staff when Sally returned. He hit send and leant back in his chair clasping his hands behind his head.

'You look pleased with yourself, slicker.'

'Well it's good to be able to get things moving. So much better than killing time here, feeling powerless. I've made a couple of transatlantic phone calls, by the way. I'll need to reimburse you.'

'Don't bother about that now. We've got more important things to worry about.'

26

Frantic barking from a sheepdog alerted Tom and Sally to the arrival of the Angels of Death. They went outside to see a column of men strolling up from the farm entrance. The nonchalant way in which they carried their weapons, their irregular grouping and the indistinct buzz of conversation and laughter which carried on the wind would have marked them out for a convivial shooting party but for the white body suits they wore. Tom felt that a funeral procession or a brisk military march would have been more appropriate until he realised that they must have become inured to emotion after visiting so many farms in similar circumstances.

As they drew close two figures detached themselves and approached Tom and Sally. Tom recognised one of them as the floppy-haired vet.

'Morning. Can I introduce Major Simmonds. He's overseeing the culling.'

The army officer came to attention and held out his hand for Tom and then Sally to shake. 'Sorry to meet you in such terrible circumstances. I don't suppose it will be much comfort to you, but I'll aim to carry out the operation as quickly and efficiently as possible. The first thing I need to do is agree the best place to dig a pit for the carcasses.'

'You better come and meet my father then,' said Sally. 'He's the owner of this farm.'

'My mother owns the adjoining farm,' said Tom. 'Should I get her and the farmhand to join you?'

'It might be a good idea. It probably makes sense to dig one large pit for all the animals from both farms, so we'll all need to agree a location. We'll need good access for the diggers and the lorries.'

'I phone them then.' Tom went back into the cottage while the others headed off to the farmhouse.

As Tom walked to up to the house after making the call he came across the white-suited culling team relaxing in the farmyard, some smoking, some chatting, others checking over their bolt guns. A couple of them acknowledged him as he passed with sympathetic nods of the head.

Inside Sally was helping her mother to brew a pot of tea while the vet, the major and Ken Hardcastle were pouring over a large-scale map of the area on the kitchen table. Listening in on the discussion it seemed that the major had decided that access to Ken's farm was much easier than to his mother's and was suggesting a field close to the entrance. The vet was concerned about the proximity of a stream to the site and worried that drainage from decaying carcasses in the pit could pollute it. Ken proposed digging in a field with poor drainage well away from streams. It seemed to be a good compromise.

Sid and Jean arrived and stood by the doorway taking in the situation, Sid shifting from foot to foot with his cap held in both hands in front of him, Jean nervously glancing around. The men at the table stood and Tom made the introductions. Rosie came to Jean to hug her and took her to join Sally who was laying out mugs on a tray. The major invited Sid to join them at the table and began to summarise the thinking about the location of the pit. Tom hung back from both groups, not feeling that he belonged to either, but he moved close enough to the table to hear what was being said. They were discussing how to get the sheep close to the pit. Ken and Sid agreed to use their sheepdogs to herd them all into an adjacent field.

Sally offered round the tray of tea and they stood in an uneasy silence which the vet eventually broke. 'Can I thank you for your co-operation? I know it can't be easy for you.'

'What choice do we have?' said Ken flatly.

'You're right. There is no choice, but some of the farmers I've had to deal with have been fairly obstructive. After you've helped us to get the sheep into the field there's nothing else you can do.'

'The killing field you mean?' said Jean, her voice cracking.

The vet looked at her with sympathy. 'If you like. I'm afraid what we have to do is not a pretty sight so it might be better for you to all stay inside and let the major's team get on with it.'

Tom went back to open his emails. Angie's latest daily report sent from New York the previous evening was among them. The lawyers had received the draft contract and were examining it. Angie and Bob had attended an initial meeting with Valco and the outline of a plan of action had been agreed. It was now up to Tiger.com to flesh it out. Tom immediately set to work, scoping out what would be required to achieve it.

A while later Sally popped her head round the office door. 'Come and look at this, Tom.' He went outside and she pointed towards the farm entrance. A low loader laden with two large earth diggers and a forklift truck was manoeuvring slowly around a bend. Behind it two lorries were visible, one carrying a load of railway sleepers, the other bales of straw. 'Fuel for the funeral pyre,' she said morbidly.

'How are our Mums?' Tom asked.

'I left them talking over old times. They're doing their best to forget what's going on.'

'What about Ken and Sid?'

'Haven't seen them. Shall we go and look?'

They walked down to the field where the sheep were being gathered. It was crowded with animals, nervously shifting around and constantly changing direction looking for a way to escape. It was as if they knew the fate that would befall them. Tom and Sally joined Ken who was holding open a gate to allow Sid and his sheepdog to herd a group of ewes in. Two white-suited men stood close by, clicking handheld counters as the sheep were funnelled through a narrow opening between aluminium barriers. The major watched from a distance, a clipboard in his hand. He finished totting up a column of figures and approached them. 'I think that's the lot. You're sure you haven't missed any?' Sid and Ken solemnly shook their heads. 'Right, thanks again for your help. There's nothing else you can do so we'll take from here.'

'You're not going to start killing sheep in full view of others?' asked Sid. His eyes were watery with tears.

'I really think it would be better if you left us to it, Mr Lambert.' The major looked round the group. 'And that goes for all you.' no one made a move to leave. He tried again. 'Look, I understand your concern, but I have to follow the procedures laid down by the ministry. What we have to do is fairly gruesome and I really would advise not giving yourself the extra pain of staying to watch.'

Ken put his arm round Sid's shoulders. 'Come on. There's nothing we can do.'

Sid was now openly crying. It proved to be contagious and Tom felt tears forming in his eyes. Sally felt for his hand and he saw that she too was tearful. Sid extricated himself from Ken's arm and approached a nearby ewe. He knelt down and made a clicking noise to it. The sheep took a couple of uncertain steps towards him, coming close enough for Sid to clasp it round the neck and bury his head in its woolly shoulders. He murmured words which were lost to the others then stood and gently propelled the ewe away. Ken went to stand beside him and the two of them stood in silence surveying the field. Sally slipped her hand from Tom's and went to hold her father round the waist. He turned to hug her. Tom saw that he too had tears trickling down his cheeks. The major caught Tom's eye and gave a strained smile of sympathy. 'I really must get things moving,' he said apologetically and turned away to speak into a walkie-talkie.

The neighbouring field was humming with activity. An area for the trench had been staked out. It looked to be a full thirty metres long and a good ten wide. Straw bales were being manhandled off one lorry while a hoist mounted on the other lifted creosote-coated sleepers on to the arms of the forklift. As they walked towards the farmhouse, they passed a group of slaughtermen walking determinedly towards the killing field with bolt guns at the ready.

Tom broke off from the others near Sally's office saying he needed to carry on working. Sally declined to stay with him, preferring to be with her parents. Tom wondered if he should be with his mother, but much as the fate of the sheep was affecting him, he felt that it could be nothing to those who had spent their whole lives with them. He had a nagging feeling that he would be an interloper, intruding on their grief.

He set to work, doing his best to immerse himself in the challenge of writing the section of the action plan that he had allocated to himself. For a while he succeeded. It was a hot day and through the open windows of the cottage came a series of dull reports. Tom saved the document he was working on and went outside assuming that the cull must have begun. He felt irresistibly drawn and walked down to a vantage point where both fields were in view. The diggers had carved out much of the trench and straw bales and sleepers were already being laid in one end. In the killing field a small mound of carcasses was visible.

Tom walked closer to get a better look and saw a white suited figure who he recognised as the vet sitting on a five barred gate and viewing the operation. The vet turned to him when he heard his approach.

'There's no need for you to be here, you know,' he said.

'I know. But I just wanted to see what was going on.'

'Why put yourself through the anguish? I've got to be here to check the procedures and sign it all off for the ministry. It's bad enough for me as a professional.'

'Maybe I've got a professional interest as well. I used to be a journalist and it's in my nature to want to observe. You have to train yourself to be detached from emotion when you're reporting on bad events.'

Tom could see that animals were being picked out one by one and dragged to the men with the guns.

'Are you detached from this?'

'No. Of course not. It's easier for me because I've not lived on a farm for many years, but I'd have to be a hell of a cold fish not to feel the pain of those that have.'

Tom saw a sheep convulse in the grip of a slaughterman and a moment later the sharp crack of the bolt gun reached them.

'So how does this rate compared to other bad events you've seen?'

'I've been thinking about that. With a natural disaster there's usually the sense that nothing could have been done to avoid it. It's the opposite with man-made disasters like wars. This has elements of both.'

'I certainly agree that much more could have been done to stop the spread of the disease. Why the hell it took so long to get countermeasures in place after the first outbreak back in February I'll never know. If transport bans and exclusion zones had been put in place immediately we'd have nipped it in the bud. Instead we had diseased animals being sent to abattoirs around the country.'

'What was it? Lack of political will? Incompetence?'

'Downright crassness, I'd say. For example, when culling started, the ministry adopted the ludicrous policy of sending all corpses which couldn't be disposed of on site to a rendering plant in Cheshire. That meant sending lorries through disease-free areas to get there. It's all been completely mismanaged. We've culled around 6 million sheep, pigs and cattle and still counting. And probably eighty per cent of the animals killed didn't have the disease.'

'Can you see an end to it?'

'Yes. Outbreaks are few and far between now. You've been bloody unlucky to probably be amongst the last to get it.'

'Will we learn from the mistakes?'

'I'd like to think so, but only time will tell. The government's just announced three separate inquiries, but none of them are going to be held in public so goodness knows what cover-ups and buck-passing from all the vested interests will be going on.'

'It almost makes me wish I was still a journalist. There's quite a story to be written.'

Engine noise from the diggers below rose and fell as they continued to excavate. A group of slaughtermen came out of the field to take a break, passing round bottles of water. Tom could see that their white suits were streaked with blood. The vet looked at his watch. 'They're due to finish for the day in an hour. I better go and check that they leave enough time to get properly disinfected before they go. See you later.'

Tom managed to finish writing his document before Sally returned.

'How is everyone?'

'Your Mum and Sid have just left to go home. Sid's a bit worse for wear I'm afraid.'

'What?'

'It was my Dad's fault. He opened a bottle of whisky and insisted that Sid join him. Sid refused at first, but your Mum said it was OK and wouldn't mind one herself. Between us all we've pretty much polished off the bottle. I'm feeling a bit woozy myself.'

'It sounds as if I've missed quite a party,' said Tom.

'A wake, my Dad called it. I wish I could have missed it. They all ended up very maudlin. At least they'll all sleep well tonight.'

The pyre was lit around lunchtime the following day. They'd been alerted to it by the major knocking on their door and suggesting that they close all their windows to keep out the smoke. Tom was doing so in the upstairs bedroom of the cottage when he saw a pillar of flame leap into the air. Sally joined him at the window. They watched in silence as wave after wave of thick black smoke mushroomed into the pale blue sky.

27

The acrid stench of burnt flesh hung in the air for days as they waited for the quarantine to be lifted. Sid and Ken occupied themselves with odd jobs around the farms, mending fences and servicing machinery, but with little sense of purpose. Jean and Rosie both embarked on an unseasonal round of spring cleaning with carpets beaten and curtains washed. Only Tom and Sally had pressing work to do. Sitting opposite each other with their laptops in the office Sally did her best to keep up with her clients' requirements while Tom was caught up in a frantic round of emails and phone calls as he kept pace with Angie's daily reports, ensuring that Valco's demands for a detailed action plan were met. He asked Sue, his Human Resources Manager to put out feelers for staff who might be willing to move to New York for a year to work at Valco's offices. The contract went through several drafts as the lawyers argued mostly over penalty clauses which Valco sought to impose. There was some concession and eventually Tiger's lawyers pronounced that they considered the terms of the contract the best that they could negotiate. Bob called Tom on several occasions to report on Angie. In his opinion, she was working hard for the deal.

A call from the vet to inform them of the date for the lifting of the quarantine came on the same day that Tom answered the phone to hear the voice of Elliott Paul.

'Hi Tom, how goes it?'

'Not bad, Elliott. I've just heard that the restrictions will be lifted. I can leave the farm the day after tomorrow.'

'That's good news because I think we're ready to sign the contract. How soon can you get here?'

Tom calculated. 'I'm free to leave on Sunday so I'll fly out on Monday.'

'Excellent, let's meet at our offices at nine a.m. Tuesday and seal the deal.'

'I'll look forward to it.'

Sally had been listening to Tom's end of the call. 'The deal's on then?'

'Looks like it. I've got to go out to sign the contract.'

She got up from the dining table and went to stare out of the window, crossing her arms. Tom was perturbed. He went to stand behind her. 'What's the matter? It's great news. It's what I've been working towards for months.'

She shrugged her shoulders.

'Come on. I thought you'd be pleased.'

'I am. For you.'

'So what's the problem?'

'What's it going to mean for us? You'll be back living in London and flitting all over the world. I'll be here, seeing you whenever you can fit in a quick visit. Some relationship that'll be.'

Tom put his hand on her shoulder but she wriggled away and went to sit down. 'I'm sorry,' she said. 'I know that we've talked about it before, but the problem's somehow been on hold while we've had to cope with all this. It's stupid really, but you said you wouldn't want to work for someone else if you were taken over and I've been clinging to the hope that it might mean that we could find a way of life that would suit us both. As it is, you're going to carry on being a city slicker and I'm damned if I'm going to leave my parents alone at a time like this.'

Tom sat down beside her, keeping a distance. 'But I love you,' he said lamely.

'Not enough to want to change what you are and what you do.'

'Couldn't the same apply to you?'

'I've got a responsibility to my parents. But then you wouldn't understand that, would you.' She flashed a defiant look at him, her eyes welling.

Tom's mind raced. He saw no gain in retaliating. It would only make matters worse. Conciliation was the only option. 'I'm not proud of having abandoned my parents but I'd like to think that I've started to redress it.'

Sally shook her head in exasperation. 'You can sound really pompous, you know. I don't want to talk to you right now.' She jumped up and exited through the office door, slamming it behind her.

Tom held his head in his hands and massaged his forehead. Nothing seemed to make any sense. Normally he prided himself on being rational, analytical, logical. Perhaps that was the problem.

He walked down to the field where the pit had been dug. Despite the layer of topsoil, wisps of pungent smoke were still escaping from the smouldering remains below. Grass which had escaped the churning wheels of the diggers was parched. Summer had spent its force. Autumn rains would be needed to stimulate the cycle of regeneration. As he dolefully surveyed the scene ideas formed in his mind.

He found his mother in her vegetable garden, harvesting the last of the season's runner beans.

'Hello stranger,' she said.

'Yes. Sorry, Mum, but I've had a lot of work to do. I should have been up here more often.'

'I'm sure you're happier down there with Sally.'

'That's what I wanted to talk about.'

Jean looked at him with curiosity. She picked up the wicker basket she'd been filling. 'Let's go and sit down,' she said.

They sat in the sun at a wooden table in the courtyard. 'Let's hear it,' she said.

Tom took a deep breath. 'Sally's the best thing that's ever happened to me, Mum. She's made me take stock of my life and I love her. But we live in different worlds and if we're going to stay together then one of us has got to change. She says she doesn't want to leave her parents alone on their farm, especially now, and my company's about to sign a big contract I've been working on for months. It should secure our future and I want to stay a part of it.' Jean regarded him fondly. 'You gave up teaching to marry Dad.' Tom said. 'What persuaded you to do that?'

'Love,' she said simply.

'Does that mean we don't love each other enough to find a way to stay together?'

'It will mean it if you don't. Love conquers all. I know it's a cliché but you'll find a way if it's the real thing. And you've got time on your side. It may seem an impossible situation now, but things change.'

'I've thought of a way to change things here on the farms. It won't necessarily solve our problems, but it'll help in other ways and it might demonstrate my commitment to Sally. Can I run it past you to see what you think?'

They all gathered at Middle Farm on Saturday evening to mark the last day of quarantine. Tom had invited them all to eat and rather than ask his mother to prepare something from what few provisions they had left he'd arranged for the village pub to deliver takeaway food and wine to the farm gates. Eating a good meal for the first time in a fortnight was enough to lift spirits and the mood when they finished was more positive than it had been for some time.

Tom called for silence. 'Can I just say a few words? We've all been through a lot in the last couple of weeks but at least we can try to restart and rebuild our lives tomorrow. I think it's time to think about the future. I've had an idea which I've already spoken to my Mum about and I'd like to see what you all think.' He had their full attention. 'The sheep are gone but there'll be compensation. Ken, do you want to spend it on buying new sheep to build up a flock again?'

Ken shrugged. 'I've got to make a living. Holiday cottages can't provide it unless they take off and all I know is sheep.'

'There's my business,' said Sally. If I can build that then it will help out.'

'Nay lass, we don't want to be a burden on you.'

'Here's my idea. What if we were to combine the two farms? Wouldn't there be an economy of scale? Couldn't they be more profitable if we pooled the compensation money for restocking and operated them as a single unit?'

They looked at him with surprise. 'Would you want to do that?' Sally asked, trying to come to terms with the implications. Tom nodded.

'I suppose it would give us more of a fighting chance,' said Ken. Sid indicated his agreement.

'I'd be happy to do it,' said Jean. 'I'm too old to start up this farm again even with Sid's help. This way I might be able to live out my days here.'

'It's certainly something to think about,' said Ken. 'What do you think, Rosie?'

'I don't know. How would it work?'

'There are several ways it could be arranged. For example, we could form a company to operate both farms with shares allocated in proportion to the compensation money, the amount of land and farm equipment. At this stage we don't need to go into detail. If everyone's interested, then I'm sure we could come to a fair arrangement. And I'll be paying off the bank so Middle Farm would start from scratch without any debts.' They all exchanged glances, looking for someone to take the cue. 'Look,' said Tom. I'm not asking for everyone to commit now. As you know I've got to leave tomorrow to go to the States. I hope to get back here in a couple of weeks. It'll give you time to think about it.'

Sally and Tom said goodnight to Ken and Rosie when they'd reached their farmhouse and walked down towards the cottage. The night was still and clear with the moon close to full. A panoply of stars shone bright in the dark sky. They stopped to take in the view over the dale. 'OK,' said Sally. 'So why didn't you discuss it with me first?'

'We haven't been communicating very well, have we?'

'You know why that is.'

'But do you think it's a good idea?'

'Well, yes. It would mean that your Mum would be able to stay on the farm rather than selling it.'

'Sid as well. And it would be good to amalgamate the farms sooner rather than later.'

Sally looked puzzled. 'What do you mean?'

'One day we'll both inherit our farms. If we were married, then it wouldn't make any sense to keep them separate.'

She stared at him in confusion. 'Is that some sort of proposal?'

Tom got down on one knee and held her hands in his. 'No this is. I love you Sally. I want us to spend our lives together. At the moment I don't know how, or where, but I know that we'll be able to find a way, even if it takes time. When we have found a way, will you marry me?' Sally continued to stare, open mouthed. 'I'm sorry. I obviously haven't been able to get an engagement ring, but I thought I'd go to Tiffany's when I'm in New York.'

She slipped from his hands and turned away. She crossed her arms and closed her eyes. 'I don't know, Tom. I love you too but I'm not sure that I can commit when there's so much uncertainty.'

'I hoped that you might think that my idea for joining the farms might have got rid of some of the uncertainty.'

'It could do. But it doesn't solve the problem of which one of us is going to change our lives. Were you thinking that by trying to create a future for the farms I'd just swoon and say of course I'll marry you and come to live with you in London?'

'No, of course not.'

'Then are you offering to come and live here?'

'Not immediately. Just like your father, I've got a living to make and I've got responsibilities to my company. Maybe in time, though.'

She turned back to him. 'Get up, slicker. You look like an idiot kneeling there.' Tom rose and they embraced. 'I'll marry you Tom, but not before we find a way to live here together.'

28

New York, Monday 10th September 2001

Tom filled Bob and Angie's wine glasses and raised his own to propose a toast. 'I hope to do this with champagne tomorrow when the contract's in the bag, but I'd just like to thank you for all the work you've done to get us to this point.' The restaurant in lower east side Manhattan was Chinese which Bob had suggested would be an appropriate choice for an eve-of-signing dinner. They clinked glasses and drank the sweet rice wine. Bob and Angie accepted his thanks. 'I'm only sorry I couldn't be here to help but it looks as if you've pulled it off without me.'

'We've been a good team,' said Bob, raising his glass to Angie who acknowledged the compliment.

The conversation turned to foot and mouth. Tom suggested that they didn't want to know the details, but they insisted on hearing the full story. Only when he had finished did they return to business matters. Angie asked for news of the takeover. Tom was immediately on his guard, and he noticed that

Bob leant in to hear what would be said, alert to the question mark over Angie's loyalty.

'It's on hold until the contract's signed,' Tom answered. 'When we announce it our share price is sure to rise and then Sinclair Rhodes will decide whether they want to make an offer which reflects it. If they do, we'll have to consider whether we can recommend it to the shareholders or not.'

'It could mean another vote among the directors.'

'Yes, it could, unless we're unanimous in our decision of course.'

'How will you be voting?' Angie asked.

Tom wondered where this might be leading. 'It depends on the offer. If it's good enough then I'm duty bound to recommend it. But with us winning the Valco business it would have to be a damned good offer. We'd have to weigh up whether in the long term the shareholders would be better off under the present management or in the ownership of Sinclair Rhodes.'

'And you'd be able to make an objective decision on that basis?' Her eyes flashed at him.

'Will you?' He held the gaze unblinkingly.

'Hey guys,' Bob said in an attempt to diffuse the situation. 'I thought we were celebrating. What's with the eyeballing?'

Tom tried to relax and make light of it. 'Sorry Bob, it's just that Angie and I have a bit of a history.'

'So it seems. But isn't tonight all about the future? And a prosperous future at that.'

Angie recovered her composure. 'Sorry, Tom. You're right, Bob. The future is what matters.' She toyed with her drink. 'Look, I'm feeling a bit tired and I want to be at my best for the signing tomorrow. Would you excuse me?'

'Of course,' said Tom. 'You've been working hard.'

'I'll get a cab back to the hotel if that's alright and meet you in reception tomorrow morning to go to Valco.' She retrieved her handbag from under her chair and stood. 'Thanks for the meal, guys.' They watched her walk out of the restaurant.

'Great ass,' said Bob when she was out of earshot. 'Strange lady.'

'Right on both counts.'

'I can't get my head round her. She's been working that delectable ass off these past few days to get the deal agreed. I've been watching her like a hawk for signs that she's got another agenda but if she has, she's fooled me. But she's obviously got a bee in her bonnet about something.'

'I'm not sure it matters any more. You can't change the past and we are where we are. Contract coming, takeover bid likely. I just have to live with it.'

'Would a takeover be such a bad thing? You'll presumably do a good deal over your shares and you'd still get to run the company. New owners are not going to want you to leave.'

'But I might want to.'

Bob reached for the wine. Tom refused the offer of a top up. 'Why would you want to do that?'

'Maybe I'd like to something more worthwhile.'

'Like what?'

Tom regretted having opened the line of conversation. 'No, forget it. It's just been such a fight to get where we are and you know, thrill of the chase and all that. Not as fulfilling as the kill.'

Bob sensed that Tom would not welcome pressing on his part. 'You're a bit of a strange one as well.'

'Let's just say that I've had a lot to deal with recently.'

The yellow cab dropped Tom and Angie at the entrance to the World Trade Centre at twenty to nine, in good time for their nine o'clock appointment on the 103rd floor of the South Tower. They joined the jostling throng of workers queuing for the elevators and eventually managed to squeeze into the room-sized express car which would take them straight to the 78th floor. As it gathered speed on its ascent Tom felt his ears popping. The doors swished open and they emerged into the sky lobby to transfer to an elevator which would take them floor by floor to their destination. Tom pressed the button and the doors began to close. With inches to go a broom handle was thrust between them and they drew back to reveal a smiling black janitor with a mop of grizzled grey hair. 'Sorry folks,' he grinned and came into the lift, depositing a bucket of tools and utensils on the floor. They began to ascend. Tom glanced down at his watch. Nine forty-six. They were in good time.

Suddenly a loud explosion resonated. The elevator shook violently causing Angie to cling on to Tom's arm. His briefcase slipped from his grasp and crashed to the floor spilling its contents. With a piercing grind of metal on metal the elevator juddered to a halt then plunged. Angie let out a scream, matched in volume by the expletives of the men. Within seconds they were all thrown to the floor as the elevator jerked to a stop.

'Holy shit!' exclaimed the janitor. 'What was that?'

Tom looked round at the four others in the elevator. 'Everyone OK?'

They all nodded apart from an elderly overweight man. 'My ankle. It hurts like hell.'

Angie moved over to him. 'Here, let me have a look.'

'What the fuck happened?' asked a young man in red overalls with 'Maintenance' written on the back.

The janitor started to gather up his plastic bottles. 'These mothers have got arresters. They stop the elevators falling after a few floors.'

'Yeah, but why did we fall? Did you hear the bang?'

'We better use the emergency intercom,' said Tom, approaching the console on the wall. As he went to press the button the speaker beside it crackled into life.

'Ladies and Gentlemen, this is the Port Authority. We have had a large explosion in the building. We would ask you to...' There was a burst of static and the voice fell silent. They all stared at the speaker, willing it to come to life again.

Tom pressed the send button on the intercom. 'Hello. Is there anybody there?' Silence. 'We're trapped in a lift, sorry, an elevator. Can you send help?' More silence.

The maintenance man pushed Tom aside. 'Let me try, buddy. You gonna send someone to get us out of here?' he shouted. He placed his ear against the speaker, hearing nothing. 'For

Christ's sake, we need help!' he bellowed into the tiny microphone and started to frantically press the floor buttons.

The janitor leapt across to restrain him. 'Hey, man! Cool it, right. Let's keep calm, shall we?'

'Phone!' said Tom. 'We can call the emergency services.' He pulled out his mobile and looked at the screen. 'Damn. No signal. I suppose there wouldn't be in this metal box. Has anyone got a signal?' Those that had phones pulled them out and one by one shook their heads.

'Nothing broken as far as I can tell,' said Angie, finishing her examination of the elderly man's ankle. 'Probably just strained from the fall.' She sniffed the air. 'Can I smell smoke?'

Tom inhaled and caught a whiff which took him back to the pyres on the farm.

'Oh shit!' exclaimed the janitor, pointing to smoke which was wisping through the narrow gap between the elevator doors. 'That's all we need!'

'What are we going to do?' wailed the overweight man still prostrate on the floor.

'We're going to weigh up the options,' said Tom as calmly as he could manage. 'We know that there's been an explosion of some sort and it looks like it's caused a fire. We can assume that the emergency services are on their way but getting us out might not be a priority, particularly if they don't know we're here.' The elevator was beginning to fill with smoke, and the elderly man started to cough.

'Couldn't we block the gap to keep the smoke out?' suggested Angie.

'Good idea.' Tom and Angie both pulled off their jackets and began stuffing the edges into the gap. The janitor grabbed cleaning cloths and started to do the same. The flow was reduced but not abated. Smoke was still seeping through slits at the top and bottom of the doors.

'It's only going to slow things down,' said Tom. 'I'm not sure I want to wait here until either we're rescued or the smoke gets us. We've got to find our own way out.'

'How?' protested the janitor.

'What about this?' said the maintenance man fishing around in his toolbox and pulling out a small crowbar. 'We could try to open the doors.'

'And then what?' scoffed the janitor.

'I don't know, but I'd rather try something than stand here and wait to die.'

The maintenance man inserted the end of the crowbar into the gap and levered it apart. It opened a few inches and smoke poured in. He let it the doors snap back.

'You sure we want to do this?' said the janitor.

Tom had been searching through the toolbox and had found several screwdrivers of various lengths. 'It's worth a try. We can hold it open with these.'

The crowbar levered the doors apart again and Tom wedged them with a screwdriver. Bit by bit they were forced further open and longer screwdrivers were inserted.

The janitor brandished his broom handle. 'I spend my life pushing this around. It's time for it to save my life.'

They leant shoulders against each door with feet on the other to gain purchase and succeeded in pushing them far enough apart to prop them open with the broom handle. They stood back, panting from the effort and spluttering from the smoke.

'Great!' said the maintenance man. 'A concrete wall.' He kicked against it in frustration with a steel toe-capped boot.

'Hang on,' said Tom. 'Funny concrete wall that you can make a dent in.' He grabbed a screwdriver and scraped at the wall. Flakes began to come off. 'I think it might be plasterboard.'

The janitor thrust a screwdriver at the wall, making an indentation. 'Shit, man. You're right. We can dig through it.'

There was only room for two to work at creating a hole, so after Tom had done a stint he handed over and saw that Angie was tending to the elderly man. He was wheezing and coughing from the smoke and she loosened his tie. Angie moved away from him and slumped down beside Tom. 'He's in a bad way. I'm not sure he's going to make it.' Tom felt exhausted from his efforts and his hands were blistered and raw with cuts. He looked at his watch. 'We've missed our appointment,' he said with a hollow laugh. 'I can't see how we're going to make it either. We won't last long in this smoke.' Tom shrugged. Angie did her best to supress a fit of coughing and leant her head on his shoulder. 'I want to say sorry.'

'What for?'

'I've been a bitch. I've betrayed your trust.'

'You mean being in league with Ranjit in trying to set up a takeover?'

'Yes. You knew all along, didn't you? Why didn't you confront me?'

'Never had the proof. Perhaps I didn't want to admit to myself that I was being taken for a ride.' Tom too had a fit of coughing. His eyes were now watering from the smoke. He recovered and turned to look hard at her. 'Is that why you went to bed with me in the first place?'

'One of the reasons. It wasn't any hardship.'

Before Tom could follow up what she had said, the old man let out a cry of pain and clutched his chest. They rushed to his side. His continuous coughing had stopped. His head had lolled to the side with eyes closed and mouth wide open. His face was pallid and beaded with sweat. Angie pulled his head up and tried to revive him. 'He's unconscious. Do you think it's a heart attack?'

'Looks like it. Any pulse?'

She grasped his wrist. 'Not that I can feel. Do you know how to the give the kiss of life?'

'CPR's better - pressure on his chest. I learnt it from a medic when I was in a war zone out East. Help me lay him out flat.'

Tom pulled the man's head back, checking that his tongue was not obstructing his airways, and put his ear to the mouth to check for breathing. Detecting none he placed both hands on his chest and began to give a series of regular sharp jabs. He paused and blew into his open mouth and once again listened for any breathing before continuing with more jabs. He repeated the cycle several times before rocking back on his heels. 'I think we've lost him.' Angie sunk her head into her hands and began to cry.

Tom stood and went to see the progress on the hole in the plasterboard. It was about a foot wide, and the janitor had put his head through it.

'Can you see anything?'

'Yes. Another damn wall.'

'What's it made of?'

'Don't know. I can feel ridges. Could be the back of tiles.'

The renewed their efforts to enlarge the hole, now able to break off larger pieces. Before long it was wide enough to be squeezed through. The maintenance man called for them to stand back and he kicked hard through the hole. There was a loud crack and a light shafted through the smoke. He went down on his knees down to peer through. He crawled back and gave a wry laugh. 'Anyone want the john?'

'What?' said Angie.

'Sorry lady. It's the men's room.'

With a few more judicious kicks enough of the tiles were removed to allow the maintenance man to wiggle through the narrow opening. 'Jesus that's good,' he called back. 'Fresh air. Come on through.'

'What about the old guy?' asked Angie.

'We'll have to leave him,' said Tom. 'We'll get the emergency services to come for him.'

They emerged into the toilets opposite a row of urinals and sat on the tiled floor breathing in the smoke free air. Angie's black tights were in shreds from the sharp edges she'd caught them on. Her legs were bleeding. Tom had fared better with trousers, but not as well as the other two wearing overalls. They were all covered in dust and dirt.

'OK,' said the janitor, 'I don't know about you but I'm getting my sweet ass outa here.'

They opened the restroom door gingerly, fearful of fire, but the corridor was clear of any obvious danger. Tom led the way following the evacuation signs. They heard a voice calling and saw a fireman opening doors one by one to check they were empty.

'Hey guys – you all OK?'

'Yes,' said Angie, 'but there's a man back in the elevator where we were trapped. He seems to have died of a heart attack.'

'Can't worry about the dead right now,' said the fireman. 'God knows there's enough of them.'

'Why – what's happened?' asked Tom.

'Planes flew into both towers. Just heard they attacked the Pentagon too. Damned if I know who we're fighting but by Christ we're at war.' His walkie-talkie crackled and he pressed send. 'This is rescue 14 on floor 68. Do you copy?' A voice acknowledged. 'I got four people here. I'm sending them down the stairwell. What's with the elevators?' He held the walkie-talkie to his ear to catch the reply. 'OK, roger and out.' He pointed to an evacuation sign. 'The signs will take you to the stairwell. Go down to the 50th floor and then take the elevator. They're still working from there down. And don't hang around – we don't know how safe this building is. Understood?' They all nodded. 'OK. I gotta go.'

The fireman resumed his room check and they found their way to the stairwell. Initially they saw no one as they began to descend the narrow concrete stairs, but there were plenty of signs that people had been using the stairs recently – discarded high-heeled shoes, abandoned briefcases and every now and then bloodstains. Around the 60th floor a team of firefighters were taking a breather, their faces red from the exertion of climbing in full equipment. They stood as close to the walls as their breathing tanks would allow to let the descending group squeeze past.

At the 50th floor they made their way to the elevator lobby. A fireman was standing by an open lift and he beckoned them over. 'There you go guys,' he said. 'It's still working.'

Tom, the janitor and the maintenance man entered but Angie hung back shaking uncontrollably. 'What's the matter?' Tom asked impatiently.

'I'm not getting in a lift to get trapped again. I'll take the stairs.'

She went to walk away but the fireman grabbed her arm. 'Sorry ma'am, but you gotta take the elevator. We don't know what structural damage there's been to the tower and it'd take you twenty minutes to walk down. Get in, and you can be safe outside in two.'

Tom went to put an arm round her shoulders and guided her into the lift while she shook with fear. 'Let's go, folks,' said the janitor, pressing the ground floor button. 'Going down!'

The doors opened on to the entrance foyer and the janitor and the maintenance man leapt out and high fived. Tom was still holding the shaking Angie and gently ushered her out. 'Come on Ange. We're safe now. Let's get away from here.' She continued to take big sobs of breath, still in shock.

The scene which greeted them as they emerged into the dusty sunshine reminded Tom of the aftermath of earthquakes he'd reported on. The ground was strewn with debris and fire hoses. Charred paper fluttered down from above. Firefighters and police milled around in purposeful activity while paramedics treated casualties too injured to be moved. They began to pick their way towards the street and Tom's mobile rang. He stopped, retrieved it from his pocket and answered it, hearing Sally's voice.

'Tom? Thank God! Are you alright? I'm watching it on television.'

'OK now. We were trapped but we've just got out. I'm fine.'

'I've been mad with worry, I …' A deep rumble from above drowned her words and he looked up to see an exploding plume of dust encircling the top of the tower. A fireman sped past screaming 'Get outta here! It's coming down!' Tom dropped the phone, grabbed Angie's hand and ran for his life.

They'd almost reached the safety of the street when the storm of debris engulfed them.

29

Bob Schwartz poked his head around the curtains surrounding Tom's hospital bed.

'Couldn't find any grapes. I brought some bagels. How are you?'

Tom still felt woozy from medication but made an effort to pull himself together. 'Fine. Apart from the broken leg and ribs, a collapsed lung and what else? Ah yes – severe concussion and multiple lacerations.'

'But you're going to be OK?'

'That's what they said.'

'Thank God for that.'

'What's going on out there, Bob? Nobody's telling me any-thing. I had to create a hell of a fuss even to get to make a phone call to my girlfriend to tell her I was alive.'

'They're rushed off their feet. The hospitals are overflowing. I had a bit of a fight myself to persuade them to let me visit you. Had to tell them I was your American uncle.'

'Well thanks for coming,' said Tom. 'Any news of Angie? Is she OK?'

'Not too bad – just cuts and bruises. She phoned me to say she was alright and to see if I could find out which hospital they'd taken you to. She wants to visit you. Said she hadn't been able to finish her apology – what's that all about?'

'She confessed to betraying my trust when we were trapped and didn't think we were going to get out.'

'So you were right about her. And was she doing it for money?'

'Never had the chance to ask her. Everything was happening so quickly. Look, tell me what happened. I only heard about the planes in the towers and some sort of attack on the Pentagon.'

Bob sighed and crossed his arms. 'OK, the facts are that four planes were hijacked. Two of them were flown into the towers, one crashed into the Pentagon and another came down in in a field Pennsylvania en route for Washington D.C. No handle on the numbers killed yet but it's well into the thousands. The speculation is that it was a coordinated terrorist attack by Al Qaeda. The country's in a state of shock right now. No flights, military on red alert. People are saying it's Pearl Harbour all over again.'

Tom tried to take it all in and shifted position in his bed trying to make himself more comfortable. He winced as pain coursed through his body. 'It's probably irrelevant now, but what about Valco?'

'The first plane hit the tower pretty much where their offices are. It looks like no one got out on those floors or above them. They've probably lost hundreds of employees.'

'Including Elliott, I suppose. We can say goodbye to the contract for the time being. The attack's not exactly going to encourage international trade. A war more likely.'

'I guess so.'

'Sorry. There are thousands dead and I'm fretting about losing a business deal.'

Tom had still not taken in the enormity of it all. He closed his eyes and thought of the thousands of children who would be without a father or mother. The parents who would be grieving a child. The friends who would never be together again. 'Have you lost anyone?' he asked Bob.

'Yeah. A nephew. And a friend who used to work on a paper with me. I guess half of New York knows someone who was killed.'

'It's all so senseless. That's what I always felt when I was reporting on disasters. And so random. I mean if we'd arrived a few minutes earlier we'd have been in Valco's offices.'

'And you invited me to the signing, remember? If I hadn't taken a rain check, I could have been there with you. There is no sense to it.'

Tom closed his eyes and thought about the symmetry of disaster in the two worlds which he and Sally inhabited. Both gone up in fire and smoke.

'Right now, there's only one thing which makes any sense to me. Will you do something for me Bob?'

'Sure thing. What is it?'

'I was going to go to Tiffany's to get an engagement ring for my girlfriend while I was here. I doubt I'll get the chance before they put me on a plane home. They say I can leave in a few days. Could you get hold of a catalogue so I can choose a ring and then get it for me on my credit card?'

'Hey! I'd be delighted to. So you're going to be married. Congratulations'

'She hasn't said yes yet, but I know how to make her.'

When Angie visited an hour later, it was the first time that Tom could remember seeing her anything less than immaculately turned-out. She wore jeans and a T-shirt. There was an angry bruise on her cheek and surgical dressings on her arms.

'How are you feeling, Tom?'

'Like shit. How about you?'

'Could be a lot worse. Just a few stitches. You're going to be OK, are you?'

'Yeah. A few broken bones, but they'll mend.'

She smiled weakly at him then lowered her eyes.

'What happened to me?' Tom asked. 'We were running away from the collapsing tower and the next thing I remember is waking up here.'

'Something must have fallen on you and knocked you unconscious. I don't know what. It was difficult to see anything in that dust. I stopped running when you let go of my hand and I felt you fall but I couldn't see a thing. I'm ashamed to say that I left you there. I thought you might be dead. I just wanted to save my own skin.'

Tom looked at her without rancour. 'Don't feel bad about it. It was probably the only thing to do in the circumstances.'

'It was pandemonium when I got out into the street,' Angie continued. 'People screaming and running everywhere in the dust storm. We were so close – a few more yards and we would both have made it to safety. I sheltered in a shop doorway until the noise of falling debris stopped. When the dust began to clear I saw a fireman and screamed out for him to help me find you. I was probably a bit hysterical and didn't really give him any choice. We found you half-covered in rubble. He checked that you were alive then called in a paramedic. They said they'd look after you and told me to go to an A & E to get my cuts seen to.'

Angie looked pleadingly at him, as if asking for forgiveness. 'Look, I'm sorry I abandoned you, but at least I got you rescued.'

'I've already said that it's OK,' he said flatly. After a lengthy silence he spoke again. 'Anything else you want to apologise for?'

She shifted uneasily in her chair.

'Why?' questioned Tom. 'Why did you do it? For money?'

'Initially. He offered to invest a hundred grand for me to set up my own business if I could get the company sold and he could cash in from selling his shares.'

'And did he suggest that you seduce me?'

'No. That was my idea. I quite fancied you anyway and thought that it would be a good way to get close to you and plant the idea of a takeover.'

'But you were seeing Ranjit at the same time, weren't you?'

Angie's eyes flashed defiantly. 'Yes. What of it? Nobody owns me. I sleep with whoever I want, whenever I want. And there's no shortage of candidates, I can assure you'

Tom recoiled from the cold, manipulative side to her character which had just resurfaced. 'And did Ranjit know about us?'

'I told him. He wasn't bothered. He knew my relationship with him was based on money, sex and little else.'

Tom suppressed a desire to tell her to get out of his sight, but he needed to know more. 'You said you did it for money initially. What did you mean by that?'

'I had a change of heart. At first, I didn't think that Tiger could survive in the long term, so it didn't worry me too much about hastening the inevitable. Then you came up with your initiative to save the company and I could see that it might succeed. Sir Giles was absolutely right in saying that it was in everybody's interests to keep all the options open. Ranjit couldn't see the logic of it. He was hell bent on cashing in his shares as soon as possible. He said the only way I'd get the money would be to do everything I could to hinder and delay you getting a deal.'

'So that's what you did?'

'Not immediately. I could tell that you were suspicious of me, so I decided to throw myself into working for your deal until I spotted a way to scupper it. The confidentiality clause in the Valco agreement gave me the opportunity. I suggested to Ranjit that he should leak details of the potential deal to the US trade press.'

'Ben and I guessed as much. We found an email from Ranjit thanking you for passing on the information.'

'You were reading my emails!'

'We had a right to under the terms and conditions of your employment.'

Angie shook her head in disbelief. 'Then I was right to tell Ranjit where to stick his offer. After the magazine didn't run the story, he said I'd have to try something else. I was too worried about being found out. I told him I might consider it if he would guarantee the investment if I ended up being dismissed for gross misconduct. He said I could whistle for the money unless I wrecked your initiative. We fell out big time and I assured him that I'd work my butt off to win the Valco deal and stop the takeover. Just to spite him.'

Tom gingerly shifted in his bed to turn away from her. He felt a mixture of emotions. Humiliation that he'd been suckered into her honey trap, but vindication that his suspicions had all been confirmed. Contempt for her callous money-grabbing coldness but a grudging respect for her full and frank confession and eventual rejection of the disloyalty. He felt her hand on his shoulder. 'I'm sorry, Tom. That's all I can say.'

He rolled over to face her. She was unable to hold his gaze. Instead she delved into the bag at her feet and retrieved a copy of the New York Times. 'I brought this for you. I thought you'd want to catch up on what's been going on.' Tom said nothing so she placed the paper on his bedside table. She clasped her arms around her midriff and rocked back and forth. She pulled herself together and took a deep breath. 'I suppose I should offer my resignation.'

'And suppose I should accept it.' She nodded in acquiescence. 'What will you do?' asked Tom after a pause.

Angie perked up. 'Well actually, I met someone when I first came over to New York to work with Bob. He's an investment banker with a duplex on Fifth Avenue to die for. I've been seeing quite a lot of him and he's asked me to move in. Says he can fix me up with a job on Wall Street.' She smiled cockily.

'Well I hope you'll be very happy together,' Tom said coldly. 'I think you better leave now.'

30

'Let me sum up,' said Sir Giles surveying the remaining directors of Tiger.com seated around the boardroom table. 'We have on the table an offer from Sinclair Rhodes. The price per share is not what we might have hoped for. But it reflects the fact that Valco have put their expansion into China on hold in view of their tragic loss of employees and the current international climate. Instead of the hoped for rise with the deal in place, our share price has fallen significantly, along with that of so many other companies, in the aftermath of 9/11. I understand from Lin that the interest shown by Huang Li has also been withdrawn. He too has suffered major setbacks in his business from the downturn in confidence that the terrorist attacks have provoked. He no longer wishes to or is able to acquire our company. Therefore, in the absence of other offers we need to decide whether or not to recommend the current one to our shareholders. Our decision should be based solely on whether or not we believe it to be in their interests.' Sir Giles leant back in his chair. 'Your thoughts please.'

Tom eased himself as close to the table as his plaster-casted leg would allow. 'It was only a few months ago that we sat round this table discussing Angie's paper. At the time I was totally against the idea of a takeover, believing that we could revive the company's fortunes. We came very close to doing so, but events have overtaken us. As it is this offer gives us a lifeline which I think we should grasp.'

He looked round the table to gauge reaction. Both Lin and Ben who had previously supported his fight against a takeover showed no sign of dissent. He continued. 'There's something else I want to say which may be relevant to the takeover but not, I think, to our decision. I apologise for not having discussed this with you, Sir Giles, but having only just returned from the States there's been no opportunity. I did a lot of thinking when I was in hospital in New York and I came to a conclusion. I've decided that I want my future to lie elsewhere and I'll be resigning my directorship in due course. I'll be happy to stay on for a handover period with the new owners if we have them and if they want me to. I want to make it clear that it's not sour grapes on my part because I'll be losing control of the company. It's simply that I've decided to change my life.'

Sir Giles broke the stunned silence which followed Tom's speech. 'We respect your wishes Tom and perhaps we can learn more of them later, but can we bring the formal proceedings to a close first. Does anyone want to speak against a recommendation?' no one spoke. 'In which case can I assume that we will recommend the offer?' All around the table nodded.

A buffet lunch had been laid out. Tom grabbed his crutches and began to struggle to his feet. Lin came to stop him, saying that she would bring him a plate. 'Change your life? What's all that about?'

'I'm going home to marry Sally if she'll have me. Maybe I've got a new perspective on what's important after what I've been through.'

'You're going to settle back in Yorkshire? And do what?'

'Who knows? Maybe learn to farm again.'

'Well congratulations. She's a great girl Tom. Can we come to the wedding?'

'You and Chong will be guests of honour providing you don't bring any fireworks with you.'

She gave him an affectionate kiss and went off to find a plate of food for him.

Tom felt as if he was holding court as Sir Giles came to sit beside him.

'You're full of surprises Tom. You're sure about resigning, are you?

'Yes. I've thought long and hard about it.'

'You're sure it's not just a reaction to the trauma you've been through in the States?'

'It may have been the catalyst, but it's not the reason. I'm going back to help run the family farm.'

Sir Giles expressed astonishment. 'Well I never. I wouldn't have put you down for a farm boy.'

'There's a girl involved as well.'

'Ah, now we're getting there. Cherchez la femme, eh?'

'She lives on the next-door farm and I'm hoping to marry her,' Tom said.

'Well, may it all work out. I'll be sorry to see you go, but if your mind's made up, so be it.'

Ben was next. 'Lin just told me. So you're marrying Sally. I did my best to warn her off, but it can't have worked. Congratulations mate! I'm going to miss working with you.'

'I'm going to miss it too. But we'll keep in touch. In fact, I don't suppose you'd do me the honour of being my best man?'

'The honour would be all mine. I'd love to. What are the bridesmaids going to be like? You know what they say.'

They talked for a while about Tom's plans for the farm until Tom noticed Ranjit hovering uneasily. 'Can I have a word, Tom?'

Ben stood, offered Ranjit his chair beside Tom, and returned to the buffet. Tom regarded him coldly. 'You've got what you wanted,' he said with hostility.

'I think we've got what's best for the company,' Ranjit replied.

'Oh come off it. You've only ever been concerned with your investment, never with what the company achieved.'

'And what did it achieve? Certainly not decent profits.'

Tom felt anger rising but held it in check. 'I've known for months about you and Angie.' Ranjit looked at him in astonishment. 'I came so close to dismissing her, but I just didn't have conclusive evidence. She confirmed it all when we were trapped in the tower. She told me she was sorry. Even told me about the hundred grand you'd offered her. Well you've got what you wanted for nothing now.'

Ranjit's face fell and he squirmed in his seat. 'I needed to cash in my investment in Tiger. I lost a fortune in the dotcom crash.'

'My heart bleeds,' said Tom scornfully. He felt nothing but distain for him. His mind raced with thoughts of exposing Ranjit for the heartless bastard that he was but what purpose would it serve? He had no stomach for it. He wanted out of the world the likes of Ranjit inhabited.

'What are you going to do about it?' Ranjit asked.

'Nothing. But an apology would be appropriate.'

'OK, I'm sorry.'

'For what?'

'What do you want me to say? I'm sorry you're going to lose your company. But I'm not sorry I'm going to get most of my money back.'

They locked eyes. There was defiance in Ranjit's. Tom turned his back and waved his hand over his shoulder in contemptuous us dismissal.

31

The solicitor stacked his papers together on the farmhouse kitchen table. 'Everything's in order. We just need a few signatures.' He passed a sheet of paper to Tom. 'After what few assets could be realised, this is the final total of the estate's debt, all of which is owed to the bank. You're happy to write a cheque for it, Tom?'

Tom had his cheque book at the ready. He filled it in and as he signed, he couldn't help thinking of the contract he'd been so close to signing in New York. Sally clasped his arm and gave him a warm smile as he passed it to the solicitor.

'I'll drop it into the bank back in Richmond. It's not going to bounce is it?' he asked jovially.

'No, I confirmed the transfer of funds this morning and they're in the account,' said Tom.

'In which case, as executor, I can sign off the will.' He signed with a flourish. 'Mrs Keardon, you are now the owner of Middle Farm.'

Jean had tears in her eyes. 'Thank you, Tom. Your father would be proud of you.'

'Aye,' said Sid. 'It's a fine thing you've done, lad.'

'And this is the agreement we've drawn up to operate the two farms as one. I need signatures from Mrs Keardon and Mr Hardcastle here and here.'

They signed. The solicitor gathered the papers and put them in to his briefcase. 'It's been a pleasure to do business.'

Tom paused on his laboured walk on crutches back to the cottage with Sally. He leant on a gate and gazed at the view. An Indian summer had brought back the good weather and the gentle undulations of the dale were picked out in sharp contrast by the long shadows cast by a low sun. He watched a formation of migrating birds flying south across the sky.

'I've been waiting for the right moment to tell you and I can't think of a better time than this.' He turned to look at Sally. 'I've handed in my resignation at Tiger. I'll have to stay on long enough see the handover through but before long I'll be able to come back to live here.'

Sally face broke into the widest of smiles and she threw her arms round him. 'Oh Tom. That's wonderful. Are you sure? What will you do?'

'Learn to farm. And maybe you'd let me help to build up your business.'

'I'd love you to. But what made you decide?'

'I don't know. I thought I'd got away from death and destruction when I gave up reporting. Then I found myself right back in it. But that wasn't the main reason. You were.' He fumbled in his pocket for the Tiffany's ring. 'I'm afraid that I can't get down on my knees this time with this plaster cast on, but can I ask you again? Will you marry me now?'

'I can't think of anything I'd rather do.' She kissed him tenderly and Tom placed the ring on her finger. 'It's beautiful,' she said. 'I love you.'

'There's only one thing missing now.'

'What's that, slicker?'

'Sheep. I was thinking we could buy some ewes before the compensation money comes through to get the farms going straight away. This place doesn't seem right without them.'

'That's a good idea.'

'And maybe a couple of rams. I think we've got some breeding to do.'

She nuzzled into his shoulder and whispered into his ear. 'That's an even better idea, country boy.'

# # #